WHAT READERS SAY ABOUT THE AUTHOR

"Dianna Benson's **Persephone's Fugitive** is an interesting, tense-filled story about a desperate man who takes a hostage. Ms. Benson does a good job getting inside the heads of the multi-dimensional characters. Enjoyed!" -**Margaret Daley, USA Today Bestselling Author**

"With **Persephone's Fugitive**, Dianna T. Benson writes a stunningly suspenseful high-seas adventure with pulse-pounding action inspired by her medical roots. If you love thrillers then you must read all of Dianna's novels." -**Jordyn Redwood, Author of the Bloodline Trilogy**

"This is the second book I've read by Dianna T. Benson, and once again she doesn't disappoint. Well-drawn characters, plenty of action, and a fast-paced story kept me turning the pages late into the night. **Persephone's Fugitive** is a solid second book in Benson's Cayman Island's Trilogy and left me wondering how much more trouble her characters will find themselves involved in once the third book in the series is finished. Grab your favorite drink, sit back in a comfortable chair, and prepare to be entertained . . ." -**Michael J. Webb, Author of The Master's Quilt, The Oldest Enemy, and Infernal Gates**

"Grab your oxygen mask, you just might need it as you turn the pages of Dianna Benson's latest novel, [*Final Trimester*]... a fast-paced and psychologically thrilling suspense story with an unexpected twist. Though a dark tale at times, the story contains elements of hope and faith and points readers toward the Light (of the World)" – **Heidi Glick, Author of *Dog Tags***

"More twists and turns than a mountain road! If you're looking for a thrill ride, this book [*Final Trimester*] is it. Benson delivers not only a great story but one with wonderful characters and great dialogue. Along with that she has a unique writing style that keeps the book moving forward. Her real-life knowledge of medicine comes through time after time. All in all, a story not to be missed" – **Lillian Duncan, Author of *Betrayed***

"Benson hits a home run in this debut thriller [*The Hidden Son*] that grabs readers from the first page. Fans of Joel C. Rosenberg will thrill to the twisty, fast-paced action and suspense." -**Copyright 2013 Library Journal, LLC Used with permission. April 15, 2013**

"I loved *The Hidden Son*. I couldn't put it down. I'm not a fiction reader typically, but I thoroughly enjoyed this book. It was completely believable yet suspenseful. I can't wait for Dianna T. Benson's next release." -**Brandon Gayle, Haz-Mat Specialist and Firefighter**

"Did you ever watch a movie or theatre performance after which instead of just clapping, words like 'bravo' and 'encore' should be shouted? Be prepared to do both with *The Hidden Son*. What drew me to this novel was the cover and the title that I figured was a purposeful play on words. The novel grabs a hold from the first chapter till the last. The characters, scenes, action, and faith-based novel will keep you turning pages and losing track of time. The plot was rich as well as entertaining. The suspense kept building as I prepared myself with what I saw would be a breakthrough or victory for the characters only to have the author throw a curve ball and get me thinking about the plot's direction all over again. Don't miss this one. My rating is 5+ stars." -**Lisa Johnson, Book Reviewer**

"Even though *The Hidden Son* is Mrs. Benson's debut novel, it reads as though she had written dozens before it. Each page leaves you wanting more. The characters are well-written and I found myself thinking of them as if they were real people. I definitely recommend *The Hidden Son* to anyone who loves a good action novel." -**Cassie Snow, Rocky Mountain Reviews**

"Dianna T. Benson's *The Hidden Son* has all the makings of a great suspense novel with plenty of action to keep the reader turning pages. I'm excited to read more of her books!" -**Jordyn Redwood, Suspense Author of *Proof, Poison* and *Peril***

"Once you start Dianna T. Benson's *The Hidden Son*, don't plan on sleeping. Packed with action, this thriller is a gripping edge-of-your-seat read!" -**Alice J. Wisler, Award-winning Author**

"Get ready to discover your new favorite author of riveting thrillers! You'll love the characters, lose yourself in the action-packed plots, and be desperate for Dianna T. Benson's next book as soon as you finish the first!" -**Diane Reeves, Non-fiction Author and Editor at Regnery Publishing**

"I started reading *The Hidden Son* and looked up three hours later, having hardly put it down, stumped by the mystery and intrigued by the complicated characters." -**Faith Farrell, Book Reviewer**

"I'm amazed a debut author wrote such an enthralling, engrossing and exciting book." -**Vera Godley, Book Reviewer**

PERSEPHONE'S FUGITIVE

PERSEPHONE'S FUGITIVE

Cayman Islands Series, Book Two

Dianna T. Benson

Ellechor Publishing House

CONTENTS

Inspired by real events   xi

Books by Dianna T. Benson   xiii

Acknowledgements   xv

Chapter One   1

Chapter Two   13

Chapter Three   23

Chapter Four   27

Chapter Five   33

Chapter Six   37

Chapter Seven   45

Chapter Eight   53

Chapter Nine   59

Chapter Ten   69

Chapter Eleven   85

Chapter Twelve   95

Chapter Thirteen   99

Chapter Fourteen   105

Chapter Fifteen   113

Chapter Sixteen   121

Chapter Seventeen   135

Chapter Eighteen   141

Chapter Nineteen   151

Chapter Twenty   167

Chapter Twenty-one   171

Chapter Twenty-two	181
Chapter Twenty-three	185
Chapter Twenty-four	197
Chapter Twenty-five	207
Chapter Twenty-six	215
Chapter Twenty-seven	225
Chapter Twenty-eight	235
Chapter Twenty-nine	245
Chapter Thirty	249
Chapter Thirty-one	255
Chapter Thirty-two	263
Chapter Thirty-three	269
Chapter Thirty-four	287
Chapter Thirty-five	295
Chapter Thirty-six	299
Chapter Thirty-seven	309
Chapter thirty-eight	313
Chapter Thirty-nine	321
Chapter Forty	325

INSPIRED BY REAL EVENTS

BOOKS BY DIANNA T. BENSON

Cayman Islands Series
The Hidden Son
Persephone's Fugitive

Quigley Triplets Series
Final Trimester

ACKNOWLEDGEMENTS

I dedicate this book to my family: My husband, Leo, and our three children, Sabrina, Curtis and Fiona. I treasure their love and enjoy their individualities. My life is rich and beautiful with the four of them in it.

I thank my beta readers for their time and insightful input: Leo Benson, Sabrina Benson, Curtis Benson, Fiona Benson, Laura Fischler, Rebecca Lockhart, Michele Watson, Allison Cain, Carol Baldinelli and Gillian Nicol.

I thank my loyal critique partners: Pamela Pruitt, Derrick Tribble, Jordyn Redwood, Lillian Duncan, Lynda Quinn, Carrie L. Lewis and V.B. Tenery.

The following experts in their field of study assist me to create believable fiction: Brandon Gayle, Haz-Mat Specialist; Adam Tanner, SBI Special Agent; Bridget Mulder Way, EMT-P; Leo Benson, computer expert; Brian Grover, PsyD; Steve Colgate, Sailing Expert; Reyna Miller, El Salvador native; Lorna Puerta, Colombia native; Monica Ospina, Colombia native; Michael Clark, addiction counselor and recovery specialist; Scot Rademacher, Wake County 911 supervisor; Brent Myers, MD, MPH, FACEP; and North Carolina Chief Medical Examiner John D. Butts, MD.

Thank you to my agent, Mark Gottlieb, and to the entire team at Ellechor Publishing House, especially CEO Rochelle Carter and my editor Veronika Walker, and to my publicist, Gillian Nicol, who works diligently in the best interest of all my books.

Above all, I thank God for everything in my life and the amazing world we call home.

I truly appreciate you all!

Dianna

CHAPTER ONE

Dead or alive, I'm ditching this place.

Sweaty and hunched in a flimsy wooden chair, Jason Keegan stared off, continuing to pretend he suffered a catatonic state. The dismal patients' lounge inside the locked doors of the Grand Cayman Island mental hospital droned with haunting moans, cries, and incoherent mumblings of twenty-plus patients. The morning sunlight filtered through the few tiny windows near the ceiling. The stench of body odor, mixed with a stale medicinal scent, clogged the under-air-conditioned room.

Get me out of here.

The greasy-haired man next to him—Card Guy, he was called—peeled the front side of a king of spades from the backside of the card. A full deck of playing cards lay stacked in a precise arrangement in front of him on the table, awaiting their mutilation. Jason didn't know the man's story, and didn't want to know. The last day and a half inside this hellhole, he'd witnessed Card Guy's violent streak and hostile personality.

It was the key to Jason's escape.

Without moving his head a millimeter, he scanned around the room to spot each nurse's location. All of them busy at some task, and far from him. A lone phlebotomist drew blood from a female patient two tables over. No security guard in sight.

Ideal opportunity.

Like a spider in motion, Jason crept his fingers on the tabletop. He snatched a card from the top of Card Guy's deck, and flicked the nine of clubs to the ground.

The weirdo pierced Jason with a glare, nostrils flaring on his giant freckled honker. Bushy, unruly brows pinched together, the man's cobalt blue eyes warned Jason against stealing another card.

It was the exact dare he'd hoped for.

Without spider fingers this time, he snatched several cards from the top. With them cupped in his upward palm, he curled the tiny stack. Crushed it.

Wild-eyed, teeth clenched, Card Guy lurched toward the phlebotomist's cart and grabbed the tray filled with tubes and vials. He threw the entire thing at the glass partition that separated the patient lounge from the nurse's station.

Fluid sprayed. Glass shattered. Card Guy picked up a large shard and lunged at Jason. Jason didn't move.

Bring it on, Card Guy.

The maniac stabbed Jason in the right forearm, just missing bone. Sharp pain froze his entire arm, especially his wounded muscle, but he mentally shook it off.

I'm left-handed, so no big deal. No big deal.

Blood gushed out around the embedded glass, dripped off his arm and onto the table in a red pool, as he continued to sit motionless, determined to convince others he suffered catatonia.

A nurse grabbed Card Guy from behind, but he shrugged the woman off and snatched up another piece of glass. The deranged lunatic aimed it at Jason's face; he braced for the impact.

Three male nurses tackled Card Guy to the floor, stopping the assault.

The chaos of noise and action milled around Jason. He sat unresponsive, staring off as if nothing more than a corpse with opened eyelids.

He deserved an Academy Award for his performance.

Several security guards rushed into the room. They bolted straight for Card Guy, who was wrestling on the ground with the three nurses.

The phlebotomist wrapped a towel around the glass sticking out of Jason's wound, covering his skin with the cotton. She pressed down with a strong force; he fought the reaction to cringe at the pain.

No pain. No pain.

He said nothing and continued to stare straight ahead, stationary and unfazed.

"Sir, are you okay?" the beautiful young brunette asked him.

A red-haired nurse with pink funky glasses rushed over. "He's nonverbal and unresponsive," she filled in the phlebotomist, "been so since admitted night before last." She peeked under the towel and examined Jason's stab wound. "Call 911," she shouted to the other nurses behind the shattered partition. "He needs to be treated at an emergency department."

Jason ignored the urge to smile. A dispatched EMS crew was the exact result he'd aimed for.

Within minutes, sirens sounded outside in the distance. Each second they grew louder as an ambulance and Cayman Island cops neared the psych hospital. Inside the patient lounge, chaos rumbled around him, yet he remained silent and motionless, and bleeding from a throbbing stab wound. The white towel was no longer all white. Red stained a huge percentage of the terrycloth cotton.

Yep, I'm escaping out of here today, just as I'd planned.

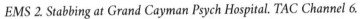

EMS 2. Stabbing at Grand Cayman Psych Hospital. TAC Channel 6.

In the back of her ambulance parked in the bay at EMS Station #2, Paramedic Sara Dyer listened to the computerized voice dispatch her unit to a stabbing call. Sara snapped the plastic narcotics medication box sealed and locked it inside a tiny cabinet. Excellent timing for a call; she'd just completed the midmonth check on med expiration dates and replaced all the expired ones with fresh vials. On occasion, she wasn't able to finish the entire daily ambulance and station check-offs before being dispatched to the first call of her shift.

After she flicked her waist radio to the designated tactical—TAC—channel, she stuffed her half-eaten sausage egg biscuit into a paper bag and dumped it into the trashcan.

Yuck. Bland and dry.

She ran her tongue on her teeth and inside her cheeks to clear the nasty taste, then zipped her backpack stuffed with personal items for her twelve-hour shift. As she crawled over her backpack and into the passenger front seat, her EMS partner rushed through the door between the station's crew quarters and the ambulance bay.

Russell slipped behind their ambulance's steering wheel and cranked on the truck's engine. Sara flipped on the lights and sirens. Within seconds they shot out of the garage, en route to their call.

On the left side of the road, they wailed through the British-owned island toward the psych facility. As Russell drove, Sara perused the laptop nailed to the dashboard for further information on the stabbing at the psych hospital.

"Fifty-one-year-old male stabbed by another patient," she informed her partner, reading the computer screen and preparing in her head how she'd handle the scene, no doubt some sort of a mental crisis for the stabber. "Our patient has a pulse. Is breathing. Stab wound in right forearm. Law enforcement just arrived on scene."

Russell didn't say a thing in response. Not at all shocking.

The normal silence between them settled inside the ambulance's cab. They'd only been partnered for a few months, since the day he was fresh out of medic school. They worked well together—they both enjoyed silence, didn't converse much, rarely shared anything personal. The most personal thing she knew about him? His fiancée was pregnant.

Every partner of hers called her the quietest woman they'd ever known, something all of them appreciated, except one—Boris, the annoying chatterbox. She'd simply responded to them: *I have nothing to say.* More to the truth? She didn't like ticking anyone off. It seemed too many people were overly sensitive and defensive about everything. It was safest to keep her mouth shut.

Sara yanked out a handful of medical gloves from a box and stuffed them in the empty left front pocket of her EMS pants for quick access; her right pocket was full of her dad's business cards. She handed out Inspector Alec Dyer's cards on scenes to those who needed encouragement to contact a cop, like an abused wife, a frightened homicide witness, etc., etc..

The morning sun warmed the cab of the ambulance in motion and made the black pavement of the four-lane road glisten. The view of the serene ocean on the left calmed her firing nerves in anticipation of what they'd encounter on scene. The near-empty beach of the weekday morning was a welcome invitation to savor the white sand and crystal-clear blue ocean water, which she planned to do later. To decompress after her shift, she'd walk the beach in peace.

Less than two minutes into their drive, Russell pulled the ambulance up alongside the curb in front of the Cayman psych hospital and behind four RCIPS—Royal Cayman Islands Police Service—patrol cars, all four empty. One uniformed cop rushed through the front doors and inside the building. Sara jumped down from the passenger seat and bolted for the ambulance's back doors to gather all their portable EMS equipment—airway bag, jump bag, cardiac monitor/defibrillator.

Packed stretcher out and wheels on the asphalt, she and Russell rolled it inside the first door of the mental hospital. A security guard buzzed them through the second.

"Psych calls are always so fun," Russell whispered sarcasm over his shoulder as he pulled the head of the stretcher through the double glass doors.

"They are?" Sara teased in return, pushing from the foot. She zeroed in on his short black hair curled tight to his head.

The hairstyle seemed out of date, a Greg Brady fashion from the seventies television show. Then again, what did she know about current fashion statements? Every work day she wore her straight brown hair in a ponytail, up and out of her way.

At a swift speed, they rolled down the hallway toward the patient lounge, trailing the cop. They caught up to him.

"Hey, Sara," Owen said to her in his typical somber tone as they neared the metal doors to the patient lounge.

"Hi." Sara had known the officer for years, since the day he'd joined the RCIPS and begun working with her dad.

Last year she and Owen had gone on a date, but he never asked her out again. Although…she'd never hinted she wanted a second date. Still, she couldn't help wonder why he wasn't interested. Maybe her turbulent personal history had scared him off. She wouldn't blame him. It scared her, so much so she was scared of the dark. At nearly twenty-six years old, she slept with her studio apartment bathroom light on every night, as well as the balcony deck light outside.

No one knew the reason she refused to work night shifts, although it seemed no one ever noticed. She simply signed up for twelve-hour day shifts only, and mentioned one time to her chief she had difficulty falling asleep in the daylight.

With authority Owen pounded his fist on the locked double doors to the lounge. "RCIPS and EMS," he shouted.

A psych hospital security guard cracked open one of the doors and studied the three of them. As he eyed Owen, he opened the door wider. "The perpetrator is contained down the hall," he pointed over their shoulders, "by RCIPS. I'll lead you there, Officer." He swung the door wide and trekked off down the hallway, jammed key ring rattling at his waist and Owen on his heels.

Russell rolled his end of the loaded stretcher inside the lounge. Sara followed, rolling the back end in front of her. The huge room was empty except for two nurses—one petite female, one mammoth male—standing over a man hunched in a wooden chair, his salt-and-pepper long hair banded at his nape. A towel blotched with blood covered his right forearm from his elbow to his hand. The huge male nurse, approximately the patient's age of fifty-one, pressed his hand down on the towel. The patient sat in stiff utter silence like a mannequin, face blank, limbs lifeless.

Catatonic?

From her pocket Sara whipped out a pair of blue medical gloves and snapped them on. "What happened here?" She approached the two RNs and the patient.

The frail female nurse, appearing to be over retirement age, pointed to a shattered mess of glass to the right. "Another patient stabbed him with a large shard. Looks like smack in between the radius and ulna but deep in muscle. Vital signs are all within normal range. BP and pulse a little on the higher end, understandably due to the trauma."

As Russell dug out equipment and supplies, Sara pressed her hand on the towel and next to the male nurse's hand. He withdrew his thick muscled left arm with a cross tattooed on his wrist.

"Let's take a look." Sara kneeled in front of her patient, peeked under the blood-moistened towel, and examined the trauma wound—a three-inch gash. Blood oozed and coiled on his skin. Hemorrhaging under control, but *not* controlled—meaning if she released pressure, this man would eventually bleed out. "This needs stitches. An x-ray of his forearm is the only way to confirm bone is uninvolved." She pressed her index and middle fingers to his right radial artery and found a strong regular pulse within a normal beat count. "Sir, we need to take you to the hospital for x-rays and stitches. Okay? Do you understand?"

No verbal response. No movement of any kind. All four of his limbs stiff, fingers rigid. Head drooped forward. His mud brown eyes stared off without purpose, somewhere at the worn linoleum tiled floor. His gaunt frame indicated regular illegal drug use and a lack of nutritious diet.

She eyed over her shoulder. "Is this patient catatonic?"

"Yes," the male nurse replied in a deep voice matching his stature. The guy looked more like a night club bouncer than an RN. He could squash the petite female nurse with his thumb.

Russell handed Sara a large clean towel. She tossed the bloodied towel onto an empty chair at the next table over. "What is his name?" she asked no one in particular, as she studied the sharp thick piece of glass sticking straight up out of the patient's arm.

"Jason Keegan," a feminine voice behind her supplied the name.

"Mr. Keegan?" Sara covered the wound with the fresh towel, circling the jagged glass piece, and pressed down with deep pressure. "Sir, how much pain are you in?"

Beyond the rise and fall of his chest, still no response. She didn't expect any, but it didn't hurt to try to communicate with him again.

Russell pointed to the glass chunk poking out the opening of the towel. "You wanna leave it in place or take it out?"

"I'm deciding." Sara paused to think. "Stabilizing it may not be best. The sharp edges could cause additional injuries to him and to others."

Plus, the patient could yank it out of his arm to use as a weapon. His stiff limbs could be a purposeful control by him, his mental state an act.

Anything was possible.

Years ago, as a Florida cop, she'd learned never to trust psych patients. That lesson was a continual confirmation during her three-year paramedic career.

The potential danger of a psych patient holding a sharp weapon outweighed the concerns of a hemorrhaging forearm wound, especially since the hospital—thus a surgical room—was only a two-minute drive.

In the EMS field—an uncontrolled setting, unlike inside the controlled environment of a hospital—safety decisions overruled.

Russell circled his index finger in the air above the glass shard. "You're thinking even taping towels around it won't be efficient enough?"

"The jagged ridges and crooked angles will tear the cotton. Any cover we give it probably won't hold on a moving stretcher to the parking lot and then in the back of our ambulance en route. Hook up a four lead."

"I'm on it." Russell scooted their cardiac monitor—the size of a boom box—on the floor next to their patient's feet and whipped out the ECG lines to connect Mr. Keegan, four lines on each of his limbs.

Sara turned to the two RNs. "Can one of you keep pressure over this towel?"

The petite gray-haired nurse moved into position. "Sure."

Russell attached the patient to the cardiac monitor via electrode patches.

Sara wrapped a blood pressure cuff around his uninjured arm and clipped the pulse ox to his index finger for a blood oxygen saturation reading. She shined a penlight in his right eye, then his left. Pupils equal and both responsive and reactive to light. Slight dilation. The increase in pupil size suggested possible stimulants in his system. Hmm, illegal drug-induced catatonia? Only possible if he'd been in the facility a short time.

"How long has he been a patient here?"

"About thirty-six hours," Bouncer Nurse answered her.

"Was he brought in catatonic?"

"Yes."

Maybe the patient's caregiver accidentally overdosed him with his prescription meds.

From the trauma pocket in the EMS jump bag, Sara withdrew a handful of 5×9 gauze pads and five roll bandages. She ripped open several of the 5x9s, and kneeled in front of her patient. "Thanks, I'll take over again."

The petite RN backed away, giving Sara space to work.

After removing the new towel, she placed four 5x9s over the wound, surrounding the glass piece. With one hand she anchored the gauze pad; with her other, she gripped the top of the glass with yet another gauze pad and eased the piece out. No squirting blood, so no arterial damage. Relieved removing the glass didn't turn out to be a bad medical decision, she pressed three more 5x9s over the opened wound.

"Retain this for RCIPS." She held the glass shard out toward Bouncer Nurse for evidence preservation as necessary for the police's case against the stabber.

With a gloved hand, he gathered it from her, placed it on a clean towel. Folded it inside the center of the cotton.

Russell tore off a strip of thin white paper rolled out from inside the monitor and reviewed it to interpret their patient's cardiac waves printed on it.

"Wave pattern?" Sara asked him, not that she was concerned. Mr. Keegan was a stable trauma patient, not a cardiac patient.

Still studying the strip of paper, Russell said nothing.

With her left hand, Sara maintained pressure to the wound over the gauze pads. With her right she wrapped a roll bandage around and around Mr. Keegan's wounded forearm, covering every 5×9 pad and the patient's skin from his wrist to his elbow. She wrapped a second roll bandage over the first. Then a third. She pressed her fingers to his right radial pulse to verify circulation efficiency post-bandage placement. It was strong.

"Vitals?" she asked her partner.

"All within normal limits. ECG is solid, too. Normal sinus rhythm. Do you want to see the wave pattern?" He held out the paper strip toward her.

"Russell?" she spoke in her field training officer tone. "Do you trust your interpretation?"

A slight pause. "Yes," he spoke with confidence.

"Then I trust you." And she did. "What is this patient's medical history?" she asked without facing either of the nurses.

"Nothing," Bouncer Nurse answered.

"What meds does he take?"

"None."

Stunned, Sara eyed the pair of nurses standing side by side, their height difference well over a foot. "What's his mental diagnosis? Why is this man a patient here?"

"He's charged with murdering his wife Monday night." Petite RN shrugged with a hint of sadness. "Cops found him in a catatonic state next to his wife's body."

"Less than two days ago, this catatonic committed murder?"

Sara had seen that one other time firsthand, years ago as a Florida police officer. That night, a forty-seven-year-old man had murdered his wife and two young daughters, then curled up next to their lifeless bodies and fell asleep. His brain never woke up to the land of the responsive.

Bouncer nodded. "Yep. The attending psychiatrist's evaluation was cut short yesterday for an emergency on another floor. He scheduled a detailed eval for this afternoon and ordered a brain CT and full blood work to ascertain toxicology."

"We're awaiting those labs and radiology report." Petite RN snatched up a manila folder from the table behind her. "Here's the doc's report." She held it out to Sara. "First page."

Sara slipped the folder from the woman's fingers. "Thanks." Any and all obtainable information assisted her in the treatment of her patient until she transferred care to the emergency department.

She flipped it open and read…

May 16: After a brief initial assessment, it appears the patient is in a cata-tonic state, perhaps schizophrenic catatonia. Unlikely, yet possible. Illegal drug-induced catatonia? Full blood work and CT scan ordered to rule out physical causes. Full evaluation scheduled for tomorrow, May 17 at two o'clock in the afternoon.…

Sara scanned the psychiatrist's patient assessment notes, which mir-rored her own findings in her physical exam of Mr. Keegan. She read the doc's explanation behind why his evaluation of Keegan yesterday was cut off far too short.

A swirl of unease coated her gut. In glancing at her stretcher's metal bars, she wished she could restrain the patient en route, just in case, but at this time she had no legal medical basis to do so since the MD docu-mented the patient was suffering in a catatonic stupor and Sara's assess-ment matched that diagnosis. Handcuffing him would be at the discretion of the police.

Bouncer Nurse pointed over his shoulder at the steel double doors. "The MD on staff today hasn't yet arrived for her shift, but the hospital administrator may be able to answer any questions you have. He's with RCIPS right now."

"Can he supply me with any more information than you two?" She handed the folder back to Petite RN. "Or than what's inside the file?"

"No." Bouncer shook his head. "Can't think of a thing."

Petite shrugged. "Me neither."

Sara turned her attention back to her patient. No blood seeped through the dressings. If it did at some point, she'd simply apply another roll ban-dage. And another, if necessary. And another, and…so on.

She grabbed the IV kit from their opened jump bag. Russell hopped in to assist. "Don't spike a bag," she told him. "I'll just insert a lock."

Within two minutes, via an eighteen-gauge needle, she inserted an IV lock on their patient's stiffened left arm for the administration of any nec-essary meds en route to the hospital. The first meds in the forefront of her mind? Versed, a psych drug to subdue and control a ballistic-behaving patient. Haldol, another med she could jab into him, if necessary.

"Is he ambulatory at all?" Sara asked no one in particular.

The petite RN shook her head. "Nope."

"Rigid immobility," Bouncer filled in. "Unresponsive to any physical encouragement."

"Appears so." Sara nodded. "Mr. Keegan? Sir, we're gonna load you up in our ambulance and drive you to the hospital, okay?" She didn't expect a reply, but she'd never simply ignore him. Patient care was more than medical procedures; it included reassuring an ill or injured patient. Maybe somewhere inside his brain, he heard and could comprehend. A high number of patients in a catatonic stupor were conscious of happenings around them.

Sara and her partner lifted their stiff patient onto the stretcher with the head in the vertical position to accommodate his rigid body posed in hunched posture.

Owen popped into the room, wiped his brow, then readjusted the police cap on his head. "What's the status in here?"

"He's stable," Sara responded. "We're about to head out to our ambulance. Are you or another officer escorting him? He's charged with homicide."

"I'm aware of Monday night's murder scene. It'll be me."

As they wheeled Mr. Keegan through the double metal doors and into the humid hallway, Sara studied her patient. His stare was still unfocused and undirected, like the soul inside had vanished.

When they reached the exit doors, the security guard in the enclosed booth buzzed them through. Without further ado they wheeled the stretcher out of the psych facility. The morning sun of late spring was now blocked behind storm clouds rolling in from the east.

At the back of the opened ambulance, they rolled the stretcher inside through the double back doors. Owen leaped in, ducked, and made his way to the head of the stretcher.

Russell climbed in next. Sara followed behind, then closed the doors to allow for privacy. In silence they worked as a team, arranging their equipment and reevaluating their patient.

Sara turned to Russell. "You want to attend or drive?"

He checked the efficiency of the bandage. "I'll take this one."

"I'll drive then." Sara opened one of the double back doors, jumped to the ground. Shut the door.

After she slipped behind the steering wheel, she twisted around to verify the position of her passengers. Owen was sitting next to Russell on the bench seat.

"Are we good?"

Russell nodded. "Ready to roll."

Sara pressed the en-route-to-hospital button on the laptop. She flipped off the emergency lights and pulled away from the curb. Turning out of the parking lot, she hung a right into traffic.

The cloud cover thickened each passing minute, darkening the morning sky. Meteorologists forecasted rain all afternoon from a heavy storm moving in from the Eastern Caribbean, pre-hurricane season weather. The season started June 1, only two weeks away.

Whoa, it was the middle of May. Her birthday was only three weeks away, and she'd be twenty-six. Her thirtieth birthday hung in the near distance, mocking her, reminding her she had no one in her life beyond her dad, her stepmom, and her two little brothers.

She lived in a perpetual state of fear. Fear of the dark. Fear of relationships. Fear of...life.

Fear of being me. I wish I was someone else. Anyone but Sara Dyer.

Pop! Pop!

Gunfire in the back of her ambulance caused a sharp pain of panic to lodge in Sara's chest. *Naw, couldn't be gunfire.* She steadied her hands on the steering wheel and glanced in the rearview mirror.

The end of a .357 barrel stared back at her in the mirror.

Owen's duty weapon?

She lifted her hand to push a button to send a distress signal.

"Don't touch a thing on that dashboard."

She stilled, her arm frozen in midair.

CHAPTER TWO

Sara couldn't breathe.

It was as if the gunman's hands were wrapped around her throat and squeezing. Panic swarmed her insides with a heated rush. Wide-eyed, she stared into the rearview mirror.

Squatted down behind her, patient Jason Keegan stared back, his eyes wild and cold. Deranged. No longer unfocused and out of it.

Sweat bubbled on her hairline. Her respirations turned to shallow pants. Arm still frozen in midair, she gulped down suffocating fear. With her right pinky and thumb, she twisted the pearl ring Dad and Lelisa had given her around and around her finger.

The man was quite the actor. For over thirty-six hours, he'd fooled a bunch of law enforcers and medical professionals—her included—into believing he was stuck in a catatonic state.

Via the rearview mirror, Sara caught glimpses of two bodies in the back of her ambulance. Her partner slumped over at the waist onto the empty stretcher. The cop's right leg up in the air, caught in the netting that separated the bench seat and the side door.

No doubt, both Russell and Owen were unconscious...or dead.

She blinked back the sting of grief and ignored the spasm in her heart.

"Don't even try to alert no one of nothin', got that?" Keegan spoke intense yet poised and confident.

If she were in the back of the ambulance, she'd reach for some Haldol to inject into this lunatic's muscles. Better yet, she'd jab Versed up his nostril and spray to render him subdued in only a few seconds.

But...if I were in the back of the ambulance, I'd be dead.

Like Russell. Like Owen.

With her arm still hanging in the air not far from the distress button, she nodded. "Got it."

She divided her focus between the road and the psych patient pointing a gun at her—both tasks equally important. If only she had her duty weapon clipped at her waist...but she was no longer a cop. Hadn't been a cop for nearly eight years, since the day she'd left the Florida State Patrol for college and then medic school.

Even without a badge and duty weapon on her person, the armed lunatic couldn't take away her ability to think and react like a former cop, something he had no clue she was.

His oblivion, her advantage. A pointed gun in her face didn't render her under his control like he assumed.

Once a cop, always a cop.

God? I take it back. I'm okay with being me. I'll stop complaining. Help me stay strong here. Help me survive this.

"Lower your arm, Paramedic." With his free hand, Keegan yanked on her ponytail, jostling her rainbow-colored cotton scrunchie. "You're not gonna touch any sort of button."

Sweat trailed down the back of her neck and slid between her scapulas. "I'd just like to up the AC. Is that okay?" Slick with moisture, her left palm wet the steering wheel. "I'm hot, aren't you?" She inched her hand toward the air condition switch on the dashboard but held her position, awaiting his response, his reaction. "Just the AC button, nothing else."

"Yeah, okay." Gun still trained at the back of her head with his left hand, he bounced it in the air, obvious intimidation to remind her who was boss here. The IV lock, secured via tape, jiggled in place. He was either left hand dominant or his wounded right arm was causing him too much pain. "Just watch your hand or I'll shoot it off."

The bandage from his elbow to his wrist was still intact, still in place and still white. No red showed through. Thanks to her, the bleeding continued to be under control.

Too bad she'd done an excellent job wrapping the stab wound.

One of the four-lead cables hung off just below his left clavicle and dangled around his hospital gown. Apparently, as he'd scrambled around back there, shooting a cop and paramedic, the main line from the monitor and the right clavicle line had popped off, probably the two ankle ones as well.

Sara nodded at him. "Sure, sure. Only the AC controls." She flicked up the air conditioning to high, then grabbed the steering wheel with both her shaky hands. "Mr. Keegan, if you blow me away, this ambulance will crash and you could—"

"I'll take my chances. Dead is better than prison."

"Which is where you would've headed once a doctor figured out you aren't catatonic?"

"You're quick." He sniffled.

She eased to a stop at a red light and empty intersection. "How'd you snow the psychiatrist?" The fact he had wasn't shocking. It sure wasn't the first time a psych patient had tricked his psychiatrist, and it wouldn't be the last.

"The doc checked me out for only a few minutes. He's suppos' to see me again for much longer this afternoon." Keegan laughed. "Not gonna happen."

"You know you're not telling me anything I'm not already aware of, Mr. Keegan. You heard the nurses explain everything to me." She hoped he'd reveal more details. Anything to help her understand him and his background.

"Again, you're so quick."

"How about you tell me how you faked catatonia so well?"

"How about you drive and shut up?"

Shutting up was typically in her repertoire. But this wasn't a typical situation, even for a paramedic and former cop. Tactical negotiations in a hostage crisis required honed skills and experience, neither of which she possessed; a third element was a lack of emotional attachment to the individuals involved.

Yikes. Zero for three. Strike out.

But the game wasn't over. She wasn't willing to give up.

The light turned green. She pressed her right foot to the accelerator and dropped her left hand to her lap. If she could reach her radio attached at her waist—

"Keep your hands at ten and two on the steering wheel," Keegan shouted. "No touching any buttons on your waist radio or dashboard console. Got it, Paramedic?"

Got it.

"What do you want from me?"

"Drive. Just drive." He sniffled again.

"Okay. What's your plan? You're on an island, remember? You can't just drive to escape. It takes only minutes to drive from one side of Grand Cayman to the other."

"I know that," he spoke as if bored with their conversation, the gun still pointed to the back of her head.

Keep him talking. Earn his trust. Talk him out of his plans, whatever they are.

"Mr. Keegan, we'll be at the hospital in about thirty seconds."

"I can see that." A breathy nasal pause from him. A whistle sounded from inside his nose, a sign his septum might be perforated from cocaine use. "Turn the ambulance around. Stay on this street." The guy spoke cool and calm, as if giving her directions to a restaurant.

Discover his plan. Understand it. Understand him.

"And head where, Mr. Keegan?"

"Just turn around. Without the lights and sirens."

"I'm not running the lights and sirens."

He looked off as if focused on listening. "Right. Why not?"

"We rarely run them en route to the hospital. We only do in a true emergency like major trauma, active stroke—"

"Whatever. Just turn around. Now."

She whipped a right and veered around a flowered island in a strip mall. With the traffic light green, she turned back on the road and headed in the opposite direction. The AVL—automatic vehicle location—inserted on her ambulance would alert dispatch she had averted off her route.

Dispatch? Recognize something is wrong and take action.

Was this really happening? She wasn't complaining; she was incredulous. Wasn't what she'd endured at the hands of her lunatic mother enough for at least half of a person's lifetime?

Sara's ex-boyfriend, Florida cop Scott Holland, had dumped her because of it. Not immediately, but he had nonetheless. He couldn't handle what had happened to her. It was too much.

Too much for you, Scott? I'm the one who went through it.

Yeah, and now she was the hostage of another lunatic, a stranger this time.

How could she be stuck in a second horrendous and deadly situation? It seemed inconceivable and too cruel.

"Stay in the right lane, Paramedic. Make a right at the second intersection."

"Where are we going?"

"You'll see. Don't you have any patience?"

"Not with that gun pointed at me."

"Quit whining."

She twisted her pearl ring some more. Around and around on her finger. And around.

Now what?

I have no idea.

On the beach to the left, a boy about eight years old flew a rainbow-colored kite in the gray sky. It fluttered in the forceful wind gusts as his dad stood by assisting. If Sara's hostage situation continued much longer, her dad would soon learn about it...and Inspector Alec Dyer would freak out big time.

Maybe this guy had someone who loved him. Who cared about him. Loved ones were excellent leverage to control perpetrators.

Just don't mention the murdered wife. Not yet.

"Do you have any children, Mr. Keegan?" Sara hung a right at the green arrow.

"What do you care?"

"Just making conversation." She shrugged with faked nonchalance. "You got any kids?"

"Yeah. One." Keegan waved the gun to the left a little. "Get in the left lane. Turn at the next left. Up there."

She turned into a parking lot of a small private pier. An array of sailboats and motorboats in rows swayed in their slips at three separate wooden docks. The three piers bobbed back and forth with the ocean surface as wind and incoming waves rocked them. No cruise ships; the cruise ship marina was on the other side of the tiny island, just minutes away. As she drove down the row of parking slots sparsely filled with various vehicles, Sara eased the ambulance's speed to under ten miles an hour.

"Mr. Keegan? What now?"

"Just keep driving." He sniffled, something he did frequently—probably a nervous tick, and certainly another indication of cocaine use. "Straight back, toward the docks."

If she gave him an inside view of reality, maybe she could convince him he was digging himself deeper and deeper into a dark cavern he could never escape. Maybe she could talk him out of his plans, whatever they were. Maybe, just maybe.

"Dispatch already knows something went wrong, Mr. Keegan. I should've reached the ambulance bay at the hospital by now and informed them of our arrival."

"I assume so, and ambulances have some sort of location device thing, don't they?"

"Yes."

"So your 911-dispatch knows exactly where this ambulance is at every second, right?"

Why lie? He obviously knew. "Right."

"That's why we're gonna make this fast."

"Make what fast?"

"By the time your dispatch figures out something is wrong and sends out cops to this location, I'll be long gone."

"And I'll be dead, shot to death. That is your plan, right?'

"Not if you listen to me. Do exactly what I say."

Yeah, right. What a gigantic liar. His plan, however, didn't account for the possibility the paramedic driving the ambulance was a former police officer.

She eyed him in the mirror. "Mr. Keegan, listen to *me*. In minutes this ambulance will be surrounded by cops. You'll be trapped with no way out of this. Think about your kid. If you don't lower the gun and let me out of here, they'll set up camp in the near distance and gun you down."

"If I give up, I'll be locked away in prison for the rest of my life. No—" he shook his head "—that's never gonna happen." He scanned out the windshield to the right, in search of something.

Ten seconds later he still searched. "Where is it?" he shouted. "Where's the *Persephone*?" His balled fist punched the air.

Ben was more than four hours behind schedule.

Vigorous winds flapped the sails and tossed his shaggy blond hair, overgrown from several weeks of needing a pair of scissors at a cheap salon. In all surrounding directions, open nothingness except seawater and sky.

The smell of sea salt and fish drifted up his nose, compliments of the windy air. On the starboard side about thirty yards, a school of dolphins jumped out of the ocean and dove back in, their flight an arched curve, matching the shape of their bodies. In the sky above the four dolphins, the wings of several birds grouped together swished in flight, then stopped for a break, each animal gliding a bit—the innocence of bird life, flying aimlessly with no goal beyond snatching a fish when one popped up near the surface.

A couple of hours ago, the weather had improved, allowing Ben to kick up the boat's speed some. Fortunately, not too many more nautical miles left to travel. The old man wasn't big on punctuality anyway. Jamaica Dude had instructed Ben to arrive at Grand Cayman Island between midnight last night and six this morning. It was approaching ten a.m.

The extreme lateness had been out of his control.

First, his flight arrival delay from Miami into Jamaica yesterday. Then, the harsh rainstorm swelled the ocean waves and soaked the boat, causing a twelve-hour trip over the sea to extend well beyond.

No huge problem, though, since the old man's court hearing on drug possession charges wasn't for five more days. In no time, Ben would reach Grand Cayman and ditch the island far behind the boat's stern, with Old Man in tow.

Plenty of time. Nothing to worry about.

* * *

Sara shrugged in response to Keegan's sentence. "What's the *Persephone*?"

"I wasn't talking to you, Paramedic." Keegan pointed to the windshield off to the right. "Park this thing. Over by the first dock."

Going with the flow, the guy was improvising with calm callousness. A criminal, a murderer with a confident demeanor in every word and every movement. She needed to be extra calm herself, and way ahead of him. Somehow predict his moves.

I can do this.

To carry out his demand, Sara drove deeper into the lot, closer to the docks. In a large open space in the corner, she rolled the ambulance to a stop. No cars or people around.

Whew. She didn't want an innocent bystander caught up in any danger. She shoved the gear into park.

"Now crawl back here."

Obviously he still needed her, or he'd have killed her in the driver's seat a second ago.

Don't be stupid. He'll shoot me in the back of the ambulance, where no one will see my lifeless body.

If she bolted out the driver door, he'd fire a bullet into her spine as she ran. Instead of panicked actions, she needed to plan and execute well every step she initiated.

Her life depended on it.

She left the keys in the ignition, even left the engine running to maintain power to the ambulance, thus power to everything onboard. It might come in handy for her to defend herself and take down this guy.

Like him, she could improvise well.

Crouched, she crawled into the open space between the two front bucket seats. She held her position there, her eyesight glued to her two friends, collapsed dead.

One bullet wound in his right temple, Russell's body lay scrunched up at the foot of the stretcher, his chest and left cheek pressed to the mattress. Owen's head was pinned at the bottom of the two steps leading down to the side door, his right leg entangled in the thick netting.

Tears stung behind her eyes. Fresh out of medic school, Russell had been her responsibility. She was his field training officer, and now he was dead, leaving behind his pregnant fiancée.

Sara's nose tingled with a burn of emotion. As she blinked to keep the tears from spilling out of her eyes, Keegan backed up and sat down on the bench seat, gun pointed at her.

Hunched over, she shuffled her feet through the tiny walkway, stepped over her backpack, easing her way into the back of the ambulance.

As she swung her arms forward, she pressed her left index finger to a red circular button on her waist radio. It was now open for a one-sided conversation from her end to all rescue crews on the island, including dispatch.

The half-second task accomplished, she continued to swing her left arm forward. She gripped the back of the bucket seat behind the head of the stretcher.

With a press of that red button, all EMS, fire, and law enforcement personnel on radio airwaves had audio of the interior of her ambulance; her radio waves, however, didn't indicate who she was, where she was, or her unit type or number.

"Signal 25," she said aloud to alert all listening she was in immediate harm. Grave danger. The Signal 25 message would cause dispatch to send everyone available to her aid.

"What?" Jason Keegan snapped at her, the gun pointed at her face. "What did you say?"

She slipped into the bucket seat. "Signal 25. It's what dispatch will assume, since EMS #2 never reached the hospital." She raised her hands up in surrender. "Do you really need to point that gun in my face? Look, Keegan, I'm just the EMS unit dispatched to the psych ward to help you with your stab wound, okay? No one else needs to die here. I can help you—"

"I know what you're doing."

Her stomach bottomed-out; her labored respirations kicked into a rapid speed.

She shrugged as if confused. "What do you mean? I'm just telling you the truth. I thought you'd want to know we probably won't be alone here at the pier for much longer."

"Do you think I'm stupid?" He ripped her waist radio from her pants, twisted the power knob to off, and tossed the device behind the cardiac monitor on the bench seat. "Giving information to your dispatch might be smart but it's useless."

CHAPTER THREE

"Signal 25."

Inspector Alec Dyer heard a faint female voice over the portable radio inside his car as he pumped gasoline into his empty tank at a station across from Cayman's white sandy Seven Mile Beach.

Signal 25? Someone on the island was in grave trouble. Cop? Firefighter? It was some type of rescue crew.

His ears strained to listen further.

"—since EMS #2 never reached the hospital. Do you really need to point that gun in my face? Look, Keegan, I'm just the EMS unit dispatched to the psych ward to help you with your stab wound, okay? No one else needs to die here—"

Alec stilled. Ice hardened his blood, clogging his vessels.

Sara. EMS #2 was Sara's unit. He didn't keep track of her shift schedule, so he had no idea when she was on shift this week. But without a doubt, that was his daughter's voice over the radio waves sending a Signal 25 alert, and conveying facts to aid and inform law enforcement.

Adrenaline spilling into his veins, he shoved the gasoline nozzle back into place at the pump and leaped into his car. As he sped away from the gas station, he dialed his commander with his free hand.

"Dyer?" Commander's voice glossed with tension after only one ring, as if he already knew.

"Sir, Sara's ambulance was taken hostage. Sounds like someone was killed, possibly shot." Alec pulled over to the curb since he had no clue where to drive to.

"I heard. Just handed some info on it." The sound of paper rustling grated through the phone line. "The patient is a stab victim at the psych ward. Guess his wound isn't serious."

"The perp is a psych patient?"

"Yes. Name's Jason Keegan. The drug addict charged with homicide night before last."

A liquid wall of panic washed over Alec's head, drowning him. "The catatonic? How's that possible?"

"Apparently the catatonia was a brilliant act. A plan to escape incarceration. He obviously knew exactly what he was doing."

"Obviously." Alec's temples pulsed with each beat of his racing heart. "Ask Craig to find out background info on this guy and get it to me ASAP." He gripped the gear shift, anxious to shove it into drive and speed off. "Sir, where's Sara's ambulance? Is it parked? On the move?"

A pause with heavy breathing. "Ah...I'll get back to you on that."

Alec's gut churned with the idea of waiting. "It can't be far, sir. This is a tiny island."

"I hear you, Dyer. Stand by."

A dial tone. The sound haunted Alec.

Ten silent seconds later, it seemed like ten hours had passed.

"Come on, Commander!" he yelled inside his unmarked police car, clawing his cell phone as if he could will it to ring.

Lelisa Dyer handed her kindergartener a plate of dry toast as he lay curled up on the loveseat suffering from a stomach virus that landed him in the bathroom more than anywhere else in the house for the last day. His older brother by two years lay sprawled on the couch adjacent from the loveseat, watching Sponge Bob and struggling with a raised temperature of one hundred five. Both her sons suffered with high fevers when sick, something they'd most likely outgrow.

"Baleigh?" She whistled at their black Labrador as she slid the back door open. "Out." The dog leaped through the threshold and outside to their backyard.

The house phone rang. Alec's cell phone number registered on the caller ID.

"Hi there," Lelisa answered on the second ring.

"Hey," her husband of eight years responded, his voice strained. Panicked. "Turn on the local news, will you?"

"What's wrong?" On sudden alert Lelisa dashed out of the family room, crossed through the kitchen, and headed for the staircase.

"Honey...Sara was taken hostage under gunpoint by a psych patient charged with homicide. She sent out a Signal 25 from inside her ambulance."

The punch in the gut rendered Lelisa breathless for a couple of seconds. *What? No.* She bounded up the stairs two at a time, in a rush to reach their master bedroom. Once she crossed the threshold, she lurched toward the remote on her nightstand, punched on the television, and switched the channel to the local news.

"Alec, there's nothing on but the meteorologist. When did this happen?"

"Minutes ago. Obviously the media hasn't yet heard."

Obviously. "What all do you know? Alec, is Sara okay?"

"I don't know," he spoke in a soft whisper, a cop-father barely holding it together. A parent herself to their two young boys, she well understood.

Years as a US DEA agent, and the last eight as a RCIPS drug task force agent, Lelisa knew how to shove aside emotion, but she was struggling with that a bit now—*Sara* was involved, her beloved stepdaughter.

"Do you know anything yet about the UNSUB?" she asked, her heart bounding.

"Actually he's not an unknown subject. His name is Jason Keegan. Lelisa, he murdered his wife on Monday. Faked catatonia at the side of her dead body so well that arresting officers committed him to the psych ward."

"Jason Keegan? Whoa, Alec, we've been trying to sweet talk him for years."

"Drug dealer?"

"No, user. His dealer is Coco Byers, called Drug King on the island. You know—"

"Yeah, yeah, Drug King."

"Mommy?" Kyle shuffled into the bedroom in his fuzzy socks, cuddling his stuffed bear, one of his presents on his fifth birthday this year. "What's wrong?" Wide-eyed, he stared at her face.

Lelisa clicked the television set off in case the news popped on with a report of Sara's predicament. Their sons didn't need to know. It could all be over in a few minutes, ending well, so no need to scare them.

"Hi baby. How you feeling?"

"Yucky." Eyes narrowed, he pointed his tiny finger to her face. "Mommy, are you crying?"

She plopped on the edge of her mattress and didn't bother faking a smile.

Should I tell him something basic about his half-sister's situation or wait until I know more?

With a wave of her free hand, she urged her intuitive kindergartener into her awaiting lap, the cordless phone still pressed to her ear. "I just heard something a little scary."

Eyebrows furrowed deeper, Kyle chewed on his lower lip. "Is Daddy okay?"

"Daddy's fine. I'm actually talking to him on the phone."

"Hi, buddy," Alec said on the line in response to overhearing their son. "I gotta go, hon. Commander's calling to give me the scene location."

"Alec? I love you. We'll get through this."

"I love you too. I'll call you later."

Lelisa pushed Talk on the cordless phone and tossed it behind her on their queen-sized striped pastel comforter. "Daddy says hi."

Kyle climbed into her lap. "Whew." He wiped his cute little brow with the back of his hand. "It's kinda scary Daddy's a policeman." He lowered his head, eyeing the carpet with his lips turned downward. "You're a policeman too. I mean police girl. It's scary."

"I'm sure it is scary, little buddy." Lelisa swallowed the lump clogging her throat. "I'm so sorry about that."

"Jeremy calls me a baby, says there's nutin' to worry about. That you and Daddy have all kinds of trainin' and expericy."

"Experience?"

"Yeah."

"And your big brother is right." She smiled close-mouthed, desperate to click the television back on and at least view the scene through the eyes of the media. It was better than nothing.

Would Sara's cop training and experience from years ago bail her out of this alive?

CHAPTER FOUR

The distress alert message the paramedic had managed to send out didn't concern Jason in the least. Nope, nothing more than a little speed-bump on his road to freedom.

He plopped down on the ambulance's bench seat and glanced at Paramedic in the high-backed chair behind the stretcher. He kept the gun aimed at her with his left hand. With his right he ripped off the tape over the IV jabbed into his left arm. He snatched a small towel from inside one of the glass cabinets and pressed the cotton over where the thing pierced his skin.

"If you're gonna remove your IV lock, don't just leave it on the bench. Put the catheter, the tubing—all of it—inside that red bin." Paramedic pointed to a container labeled "Sharps" hanging on the wall above him. "The opening is at the top."

"Worried I have AIDS? Don't want to catch it from the drug addict?"

"The HIV virus dies the second it hits light and air, so that would be impossible."

"Hepatitis then."

"Do you have hepatitis?"

"No." He eased the IV lock out, dumped it along with the attached tubing and connections inside the bin, but only because he couldn't spot a trashcan to dump the disgusting thing in. He pressed three fingers deep onto the towel over the area now free of an IV. A few seconds later, he peeked under the towel, noted oozing blood. He snatched a bandage from inside one of the cabinets and stuck it to his skin.

"You still need me alive, huh?" the annoying paramedic droned on in her pathetic attempt to negotiate her own hostage situation.

EMS hadn't trained her well in the art of the tactic. Either that or she had no idea who she was dealing with here. He wasn't just a drug addict, not just a murderer either. He was a man willing to do anything neces-sary—even dying—to get what he wanted, and he wanted nothing more than to never be forced to live inside a prison.

He rolled his eyes. "You really are proving to be a quick wit." He pointed to the cable dangling off near his left collarbone. "The other three EKG things fell off easy. How do I get this one off?"

"ECG. EKG is the acronym for the European spelling of the same med-ical term. I graduated from medic school in America."

"Yeah? But you work in the British-owned and government-operated Cayman Islands. Furthermore, I don't care. How do I get it off?"

She didn't respond.

"You really think there's hope in me strangling on it or something?"

Not moving an inch to help him, she just stared at him.

"You honestly think you'll be able to use it against me somehow? You really have no clue, do you?"

"Just pop it off from the patch stuck on your skin."

He slid away from her, out of her reach. With his throbbing arm, he grabbed the one black cable hanging off of him and yanked. It snapped off with a click, leaving the patch stuck on his skin. He tossed the bunch of bulky cords behind the heart monitor.

"Done." He stood up.

He stepped in front of the woman and leaned over her. Snatched her cell phone off of her waistline and tossed it at the pile of black cords.

Still aiming the gun barrel at her, he leaned over the dead cop. The guy's head was jammed between the side door and the bottom step, his neck and back twisted in the doorway, his leg entwined with a netting made of seat-belt material.

Jason snagged the handcuffs off the cop's beltline.

A grip on the gun twisted his arm backward.

He whipped his head around toward the paramedic; she was twisting his arm holding the gun. With his free hand, he shoved her into the wall of glass cabinets. Her body bounced, then crumbled onto the stretcher. Suck-ing in air, blinking a dozen times in a five second span, she attempted to stand. One-handed, he grabbed her by the shoulders and shoved her down into the bucket seat again.

"Seriously?" He laughed. "You thought you could take the gun from me?"

"Yeah." She breathed two quick breaths. "That was my plan."

"What a joke."

After he lowered the head of the stretcher, leveling the mattress flat, Jason sat down on the scrawny thing, facing the woman. He grabbed her hands, squeezed them together. Circled the cuffs around her wrists, but didn't lock the metal closed yet.

She said nothing, pleaded nothing. No fear flashed across her face.

Did anything rattle this woman?

He yanked her forward, toward him, their faces mere inches apart. He held their positions for a few seconds just to incite some fear in her.

Her eyes indicated nothing of the sort.

Fine.

With a click, he cuffed her hands to the stretcher's metal railing. She glared at him but said nothing.

He switched the gun to his right hand and ignored the throbbing pain from the stab wound. One-handed, he grabbed hold of the dead paramedic's uniformed shirt, dragged his limp upper body from the foot of the stretcher. Dropped it on the floor near the back doors of the ambulance and out of his way.

A slight sniff from behind him.

Jason turned around to eye Paramedic. Grief filled the corner of her eyes. "You gonna cry?"

"I might," she snapped back. She kicked her leg out, smacking him in the shin.

He backhanded her across the face. "Don't try to fight me. You won't win."

Still no sign of fear, no pleading for her life. With a lifted shoulder, she wiped blood from her nose and sliced-open lip.

Jason cringed at the pain in his left shin, then perused the cabinets.

"Are you looking for pain meds, Keegan? Stab wound hurting, huh?"

"You wish."

"Looking for a narcotic? Needing a fix?'"

He slid open one cabinet but didn't find what he wanted. He slid open a second cabinet. A third. A fourth. Dug around in that fourth one.

Excellent.

He whipped out soft restraints from inside. Straddling the stretcher, he sat down in front of her again, this time to wrap the cotton restraints around her ankles with the attached Velcro. He tied the dangling straps to the stretcher legs. Then tied it in a double knot. She had no room to move, not even a centimeter.

Emergency sirens sounded outside in the distance.

The sound gained volume with every second.

Out the window of the ambulance's side door, he scanned the docks. Still no white sailboat with the name *Persephone* written in red paint.

Where are you?

He set the gun down on the bench seat, and undressed the dead cop out of his navy pants and uniform shirt dotted with blood on the collar, leaving the pig in his underwear.

After removing the cream-colored hospital gown, Jason dressed in the cop uniform in haste. The uniform hung on him a little baggy in the shirt, the pants too long, but it sufficed. He dug around in the front pants pockets and found the handcuff key. He kept it there and grabbed the paramedic's radio he'd stashed behind the heart monitor, clipping it onto his waistline, onto the cop pants.

He flicked the radio back on to hear any chatter. To listen in to conversations between cops determined to bring him down—even more determined, he assumed, after his actions that morning.

Complete silence.

He switched channels. Same thing.

All channels were silent.

Must be hiding their activity from me.

He dug his hand into the back right pants pocket. Empty. He dug in the left. Found it. A lighter. He'd first smelled cigarette smoke on the cop back at the hospital.

The sirens wailed louder, nearing him.

Where was *Persephone*?

The sailboat should've been here waiting for me hours before I even drove away from that psych ward!

The roar of sirens intensified, the cavalry incoming.

Crouched down low, Jason eyed through the driver window. Three police cars lined up at the front of the marina parking lot, red and blue lights flashing and spinning.

The initiation of a standoff.

"Huh." He breathed out the word.

"You didn't plan on facing the cops *at all* before you made your escape?" Paramedic shot off her mouth.

It didn't rattle him in the least.

"Nope," he replied with a shrug, still staring out the window.

"Wow. You assumed you'd have no resistance, yet this turn in events doesn't seem to bother you even a little? Sounds like there's a standoff against you out there, Keegan."

"It's just a little speedbump on my escape road, nothing more."

"Speedbump? A standoff with the cops is more than a little speedbump. I assume your escape vessel is some sort of boat, but it isn't here. Keegan, you're trapped in a vehicle that is cornered by law enforcement. At a dead end parking lot."

"Yeah, but I have you. I'm guessing a paramedic for a hostage is high-stake leverage with cops. You're not a civilian. They see EMS as on their team, as one of their own. Am I right?"

"So what?" she snapped back. "That doesn't change the fact you're way outnumbered with nowhere to run and escape."

"Haven't you ever heard of think-on-your-feet action?" Smiling, he winked at her.

Her jaw dropped. "You're enjoying this, aren't you? You find it...thrilling. Like the high from the drug of your choice."

He glanced at the docks again through the cloudy morning. Scanned the marina water for boats sailing in.

No *Persephone* in sight.

Soon. It would arrive soon. His Jamaican buddy wouldn't let him down. No way. The knowledge in Jason's head and the proof he could supply to the authorities was his insurance that Jimar Malcolm would execute his part of this escape plan with success.

With the cops piled up outside, Jason just needed to adjust the plan.

"New plan, Paramedic. You're coming with me."

"What?" she snapped back with stunned fear. Finally, he had rattled her. "Your escape boat is here? It docked?"

"No, but it will. It will."

CHAPTER FIVE

With a clog of fear knotting his gut, Alec cruised around a parked fire truck, and slammed on his brakes behind three patrol cars horseshoed at the only exit/entrance of the marina parking lot.

Blood pumping in his veins, he darted around the firefighters staged on-scene, and marched up to the three officers who were securing this side of the perimeter. "Catch me up to speed."

Young Officer O'Brian's blue eyes flashed wide. "Inspector Dyer—"

"I already know—" Alec pointed to the parking lot "—that's Sara's ambulance. Anything yet from this guy Keegan?"

"Nothing," O'Brian answered in his Irish accent as the two older officers stood by listening to the exchange. "He's quiet, and no movement."

Alec studied the ambulance at the far end of the parking lot. "How do you know Keegan is still inside? How—"

"I've spoken with an eye-witness, sir." O'Brian pointed over his shoulder to a little old man.

The gaunt elderly man hid behind a palm tree. The tree's branches and leaves blew in sustained wind that had gained force over the last few hours, the approaching storm nearing. A leashed German Sheppard sniffed the ground near the man's feet.

"Says he saw the ambulance drive in here," O'Brian went on, "a woman behind the wheel. He was walking his dog, stopped to watch the action, but no one ever entered or exited the ambulance. He waited. We arrived on scene."

Alec waved his fingers at the binoculars in Officer Davis's hand. "Gimme those."

Davis handed them over. "Sir, she's not in the driver's seat. Both seats are empty."

Alec spied through the binocs. "I see that."

"Inspector Dyer? Agent McRoy just arrived."

Alec turned to find the island's only sharpshooter striding up to him. "Dyer."

"McRoy. What's your plan?"

The agent pointed to the roof of a store up on a hill alongside the road. "Stage up there. Wait for the opportune time. Take the clean shot and drop him."

Alec noted the row of cop cars lining the road on the street-side of the parking lot to neutralize the situation.

At the sound of a screech, Alec whipped around. Inspector Craig Hillman's unmarked four-door RCIPS car jerked to a halt on scene. To be out of everyone's earshot, Alec strode up to his long-time friend as he leaped out from behind the steering wheel.

"You okay, man?" Craig's chest heaved in and out with a raw emotion Alec felt himself.

"What do you think?" Alec snapped back at his best friend who loved Sara as if she were his own daughter. Instead of speaking a lame apology, he rubbed a hand over his face to calm down.

"I think it's nuts, Alec. Nuts that Sara is going through another round of hell." Craig scoffed as he perused the parking lot.

Yeah, first her crazy mother tried to kill her and nearly succeeded, and now a charged murderer desperate to escape is holding her hostage.

Alec couldn't believe another real-life nightmare threatened Sara's life. *Why, God? Why?*

"What's the deal out there, Alec?" Craig pointed to the ambulance. "I heard Sara indicated in her Signal 25 that Keegan killed someone."

"That's the interpretation."

"Anything else?" Craig clearly avoided voicing his underlining question.

"She's still alive in there, Craig. Keegan wouldn't have any leverage without her alive."

Craig nodded. "Right. More than hope, Alec, that's the truth."

Alec pushed aside the swell of paternal fret choking his windpipe, and dug into being a cop working a case. "Talk to me about this guy Keegan. What'd you find out?"

Craig folded his arms over his chest and stood erect. "Jason Keegan. Grew up in Southern California. Cocaine addict since college at the University of Idaho over three decades ago. One possession charge his sophomore year, then he dropped out. Second possession charge about fifteen years ago as a Florida resident in Miami-Dade County. Moved to Cayman in 2006 after Hurricane Ivan damaged the Hyatt Regency Grand Cayman in 2004, and the Beach Suite was rebuilt in its place, which is where he and his wife are employed. He's one of the hotel's mechanical repairmen. Wife works...*worked* in the restaurant before he beat her to death Monday night inside their home."

"Any drug charges here on Cayman?" Alec had forgotten to ask Lelisa the same question.

"Two. Both possession. His buyer—"

"Coco Byers."

"Yep, our friend Coco. We're working on concrete proof to nail him. We know Coco sells to countless Cayman residents and visitors to the island. Alec, did you know he's not even a user?"

"I do. Lelisa and her team have been trying to prosecute the mass dealer for years."

"He's crafty. So is Keegan. Alec, Jason Keegan is an explosives expert."

"That's comforting." Alec didn't want to hear one more word, but that wasn't an option. "Anything else?"

"His skills and connections saved Coco Byers grief many times over. Keegan has a ton of buddies in low places. Drug addicts and dealers. Criminals of all varieties throughout the Caribbean and in the US."

This guy has scummy friends, no doubt.

Sara kept a watchful eye on Jason Keegan as he stared out the side door window. The last few minutes, his relaxed and confident demeanor slipped a notch, maybe two, which made him unpredictable, thus even more threatening.

One by one his fingers on his left hand curled into his palm, his thumb overlapped the wall of fingers, completing a tight fist.

Had his shady rescue buddies seen the lights of cop cars from a distance? So instead of sailing to Cayman, Keegan's scummy friends sailed their boat away?

Made sense.

"Looks like we're both having bad luck today," she spoke in a soft tone and with sympathy, striving not to tick him off. The silence in the ambulance unnerved her, so she found her mouth rambling. With thoughts of super glue, she pressed her lips together.

With his back to her, his lack of movement creeped her out. What was he thinking as he stared out the window? The rigid stance was indicative of a volatile man with a tight lid on trapped and explosive emotions. If she didn't play this with caution, she'd crack that seal. To her knowledge, he'd murdered three people, the first his wife two days ago, then...

She eyed Russell's and Owen's contorted bodies, their skin pallid.

Am I next?

Could RCIPS neutralize the situation enough for her to get out of this alive?

Once again she toyed with her pearl ring, a little bit difficult with her hands cuffed but she found a way. Somehow the habit always eased tension inside her.

Two approaching sirens wailed outside, gaining in volume. By the sounds of them, Sara assumed a fire truck and a patrol car joined the scene of the standoff.

Keegan darted behind her bucket seat, probably to spy out the windshield. "Is there nothing else going down on the island today?" he spat under his breath. "Not one other thing?"

"If you want to get out of this alive, Keegan, surrender."

He sniffled. Again, it caused a whistling inside his nose.

Bent over at his waist, he leaned within her personal space. "Shut. Up!" He shouted both words at her, spitting on her cheeks and nose. "I'd rather be dragged out of here in a body bag than give up. Get it?" His chest panted as his diaphragm expanded and retracted; his panicked eyes glared at her with venom. "I won't live my life in prison. That's not living!" he yelled, the tendons in his neck bulging.

For the first time in front of her, Jason Keegan lost his cool. If she were in Vegas, she'd bet the change in his mood wouldn't work in her favor.

CHAPTER SIX

Dread, anxiety and hopelessness coiled together and latched on to Sara's nerve endings like a claw dagger. For the umpteenth time, she yanked her hands backward, hoping somehow this time the cuffs would magically unlock to free her wrists. She wiggled her feet yet again. No luck there, either. She was bound to the head of the stretcher that was locked into the railing nailed to the ambulance floor.

And there wasn't a thing she could do to change that.

Keegan's outburst moments ago had ended as abruptly as it started, and he regained his calm and confident composure. In his brief show of desperation, she'd seen the murderer in him, the rupture of anger underlining the drive that led him to kill. If she gave him no reason to jump to anger, she could stay alive.

Until he no longer needed her.

This man had nothing to lose, and his means to achieve his escape from law enforcement seemed like a game to him, excitement. A temporary high.

Dangerous combination.

With Sara's waist radio in front of his face, Keegan depressed the button on the side of the oblong device with his index finger. "Cayman Police? This is the man inside the ambulance. The one I took hostage." He clicked his finger off the button. Paused, obviously waiting a reply over the radio. He depressed the button again. "Anyone listening? Someone answer me."

Silence over the radio waves.

Then a crackle.

"Mr. Keegan, this is Inspector Hillman of the Royal Cayman Islands Police Service," Craig's voice boomed with authority over the radio. "I'm listening to you."

Sara envisioned Craig holding Dad back with a warning glare and raised palm to prevent him from spouting over the radio waves. If Keegan knew Sara was a cop's daughter, it would only serve in his favor—more leverage against the police. Dad would no doubt understand that, she was certain. Even though he'd be revved up, he wasn't stupid.

In a creepy laugh, Keegan cackled into the radio. "You've got nothing more to say to me than that?" he snapped at Craig, then lifted his finger from the button to listen.

"What do you want me to say?" Craig's voice answered over the radio.

Keegan pressed the button again. "Tell me if you want to save the woman paramedic's life."

"Is she still alive?"

"Yes."

"Prove it, or this conversation is over, Mr. Keegan."

Keegan stuck the radio in front of Sara's face. She awaited instruction from him on what he wanted her to say or not say.

Nothing came from him but heavy breathing and blank eyes. He depressed the button.

"I'm here, Inspector Hillman," she spoke into the radio and kept it professional to hide the fact Craig was someone close to her. Her dad's best friend, Craig had been Dad's partner in Fort Lauderdale back when they both worked on the FLPD over ten years ago.

Keegan yanked the radio away from her face.

"All right, you heard she's alive. Inspector, do you know anything about ammonium nitrate?"

"What about it?" Craig responded, a hint of fear in his tone.

"That's the dry solid component inside cold packs. You know, medical ice packs on ambulances? I just pour isopropyl alcohol onto several cold packs...do you know what isopropyl alcohol is?" He spoke in a patronizing tone.

"Rubbing alcohol. Another medical supply on ambulances."

"Yep, and it's a fuel source. Get where I'm going with this, Inspector? If I turn on the stationary oxygen tank onto full and without an O2 tubing attachment, then 100% oxygen will fill this ambulance."

"Too bad for you I know something about explosives, Keegan. You need a heat source."

"Inspector, I swiped the cop's cigarette lighter. So, if I set isopropyl alcohol drenched cold packs on fire in the O2 enriched environment and I fire a bullet into the oxygen tank, breaching it, that will cause a rapid release explosion. That insult alone—the bullet into the oxygen tank—wouldn't be enough for an explosion, but it would be in an oxygen enriched environment. Got it now? You'd be unwise to doubt me, Inspector. If you don't stay far back, I'll blow this ambulance to pieces. Explode the entire truck. Boom goes your precious paramedic. You'll be picking her body parts off the parking lot asphalt and the wooden docks, even out of the ocean water. So, back off."

Gulping, Sara squeezed her eyes shut.

She'd believed leaving the ambulance engine on would work to her advantage. But the exhaust from the diesel fuel would only serve to assist Keegan in his plans.

Huge backfire.

"I hear you, Mr. Keegan." Craig's voice over the radio waves. "But we're already far back in the distance from the ambulance."

"It's not far enough, Hillman. Back up more."

"Okay. We will."

"Also, any of you law enforcement types step foot on the docks or sail around into the marina, I'll blow this ambulance. You gettin' all this, Inspector?"

"Yes, Mr. Keegan, every bit of it."

Keegan dashed to the front of the ambulance and back behind Sara. Restrained and cuffed with only a centimeter of space to wiggle, she couldn't see around her high-backed chair. So, she pictured him squatting just behind the driver's seat as he eyed out the driver door window.

Several silent seconds passed. Several more. Even more.

"That's good, Inspector." Keegan's voice behind her. "Real good. You take orders well."

Sara pictured all the cop cars and rescue vehicles backing up out there.

"I'm holding up my end of the deal." Craig's voice again. "You hold up yours, okay? Mr. Keegan, is the other paramedic or the police officer in need of medical care?"

Keegan didn't answer Craig.

Another moment passed.

Still, she heard no response.

What's he doing behind me?

"Hey?" Sara shot over her shoulder, her nerves firing just under her skin, her heart pounding against her ribs with a banging sensation. "Keegan?"

"Keegan, talk to me, man," Craig spoke over the radio. "I can't help you if you go silent on me. You initiated this conversation. What is it you want?"

Still no response from Keegan. No sounds at all behind her.

Silent seconds continued to tick on. And on.

A cell phone rang inside the ambulance, from over behind the cardiac monitor. The simple ring tone sounded like an old fashioned home telephone.

"Keegan?" Sara craned her neck over her shoulder. "Hey, that's my cell phone ringing."

"So what?" he barked back as he moved into her line of vision and stood over her.

She shrugged. "Answer it, will you?"

"Why?"

"'Cause I'm guessing it's the Cayman police. Easier to talk on a cell phone than over radio waves, don't you think?"

The phone continued to blare its rings. Keegan dug around the bunched up ECG lines in search of it. After only five rings, her cell silenced.

Ten seconds later, it rang again. A second ring. A third. It was set to eight rings before switching to voicemail.

After Keegan untangled the cell from the corded mess, he eyed the LED panel. "It's the Cayman country code number. No name."

"Answer it, Keegan!" she yelled at him with fury biting at her.

"Watch yourself, Paramedic," he warned, pointing her ringing cell phone at her.

"Just answer it," she said in a calmer tone. "I'm sure it's the police."

"I have nothing more to say to them."

Ring.

"Answer it anyway. Aren't you a little curious what they have to say to you? Besides, you have nothing else to do but wait for your ride, right?"

Ring.

He glanced out the side door window. Placed the ringing cell phone to his ear. "Yeah?" Silence in the ambulance as Keegan obviously listened to the caller.

Was it Craig?

Grrr...with the radio I could hear both sides of the conversation.

"What do you want?" Keegan spoke into her phone.

Silence again for several annoying seconds.

"Hillman, I already told you what I want. Stay far back and be cool, that's the only way your paramedic stays alive."

More irritating silence for about five seconds or so.

"No, Inspector, there's no negotiating here. Stop trying. Just keep your end of our little deal, and I won't blow the O2 tank."

Pause.

"That's the idea, Hillman. I'd rather die than be captured and in custody. Don't you get that? You will never imprison me. You hear me now? Understand what I'm saying?"

Silence.

"Good." Keegan clicked off, then pocketed her cell phone.

Sara's stomach flipped-flopped. Her head swarmed with the reality of her plight.

God? Dad wouldn't survive me dying. He went through so much after I disappeared when Mom dumped me beaten and left for dead. For Dad's sake, get me out of this. He's so devoted to You.

The God she knew—thought she knew—was loving. Comforting. So, why was she facing another crazed killer? Was God truly harsh, like many believed? Was her faith only a fantasy?

Keegan eyed out the ambulance's side door window again.

Lingered there.

He high-fived the ambulance's wall, whipped around toward Sara. "Bingo, Paramedic." He winked at her. "That's my cue." Looking off, he beamed a creepy smile. "It's about time."

Right hand on the wheel, Ben steered the *Persephone* toward the Cayman marina in the near distance. Sustained winds quivered the mainsail. Spotty rain trickled the wooden deck, the sail, and dotted his t-shirt and shorts. It seemed the storm he'd braved crossing the Caribbean Sea was tailing him and headed here.

Jamaica Dude had told Ben if the old man didn't show up at the Cayman docks sometime that morning, then wait. The slip was rented for the *Perse-phone* from midnight last night for the next two days, as needed. If Old Man didn't appear within the two days timeframe, Jamaica Dude told Ben to call him for further instructions.

Easy enough.

Ben sailed into the marina and headed toward the first dock and the empty slip second from the far end, as prearranged by Jamaica Dude.

Red and blue flashing lights in the distance caught Ben's attention. An array of cop cars and rescue vehicles crowded the only exit of the parking lot as well as the street lining the lot.

"What's up with this?" Ben spoke his mind out-loud. A sense of intrigue swirled in his racing brain.

It can't have anything to do with the old man. That doesn't make any sense.

Ben's gut clenched. "Or does it?" he whispered to the wind.

Is there more to Old Man's court hearing in five days than drug possession charges?

Nearing the shore, Ben decreased the speed on the motor to low, then to neutral. He curved into the empty slip. The sailboat's bow bumped to a stop on the dock's edge. He jumped out onto the rain soaked wood to tie the *Persephone* down.

A quick eight-knot with rope from the dock onto the port and starboard sides of the boat's bow, and the *Persephone* was secured.

Standing on the dock, he scanned through the drizzly rain and at all three piers, but didn't spot anyone. Back behind him, the marina and the ocean beyond was empty of any vessels.

"What is going on here?" he muttered as he eyed a lone ambulance parked near the dock, maybe twenty yards away. Back in the distance, several cop cars, two fire trucks, and another ambulance. A bunch of people in various uniforms stood around. The area bustled with activity and blinking rescue vehicle lights.

No sign of the old man anywhere.

Maybe several people suffered severe injuries in an accident of some sort, or some kid drowned or something. Maybe all the commotion had nothing to do with the old man.

"Maybe," Ben muttered to himself.

Too coincidental, though?

Should I sail back out of here?

Unease crept into Ben.

He hopped back onto the boat and headed down below deck to retrieve the cell phone Jamaica Dude had handed him yesterday, minutes before Ben had departed Jamaica for Cayman. After he stepped down two metal stairs called the companionway, he landed in the main salon, a tiny area that branched out to two cabins, one at the bow and one at the stern. Back behind the companionway was a head—a bathroom—adjacent to the stern cabin. Across from the head was a countertop built into the boat hull and a folding chair in front of it. He snagged the iPhone off the counter to connect to the Internet and research Grand Cayman Island's breaking news.

CHAPTER SEVEN

"Paramedic? It's time to leave."

Sara wiggled her pearl ring with her thumb; her mind raced for a plan of action to save herself. "Your escape boat is here?" she spoke the obvious out of nervous energy, not knowing how else to respond.

"And you're coming with me." Keegan tucked the gun into his pants at the waistband in the center of his back, and untied the ankle restraints from the steel stretcher railings.

Unrestrained, she kicked out at him but missed.

"You don't ever give up, do you?" he said, squeezing her feet together. He knotted the loose straps to one another, leaving maybe a quarter of a foot of space between her ankle bones.

After unlocking the handcuffs with Owen's key, he unhooked them from the stretcher, then pulled her arms behind her back. With a click, he snapped the handcuffs locked.

Butterflies flitted inside her stomach. "Keegan, you do *not* have to drag me along. You don't."

"Of course I do. How else could I reach the sailboat from this ambulance without the police firing countless bullets at me? How else could I sail out of here without them descending on me, surrounding me like sharks in bloody water?"

Her abdominal muscles locked up, her lungs panted each breath. "You're gonna use me as your human shield? Keegan, that's crazy."

"That's exactly what I'm going to do, and it's smart."

"Smart?" Torrid dread encased her with a strangling hold. "No. It isn't." She scrambled for words of a hostage negotiator. "Using a paramedic as leverage? Taking a paramedic captive? Keegan, that won't guarantee your escape. Just the opposite. You won't get out of this."

He slid open a glass cabinet door and snagged a roll of tape from inside.

After ripping a strip off the roll, he stepped toward her. "You've forgotten I'm willing to die. Now shut—"

"Don't—"

He slapped the tape strip over her mouth. "—up."

With a clenching grip on her bicep, he yanked her to her feet. Dragged her to the side door of the ambulance, her feet shuffling forward one inch at a time with her ankle bones smacking each other. He shoved her in front of him, pressed her back up against his chest, then wrapped the crook of his left arm around her throat in a chokehold. With no wiggle room, her cuffed hands were trapped between her lower back and his lower abdomen.

Keegan's bandaged arm reached behind his back and withdrew the firearm he'd stashed there minutes ago.

"We're gonna step around the dead cop and out the door. Then we'll walk to the *Persephone*. She's a fifty-foot monohull. The second boat on the first pier."

Even if she could speak, she wouldn't. This guy had nothing to lose and didn't care about anything beyond ditching the Cayman police.

With his foot he shoved Owen's body to the side like a bag of trash, blood pooled around his body and the ambulance floor. Then Keegan lifted the ambulance side door handle. The door popped open with a loud snap.

The sound echoed in her ears, haunting her.

How can I get myself out of this?

He nudged her outside into the drizzle, causing her to jump out with her feet tied together. She landed on the wet asphalt with a bounce, her ponytail flopping and loosening from the day's events, her scrunchie slipping farther down from the top of her head.

Once Keegan's feet hit the ground behind her, she went lax, forcing him to hold up her body weight.

"Nice tactic, but it won't work," he hissed into her ear. "If you don't stand up and walk on your own, I'll shoot you in your arm and drag you. Bullet in the arm is the perfect place to cause you tons of pain but keep you alive. You want to bleed out on the boat? I'll have to dump your dead body out at sea somewhere."

She shook her head, then held herself upright on her feet.

"Smart girl."

I don't want to end up like Russell. Like Owen.

Could she really prevent that?

The rain shower intensified in thickness, the speed to a steady flow, soaking Sara and her captor. Through the warm, wet stream, she noticed a white sailboat with "Persephone" written in red cursive docked in the second slip at the first pier. The mainsail flapped in the wind and rain. Attached at the stern, the motor rudder dipped down into the ocean water. The boat wasn't ancient and rundown, but it was far from a lavish yacht.

Off to the left and up, Sara spotted the only sharpshooter on the island, crawling on the rooftop of a store situated on a hill lining the road up from the parking lot.

High precision rifle in hand, Agent McRoy hunkered down on the metal roof. The agent typically didn't have anything to do but wait for a situation just like this. The former British Army sniper was well trained. Mass experience. Flawless record. Sara knew and trusted him with her life. If he fired, if by chance he somehow found a clean opening, he wouldn't miss Keegan.

A clean shot in this case, though, would be tough to find. Especially since Keegan's height nearly matched hers.

With his back to the docks, Keegan dragged Sara toward the first pier, maybe fifteen yards from the parked ambulance, its motor still running. Baby step at a time, he backed them up, the gun barrel pressed to Sara's left temple. He kept his head directly behind hers. The ambulance blocked the view of most of the cops and other rescue crews on scene.

A quick glance at Agent McRoy, and Sara found him lying on the roof on his stomach. Rifle pointed at her and Keegan, aimed to fire when a clear path presented itself.

She leaned to the right, shifting her body enough to allow for a possible headshot.

Keegan pushed her back inline directly in front of him.

"You think I don't see that guy?"

He left McRoy no clear shot. Dad and everyone else on scene would agree. No way the marksman would fire. A moving target was difficult enough to hit. Add the poor visibility in the rain, plus a human shield, there'd be no way McRoy would risk hitting her. No way.

Don't risk it, Agent McRoy. Please don't fire.

Keegan shuffled their steps backward onto the wooden dock. "We're almost there. You've listened well, Paramedic. You know how to stay alive, how to keep me from firing a bullet into you. That's good. Real good. Just keep remembering who's controlling who."

She nodded.

Nope, no denial on her part. She knew he held the reins alone.

Alec couldn't stop pacing. Couldn't stop from reeling around in hyper energy. He'd lost his cool long ago, the second Jason Keegan radioed in and demanded to be heard.

Dressed in a cop's uniform, the scumbag dragged Sara under gunpoint out of the ambulance and toward the docks as Alec stood by helpless. Useless.

His blood boiled in his arteries. Rage consumed him. He craved to kill Jason Keegan with one shot to the face.

"Alec?" Craig tapped his shoulder. "He doesn't have it. McRoy doesn't have a clean shot."

"I see that," Alec snapped back.

They stood amongst the grouping of patrol cars horseshoed at the exit, watching a charged murderer kidnap his only daughter.

Alec was powerless. So were all the countless cops around him. It was Sara's disappearance all over again, only this time he was watching it live, a futile detective unable to do a thing to stop the killer abducting his daughter. This time he knew who was taking her against her will, but in order to save her life, he had to allow the hostage situation to continue to play out.

It was insane.

With Sara trapped in the crook of his arm, Jason Keegan backed up onto the dock and sidled his way right up alongside a white sailboat.

Alec pressed binoculars to his face, eyed through them and the misty rain. Watched Keegan drag Sara onto a boat with the name "Persephone" written on the bow in bright red, his salt-and-pepper-shaded ponytail bouncing down his back.

"We'll overtake the boat, Alec. Surround it in the water. He'll never leave the marina."

"Craig, don't feed me that bull. Don't hold out any hope on it either, man." Temples pulsing, Alec pointed at the marina. "He'll sail out of here with Sara under gunpoint. Just like with the ambulance, if we approach that boat, we're risking Sara's life. We gotta let him go."

Craig ran his hand through his hair. "I know. I know."

Alec's cell phone rang. Agent McRoy's number displayed on the screen. "McRoy?"

"Dyer, I'm sorry. I have nothing. No room to take a shot."

"I know," Alec said through clenched teeth, his legs turning to jelly, barely holding up his weight.

"My record longest range is nearly eighteen hundred yards, but he's using your daughter perfectly to block his body. Plus, in these poor conditions, visibility—"

"I know!"

Down below deck, Ben continued to fiddle with the iPhone, desperate to connect to the Internet long enough to actually read the news.

"Come on," he shouted out in frustration.

Cell service wasn't working well on this phone. Maybe the Cayman cell tower was the problem, or the rainy weather. Either way, his connection was spotty at best.

The screen flashed on, blinked off. He tried it yet again. The screen bleeped on. Stayed on. He accessed the news page. The connection stabilized.

The screen blackened again.

The boat jerked backward in sudden motion.

"No, you don't," a male voice yelled from up on the deck.

Other words followed but were garbled. Muffled.

Cell pocketed, Ben rounded the companionway and bounded up it and into spitting rain from thick clouds. As he reached the landing of the cockpit, he noticed the *Persephone* backing out of the slip, then spotted a female in an EMS uniform, mouth tape-gagged, ankles bound together and knotted to the helm pole, hands cuffed behind her. Old Man squatted smack next to her on the boat floor as if ducking behind the wheel. Hiding.

"Dad?" Ben stared at the gun Jason pointed at the woman EMT as he steered the helm with his other hand. "What...why are you dressed in a cop uniform? *What* is going on?"

Leaping to his feet, Jason's jaw dropped, eyes popped wide open. "What the devil are *you* doing here, kid? And don't call me Dad. You know I hate it."

Okay, Old Man.

"You asked me to come, *Jason.*"

"No. I didn't." Jason kept the gun on the tied-up woman as he revved up the motor to medium high and steered the boat forward with his free hand.

Confusion swarmed Ben, brewing the onset of a headache.

Dead heavy on his feet, he just stood there, not knowing what else to do. The boat's speed rocked him, unbalanced him, so he slid onto the bench seat. Then he pointed to the EMT on the ground. Ankles restrained, she sat in a groin-stretch position, the soles of her boots together. "What's up with her? Who is she?"

Jason cranked up the motor to high and sped the boat out to the open sea. Heavier rain fell on the hazy horizon. "A friend."

"Friend? You hold your friends at gunpoint? Handcuff and gag 'em?"

"You don't understand."

"Understand? Are you saying my vision is flawed without my knowledge?"

Silence.

Ben studied the EMS woman bound up on the ground. Her face flushed, hair tousled. A multi-colored hair band dangled halfway down her ponytail as if she'd had a rough morning. The lingering rush of sympathy for her walloped him with a smack, but he couldn't help wonder if neither she nor Jason could be trusted. Were they both dressed up in disguise and running from the law?

Face blank and unreadable, she seemed indifferent to the situation. She was handcuffed and tied up, yet didn't seem scared at all.

Why isn't she terrified?

He didn't know what to make of her. He didn't know what to believe. What to think. Of either of them.

"Jason?" More confusion spun Ben's mind; his lungs panted his breaths with fear of the unknown. "Explain to me what's happening."

More silence.

A dark blanket of apprehension dropped over Ben, covering every inch of him and seeping into his core like a hundred pounds of lard.

This is not what I agreed to, whatever it is that's happening.

"Hey, I'm talking to you!" Ben yelled at the man who'd fathered him, the man who raised him alongside Mom, but whom he'd never really called Dad. Per the man's demand since Ben had been a small boy, he called him by his first name. "Jason, answer me."

"Watch it, kid," Jason snapped. "I'm the one holding the gun here."

"Yeah, and why is that?" Ben shouted. "What's the deal here?"

"You aren't supposed to be here, college boy," Jason yelled back, racing them deeper out to sea at the boat's top speed. "You were sent to do someone else's work. Do you get that now?" he yelled louder. "Huh?"

Jamaica Dude duped me. Manipulated me.

Ben scoffed. "Yeah, Jason, I get it," he said, his jaw so tense it ached.

Jason's focus remained on the wide-open ocean stretched out before them; his left hand clutched the gun like a lifeline, his right guided the wheel. A thick bandage covered his right forearm, from his elbow to his wrist.

"What happened to your arm?"

"Just a little wound, kid. No big deal."

"That's a large bandage for just a little wound."

With the tip of the gun barrel, Jason touched the woman's shoulder. "Paramedic here fixed me up. She's overzealous about her job."

"O…kay." None of this made any sense, especially…

Ben eyed behind his father at the marina parking lot decreasing in size as they charged away from Grand Cayman. Lights flashing, tons of cop cars and other rescue vehicles still horseshoed the exit, blocking it off.

"What happened back there?"

No answer.

Heightening fear of the unknown slicked Ben's palms and coated his armpits with sweat. He glared at Old Man. "Answer me!" he shouted. "What happened at the marina?"

"Kid, don't you think if that mess back there had anything to do with me, a dozen law enforcement boats would be rushing after us?"

The Grand Cayman shoreline continued to diminish in size. The entire seventy-six-square-mile island would dwindle and soon disappear from his sight, sooner than normal with the poor visibility. No boats charged after them. Not one.

Still. Too many unanswered questions bothered him.

"Jason? Why are you dressed like a cop?"

"Man, college boy, you're full of questions."

"Start answering them, and maybe we'll get somewhere."

"Watch it, kid."

"Or what, you'll shoot me?" Ben snapped back as he eyed the revolver in Jason's hand.

The only gun the old man ever had when Ben was growing up had been locked away in their house somewhere out of his sight. As far as he knew, Jason had never used the revolver, had said it was only for protection, which had never been necessary, to Ben's knowledge.

Seeing a gun now in Jason's possession, in position to fire, seemed so foreign. So bizarre. So out of place. The man before him was not the man he'd known for twenty-six years.

What changed?

"Put that gun away."

"You giving the orders, kid, is not how this is going to play out."

"Then how's it gonna play out, Jason? Tell me!" Ben yelled, fists balled at his sides. A fresh course of anger and confusion thrust through his veins.

"I don't owe you any explanation or any information."

"Turn this boat around." Ben pointed over Jason's shoulder. "Go back to Grand Cayman."

"Or what, Ben? Kid, if you don't want to be here, jump overboard and swim back. We're only three or four miles from shore."

Ben was fit, sure. But an Olympic distance swimmer? Not even close. "You're hilarious," he snapped back. "An above-average comedian."

"I'm not joking," Jason spoke with venom.

The coldness in his tone, the iciness in his eyes, shot a chill through Ben.

The man standing behind the boat's helm wasn't the man he remembered. The man he knew was a cocaine user, yes. Often drugged-out, yes. But he'd never hurt anyone, only his own body via his drug of choice, only stood by as Mom had done the same to hers.

Had the white powder destroyed his mind to the point he was no longer in control of himself? His brain so fried and jittery, irrational seemed rational?

"Jason? What happened to you?"

"Life."

CHAPTER EIGHT

Alec bolted for the ambulance, its motor still running. As he ran across the rain-wet marina parking lot, he dialed his scuba friend out in the ocean. Earlier he'd spotted the man's boat anchored a few miles off the shore. It was still there.

"Hey, Alec. What's—"

"Ronnie, listen. Do you see that white fiberglass sailboat flying out to sea? *Persephone* written in red cursive at the bow? It's not far from you."

A silent pause. "Yup. What about it?"

Alec reached the ambulance. Gun drawn, he popped open one of the double back doors and found two lifeless bodies. Russell lay on the floor at the foot of the stretcher. Alec grabbed the paramedic's body to prevent it from spilling out onto the parking lot ground. He checked for a carotid pulse.

Sara's partner was dead.

"Alec? You still there?" A voice in his ear over the phone.

"I'm here. Ronnie, keep tabs on the direction of the *Persephone*. Police business."

"Uh-huh. I see all the rescue lights at the marina. You want me to follow the *Persephone*?"

"No, Ronnie," Alec snapped back at the guy's burst of excitement. "Stay put."

"That makes keeping tabs on its whereabouts a little impossible, Alec. Doesn't it?"

The side door of the ambulance jerked open. Alec watched Craig reach in to examine Owen's body.

"Ronnie, just watch the general direction the sailboat heads. That's all I need."

"I'm your man, buddy. Count on me."

"Thanks." Alec disconnected with Ronnie as an aircraft zoomed low overhead.

Craig shook his head. "He's dead, Alec. Bullet in the neck."

Alec dashed to the driver door, opened it, and shut the truck's engine off.

Craig's cell phone rang via the latest Dave Matthew's Band song. "Alec? It's Sara's cell."

Alec lurched around the hood of the ambulance and joined Craig at the opened side door.

"Inspector Hillman," Craig said, answering his phone. "Mr. Keegan?"

Alec braced for what would follow.

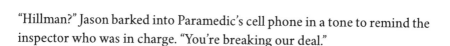

"Hillman?" Jason barked into Paramedic's cell phone in a tone to remind the inspector who was in charge. "You're breaking our deal."

Eyes narrowed and brewing with suspicion, Ben stared at Jason. The college boy was studying his every move, and it seemed he hung on every word he spoke to the inspector over the phone.

My own kid doesn't trust me.

Smart kid.

"How's that, Mr. Keegan?" Hillman replied, tone calm and steady.

"Second aircraft overhead in only one minute. Two boats are curving around from the north side of the island, another one from the west. All are headed in the *Persephone's* general direction. Hillman, there are hard-core explosives aboard this boat just beggin' me to set 'em off. You're giving me reason to oblige."

At his words, Ben's eyebrows shot up, head jolted back in stunned shock.

Well, some of the truth was out for the kid to hear. So be it. It couldn't be helped. Jason couldn't sugarcoat this conversation for listening ears.

Ben's fingers flicked in nervous energy. Mistrust swirled in his eyes as he fired suspicious glances back and forth between Jason and the paramedic tied up at his feet. Jason continued to point the gun barrel at Paramedic to keep Ben in line and under his control.

It had worked thus far.

"Mr. Keegan, I can't—"

"Same deal here as at the marina," Jason cut off the inspector. "You know what happens if anyone comes near the *Persephone*. Don't forget it. This conversation is over."

"Mr. Keegan? I can't shut down commercial flights scheduled in and out of Cayman or aircraft flying in the area. I can't control all vessels traveling the Caribbean Sea in your vicinity."

"Don't play me, Hillman."

"I'm not. You're asking the impossible. It's inevitable—you will see other boats out there, as well as aircraft overhead. There's nothing we can do to change that. Be realistic."

"Come on. You know exactly what I mean. Guarantee that no one tails me, and I'll know if they are, Hillman. Don't push me."

"Relax. I won't. We know what you're capable of, and we don't want anyone else dying. Mr. Keegan, do you have some sort of life raft onboard?"

"Where are you going with this, Hillman?"

"How about putting the paramedic on the raft, allow her to drift away from the *Persephone*? You don't need her anymore."

"The heck I don't. Do you think I'm stupid?"

"No, not at all."

"Then why would you suggest such an idiotic thing?"

"Just an idea. Mr. Keegan, what is your plan with her? How about we make a deal?"

"You know the deal. We've been through this. There's nothing else to say."

"Is the paramedic still alive?"

Jason glanced down at his prisoner. She stared back up at him, her squinted eyes like ice daggers firing at him.

She was a feisty one.

"Of course, Hillman, otherwise I'd have zero leverage. Man, you're just not getting this, are you? Lack of intelligence, or do you have a learning disability?"

Lightning cracked. The downpour continued. Thunder boomed.

The line went dead.

Cell service out, gone—either too far from shore or the boiling storm overhead, or the combination of the two.

No matter. Message sent to the inspector. Task accomplished.

Jason pocketed the paramedic's cell phone.

"You have lost your mind." Shaking his head, Ben glared at him.

Near the back of the ambulance, Alec stepped forward, toward the ocean.

The *Persephone* decreased in size as it blended in with the hazy horizon. It would soon disappear into the open seawater and the looming storm above.

"What's the call, Dyer?"

Alec whipped around upon hearing his commander's British-accented voice. His superior stood next to Craig, who leaned against the ambulance, arms crossed in effort to keep himself under control.

Commander pointed to the ocean. "Your daughter, your call. How do you want us to proceed?"

In Sara's disappearance ten years ago, the FLPD had given Alec little control in the beginning, then shut him out of the case completely. The Cayman police handled things differently. The refreshing change terrified him

So this is what FLPD meant by too emotionally involved to be competent on the job.

Alec cleared his throat. "Sir, we let the boat go. Sara stays alive that way."

"I agree," Craig chimed in. "I don't like it, but it's the only way. For now."

"So what's the plan?" Commander asked, his attention focused on Alec.

"We keep tabs on the *Persephone's* direction from a safe distance. I have a diving friend already on it from his boat out there, but I ordered him to stay put and simply watch. Sir, I've contacted Interpol and the US Coast Guard for assistance."

Commander nodded.

"And RCIPS is on two unmarked boats out there, a safe distance back from Keegan."

Clipped at Alec's waist, his cell phone rang. His wife's cell number popped up on the screen. He turned away from the crowd of cops who—as useless as he—couldn't do a thing to rescue his daughter.

"Lelisa?"

"Alec, honey. How are you?"

Fired up to kill someone with his bare hands. Beat them to death. "Hanging on."

"I'm watching it all live on TV. I had to tell the boys something, but I'm keeping it simple. Not allowing them to watch the news or talk to anyone. What is RCIPS doing?"

"Keeping tabs on Jason Keegan's whereabouts out there from a safe distance back."

"You have no other choice?"

"Keegan's escape boat is loaded with explosives, Lelisa. He's willing to die to avoid being apprehended."

"Then, yeah, you have no other choice. I kinda figured that by how you were playing it at the marina. Alec, no matter what, never ignore the fact he's an explosives expert."

"That's why we let him go." He pressed back up against a lone palm tree, wishing the Batmobile was real and he had access to it so he could whisk out to the *Persephone* and snatch Sara away from Keegan, since actual police work was failing.

"Alec? Honey, keep positive."

Keep? I don't feel positive at all.

"Lelisa, I had to stand by and watch this guy abduct my daughter. He's desperate to be left alone, and leaving Sara in his hands is keeping her alive."

"That won't work forever."

"I know." He squeezed his eyes shut, drew in a deep breath to slow his racing heart.

It took the rest of his dwindling strength to keep himself grounded where he stood instead of hopping on some boat to chase down the *Persephone* and blow Jason Keegan's head off. But if he raced after the sailboat, it would only get Sara killed, plus it'd be too limiting—he'd be most efficient working onshore to find the best way to get this guy under authority-control and Sara safely away from him.

Sure, yeah, but…how?

"So what's your plan?" Lelisa asked him.

I. Have. No. Idea.

"I'm working on it."

CHAPTER NINE

Streaks of clouds dusted the sky in random beauty over the endless stretch of sea. In the far distance, the distinct line, perfectly straight, defined where the ocean ended and the sky began to the human eye. Wind gusts, strong and steady, moved the ocean surface, churning it. The roll of white caps danced in the water, shaded by variations of blues and greens.

The Caribbean Sea looked as angry and turbulent as Ben felt.

Heavy angst filled his gut as he continued sitting on the bench seat, torn by what move to make next. He envisioned attacking Jason. Coming at him full force, full body, and tackling him to the boat deck to wrestle the gun away from him.

The gun barrel pointed at the woman's head stopped him.

Regardless of how exactly the EMT was involved in all of this, Ben couldn't put her life at risk, especially since apparently she was nothing more than an innocent victim. He'd be less in the dark if he'd heard more than just Jason's end of that telephone conversation with some person named Hillman.

Instead of allowing his emotions to control his actions, Ben had to remain in control of his emotions. It was essential.

Jason let go of the wheel. The boat continued on-course with a slight zigzag.

"What are you doing?"

Ignoring Ben's question, Jason snatched up the boat's radio mic. Gun still aimed at the EMT with one hand, he twisted the radio knob to a certain channel frequency with his other. "This is the *Persephone*," he spoke into the mic. "Need to speak with J.M." He waited for a response.

No doubt to Ben, J.M. was code for Jimar Malcolm, and Jason used the initials in case of any listening ears over the radio waves.

Ben waved the radio mic his way. "Let me talk to Malcolm." *The Jamaican jerk.*

"Just so you can tell him off for getting you involved? Don't think so, kid. I'd like to do the same, but we don't have time for that."

No response over the radio waves.

"J.M.?" Jason said into the mic, then steered the boat for a few seconds. "You hearing me?"

A crackle over the radio.

"Cayman Kee?" The voice over the radio spoke in a thick Jamaican accent Ben didn't recognize.

"You're not J.M.," Jason said. "Who is this?"

"A pal of his. Give him a second."

Silence.

More silence.

Rustling sounds. Whispers.

"Mon? Dat you?" Malcolm's voice, Ben recognized.

"Yeah, it's me." Jason took a brief moment to steer the boat. "Who was that guy?"

"Don' worry. We can trust 'im. Wha'appen?"

"I need another boat. I've gotta ditch this one. ASAP. Go backup."

"Yeah, mon. I get you one. Sail to de backup plan coordinates. Wee swap boats der."

"Yep. Plan Backup. Jamin? Hey, are *you* actually gonna be there this time? Don't answer. We'll discuss it later."

"No' 'appy wid me?"

"Later."

Jason kicked the speed of the boat up to thirty-five knots.

Ben watched the outline of Grand Cayman Island disappear into the horizon behind them.

With a crashing boom, Jason slammed the handheld mic piece into the tiny radio over and over again, with a force determined to destroy the box.

"What are you doing?" Ben yelled, jumping to his feet. He swayed from the boat's speed.

Jason aimed the gun barrel at his face. "Back off. You aided my escape, so unless you want to serve time or die by my hand, shut up and do what I say when I say it. Got that straight?"

As Grand Cayman Island drifted out of Sara's sight, she watched the Ben guy step up to stop Keegan from killing the radio, but the end of Owen's .357 Magnum in Ben's face halted him in midstride, and he sat down again.

Keegan's bizarre action reminded her of a scene from one of her favorite old movie, *Jaws,* when Robert Shaw's lunatic character smashed the boat's radio, terminating the only onboard communication connection with the shore.

"Why would you do that?" Ben shouted out, pointing to the chaotic brokenness of metal and damaged wire, yet staring at the gun aimed at his face.

Keegan dropped the hand mic. It dangled from the radio, the black curlicue cord swinging back and forth in the air mere inches from the ground. He gripped the boat's wheel again and steered them ahead straighter.

"If you would've arrived at the marina on time," Keegan yelled back, changing the subject, and losing his cool for the second time in front of Sara, "this would be smooth sailing. *Literally!"* he shouted the last word in an even louder volume, his finger on the trigger.

The rage in his eyes caused a chill to shudder through her.

"What's that have to do with destroying the radio?" Ben shot back at him.

"Everything," Keegan spat the one word with venom in his tone.

It creeped Sara out.

Ben pointed to the gun in Keegan's hand. "You gonna shoot me, *Dad?* You're that desperate, you'd kill me?"

Sara didn't know what to think of Keegan's son. While he seemed stunned by his father's volatile behavior, he'd sailed to Cayman to pick Keegan up. In Keegan's words, Ben had aided his escape.

"I don't want to hurt you, kid, but I will if you force me."

Restrained and bound, Sara could do nothing but sit there and witness the family drama unfold.

"Jason, why are you so panicked?"

"Panicked? Your old man doesn't get panicked."

"I know, so what's the deal?" Ben shrugged on a scoff. "Who's got you so freaked? Is it the guy you spoke with on the phone? Hillman? Who is he?"

As if she weren't onboard the boat, an awkward silence settled in between the two men.

And stretched on.

"He's a Cayman cop, right?" Ben broke the silence, fresh anger and accusation in his tone as well as in his stiff body language as he sat ramrod straight. "Now it's clear why the cops aren't rushing after you on this boat. You threatened them."

"Good, Einstein. You can add two and two."

"Cut the crap." Ben's volume raised several notches. "What else did you lie to me about today? Huh? Are you running from more than just drug possession charges? Is that it?"

Drug possession? How far in the dark is this Ben guy?

"You're the one with the fancy college degree. You figure it out."

"That's what I'm doing, Jason. Trying to figure out what's going on here." Ben eyed the gun still pointed at him, then glanced at Sara.

She simply stared back at him. Not that she could do anything else anyway.

Ben broke their eye contact. "This all seems too elaborate to simply avoid three to six months in prison for possession."

"Kid, this is my third possession charge just on Cayman alone. There's no such thing as a quick three to six months for me anymore. Try several years. Maybe a decade. Maybe more."

Smooth, Keegan. Convincing. The guy can sure think on his feet. Impressive.

Ben studied Keegan, as if trying to read through his father's facade. "What's up with her?" he said, pointing down at Sara. He bolted up and toward her. Squatted on the balls of his feet in front of her and lifted his hand.

Unsure of his intentions, she pulled her head away.

"Don't." Keegan pushed him with a hard shove to his shoulder via the gun barrel. "Stay away from her," he warned, a flash of panic in his eyes.

Ben stumbled backward, righted himself back up on his feet. "Take the tape off her mouth, Jason, or I will."

That's what he was gonna do? Ungag me? Huh. To help me or get info out of me?

"No, you won't, kid." Keegan aimed the gun in his son's face again. "It stays on."

Ben cleared his throat; he sounded ticked. With an angry slap, he grabbed onto the horizontal metal bar holding the sail. It seemed to steady him on his feet, apparently the purpose. "And why is that?" he hammered back at Keegan.

"'Cause I say so."

Ben scoffed. "That is a brilliant response, Jason. Just brilliant."

"Glad you see it that way."

Scoffing again, Ben rolled his eyes. "Cut it out." With his free hand, he pointed at Sara again. "You're treating her like a rabid animal."

"It's your fault she's even here."

Ben laughed but in a tone that held no humor. "How's that?"

"You arrived at the marina more than four hours late, remember? Let it go, Ben. She's fine. None of this is your business."

Anger seethed deep inside of Ben. It churned with a boiling mixture of raw emotions. "None of my business?" He snapped back at Old Man but stayed cognizant of the gun. *Don't get too fired up.* "How do you figure that? Jason, I'm on this boat. You bet it's my business. So spill it. What happened exactly?" Ben knew nothing, other than the old man was in a heap of trouble and desperate to disappear. "What is going on? Nothing is clear." Nothing added up. Nothing made sense. "I want answers." He clawed the boom even tighter to keep his anger under control.

"Kid, you've forgotten who's holding the gun. Don't push me!"

Jason aimed the firearm over the ocean and fired a round. A bird plunked in the water, his shot body lifeless on the surface.

"Last warning, Benjamin. Next time I fire, I'll aim directly for your head."

My own father, threatening to kill me.

The harder Ben tried to process it, the more he couldn't.

"Don't look at me like that, kid. You always thought I was a crappy father. Why bother to try to change your mind now, right?"

Old Man's rationale was as crazy as his actions.

"Back off and sit down," Jason shouted.

Ben again studied the bound and gagged woman on the deck. Face still blank, she stared back up at him. She hadn't once tried to untangle herself from the restraints or get away from Jason's side. Not once had she even moved beyond simple squirming. She'd often stared at Ben as if studying him to figure him out, like now. Other than that she did nothing but sit there like a good little prisoner.

It baffled him.

"Kid, it's not just you I'm willing to hurt." Jason let go of the wheel, and backhanded the woman at his feet.

"Stop it!" Ben shouted out his shock, his pulse throbbing in his temples as he noticed her eyes tearing up from the blow. He backed up and dropped down on the bench seat again. "All right, all right, I've backed off. Don't hit her again."

He'd never once seen his father so agitated, never seen him resort to violence.

"Why'd you do that?"

"To show you nothing is beneath me." He spoke with a piercing glare in his narrowed eyes.

"Wow," Ben responded, stunned by the confession. "What is it you want from me?"

"Just stay out of my way, kid."

"And how do you suggest I do that? We're on a sailboat, Jason. No land in sight."

"Just quit fighting me!" Old Man yelled. "And shut up. I'm tired of listening to your incessant questions. Your demand for answers."

In exasperation Ben rubbed a hand over his face. He drew in a deep breath. Released his pent-up emotions in an exhale.

Another ping of sympathy for the tied-up woman hit him. Not only did he want to remove the tape over her mouth but also to unbind her and allow her off the boat and onto land somewhere. Her presence didn't sit well with him, for her sake or for his own.

The felonies were racking up today, and the cops would view it that he was an accessory to every one of them.

Not only was this bizarre situation nothing like the old man—at least the man Ben had known his whole life—this was not what he'd agreed to on Monday night, two days ago…

Ben noted the time of eight o'clock on his wristwatch, grabbed his soda can off the lab counter, and headed for the door to leave work for the night. The telephone rang.

His boss, Professor Evert, answered it.

"Ben, wait," Evert said a few seconds later. "Don't leave yet. Someone's calling for you. Says it's important."

Ben turned around in the doorway to take the call. He couldn't afford a car, let alone a cell phone, and he didn't have an address beyond the apartment couch his three buddies allowed him to crash on nightly, so this was his only phone number.

"Thanks." Ben took the cordless phone Professor Evert held out. "This is Ben Keegan."

"Little Keegan," a male voice in a sneaky Jamaican accent spoke over the line. The only person who called him that name was Jimar Malcolm.

Ben stepped farther away from Professor Evert and slipped inside the tiny office set off from the lab. "Jamaica Dude?" he said, calling the older man by the name he'd referred to him since Ben had been a young boy.

"You gott it, Little Keegan."

"What do you want?"

"Offer you ten thousand dolla' deal. You say yes, an' once we 'ang up, I transfer two of de ten in yo' bank account. Jus' gimme de routing numba and account—"

"Goodbye, Malcolm. Don't call me again—"

"Yo' paren's need yo' help."

Ben was a sucker for helping Mom and Dad, the reason he kept his distance. Far distance.

But what if this time they'd finally listen to him and end their self-destructive lives? If he agreed to help, maybe this one last chance to persuade them to quit cocaine would succeed.

Was he kidding himself?

Would the stakes be too high?

All he knew for certain was he needed the money. His paycheck from his part time job as a lab chemist paid his graduate school tuition and his student loan on his bachelor degree, plus bare minimum living expenses, including bus fare for transportation. Top Ramen, Totinos frozen pizzas, pop tarts, and water were his standard for daily calories and nutrition intake. Life would improve after he graduated next year. Just one more year.

"You wanna hear more, Little Keegan?"

Did he?

Even if his encouragement finally ended his parents' drug life, and he certainly needed the money, continuing this conversation may tempt him down paths he refused to ever head.

But...it didn't hurt to learn the details.

Ben closed the tiny office door off from the lab. "I'm listening, Malcolm."

"Yo' paren's, dey cleanin' up. Dey 'ave decided to go clean an' start de fresh life somewhere else."

What? *"I don't believe it."*

"I's true."

Hope filled Ben, but doubt invaded and took over. "Why the change?"

"Yo' dad was charge' wid possession."

His third just on Cayman, if Ben's knowledge was up-to-date. "Shocking," *he scoffed.*

"He due in court Monday. I's got 'im freaked. He accept de judge will hammer 'im with harsh prison sentence, so he flew yo' mum off Cayman today, but he could'na fly out wid her. His passport flagged. RCIPS would stop 'im, take 'im inno custody for tryin' to flee de charges."

Why was he still listening? "We're done here. So long, Mal—"

"De drug possession charge is bogus."

"How you figure?" *Ben retorted with skepticism.* "You expect me to believe that? All the others in Cayman and the US weren't."

"Jason was at de wrong place at de wrong time when de cops raided. He was der only to sell de last o' his stuff back, an' cut ties wid Coco. You know CC?"

"Yeah. I met the Drug King the last time I visited my parents. What do you want from me, Malcolm?"

"Fly to Jamaica tomorro' morning an'—"

"Tomorrow?" *The ideal excuse popped up in Ben's mind.* "No can do. I gotta work."

"Get de nex' couple days off. Can you do dat?"

He had nine vacation days left, and two weeks ago the spring semester had ended. The second session of the summer term didn't start until July, and he wasn't taking classes the first session. If he wanted to, sure...he could make it work.

Ben leaned back against the edge of the desk, toyed with the group of pens stuffed inside a chipped coffee mug. "I need more information, Malcolm."

"I will arrange prepaid airline ticket for you. Once you land in Jamaica, you sail a boat to Cayman an' pick 'im up."

"Take him where?"

"I don' know. He tell you dat."

Hang up the phone. Now.

"What do you say, Little Keegan?"

"I say this is illegal."

"He runnin' from a drug possession charge, Ben. Cayman police will be glad 'is cocaine butt is gone, off dey island. Out of dey hair. You be doing de RCIPS a big fava."

Huh. Solid argument.

Plus, his father wasn't a drug producer or dealer. Just a user. It was his body to destroy as he so decided. The man needed rehab, not a prison sentence. Serving time would only mess him up even worse.

More than all that...could Ben live with the regret of turning away from his parents' arms outstretched for him? For his help?

"You still der, Little Keegan?"

"Yup. Just thinking."

"You tink too much."

"You think too little, but since you're just the messenger—"

"I am more den a messenger. If you 'aven't notice, I'm arrangin' all dis for yo' paren's since dey stayin' low. Little Keegan? Would mo' money eliminate yo' hesitation?"

The ten thousand alone would be a tremendous relief for his life, so more would be superb, but it wasn't about the money. Ben wanted to help them, something he'd failed to do all these years.

"No. The ten is enough."

"You a good kid, Little Keegan. So you onboard wid dis?"

Ben recalled his parents' excitement when they'd told him they were moving to Grand Cayman Island soon after he'd graduated from high school in South Florida nine years ago.

"They'll never be able to return to the Cayman Islands again. Do they understand that?"

"Dey get it, dey do. Yo' mum's jus' dyin' to see you agin, kid. Be in yo' life. An' you know yo' dad give her wha'ever she want."

CHAPTER TEN

The stretch of seawater ended at the horizon in every direction of Earth's circular formation, the ocean surface and the sky both empty of anything humanized, anything manmade. Typically, Jason found the wide-open view relaxing. Now, it annoyed him. His own repetitious breathing, in and out, in and out, annoyed him. He needed a line or two of coke to elevate his mood—white powder always soothed his irritation to the point he was under control and able to tolerate other people's existence. Before cocaine entered his world, blowing up objects was the only thing that released his anger caused by others and their infuriating behaviors.

Dealing with people was the worst part of life. He just wanted to be left alone to escape everyone who knew him and live the rest of his days as someone new.

And I'll kill anyone who gets in the way of that.

Ocean water rolled under the *Persephone* with each forward glide of the boat. Various white caps popped up as the surface swells swayed and rocked. Above, thick cumulus clouds blanketed the sky. Hovering rain clouds spit their moisture, wetting *Persephone's* decks and causing poor visibility.

His bandage remained intact, and no bleeding showed through it. The pain was no biggie. He'd had worse. Things could be worse.

They could be better, too.

If the guy sitting rigid across the boat deck from him wasn't his son, he'd fire a bullet into his forehead and dump his body overboard.

I'm so tired of holding this gun.

He eyed his kid. At the edge of the bench seat, Ben sat as if prepared to lunge at him at any given second. Not like him at all. Typically, he was slouched, legs stretched out, feet crossed at the ankles.

"Relax, Benjamin. We've got tons of nautical mileage to cover."

Ben glared at him. "Where are we headed?"

"South."

"Thanks for that, Captain Obvious." Ben's lashed tone continued from earlier. It stemmed from the kid's frustration of not knowing what was going on.

I should tell him something, just to keep him calm for the next seven hundred miles.

Fine, but make it good.

"Ben, I was shocked to see you today."

"Yeah, I picked up on that." Ben rubbed a hand over his face with an angry jerk.

"Things didn't go as planned. *You* arrived and hours *late*. I had to improvise at the last second. Big time. Get it?"

"No. Not really."

"I was forced to involve Paramedic here since you weren't on time."

"I can't control commercial flights, Jason, or the weather. My flight from Miami landed over two hours late into Jamaica. Then the weather over the ocean sailing to Grand Cayman was one intense storm after another."

"Excuses, excuses, college boy. You—"

"Hey, I don't need to explain myself to you," Ben snapped, "this is—"

"Point is, Ben, you were supposed to be at the marina no later than six this morning."

"No. Jimar Malcolm was supposed to be there, not me."

"Exactly. Malcolm, not you. And because *you* showed up *late,* this woman is involved. *You* put her life at risk."

"Don't put this on me," Ben lashed back, pointing at him with a stiff index finger and balled hand. "Your actions back at the Cayman marina did."

Jason shrugged, going for indifference. "Told you—none of that has anything to do with me."

"You're still sticking with that lame story? I didn't buy it the first time."

"You think I care? No, kid, I don't. I don't care."

"You're a piece of work." Ben shook his head. "Why'd Malcolm call me?" he asked in a yell and with an intense face. "Why'd he send me? What's up with that?"

And what did he tell you, kid?

"I don't know why Malcolm sent you." Jason thought back to Monday, two nights ago. "I really don't."

Pacing his kitchen floor, mindful of stepping around the blood, Jason dialed on his cell phone at 6:05 p.m.

"Yeah?" Malcolm answered after what seemed like endless rings.

"Malcolm? I offed my wife. Get me out of Cayman."

Pause. Long pause. "How you sugges' I do dat?"

"Sail here on the Persephone. *I'll meet you at the marina."*

"Dat's almos' tree hundred miles."

"Like I don't know that. Leave now. I'll make it worth your trouble."

Silence.

"If you don't come, Malcolm, when I'm arrested, I'll turn evidence over to the cops. You'll never again see the world outside maximum security prison fences."

A breathy pause. "I'll be at de Cayman marina Wednesday morning."

"Wednesday? That—"

"I's de soonest I kin make it 'appen, Jason. Until den, dump her and lay lower dan low."

"Yeah, okay." Jason's mind plotted. "Okay. Later tonight I'll weigh her body down and toss it in the ocean a few miles offshore, and stay out of sight for the next thirty-six hours. No problem."

He'd been successful at this before. He could do it again.

"Sounds like a plan," Malcolm said.

"Be at the marina no later than six in the morning on Wednesday."

"Fine. I'll be der."

"Malcolm? If you hear from the kid, tell him his mom and I decided to clean up. For him."

"Why would Little Keegan call me?"

"You'd be the first person he'd call if he gets wind of a news report that his mom and I are missing and he can't reach us. Tell him this last possession charge will land me a long prison sentence, so I flew his mom off Cayman and plan to meet up with her."

"Wha'ever you say, Jason."

Ben studied Old Man, who seemed deep in heavy thought after giving a lame answer to the question. "You don't know?" Ben repeated the answer, continuing their conversation. Boiling anger coiled inside his pent-up gut. Maybe he could catch his father in a lie that would then lead to the truth. "So, if you don't know why Malcolm sent me, then you don't know what he told me, do you?"

In a cold silence, Jason steered around a piece of bobbing drift wood. "Um..." He shrugged, his shoulders and back stiff. "I'm...guessing he told you the truth." He scraped his front upper teeth with his fingernail, something he often did. In quick reflection of those times, it seemed like it was out of nervousness. "There'd be no reason not to."

"Uh-huh. Which is?"

Jason smacked his lips. "The truth?" he said in an obvious attempt to stall.

"Yeah, that's what I'm asking."

Old Man scratched his nose—a new addition to his nervous habits, or a sign of lying? He sniffled—definitely one of his ticks—and his annoying whistle sounded through that hole in his septum. The result from years of snorting cocaine. Disgusting.

"Kid, your mom and I decided to clean up. For you."

"Just for me?"

"Yes."

Hmm, it matched with what Malcolm had told him, but Ben didn't trust Old Man. Hadn't trusted him for a long time. After today it looked like he'd never trust him again. "Both of you?"

"Yes."

Ben didn't say anything. He didn't know what to believe. Old Man seemed nervous.

"Kid, I refuse to put your mother through another possession charge, and there's no way I'll put her through me being a prison inmate for who knows how long. We decided to leave Cayman, start fresh and clean together somewhere else. The plan is we'd contact you once we were settled. We faked a fight about the possession charges I'm facing. Made the neighbors think she was leaving me. After she flew off from Cayman—supposedly because she left me—I was still around on Cayman, waiting for my court date. Again, supposedly."

Huh. Made sense. But Ben didn't trust it. It was too vague.

"You don't believe me, kid, do you?"

"You figured that out, huh?" The man was so maddening. "Yeah, Jason, I find your story difficult to believe. You say it's the truth, so where's Mom? Where are we meeting up with her?"

"Let's leave the final destination for my knowledge only."

Old Man has an ambiguous answer for everything.

Ben jumped to his feet, gripped the boom for support. "Why?" he fired back.

Eyes wide, Jason jammed the gun tip to the EMT's temple. "Stay back, kid."

Ben raised one palm. "Take it easy. I'm staying right here."

"Keep it that way. One step, and I fire. She's gone."

"I get it," Ben snapped out. "Get the gun away from her head, Jason."

"Sit back down. Now."

After Ben released his hold on the boom, he stepped back. With his stub fingernails digging into his palms, he plopped back down on the bench seat.

Jason lowered the gun to the paramedic's arm. "Ben, your mother's safety is priority one. The less you know, the better for her. If you don't know where she is, that info can't be used against you."

"How could it be used against *me?*"

"Because you're on this boat!" Jason yelled. "You're stuck here, so quit the whining."

Another round of frustration and anger commingled inside of Ben, and there wasn't a thing he could do to ease the build of rage it caused. Out on the vast ocean with nothing but surrounding water in every direction, plus a gun in the EMT's face, he had no options.

He took in a deep breath. It helped to calm him. "Why don't you tell me what exactly I'm involved in here, Jason."

"It's not what you're thinking."

"And what is it I'm thinking?"

"That I've committed a crime today."

"Are you delusional?" The calmness evaporated in a flash of an instant. "Abducting that woman isn't a crime?"

"It's not what it seems," Jason went on as he steered the boat around some sort of garbage heap dropped by trash barges. "This is Bubba's mess, not mine. You remember Bubba?"

A familiar ache formed in Ben's forehead. "Bubba? One of your stellar drug buddies? Yeah, I remember him."

"This morning he followed me to the pier. I didn't know that. The cops were tailing him. I didn't know that either."

Blowing out a sigh, Ben rubbed the skin over his growing headache. The last time he'd suffered one—after being plagued with them since middle school—was the last time he'd seen his father. "Why are the cops after him?"

"Maybe the cops believed he was planning a deal down at the docks? I don't know. What I do know is he found out from Coco—"

"Another stellar criminal friend of yours."

"Watch it, kid," Jason shouted.

Why, yes, sir.

Ben fought the desire to salute Jason on a condescending laugh and smirk.

"Ben, Coco told Bubba I was leaving the island to avoid drug possession charges from turning into a conviction and a prison sentence. Bubba ran up to me in the marina parking lot, said he's leaving with me. Said the cops are after him, we gotta go now. Cops started running for him, closed in on him. Demanded he put his hands above his head. He went all crazy. Pulled a gun out and started shooting. He hit a cop."

Ben felt his eyes flash wide open. *"What?* Bubba shot a police officer?" Mortified, he squeezed the bridge of his nose between his thumb and middle finger.

"He did, and killed the guy."

This story grew worse with every word. "Bubba is a cop killer," Ben uttered, still shocked.

"He is as of today, kid. I dragged the dead cop behind a car, took off his uniform, and dressed in it to blend in with the action, so I could slip away unnoticed."

Huh. Makes sense, I guess.

"What happened to Bubba, do I dare ask?"

"He was shot in the head. Half his face—"

"Got it."

Ben took a silent moment to think, to allow what all he'd just heard to soak in and process. A visual memory of the crowd and flashing lights at the marina formed in his mind.

"You're saying none of the activity in that Cayman parking lot had anything to do with you? That you were just caught at the wrong place by the wrong friend?"

"That's what I'm saying, kid."

That's an incredible story, Old Man.

Yet it is plausible.

Everything Jamaica Dude had told him fit with the old man's story.

Ben pointed down at the woman with tape across her mouth. "Who is she, Jason? You took a hostage in order to escape? Is that it?"

"Ben, the cops know Bubba and I are friends, so they assume I'm involved in whatever he's running from. An ambulance was dispatched out for the shot cop. Paramedic here ignored shouts to stop as she went off on her own to help the cop. Guy's her boyfriend or something." Jason poked her shoulder with the gun. "Right, Paramedic? But there was nothing she could do for him. Bubba took advantage of Paramedic being there—he grabbed her for a human shield, held her at gunpoint. I told him to let her go and surrender. He started to take off with her, but I snatched her away from him. Then I grabbed his gun. He stabbed me in the arm with his Swiss army knife, and ran off. A sharpshooter shot at him, took him out."

Makes sense. But...

Was it a web of lies weeded into the truth? How much was true?

Any of it?

Ben sighed, mind racing. Why should he trust anything Jason said?

"Cops started moving in on me, but backed off once they realized I was armed," Jason continued. "They'd never believe I had nothing to do with it all, so I made a decision to run. After Paramedic bandaged up my arm, I grabbed the dead cop's handcuffs and cuffed her, tied up her feet with restraints from the ambulance. That's when you showed up, kid. I held the gun to her head to keep the cops back as I dragged her to the boat."

"The sharpshooter missed you?" Ben hadn't heard any gunfire.

"He didn't fire at us. I blocked myself well behind Paramedic. Enough to make sure he wouldn't even chance it." Jason nudged her upper arm with the side of the gun. "Hey? I bet you'll never ignore cops yelling at you to not jump in to help when you shouldn't, will ya?"

With narrowed eyes, she shouted something in a loud muffle, but Ben couldn't understand through the tape. She thrashed around, yanked her legs back away from the pole restraining them, to no avail. Slumping, she gave up.

Her sudden burst of desperation bothered Ben. How could he help her?

"That's why I gagged you." Jason shook his head at her. "No one here wants to listen to your blah, blah, blah. Now behave. Understand?"

Ben had never seen his father treat another human with such ridicule and disregard. "Unbind her, Jason. Way out here, there's no where she can run."

"You're not as smart as you think you are, college boy. I abducted her. Regardless of the situation, regardless of my intentions, I've taken her against her will. She's not happy with me, okay? Any chance she'd get, she'd attack me. Paramedic here isn't docile, I assure you."

"At least ungag her." She should be unbound completely, but Ben wouldn't win that battle. One step at a time. "There's no need for the tape over her mouth."

"Do you really want to listen to her go off on me? I don't think so. You don't want to listen to her incessant chatter, either. Believe me."

"Chatter or pleading for her life? There's a huge difference."

"Ben, we need her under our control. We need her alive, too. Think leverage."

"*We?* I don't think so. This is *your* mess, Jason." Adrenaline pumped in Ben's bloodstream; his heart pounded under his ribcage like a gong. "*You're* the criminal. I'm not involved."

"You aided my escape from facing possession charges, kid. You knew exactly what you were doing there. So, yeah, *we.*"

Why didn't I hang up on Malcolm? Why did I agree to this? Why?

For Mom.

"No, Jason," Ben shot back, defensiveness rolling out of him. The fear of facing criminal charges revved up his breathing. "You took the helm and ditched Grand Cayman." He stabbed his index finger in the air in the direction they sailed from. "I don't know what happened back there. I still don't."

"Good luck with that defense. You think the cops will believe that? Come on. You're not stupid, college boy. You have a degree from Florida. Earning another one, a fancier one. You can figure this out. Cops won't believe your story any more than they'll believe mine."

This. Is. Unbelievable.

Ben's mind struggled to clear the mess of details, somehow arrange them in an organized fashion he could process, then manage. "What are you gonna do with her?" he asked, eyeing the restrained EMT again. Redness rimmed her lower eyelids—from anger? Frustration? Sorrow?

"I don't know. I was forced to improvise at the last minute and under major gunfire. This wasn't the plan, Ben. Remember, she's not supposed to be here. Neither are you."

"Why didn't you simply tell the cops what happened?" Ben shrugged hard and quick. "Why'd you take this woman hostage and leave the island?" He jerked his head at the EMT. "I'm guessing she would've vouched for you. She'd have no reason to lie about what happened."

"Kid, I'm ditching Cayman to avoid drug possession charges. You know, escaping the cops to avoid an inevitable prison sentence? Get it? I don't want to deal with the cops at all. You understand? Ben, I've stopped the drugs. I'm going clean. This last charge knocked one to my head, and I realized the truth. I can't live like that anymore. But you think the cops or a judge will believe me? Not a chance."

"So what you're telling me is that it's the one-armed man to blame, not you?"

"Bubba has both of his arms."

"Cute, Jason. Cute." Ben stared out at the roll of the waves, at the endless watery surface extended in every direction and ending at the horizon.

He drew in a deep breath to calm himself. This time it didn't work. So he focused on the ominous sky high above and the darkened clouds. The wind churned the ocean, stirring the white caps to life. A storm over their heads was brewing like a monster, matching the tension on deck.

"You really expect me to believe all this?" He studied the man who'd raised him under strange conditions. Ben had known of his parents' drug habit; he knew their current Cayman drug supplier, Coco. Knew all the drug buddies over the years, like Malcolm. But the topic was never discussed in their home, only skirted. Avoided. Until Ben entered high school and started loving beer too much.

Started *needing* it.

From that moment, addiction issues in their family were recognized yet minimized. To avoid being sucked into the taunting drug world, to evade cracking, folding, and ending up like his parents, Ben drew away from them, built a brick wall around himself as they drugged up their life in order to deal with living.

But he never gave up on them.

Yeah, the reason I'm caught up in this mess.

"Kid, I really don't care if you believe me or not, remember? You asked for the truth, and that's what I'm telling you."

Ben shook his head, a wave of sadness and disgust crept over him. "I've never seen you like this. Mean and violent."

"You've only known me as a druggy, kid. When I'm sniffing, I can deal with others. I learned that back in college. See why I use coke?"

"I thought you quit. Just a bit ago you said you quit. *For me.*"

Jason blinked. "I did. I did quit. And look what happened. Look what's going down. What went down because of *you*. No matter how you look at it, Ben, this is your fault."

Huh? So Old Man was trying for the old guilt trip routine. No, not going to work. "Whatever, Jason. Whatever. Look, I don't want to be here. You don't want me here. Fine, I'm gone. Backtrack and sail to one of the other two islands. Drop me off at Cayman Brac or Little Cayman. I'm not joining you in this wild illegal adventure of yours. I'll take the EMT with me. You won't have to *deal* with either of us anymore."

"Kid, cops on both those islands will be on the lookout for this boat. We'll find ourselves under a standoff before we even dock. I'm not only facing possession charges, now I'm facing charges for what happened at the pier. The cops won't believe I had nothing to do with Bubba murdering that cop today. Do you get that?"

A crack of lightning flashed.

"I get it. Your plan is to disappear off radar. Forever."

Thunder rumbled.

"That's my plan."

More thunder.

"So, kid, tell me how that new drug production of yours is coming along."

The strange topic change threw Ben. Why did Old Man even care? Especially *now*? "You mean, medication. It's coming along."

"Bull."

Where was the old man going with this conversation? "And why do you say that?"

"Where is it, Ben?" Jason shrugged hard as if ticked off. "When will it be out?"

"It takes years to develop a new med—including testing and FDA approval—before it can be released into the pharmaceutical market." Was he asking out of desperation, hoping Ben had some samples with him in his backpack? "Are you interested in taking it?"

"Me and your mom. You gonna achieve your goal, kid? Develop the drug that helps the druggies?"

"It doesn't work that way. This med won't hold you off until your next fix. First step is you have to *want* to stop your addiction. Next step—"

"I'm not an addict, kid."

"*What?*" Ben shot back in a scoff. "Of course you are. We've been through this so many times. I'm beyond done listening to your denial and blaming—"

"Don't forget who you're talking to."

"The man with the gun. Got it."

"Good. So...what's the next step? You were gonna say something about a next step."

This was the oddest conversation. It also made no sense. "You said you're not an addict, so why would you need to know that?" What game was the old man playing now?

"I don't need it. I only snort...*snorted*...to boost my mood. I don't suffer withdrawal. I—"

"Act like a complete jerk when you're not using."

Silence. Old Man had no lash back response for that, huh?

"Jason, you're talking physical addiction versus psychological addiction—I get it, but addiction is addiction."

"Lecture over? Next step, Ben? What is it?"

"You stop using. No more cocaine. Ever."

"I told you I quit. I wanted to quit."

"Just like that? After all these years?"

"Yes."

Ben didn't believe it. The old man never once even hinted he ever wanted to quit. This whole story of his today, from the start of it, was a pile of suspicious muck. Ben had no idea what his father was trying to say, his words so convoluted and contradictory.

Maybe he doesn't know what's going on in his own head.

"Jason? What is this conversation really about?"

"I can't ask my son about his work?"

"Come on!"

"I'm done talking, Ben!" Old Man yelled back. "I've got nothing more to say to you."

More lightning skipped around in the sky. Five seconds later, the sound of more thunder. The gentle sprinkles became a shower. A downpour.

I want off this boat.

Ben ground his teeth. *How can I make that happen? How can I untie the EMT and get us both far away from my father?*

The rainfall soaked Ben's shorts and t-shirt. The wetness filtered through his running shoes and dampened his socks. To reassure the EMT in some small way, he smiled at her, a closed-mouth smile, matching the gloomy mood on the deck.

Her eyes softened a bit, as if communicating a return sad smile since her mouth was taped up.

Jason threw off the mainsheet. With only the mainsail up, it lined up with the wind and flopped around. The boat eased its speed.

In contrast, Ben's heart picked up speed. "Why did you let the mainsail luff?"

The boat zigzagged to a slow speed, then deadened in the water, clearly Jason's intention.

The old man snatched some coiled sailing rope, tossed it to Ben. "Tie your ankles together."

"*What?*" Ben yelled, stunned and filled with fresh anger. "No way."

Jason pressed the gun to the EMT's shoulder. "If you don't, I'll shoot her in the arm. A wound like that, she'll stay alive but suffer intense pain. You want that?"

In a slow movement, Ben raised his palms, giving up for now. He had no choice. "Jason, take it easy. Don't hurt her."

"I will if you don't start tying yourself up."

Sara's pulse bounded, her heart pounding against her ribs. It felt like it would pump itself to an exhausted stop, killing her in the process. She stared at Keegan's son; he stared back. It seemed he was struggling to decide on the best course of action.

If he didn't tie his feet together with that rope, Keegan would fire a bullet into her deltoid. He'd threatened to shoot her numerous times that day, but he no longer needed her unscathed and able to move. It'd be no problem for him if she were bleeding on the deck and in a ton of pain. Obviously he had a plan arranged at his destination, and it didn't include her.

She was lucky he hadn't shot her yet.

Am I just going to sit here, waiting for him to kill me and dispose of my body?

But she'd get nowhere fighting him. She had no choice but to be quiet, not make a ruckus. Not only was the creep ruthless, he was a master at lies, proficient at thinking on his feet. He'd spun a fictional tale for his son to explain the day's events, all of it believable enough if she hadn't known the truth. She'd be impressed if the lying, murdering scumbag wasn't holding her at gunpoint while he sailed them to the far reaches of the vast and stormy ocean.

Across the boat from her, Keegan's son broke their eye contact and glared up at his father. "You are unbelievable, Jason." Bent over on the bench seat, he wrapped the rope around his ankles and tied it.

He's tying himself up for my safety. Wow.

"Tighter, Ben!" Keegan shouted out in a volume that startled Sara with a flinch. "You think I can't see that loose knot from here? Don't mess with me, kid."

Keegan dug the gun barrel deeper into Sara's muscle, and she heard a muffled gasp escape from between her own lips.

Ben heard a faint intake of breath—sounded like fear was the apparent cause—come out of the EMT's taped mouth. He snapped his head up and noticed her eyes wide, chest panting. He wasn't sure what had occurred to cause her a burst of fear. It was the first time he'd seen her react scared and defenseless.

"Whatever you're doing, Jason, cool it." Ben lowered his head again and fiddled with the rope, still leaving it a little loose so he could break out of it when the time was right.

"Tighter," Old Man shouted. "No more games, Ben. Last warning."

Fine. "Relax." Ben tightened the knot, his ankle bones less than an inch a part.

Jason marched up to him, gun pointed down at him. "All right, stand up. Move it."

"Just shoot me sitting down."

"Get up." Jason pointed the gun to the companionway. "Down you go."

"You're gonna shoot me down there? What do you plan on telling Mom?"

"I don't need to tell her a thing, kid. Like me, she didn't know Malcolm involved you."

The old man was mind-boggling. "So, you'll just lie to her? Tell her you haven't seen me? Have no idea where I am?"

"Stand up, Ben!" Jason shouted. "Let's go."

I can't believe this is happening.

"When are we rendezvousing with Malcolm?" Ben blurted out something to stall.

"No concern of yours. Stop wasting time. Down under you go, kid."

"Why?"

"'Cause I'm tired of looking at you, and I don't have the patience anymore to deal with you. If you don't move," he jerked his head backward, "I'll shoot the paramedic."

"How many times are you gonna threaten me with that line?"

"As many times as I need to."

For now, Ben had no choice but to back down.

Unbalanced on restrained ankles, he climbed to his feet, his eyes not wavering from the gun barrel pointed at him. Without another option, he shuffled his way to the top of the companionway.

Would my own father shoot me in the back of the head?

Feet together, Ben hopped down the two stairs, flinching. Waiting for that bullet.

None came.

In the tiny main salon, Jason pointed the gun to the lone chair in front of the counter. "Sit down."

It was rare to have a folding chair on a boat, to have any moveable furniture not attached to the boat hull. Ben had wondered about that chair yesterday. "Why is this thing even onboard?" Suddenly, its presence seemed ominous.

"Because it is. Sit down."

"Why?"

"Do it," Jason yelled.

He needed the EMT alive, but he didn't need Ben. It would be better for Old Man if he were out of the way. Jason could kill him and throw his body overboard, never to be found.

I'm powerless over everything here.

Once again out of options, Ben eased down into the chair.

As Jason's beady eyes stared him down, with his gun-free hand he opened the storage closet and dragged out a bag. Eyes still on Ben, Jason's hand fumbled around inside the bag, then withdrew a tiny black box and held it up.

"See this, Ben? It's a detonator."

"You really need more leverage to control me here?"

"Just giving you a heads-up. I'm not messing around, kid."

"I didn't think you were." Old Man needed some coke or he'd explode from the inside out.

"Arms behind you, kid, behind the back of the chair."

"How far are you gonna—?"

"Just do it," Jason yelled. "Now!"

Ben couldn't help thinking he wanted his father dead.

With reluctance Ben dragged his arms behind the wooden slats of the chair. Squatted down behind him, Jason wrapped rope around Ben's wrists and looped the rope ends to the chair back. At least that's what it felt like. With a jerk, Jason tightened the knot as if to chafe on purpose.

Arms tied to the chair, ankles bound together, there wasn't an effective thing Ben could do to fight the monster his father had become.

Skin crawling with agitation, Alec stood in the center of the main room of the dock house, watching Higgins, the dock manager, scroll through computer files.

"On Tuesday morning, yesterday," Higgins spoke from behind the teeny room's only desk, "the slip was rented starting midnight last night for the next two days with an option to extend, if necessary. Something we agreed to since we have plenty of slip space to rent out."

Who had sailed the *Persephone* to Cayman? Someone had sailed it in here; Alec had seen another man on deck as Keegan sailed away. Who was that man helping him?

The lingering unanswered question bothered Alec.

"Who arranged the rented slip?" he asked Higgins.

"Someone claiming to be Jason Keegan." The manager shrugged, studying the computer screen. "Obviously couldn't be him since he was inside the Cayman psych facility at the time of the call. Something we didn't know until now. Whoever the guy is, he used Keegan's debit card from his Cayman bank account to pay for the slip. Used Keegan's house line here on Cayman as the telephone contact number." Higgins looked up at Alec. "What else do you need from me? How else can I help?"

"Do you happen to know what phone number the Jason Keegan impostor called from?"

"We don't have caller ID here at the pier. I'll check our records with the phone company." Higgins picked up the landline telephone. "Maybe whoever sailed the *Persephone* to Cayman is the same person who impersonated Keegan in order to rent the slip."

"Maybe. Maybe not." Alec marched off to return to the tiny office. "Regardless, whoever that person is, I will find out, and after they meet me, they'll regret ever helping Keegan."

Did I really say that out loud and in such a vindictive tone?

"Inspector, that sounds like you're an enraged father, not a dedicated cop."

Yep, I did. A few feet from the office doorway, Alec whipped around. "You got a problem with that, Higgins?"

"Just the opposite. I'd feel the same way. I have three daughters."

Inside the tiny office, Alec closed himself off from the world, a thought plaguing his mind.

Who is the man who sailed the Persephone *to Cayman, and how can I get my hands wrapped around his throat to squeeze the life out of him?*

CHAPTER ELEVEN

On the boat deck, Sara shivered in the downpour; her soaked EMS uniform clung to her skin. The sky darkened with low-hanging, ominous-colored clouds, yet it was only midafternoon, several hours from dusk. The wind picked up a bit with thrashing gusts, kicking up the quantity and height of white caps, giving the impression the water was on the move, on a quest, like the flow of a river. The high speed of the boat turned the air temperature to chilly.

For the first time in her life, Sara turned away from depending on prayer. Why bother? Obviously, He wasn't listening.

Desperate to escape her predicament, determined to help herself, and with nothing else to do, she tugged her legs backward and squirmed. Of course, it only tightened the restraints around her ankles.

Jason cackled down at her. "Oh, yeah, Paramedic. That oughta work for you. Even if you did somehow get yourself untied and away from me, where you gonna go? Huh? Jump overboard and try your chances at swimming somewhere? Go for it. Sounds like a smart move."

All she could do was glare up at him.

She couldn't kick him, hit him. She couldn't spit at him. She couldn't even yell at him.

She despised this man. Despised how he'd shot Owen and Russell like they were insignificant vermin or something. Despised what he was doing to her.

Keegan threw off the mainsheet again, an action his son had called "luff" hours ago, right before Keegan threatened him below deck under gunpoint. Like hours ago, the mainsail again lined up with the wind and flopped around. The boat slowed down and eased to a near stop.

Her chest tightened. "Keegan? What are you doing?" Her words caught behind the tape.

With the gun jammed into the waistband at his midback, Keegan kneeled in front of her, his breathing quick, eyes wide with blatant anger.

Saying nothing to her, he unknotted the ends of the restraints tying her to the pole and unbound her feet from it. She kicked out at him.

"That's not gonna get you anywhere." He gripped her feet and tied her ankles together. With a squeeze he grabbed hold of her arm and yanked. "Stand up."

Unsteady, she rose to her feet, ankles restrained together and hands cuffed behind her back.

"Let's go," he grumbled at her, then dragged her to the top of the opening to below the deck, then down the metal ladder stairs.

She didn't fight him. Not yet.

At the bottom of the two stairs, she whipped around and barreled her body into his, not sure of the outcome, not having any sort of plan.

He stumbled backward into the bottom stair. "What was that?" he asked her on a laugh, as she spotted his son tied to a chair outside a cabin at the boat's stern.

Keegan righted himself and shoved her into the corner across the main salon table and half-moon bench seat around it. She staggered, then dropped to her knees.

"Jason?" the son yelled out from across the room, his voice panicked. "What are you doing?" he shouted louder. "Don't hurt her. There's no reason to hurt her."

"Shut up," Jason yelled back. "This doesn't concern you, kid. Paramedic? Sit down with your back against the wall."

She plopped down as he asked, her arms cuffed, hands clanking together. Why fight it? What could she do, other than exhaust herself more with no result in her favor?

Squatted down in front of her, he wrapped the ankle restraint ends around a steel pole nailed into the floor in the corner and knotted them with a tight jerk. She thought about screaming at him to remove the tape from her lips, but he wouldn't listen, he wouldn't even be able to understand her muffled words.

He bolted up to the boat deck, leaving her alone with his son tied up to the chair across the room from her, staring at her. She stared back at him but couldn't read what was behind his eyes.

A few seconds later, he turned his head away and squirmed, yanking on the rope tying his arms to the chair back. He didn't get anywhere, other than tightening the knot.

Sounds familiar.

Bright red streaks circled around his wrists, clearly from the rope chafing his skin the last few hours. He'd obviously been yanking on his restraints off and on, and getting nowhere.

She buried her face into her drawn-up knees.

A half second later, the boat burst off at a speed that spurred on nausea. *Ugh.*

The day rolled past three in the afternoon. For what seemed like the hundredth time, Alec fought off the urge to allow his brain to go berserk. Just lose it. Allow the fear to swallow him from the inside out.

He'd lost Sara once before for two long years. This time, her abductor needed her alive...at least for a timeframe.

She could already be dead.

Throat clogged, heart twisted into a knot, Alec stared out the wall of windows from inside the wooden dock house. The empty ocean stretched beyond the three piers, taunting him to get out there and scour the ocean for his daughter.

Limiting. Useless. I can't help Sara out there.

The *Persephone* was one hay straw in the Caribbean Sea full of infinite hay bales.

Was she already dead?

The haunting possibility repeated in his head, over and over, an evil voice toying with his emotions, pushing him toward the brink of an ugly edge he'd never recover from if he reached it.

"Hey, you still there?" In Alec's ear via his cell phone, Craig's voice interrupted the spin of dark thoughts. "Is working this case—"

"Sara isn't a *case*. She's my daughter."

"Alec..." Craig cleared his throat. "I'm—"

"This is rough on both of us. No explanation necessary, okay? We don't need to do this. Let's just focus on being detectives." *What were we discussing?* "When did this radio transmission occur?"

"Three hours ago."

"Play it for me."

"This is the Persephone. *Need to speak with J.M."*

Radio silence.

"J.M.? You hearing me?"

A crackle over the radio.

"Cayman Kee?"

"You're not J.M. Who is this?"

"A pal of his. Give him a second."

Radio silence.

Noise of some kind.

"Mon? Dat you?"

"Yeah, it's me. Who was that guy?"

"Don' worry. We can trust 'im. Wha'appen?"

"I need another boat. I've gotta ditch this one. ASAP. Go backup."

"Yeah, mon. I get you one. Sail to de backup plan coordinates. Wee swap boats der."

"Yep. Plan Backup. Jamin? Hey, are you *actually gonna be there this time? Don't answer that. We'll discuss it later."*

"No' 'appy wid me?"

"Later."

"What do you think, Alec?" Craig asked over the cell connection.

"I think maybe it was staged."

"Huh. What did they say to make you draw that conclusion?"

"Let me hear your thoughts first."

"Sure. Did you notice the accent and dialect? I'm thinking it's Caribbean, more specifically Jamaican."

Alec nodded to the empty room. "I'll buy that."

"Sounds like this Jamaican failed to show up on the *Persephone* today. So who captained it here? It didn't sail to Cayman by itself. The Jamaican sent someone else to do his job. Alec, we find the Jamaican, we'll discover where Keegan is headed on the *Persephone*."

"You're on to something."

"Hopefully. Tell me, why do you think it was staged?"

Alec leaned on his forearms resting on the office's metal desk. "You said without a doubt one of the voices is Jason Keegan."

"Yeah. After this morning, I *know* Keegan's voice, Alec."

"Did you know he's a talented actor?"

"You're not just referring to how he avoided arrest by faking catatonia, are you?"

"During high school when he lived in Southern California, he played a catatonic patient in a low-budget Hollywood play. Earned some kind of acting award plus an acting scholarship, but turned it down to go to the University of Idaho."

"That explains the excellent catatonia Monday night."

"And led to my thinking the radio transmission was staged. Jason Keegan knows how to deliver a line. The actor also knows *what* is said is just as important as what's *not* said."

"Meaning…?"

"The caller said *Persephone* only once, not too blatant but enough for law enforcement to identify the radioing boat. And the first receiver? The pal of J.M.? He referred to the caller as Cayman Kee before J.M. raced into the room."

"As if supplying an ID confirmation to go along with the boat name."

"Exactly. The pal is a plant, used only to purposely slip up by saying part of Keegan's name. Yet the second receiver? J.M.? Only his initials are mentioned."

"No actual name. Intentional to hide the guy's identity."

"That's my thought." Alec rubbed his eyes with his left thumb and index finger. "But, Craig, it does nothing to find Sara. It doesn't lead us anywhere. We've got nothing. Nothing but an empty ocean."

The phone line quieted. Not even the sound of breathing came through. Was his friend still there? "Craig?"

"You've heard," Craig said, tone somber.

"Yep." Underneath his thumb and index finger, Alec squeezed his eyes shut. "We lost sight of the *Persephone*. She's gone."

Sara disappeared. Again.

"Hey," Keegan's son whispered at Sara, his voice low in volume but intense in tone.

She lifted her head from being buried in her kneecaps and glanced over at him.

"When Jason dragged you down here," he whispered, "did he say why? Why he wants you down below?"

She shook her head.

"Can he hear me talking to you?"

She leaned to the right to see up the short ladder staircase, spotted Keegan focused on steering the boat full speed ahead. The wind tossed his long gray ponytail hanging down his back. She eyed Ben again but made no gesture.

"So?" he whispered on a half-shrug. "Yes or no?"

She chose against responding to him. Why should she trust this guy, Keegan's son? He'd agreed to sail Keegan out of Cayman so the scum could escape drug possession charges. Aiding and abetting was criminal activity. The son was a criminal, just like his father.

But...Ben acts nothing like a criminal. Nothing like Keegan.

"You can answer my first question, but not this one?" Ben whispered, his cheeks scrunched in confusion. "Just tell me—can you see him up there?"

Even though the son had committed a crime, this question wasn't a big deal. So she nodded.

"Does it seem like he hears me?"

She shook her head.

"Jason?" Ben shouted up, to Sara's surprise.

Interesting. She'd assumed he didn't want to gain Keegan's attention, that he wanted to communicate with her without his father noticing.

"Jason?" Ben yelled again. "We need a bathroom break. You can't keep us tied up down here without—"

"Not my problem," Keegan yelled.

"You're treating us inhumanely."

"Don't care."

"He's lost his mind," Ben muttered to himself. "You're a selfish son of a—"

"You're finally catching on, kid," Keegan yelled down, cutting off Ben's tirade.

A gust tossed the boat like a plastic Fisher Price toy, heightening Sara's nausea. The whistle and hum of the wind roared down through the opening of the short staircase and buzzed in her ears. Rainwater spewed as if God turned on a faucet to full blast.

I'm not gonna escape this nightmare, am I?

Still inside the dock house office he'd holed himself up in hours ago, Alec clawed his cell phone. "That's right," he spoke through clenched teeth, sitting in the chair behind the desk and toying with a pencil in his hand. "I said *don't* approach the *Persephone*. Just locate it and keep tabs on its general coordinates," he clarified for the US Coast Guard for the second time today.

"That's what we're attempting to do, Inspector," the male officer responded. "But by keeping this far back, we can't even locate her."

"I understand that. I do. Do you understand this fugitive is an explosives expert?"

"I get why we must keep our distance, Inspector. I'm just telling you because of that forced distance, we can't locate the sailboat. From my knowledge, that's the reason law enforcement lost sight of her."

Alec snapped the pencil in half. "Anything new from Radio Direction Finding?"

"Nothing. RDF is useless until the *Persephone* makes another transmission. From the one and only radio contact she made several hours ago, we triangulated her position at that time to a few miles off the coast of Grand Cayman and heading southwest, but she's been silent since."

Nothing he didn't already know.

The desire to fire his duty weapon endlessly at a target dummy until it was a shredded mess had him leaping to his feet. Fuming, he stalked around the office space. "What about the Coast Guard's unmanned aircraft?"

"Both those high and medium altitude aircrafts tracked dozens of vessels today in the vicinity we're searching within the Caribbean Sea. The real time video showed various ships and boats. None of them are the *Persephone*. Inspector, I spoke with Interpol earlier and—"

"I just spoke with them. They've been unsuccessful locating the boat."

Everyone has.

Understandable, but it still ticked him off beyond anything he could phrase into words.

After Alec hung up with the US Coast Guard, he once again checked his messages, hoping this time one would magically appear from one of the ports he'd put on alert.

Nothing. Not a peep from any of the ports he'd deemed a possibility Keegan would dock that sailboat.

"*Persephone*—perfect name for a criminal's sailboat," Alec spoke to the grimy window in front of him overlooking the marina and vast ocean beyond.

Standing there on weak legs, he buried his face behind sweaty palms and squeezed his eyes shut. The thumping beat of the pulse in his temples lifted his thumbs.

Sara, sweetie, how could something so bad happen to you again?

A quick knock had him whipping around as he dropped his arms down along his sides. He found the dock manager standing in the doorway of *his* office.

"Do you need your office back?"

"Naw," Higgins pointed over his shoulder, "I'm good out there. Inspector, I've got some more answers. The *Persephone* is under JSR. Jamaica Ship Registry."

Jamaica. It confirmed Craig's suspicions.

"If it weren't for your daughter sending that distress alert, no one would've paid any attention to the *Persephone* sailing in here and back out. Because of her, Inspector, you law enforcement people know the ID of the fugitive's escape vessel."

And…instead of being shot to death alongside Owen and Russell, she bought herself some time.

How much time?

"You find out anything else, Higgins?" Alec asked with impatience, irritated by the dock manager's cheery disposition.

"Yeah, but you're not gonna like it. No go on that phone number. A Puerto Rico number called to reserve the slip. It's a burner cell phone. There's no way—"

"—to ever trace the person who bought that phone." Alec balled his hands into fists, his nails dug into his palms. "Thanks for the info."

Thanks for nothing.

His cell phone beeped. "Commander?" he said, answering it, as the dock manger slipped out of the office, closing the door behind him.

"Anything yet, Inspector?"

"No, not really, sir. I'm still hanging at the pier. I've set all possible ports on alert for the *Persephone*."

"Dyer, you're trying to predict where this guy will dock. That's impossible."

"I'm not guessing, Commander. I put *all* Central America, South America, the Gulf, and Caribbean ports on alert." With the help of two cops making calls, he'd been on the phone for hours with the various locations, giving specifics on Keegan's explosive expertise.

"Inspector, there's hundreds of shoreline cities and towns he could sail that boat to. Heck, he could sail to uninhabited land."

Alec punched the metal file cabinet. "I know," he barked back and didn't care his tone was disrespectful and unprofessional.

"Careful with the leeway I'm giving you here, Dyer."

Alec nodded to himself. "Understood, sir. Sorry." Staring at the fist-dented cabinet door, he drew in a deep breath to calm down. "Commander? When Keegan docks, he'll blow that boat if law enforcement swarms in on him. The scenario from earlier today is no different."

"True. So what do you suggest?"

For the first time in his career, Alec had no suggestions.

A sinking sensation caused him to sit in the desk chair to avoid swaying on his feet. The silence over the line grew past uncomfortable, but he didn't know what to say. Elbows on the desktop, he steepled his fingers together, stretched them up. Down. Up and down. Up and down.

"Anything from satellite imagery?" he said, but suspected the answer.

"Satellites zeroed in on a boat. Followed it for hours."

Alec perked up but knew it was false hope. "It was presumed to be the *Persephone*, but ended up it wasn't, right?"

"You got it. Interpol followed the wrong boat. A similar sailboat to *Persephone*."

The spark of fresh hope plummeted and disintegrated in a puff. "If only satellite technology in the movies was reality."

"I hear you there, Inspector. I hear you."

"With the distance, the accuracy on those things are so hit and miss, especially something as small as a monohull sailboat."

"Yep. So now what, Dyer?" Commander prodded, even though they both knew he was in charge of the case as much as Alec was emotionally enmeshed in it. "Tell me."

Alec had no idea, no clue which direction to head from there, although it was a comfort to be consulted, given the opportunity to step up to bat and swing.

"Inspector?"

"I don't know, sir." Alec spoke in a voice he didn't even recognize. The defeated connotation, however, was so painfully familiar.

Would Sara make it home alive this time?

Commander cleared his throat. "When do you expect to hear from your wife on the interview?"

"Last I heard, the creep wasn't flinching at bit. Interrogation is nothing new to that man."

CHAPTER TWELVE

One last wave at her boys, and Lelisa flew out the door to her garage. Cell phone in the crook between her cheek and shoulder, she crawled into her car as the line rang the number she'd dialed a few seconds ago.

"Lelisa?" her husband's voice answered.

In that one word he sounded strained. Exhausted. Anguished. She could take it away if she could just find Sara and bring her home. Yeah. Just.

"Hey." She tapped the garage door opener hanging on the passenger visor.

"How'd the interview go?"

That conversation wouldn't give him any hope, so she decided to give him something that could. "Craig's girlfriend is over with the boys. You know how the boys love Rachel. I'm headed to the helipad to chopper out to a barge—"

"What? Why? Something to do with the interview?"

Just tell him and move on.

She backed out of their two-car garage and into the late-afternoon dreary sky. "No. Questioning Coco Byers was a dead end. He says he knows nothing."

"It sounds like you believe him."

"I do, yeah. Keegan would be stupid to get that guy involved in his escape, and he's proved just today alone he's far from stupid. Coco would easily hand Keegan over in return for personal gain. I'm sure Keegan knows that." She shoved the gear into drive and took off. "Alec, I'm helicoptering to a nearby barge on the move and maybe—"

"No. That won't get you anywhere."

She hung a left and headed toward the airport on a road paralleling the beach. The storm above stirred the ocean into a volatile bubbling surface. "It's worth a shot."

In a heavy sigh, heartache coiled out of his long breath of clear defeat.

She hurt for her husband; she feared for her stepdaughter. She hated being so ineffective as an agent at rescuing Sara from a deadly situation.

"Lelisa, hopping on a barge is useless."

"Maybe not. The worst case scenario is I find another dead end. Alec, you still have angles to work on the island. I've already worked all mine. It's time for me to work with the US Coast Guard on this. They're well skilled in maritime interdiction combating drug smugglers, and they have the right to board and seize any vessel subject to US jurisdiction."

"I know that," he snapped. "Don't you think I know that?"

She bit her tongue. He wasn't lashing out at her. Understandably, fear and frustration overwhelmed him. "Alec, my point is Sara is a US citizen. Keegan's a US citizen, and a known drug offender in both the Caymans and the US. Kidnapping is a federal crime, so I'll make the law work for us."

Silence over the line.

Not wanting to push her husband, she waited the silence out.

"I don't like this," he finally spoke and in a warning tone.

"The boys are doing fine," she said, trying to reassure him about something. "Their fevers are down, and Rachel's a nurse."

"You know I'm not worried about the boys. Lelisa, this guy is a serious explosives expert. Willing to die—blow himself up—to avoid being apprehended. If he sees any vessels or aircraft tailing him from a distance, he'll explode the *Persephone* into small bite size pieces."

"Then I better maintain a huge distance." *If I even locate the sailboat.*

"What if by chance Keegan sees your chopper? He'll assume it's a threat to him."

See the helicopter? The *Persephone* disappeared off-radar hours ago and would most likely not be in eyeshot of a chopper hovering over the barge to drop her off. *Paranoid, Alec?*

"Hon, you're scared and—"

"Of course I am."

"I know. So am I." She turned right at a stop light. "I love Sara like she's my own daughter."

"I know that."

"Then why don't you trust me to do this right?"

"Because I don't know what is right on this one, but I'm sure what you're doing is pointless."

She turned into an airport parking lot adjacent to the helipad. "I *need* to try this, Alec."

"Because I'm not getting anywhere?" he snapped. "I messed this up from the start?"

"I'm not saying that, honey. At all." She hated to hear his defensive side lash out. It was a sign of defeat, of hopelessness. "Hey, I'm on your side. You know that."

A car horn honked in the background over the phone line.

"Are you on the move somewhere?" She curved into a parking space.

"Yeah. Keegan's house. The CSU worked Annie Keegan's homicide scene on Monday night, but we're digging deeper into his life, into the man of Jason Keegan."

She shut the car engine off. "Makes sense."

Alec cleared his throat. "Lelisa?" her husband spoke her name in a softened tone that crushed her.

He's hurting so much.

With one leg out the opened driver door, she stilled. "Yeah, hon?"

"Lelisa, *I* allowed Keegan to sail out to sea," he spoke in a near whisper, as if ashamed. "Now the *Persephone*—"

"All law enforcement on this island allowed Keegan to sail off to keep Sara alive. There was no other—"

"The plan was to follow from a far distance so as not to tip him off," his tone spoke full of hopelessness and guilt, "but it was a risk. *I* risked losing sight of her."

He needed to recap it in his mind, to explain his decisions as a cop out loud to her. She more than understood that. Eight years ago the roles had been reversed when she exposed her superior, a war hero and dedicated DEA superior, who'd turned criminal.

"Alec, you were forced to choose bad over worse. It's understandable that boat slipped away off-radar. It's difficult to follow a sailboat in the open sea while keeping out of its sight. With the heavy cloud cover and low visibility from the storm, it was impossible."

"Hmm," he said, sounding unconvinced.

She climbed out of her car and locked it with a click to her key fob. "How it all went down was the only way to keep Sara alive, and Alec, she's still alive."

"Maybe, but she won't be for long."

"You're working the case fine, honey. You're not God, so all you can do is your best work as a cop, and that's what you're doing." After she swung her overnight bag onto her shoulder, she marched off toward the helicopter in the near distance, its blades whirling, the pilot waiting for her in the cockpit.

"You're on the helipad now, aren't you?"

"Yep," she shouted over the noise, her hair tossing across her face from the blades in motion.

"Lelisa?" he spoke in a louder tone, obviously to be heard over the sound on her end. "Did I get her back eight years ago only to lose her again? This time to some perp just using her to escape incarceration?" His tone was sheathed in sadness.

Her heart squeezed like a twisted hand towel being rung out.

She stopped walking, turned her back on the waiting pilot to curb some of the noise. "No," she spoke in a raised tone so her husband could hear her. "She'll get out of this."

"Thinking positive isn't—"

"It's not about thinking positive, Alec. God is carrying Sara through this, just like He carried her all those years ago."

He paused, as if thinking. "Yeah," he said with what sounded like fresh hope. "He wouldn't save her life then only to take it now."

"That seems too harsh to me." But she'd seen way harsher stuff happen countless times.

"We need to focus on doing our jobs and on prayer."

Hope filled her. "Absolutely, sweetie." Upon hearing her husband's despair lift and faith slip back in place, she whipped around and stalked off for the helicopter again.

"Be careful out there in the ocean, honey. Be safe."

"Always." She ducked. Bent over, she climbed into the copter.

The pilot lifted off the ground.

Lord? Help us find the Persephone *before she disappears forever.*

CHAPTER THIRTEEN

Turbulent seas rocked underneath the *Persephone*, enough to cause Ben's stomach to lurch, waking him up. Tied up down there for the last several hours, boredom hit, especially since the EMT refused to communicate with him, so he'd dozed off for a bit.

He looked over at her and found her pressed back against the boat's hull, her head cocked to the side. Eyes wide open, staring up deck. He knew the trigger of her fear. He didn't have a visual like she did, but he heard it.

The swell of the ocean splashed water over the boat's topsides and onto the deck. Rain poured down in the drizzly late afternoon, according to the wall clock. He pictured the two cockpit drains emptying the water back out into the sea as fast as it spilled in. The boat wouldn't sink if the drains failed to keep up, but the cockpit would fill up and overflow, making it difficult to steer and control the boat. They needed to sail through this storm long before that happened.

Wind roared in his ears as his tied-up body listed in motion with the boat's movements. The *Persephone* heeled to one side, typical in heavy weather. But then she whipped direction with the wind and heeled to the other side in a vicious rocking motion.

This storm was too much for one sailor.

"Jason?" he yelled up to the boat deck. "Hey, untie me. You can't handle this storm by yourself."

"Shut up, kid. I know what I'm doing."

"It's not about skills as a skipper. If you don't let me help up there, we could lose the mast and capsize. Do you get that? This boat needs four skilled hands up there. Two bodies working the lines and rudder."

A few silent seconds passed. Ten more.

"Did you hear me? Jason?"

More silence from him.

The howl of wind kept at it and tossed the boat like a tinker toy.

Ben glanced at the EMT; her emotions were plastered on her face. "Hey, it'll be fine. Somehow I'll make it fine and keep you safe. I promise. Just hang tight."

Her scrunched-up face gave him the impression she didn't believe him, but she nodded.

"Come on, man!" Ben shouted up to Jason. "You're gonna kill all three of us."

Nothing from the old man. No response at all.

"Jason?" Ben yelled louder, not willing to give up.

It wasn't just his life on the line. If he didn't do something productive, he'd break his promise to the EMT, an innocent woman dragged into this craziness. She didn't deserve the fate of death indirectly caused by Jason's criminal activity.

A few silent seconds later, the sound of footsteps pounded across the boat deck above, then on the companionway. A couple seconds later, Jason jumped in front of Ben, a knife in his hand.

"Whoa," Ben shouted, bracing for a stabbing attack. "What are you—"

A quick swipe, and Jason knifed the rope tying Ben's ankles, cutting it, then he sliced the rope around Ben's wrists.

"You wanna help, kid? Let's go."

Without a moment's delay, Ben jumped up, uncoiled the rope from his feet and hands as Jason waved the gun toward the upper deck. For a split second he considered tackling his father for the gun.

Now is not the time.

Ben bounded up the short companionway. A gust of wind slammed into the *Persephone*, knocking him off-balance. He stumbled up onto the deck. Rain battered his body, slapped his face with a wet sting. He righted himself, as Jason grabbed onto the wheel, struggling to stay on his feet. Ben grabbed the line to the mainsail and trimmed the thick rope, stopping it from flopping around. The sail billowed out in a firm curve.

The boat heaved forward with a jolt.

Jason slipped the gun into his waistband on his left hip, then controlled the wheel with both hands, the black bag full of explosives at his feet.

Now is the time....

"Take this a minute," Ben shouted over the howl of the wind, reaching to hand Jason the mainsail line with one hand while reaching for...

Jason drew the revolver and steered one-handed. "Nice try, kid. Do you want to sail through this storm or not?"

Want? I want to toss you overboard.

Fine...now wasn't the time.

When will be? When?

After slipping the mainsail line under the sole of his running shoe, Ben released the jib furler line, his moves rough with impatience. He pulled the jib sheet and unrolled the jib. With an angry yank, he tightened the line, wrapping it around the winch. He retrieved the mainsail from his foothold and plopped down on the windward side with his feet planted on the opposite bench seat, the leeward side.

The wind heeled the boat. It stayed tilted to the point they took in seawater down the companionway. About an inch of water pooled around his feet. If the cabin filled up with enough water, a fifty-foot monohull could sink—and the restrained EMT would drown first—so he reached over to slide the tiny door closed, sealing off the companionway.

But it wouldn't budge.

"Forget it. It's broken. Something on the track is jammed."

"Of course it is." Ben scoffed under his breath. "Steer more into the wind," he shouted out.

"No."

"Jason, just do it."

"We'll be way off course. We're heading south—"

"Are you trying to kill us?"

"Shut up." Jason continued to steer southbound.

Drop dead, Old Man.

Even though he was soaked, cold, and concerned about the weather, thoughts of the handgun remained first in Ben's mind.

If I could snatch it somehow...

He glanced down the companionway and spotted the EMT's face.

"Jason?" he said, facing him. "She looks like she's gonna be sick down there. If she throws up, she'll choke with tape—"

"Then she better hope she doesn't yak."

"You are one selfish—"

"Now you're getting it, kid."

The wind gusts battered the *Persephone*. It jetted them across the rippling watery surface toward a destination unknown. The turbulent swells of the sea mirrored a pot of boiling water. The rain shattered down at an angle, like shards of dull-edged glass.

"It's only mid-May, right?" Ben said, thinking the start of hurricane season was still two weeks away.

"Yep."

"This seems like a CAT 1 hurricane. At least a tropical storm, you know?"

"Yep."

Jason, typically a man of few words. Fine with Ben. They had nothing more to discuss anyway. He was sick of listening to lies mixed in with distorted truth and some reality. How much was actually real—if any—was sheer mystery. Prodding the old man for the truth proved to be a frustrating waste of time and energy.

"We shouldn't be out here, Jason."

"I don't have a choice."

How'd Dad end up down such a dark path?

Ben glanced down at the EMT; her face wasn't so pale as before.

For two intense hours, Ben clutched the jib line and the mainsail, Jason the wheel. They cruised at a speed of eight knots. The rain soaked Ben's clothes like a showerhead. His feet swam in two inches of water, a mixture of seawater spilling in and rain water pouring down from the black-gray sky.

Even though the day's events were bizarre and ludicrous at best, sailing with the old man like this reminded Ben of the good times they'd shared on the ocean as father and son, especially the one storm they'd fought through when Ben was only twelve—a risky yet amazing adventure Mom never knew about. The contrast between today and all of those fond memories caused sadness to worm its way into Ben's heart, despite his efforts to stifle it.

Sure, Old Man had been a drug user ever since Ben could remember, but he'd never been violent, never been a criminal.

Until now.

Hatred mixed in with the churning sadness. For the first time, Ben loathed his father. The evil image of killing the old man wrapped around his brain and refused to dissipate.

After another hour of pushing through the storm southward, the sky ahead peeked through baby blue dotted with only a few string clouds.

A few more nautical miles and the winds died down. The rain flow fizzled to a mere drizzle. The seawater surface calmed. Inside Ben, however, the burning hatred for his father built to a boiling rage.

He leaped to his feet, ran two steps toward Jason, and struck his fist square in Old Man's face.

"What...?" Jason's eyes registered stunned shock. He reached for the gun.

Ben punched him again. And again. He grabbed him by his shirt, tackled him to the boat deck. Wrestled Jason under his control. He gripped the old man's gun-hand and pounded the back of his hand onto the deck twice. A third time. The gun released from Jason's hand. Ben snatched it and leaped to his feet.

"Enough!" Ben shouted out. "It's over." Standing over his father, he pointed the gun down at him. Chest heaving air in and out, Ben stood there, aiming the weapon like a crazed man.

Kill him. Now.

"Over?" Jason sniffled, nose whistling. "How do you figure that? 'Cause you're the one holding the gun?"

"That's right, Old Man. That's right."

I can't squeeze the trigger. I can't shoot my own father.

Could I ever kill anyone?

Uncertain of his next move, he continued to stand there, pointing the gun down at his father.

"I'm willing to die, son. Are you?"

"I'm not willing to risk the EMT's life."

Flat on his back, Jason grabbed the wheel and yanked it hard.

The boat darted to the right. The boom swung, smacked Ben in the side of the head. Vision blackened, his body crumbled to the deck, out of his control.

Jason bounded up to his feet and stared down at him.

The old man's body blurred; so did everything around him.

I'm gonna black out. I'm gonna black out....

Back in high school, he'd been unconscious for several hours after a hit in the head from a boom.

"You shouldn't have hesitated, kid." Jason laughed, standing over him. "You should've shot me when you had the chance." He stepped on Ben's hand, crushing it between his cop boot and the hull floor. "Hesitation is for the weak."

Ben swallowed a yell of agony to ignore the stabbing pains in his hand...his gun-filled hand.

Bending over, Jason punched him between the eyes. Once. Twice. A third time. His anger turned demented. Out of control. He snatched the gun. "I oughta shoot you right now."

"Go. Ahead." Ben's speech sounded slurred to his own ears.

"Tough words, kids. You want to die?"

Aggravating him more wouldn't do any good, so Ben decided on a different tactic. "I want. This over." His words wouldn't come out more than two at a time. "Stop with. The games."

"You think I'm playing games here?"

"I don't. Know. What. To think." Truth was, he couldn't think straight. His mind was foggy, his head throbbed.

"I don't care what you think."

"Clearly." Old Man was losing it all over again, that Ben did know. The image that popped into his aching head was him and the EMT floating on a raft, gaining a safe distance from Jason on the *Persephone*. At this point Ben would take his chances out there on the vast ocean on a pathetic life raft. With the head trauma from the boom, he couldn't protect the EMT nor could he sail a fifty-foot sailboat—he couldn't even see, let alone stand.

"Ben, when you go against me, you'll lose. Every time. Get it?" A pause of silence. "You didn't have the heart to put me down. You never will."

Ben heard the words as if Jason spoke them from inside a cave.

A sense of heaviness overcame his mind and darkened his vision to full blackness.

It's dusk. That's it.

Yeah, but I'm fading...I'm falling uncon...

CHAPTER FOURTEEN

Kicking dust up, Alec slid his car to a stop on the gravel road lining a row of tiny houses spaced together with mere feet between them. He leaped out of his car into the dreary late afternoon weather. After dodging around two parked patrol cars and the CSU's bright red SUV on scene, he marched up to the sun-faded brown house.

As he snapped on latex gloves, Alec stepped through the threshold of the Keegans' modest home. To the right, in an area serving as a study, one cop stood over the crime scene investigator as he sat at the desk, scanning the computer.

"Jerry," Alec said on a nod at them both.

The cop looked up. "Inspector."

"Hey, Alec." The CSI, the other Jerry in the room, spoke with his eyes glued to the computer screen.

"Anything?"

"Nothing that will lead to finding that sailboat," the cop interjected. "Second thought, we still have much to search here, so I'll change that to 'nothing yet.'"

"Have you two searched the desk or elsewhere in this room?"

"Yeah." Jerry the cop nodded. "That's where we started."

"Uh-huh." Alec nodded back.

"Stevie is combing through the one and only bedroom."

Alec backed out of the study area and headed into the kitchen across the hall.

Blood stained the worn linoleum flooring and the edge of the Formica counter. Blood spatter dotted the wall of the center island. Broken glass and dishes scattered in a shattered mess on the floor.

Movement outside the window caught his attention. A man with a beer in his hand stood on the weed-infested grass, lurking around like a nosy neighbor bored at the moment.

Alec palmed the front door and slipped outside. "Sir? You live around here?"

"Yeah." The guy pointed his beer can to the yellow house right next door.

"What is your name, sir?"

He blasted out a cough. Several more coughs. "D.J. Dingle."

"Mr. Dingle, do you know Mr. and Mrs. Keegan?"

"Of course. We live smack next to each other, as you can see. Kinda difficult not to know 'em, you know? Who are you?"

Alec showed him his badge. "Inspector Dyer."

"*Dyer*, huh? Same last name as that paramedic. The girl Jason took."

Alec's gut clenched. So did his hands into fists. "That's right. She's my daughter."

Dingle whistled. Coughed a few times. "Bummer."

Bummer?

Alec restrained himself from punching the guy right down to the weeded lawn.

He filed through his memory bank for neighbor names. "Mr. Dingle, you weren't questioned on Monday night. The night Annie Keegan was murdered."

"No," Dingle said with a shake of his head. "I wasn't. I called 911."

"*You're* the anonymous 911-caller?"

"That's what I said." Dingle nodded. "Yes, sir, I am."

"That call came from another address." Alec glanced across the street. "From a house over there, but the residents weren't found home that night."

"They weren't home. They leave their door unlocked. I used their telephone."

"You don't have a phone?"

"I do." Dingle coughed twice, sounded like he'd hacked up part of a lung. "I just didn't want to get involved."

Apparently Dingle suddenly wanted to spill his guts. "But you do now. What made you call 911 that night?" Alec knew the 911-call by memory but wanted to hear it in the caller's own remembered words two days later.

"Screaming. Shouting. Stuff breaking and crashing. You know, unsettling noises. Inspector, what I really want to tell you about is what's in the backyard. The Keegans' backyard."

Alec's ears perked up in hope for a solid direction.

This may lead to finding the Persephone *and bringing Sara home. Alive.*

He eyed the yard behind the Keegan home, at least what he could see of it from where he stood.

"Back there?" Alec pointed.

"Yup," Dingle said, but nothing else followed.

Alec's mind reeled images of buried drugs, explosives. Body parts. "Really? What's back there?" He texted Jerry, the cop inside searching the Keegan study.

Send the CSI out here.

"It's in the dirt. Under the huge palm tree." Mr. Dingle stepped toward the fence separating the front and back yards.

Alec rushed in front of the man to block the gate. "Sounds like maybe we need to preserve evidence, Mr. Dingle, so instead of going back there, can you just tell me?"

D.J. Dingle pointed to a lone palm tree planted in the left back corner. A broken birdbath stood underneath it in the soil. "After I called 911 and rushed back home, I watched the Keegan's house. Listened through my opened window. The hollering and crashing noises and stuff had stopped. In fact, it was silent over there, dead silent. Sirens sounded, and they got louder. Closer. I saw Jason slip outside. To his backyard. He buried something back there that night. Buried it under the palm tree, near the birdbath." Dingle wrapped his palm around the cone-shaped fence post.

"And you saw this? You saw Jason Keegan actually bury something?"

"Sure did, Inspector. He ran out into his backyard with something in his hand. He squatted down and dug around, then put whatever it was in the hole and covered it up. You know, buried it. Sirens got really loud. Big time close. He rushed back into his house then."

"What did he bury, sir?"

"I don't know, but it's the size of bread."

Bread? "A loaf?"

"No, a slice. You know, one slice of bread."

"Okay, what was it?"

"I don't know, I already told you that. Something small, though. Fits inside a hand kind-of-small. Like a piece of bread, I already said. Jason buried the thing. I didn't see what it was, Inspector. It was getting dark. And it was small."

"Sure, I understand."

CSI Jerry stepped outside. "Inspector? What's up?"

"Check the backyard. Soil around the birdbath. Keegan buried something Monday night. Small. Hand-sized." Stepping back from the gate, Alec grabbed Dingle's arm, urging him to do the same.

He did.

Jerry bolted off across the weeded lawn and toward the area in question, snapping on fresh latex gloves as he stalked.

"Mr. Dingle? Were you home alone Monday night, witnessing all of this?" Alec glanced over to the palm tree, watching Jerry digging methodically in the dirt.

"Yeah. I live alone."

"Okay. What happened then? After Keegan raced back inside his house?"

"You people showed up, and an ambulance and firefighters and whatnot."

"What did you do?"

"Watched it all out my window." He pointed his beer can to the upper floor window of the yellow house next door. "You people were in and out. A stretcher went in. About ten minutes later, EMS carried Jason out on the thing, and he wasn't moving at all. I was thinking: What? Why? What happened to him? He was fine just a few minutes ago, you know? Running outside to bury that thing, whatever it was in his hand."

That would've been helpful information that night.

"Later on another body was wheeled out, this one zipped inside a black bag. That's not good."

Gee, you think? "Mr. Dingle, sir, RCIPS knocked on your door that night. Why did you avoid us?"

"Yeah, I didn't answer." He took a swig of beer. "Look, I called 911, right? Why didn't you people realize Jason wasn't mental Monday night? A little bit ago, the news reported all the stuff he pulled, how he faked being unable to talk or whatever. It was an act, and you people didn't figure it out. You stuck him in the psych ward instead of jail, and now he escaped on a sailboat. Inspector, we all make mistakes. It's called being human."

"Mistakes?" Alec's blood boiled. "Mr. Dingle, you intentionally withheld information from the police in a murder investigation. That's called obstruction of justice."

"Well, I'm talkin' to you now."

"And why is that?"

"Over the years, I've seen that paramedic working EMS calls around the island, helping all kinds of people and saving their lives. She saved my coworker's arm last year when his hand got stuck in a roll machine. I don't want her to get hurt. If I can help bring her home safely, I can't ignore that."

Thank you for that.

Alec unclenched his fists and drew in a long breath of fresh air. "Mr. Dingle, prior to when all the rescue crews showed up, did you see anyone enter or exit the Keegan home that night?"

"You mean besides Jason? In his backyard?"

"Yeah, besides that."

Dingle's left eyebrow lifted, his lips pursed as he looked off. "Hmm. I don't know one way or the other for sure. I wasn't paying any attention to their house until I heard the screams, yells, and crashes. Then I couldn't stop paying attention. Reality TV live next door, you know? It was addicting."

Addicting?

"Was this common behavior at the Keegan home? The sounds of violence?"

"No. Not at all." Dingle shook his head with conviction. "I never heard anything like that from them. That's why it was so exciting, man. You get what I'm saying?"

Exciting?

If the public was so drawn to morbid curiosity, why didn't they get a job in law enforcement and help instead of standing on the sidelines gawking at the commotion?

"Mr. Dingle, are you saying the Keegans seemed like a happy couple?"

"That's what I'm saying, Inspector. So when I heard the noises over there Monday night, I knew something wasn't right. I'd never heard anything like that from Jason and Annie. Every time I saw them, they seemed happy together. They kept to themselves, though. A relaxed and quiet couple, you know?"

"Did you know they were into drugs?"

"Yeah." Dingle nodded, lips curved downward. "Yeah, I did. Sad. A quiet drug addict couple." He finished off his beer. "Inspector, to be honest, when I heard the loud hollering and crashing that night, I immediately thought someone else was in the house, like one of their drug friends coming on to Annie or something and she was fighting him off. So I called the cops." He crushed the can in his hand. "From what I always saw, Jason and Annie were a happy couple. At least nothing violent. Nothing like that. They weren't like that."

So what changed?

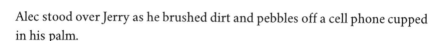

Alec stood over Jerry as he brushed dirt and pebbles off a cell phone cupped in his palm.

Okay, Keegan had buried a cell phone. Huh.

With a gloved hand, Alec took the phone from the CSI's outstretched one and turned the thing on.

This wasn't a burner cell. Must be a phone Keegan used regularly, something that was never found in the house on Monday when the crime scene unit had combed the place, and there was no record of a Jason Keegan owning a cell phone.

Alec scanned the call history. The last number dialed was only minutes prior to the arrival of RCIPS Monday night. The three prefix numbers were the Jamaica country code.

Again with Jamaica.

"I don't get it, Alec." CSI Jerry climbed to his feet. "Why didn't the idiot smash the phone before burying it? Why not render it completely incapacitated so the number and history and such would be destroyed?"

Alec shrugged. "He only had minutes to carry out his plans. The sirens were closing in on him, according to the neighbor. Heck, maybe he planned to retrieve it."

"Maybe he knew simply destroying the thing isn't a guarantee the number isn't traceable, thus the call history could be discovered."

"Another solid guess." On his own cell phone, which had the blocked number feature so his number nor his country code would display, Alec dialed the Jamaica number.

"'ello?" a man with a Caribbean accent answered.

"Hey, man, I hear you've got the stuff," Alec spoke in a hushed tone, like a sly drug addict.

"Who is dis?"

"I could give you a fake name, but that's pointless. You got the stuff or not?"

Pause. "What stuff?"

"The good stuff. You name the price, I pay. It's that easy."

"Mon, I don' know who you are, an' I don' know wha' you are talkin' about."

Click.

Alec redialed the number.

"Stop callin' me," the Jamaican said as a greeting.

"I need the stuff, man. I'm serious. I pay whatever. Where do I meet you?"

"Wrong numba. I not who you tink I am. You're confusing me wid somebodee else."

"Keegan? Is that who? Jason Keegan?"

A pause of silence over the phone. "Jason dunna have anyting you'd want."

Yes, he does, and I'm getting my daughter back. "Listen to me—"

"Sure you are no' lookin' fo' CC?"

"Coco Byer? Nah, I'm looking for Keegan. Where is he?"

"I don' know. Why would I know?"

"Is he headed to Jamaica?" Alec pressed on like a desperate father at the end of his rope of patience.

Silence from the Jamaican.

"Cozumel? Cancun? Belize?" *Tell me. For the love of God, tell me!*

"Whoever you are, is'en to me. Jason Keegan is no' stupid, an' needer am I."

Click.

CHAPTER FIFTEEN

Jason stood at the *Persephone's* wheel as the orange sun lowered its way through the striations of cloud cover and toward the watery horizon in the west.

Forty-eight hours ago he'd snorted his last lines. Forty-eight. Rage continued to build inside of him, toward a brink. No coke at his disposal created a monstrous anger in him. Monday night that rage took over him, like twenty-one years ago.

Cocaine uplifted him. With it, nothing was impossible. Without it...

The strangle-hold grip he had on the wheel ached his knuckles.

Would I kill my own son, my own child?

"You asleep down there?" he yelled down to Ben tied up to the only piece of furniture not connected to the boat hull. "Kid?"

"What?"

"It wasn't supposed to be like this."

"Like what, exactly? You flipping out?"

"I'm not flipping out."

"Oh, it's normal to abduct a woman under gunpoint? Tie your son to a chair?"

"You know why those things happened, Ben."

"Yeah, you're willing to do anything to get your way."

You got it, kid. I'm not going to prison. Ever.

Sara listened to Keegan's voice shout up on the deck.

"You asleep down there?" A pause of silence. "Kid?" Another pause. "It wasn't supposed to be like this." More silence. "I'm not flipping out." A long pause. "You know why those things happened, Ben."

Sara glanced at Ben, his body slumped unconscious from head trauma and tied to the chair.

Keegan is really losing it.

<hr />

Ben blinked four times. A sharp pain blanketed his forehead and cemented behind his eyes. His vision blurry, only vague shapes and spotty colors floated in front of him. A fog encompassed his brain.

What happened?

A rocking motion listed his body as if he were on a train or something. *Where am I?*

It felt like a golf ball was stuck to the side of his head. What was it...his arms wouldn't budge to touch his scalp and find out.

My arms are tied up to a chair. Why?

Jason, his old man.

I'm his prisoner on a sailboat.

The memory of the entire day flooded his pained head, every ugly bit of it. The golf ball was a lump from the boom whacking into him. Right.

The *Persephone* seemed to be thrusting at top speed. Jason had obviously turned on the motor and kicked it into high gear to make up for lost time and mileage due to the storm.

The woman EMT.

Ben blinked a few more times, his vision clearing. She was still across the main salon from him. Mouth still taped shut, she simply stared back at him.

"You doing okay over there?"

She nodded at him, then jerked her head forward, her eyebrows lifted.

Huh? "How am I doing?"

She nodded.

His head hurt as if his skull had been smashed in with a brick. "I'm fine. I'm good."

Her eyes narrowed.

"You don't believe me?"

She shook her head.

"You saw the boom knock me out?"

Eyes narrowed even more.

"The boom is the steel horizontal bar that holds the bottom of the main-sail."

She nodded in understanding.

Nausea from head trauma coated his gut. "I hesitated up there. I had the opportunity to shoot him, but I hesitated. I blew it. I'm sorry."

Eyes softened, she shook her head.

"I've never held a gun in my life. I knew what to do, how to squeeze the trigger. I just..." Couldn't do it. *I couldn't shoot and kill my own father.* "I'm so sorry."

Water rimmed her lower lids. She blinked it away.

Next chance, I'll blow him away.

"You forced me to kill you, Annie!" Jason shouted over his wife's lifeless body sprawled on their kitchen floor, her hair swimming in a blood pool.

Swaying at the boat's wheel, Jason shook his head, trying to clear the visual. The memory bothered him. He never wanted to remember it again, but his brain couldn't shut it off...

"You did this, Annie!" he continued yelling. "You gave me no choice." Until seconds ago, he'd never touched her in violence. Cocaine elevated his mood and diminished his annoyance with others.

But she'd pushed too far.

"You'd be alive if you would've kept your nose out of where it doesn't belong. You dug around into something that has nothing to do with you. It's not your business what happened twenty-one years ago."

Annie's dead body lay mere inches from his feet. Grief surrounded his chest and squeezed it inward. He gasped for a breath, stunned he was mourning her.

Well, too bad. He just needed to get over it. She was dead...and forever quiet.

A plan formed in his mind. To put it into action, he grabbed his cell and dialed his good buddy, Jimar Malcolm.

"Malcolm? I offed my wife. Get me out of Cayman. Sail..."

Seconds after he finished that call, emergency sirens sounded in the distance. The volume heightened...and heightened.

Coincidental, most likely. But if not, and the cops were headed there, he couldn't run and flee the scene. They'd find him on this tiny island before Malcolm sailed here.

As the sirens grew closer, another plan formed in his head.

Three words came to his mind.

This. Could. Work.

"It would've worked if *Malcolm* had sailed to Cayman," Jason grumbled under his breath. Grinding his teeth, he choked the wheel and continued to steer the boat southbound.

Malcolm will pay for this.

Exhaustion hit him, draining him. He hadn't slept in days. The sleep deprivation in the psych ward gave him a high, spurring on his acting ability to stay in role as a catatonic without a break.

The lack of sleep was catching up with him.

Now that the cops weren't in his face or anywhere in sight, he was feeling the lull. Without coke, his mood was out of control. He wanted to rip everyone's face off.

Desperation to do several lines filled him with urgency. He didn't want to hurt the paramedic, and he really didn't want to hurt his son, but neither of them should be there. Their presence changed what should've been an easy escape.

Malcolm will pay for this!

Jason envisioned snorting one line of coke. Another one.

Ah...it's kicking in. Relief.

No. He was kidding himself. Euphoria wasn't coming on. It wouldn't without the real thing.

If only he had some...he could sniff away his rage and roll with today's events. But there was no cocaine onboard the *Persephone,* and the only thing rolling was his anger.

"You'll pay for this, Malcolm!" he yelled out. The vast sea swallowed up the sound of his words. "You will pay."

Oh, yeah, he's really losing it now.

Ben couldn't help thinking it as he listened to Jason shout up on deck at a man who wasn't there. He pounded his hand on various things up there. The last time it sounded like he beat up the radio some more. Good thing the EMT was down here and out of Jason's reach.

Ben eyed her over in the corner, her upper body shoved up against the boat's hull, her ankles still bound together by cotton restraints and knotted to a pole with sailing rope. Hands cuffed behind her, her face scrunched in some sort of panic.

She stared out the window near her, then glanced at him, eyes wide and filled with fright. She squirmed as if in pain, moaned out as if...he had no idea.

I need to get that tape off her mouth. I need to drag some answers out of her.

She knew way more than he did about what was going on.

"Hey, you doing okay over there?" he whispered to her.

She shook her head, and shook it. And shook it. She jerked her shoulder at the window and groaned through the tape.

"What? What's out there?"

With her eyes squeezed shut, she pounded the back of her head to the wall, and cried out. The tape muffled her wails.

Why was she so terrified now, when all along today she hadn't seemed frightened and should've?

It didn't make sense.

With her thumb and pinky, Sara played with her pearl ring. Her throat constricted, threatening to close the airflow off to her lungs. Her uniform shirt clung to her skin. The rainwater-soaked shirt had dried a little during the last few hours, but now it was blotched with sweat. Sticky sweat coated her face, her chest, her underarms, her palms.

Out the window the sun dropped its way into the ocean as the *Persephone* chugged on toward destination unknown. A gray hue blanketed the dusk sky, full of clouds and no moonlight. Night settling in, the sky and the ocean would soon be utter black.

Plunging her into the darkness of nightfall.

With no light to turn on.

"Nooo!" she screamed into the tape over her mouth, a fresh wave of panic captivating her.

No. No. No.

She yanked her legs backward, pulling on the metal pipe constricting her feet. For the fourth time today, she planted her boot soles on the pipe, one above the other, lifted her hips off the ground, and pushed backward with a long-winded grunt.

Pushed hard.

Harder.

"Come on!" she yelled out, her muffled words caught underneath the tape.

The pipe didn't budge. Not one bit.

"Stop it," Keegan's son said, in a louder tone than he'd spoken to her earlier. "You can't break free. You'll only hurt yourself."

He was right. No way could she push or rip this steel pipe from its nailed position in the floor.

So...again for the fourth time today, she collapsed onto the worn carpeting in defeat. Energy wasted for nothing. She blew out the breath she'd held during the ineffective effort to free herself.

"Hey, what's going on with you?" Ben went on. "Something's changed. What?"

The view beyond the window...the glass floor of the black ocean water and the darkened sky tormented her. Even if she could speak, she wouldn't dare say the truth. She'd never shared it with anyone.

"What changed? Tell me. Somehow communicate it to me."

I can't stand nighttime. I'm afraid of the dark. OKAY?

She craved to cry herself to sleep, but the tears wouldn't come to the surface. They hid behind her eyes, too scared of making her weak and even more vulnerable than she already was by being bound up. If only she could fall asleep, stay asleep until bright sunlight bathed the ocean and the boat.

What am I going to do? What am I going to do?

Instead of welcomed light of any kind, a memory reel flooded her. Unlike a movie simply on replay inside her brain, this memory took her back. Back. Back.

"No, not now!" she yelled into the tape. *I can't disappear into this for the billionth time. Not now.*

God? Don't ignore me. Not now. Drift me into a state of unconsciousness so I escape the dark before I lose my mind in it.

She felt nothing from Him. Felt nothing at all but mind-numbing fear.

With the trigger of darkness, knowing daylight was multiple hours away, she lost the fight, couldn't stop herself from slipping away and experiencing the horror of that night all over again, as she'd done for years so many times before...

She opened her eyes to pure darkness.

Where am I? Why do I feel like a pretzel, like my body is constricted?

I squirm, but...I'm trapped inside...something. I pat my hands around. I sniff.

I'm sealed up in some sort of plastic.

A trash bag?

Someone rolled me up inside a huge sack as if I'm a pile of dead leaves....? *Why? Why would—*

I remember now.

A hammer. After my mom beat me, she struck my head with a hammer for the final blow.

The noise of an engine hums in my ears. The motion of rolling movement underneath me, like I'm inside something with wheels.

My sixteen-year-old beaten body is inside a moving vehicle. I'm inside the trunk of a car.

Mom's car?

Where is she driving me? She must think I'm dead.

"You okay? Hey, are you okay over there?"

Sara heard a familiar male voice. It sounded like it cared, like the person who'd spoken those words wanted to help her.

I'm hallucinating, that's it.

No one was there in the car trunk with her.

I'm all alone, trapped in the dark.

She thrashed around, kicked, desperate to find a way out and to some light somewhere. She screamed, her voice sounding muffled as the darkness swallowed up her youth and memory.

CHAPTER SIXTEEN

The pilot revved up the engine of a Cessna 170, basically a four-seater Cessna 140 with a more powerful engine. Alec shut the airplane's front passenger door and belted himself in the seat. Two Cayman drug force agents buckled themselves in the back, traveling to Jamaica for a case unrelated to Jason Keegan's escape or Sara's abduction.

The Cessna gained speed on the runway and lifted off. The small airplane flew over the seventy-six-square-mile island of Grand Cayman as the sun eased to sink into the cloudy horizon for the day. Seawater stretched, endless, in all directions. Nothing in sight except for the sister islands of Little Cayman and Cayman Brac, near each other and about one hundred miles from Grand Cayman.

Off to the right and a little lower altitude than the airplane, a grouping of seagulls glided over the ocean. Alec inhaled a deep breath and tried to draw from the peace of the birds' serene flight. His apprehension calmed a slight bit. Two of the seagulls eased to a stop and hovered in place over the water.

In search of prey? As if answering his question, one dropped straight down, face first, and dove into the ocean, disappearing underneath the surface.

Where exactly had Keegan disappeared?

Alec's nerves enflamed with a fury only another parent could imagine.

The airplane zoomed in the air southeast. For endless miles, he searched the ocean below for the *Persephone*.

Nothing. Well...nothing but two cruise ships. An oil rig. A day cruise boat. A Coast Guard cruiser. Several speed boats. Three fishing boats. Two sailboats, neither of them the *Persephone*.

Where are you, Keegan?

On the horizon behind the aircraft, the top tip of the sun inched its way into the ocean. And disappeared. A red hue surrounded the orange ball of heated light. Twenty minutes later the night sky swallowed up the watery surface. The sky and water now a blend of one flow of blackness, mirroring how he felt deep inside. Dark. Empty.

His cell phone buzzed to life. Craig's number flashed on the screen.

"Craig?" Alec yelled over the engine noise. "It's about time, man."

"Have you landed in Jamaica yet?"

"Just about to. What's up? Talk to me. You got a name?"

"First off, the media understands the safety issue behind keeping your name out of the news."

"You made it clear?"

"Alec, they get if Keegan learns Sara has any link to a cop—that she's the daughter of an inspector, no less—it would place extra risk on her life."

"And it would give Keegan the green light to demand more."

"The Cayman media understands that, Alec. They aren't going to jeopardize a paramedic's life to enhance a story's sensationalism. Come on. You gotta trust that."

I've lived here longer than you, buddy. I know Grand Cayman Island. "I do. Moving on."

"Fine. I've got a name for you."

Hope soared through Alec's system. "Let's hear it."

"Jimar Malcolm. That's the Jamaican you're looking for, Alec."

"Okay. Fill me in."

"Malcolm owns half of the *Persephone*. Keegan owns the other half. The two sailing pals go way back. Drug buddies in South Florida, according to a confidential source."

"A snitch?"

"Yep. The Jamaican number you called, the one listed last on Keegan's call history, is registered to a J.L. Malcolm, a Jamaican citizen. Jimar L. Malcolm lived in South Florida at the same time Keegan resided there. Coco Byers's brother is an inmate in the Miami-Dade prison, and loves to make statements in order to decrease his twenty-year sentence for meth cooking and supplying."

"Did the brother introduce Keegan and Malcolm?"

"Introduce? Sure, you could call it that. Malcolm had a jealous and angry husband after him. He decided to kill before being killed. You following me so far? So Coco's brother suggested he hire our buddy, Jason Keegan. Keegan blew up the angry husband and his motorcycle to tiny pieces. Think: ashen remains post-cremation. Dental records useless to supply an ID confirmation. DNA testing of various bone fragments confirmed the identity, proving one man—the jealous husband—died in that blast. You think Malcolm stays clear of married women now?"

"Probably not. You got an address for this guy? This Jimar L. Malcolm?"

"Yup. He's a bartender at Parakeet's."

"Parakeet? Like the bird?"

"That's it."

"Gotcha. Thanks, man."

"That's what I'm here for, Alec."

Lelisa Dyer scanned the sea below her as the helicopter flew toward the barge awaiting her arrival. According to the coordinates, the barge should come in to sight in the southeast within a few minutes.

Just as she'd done the entire flight across the dusk-lit ocean, she scrutinized everywhere visible for a sighting of the *Persephone.*

The empty and endless water below haunted her.

Keegan, where are you? Where have you taken Sara?

Ten minutes later the pilot pointed. "There's the barge," he shouted over the rumble of the helicopter's engine.

In the near southeast distance, some sort of huge floating vessel came into view. Wispy rain clouds hovered high above it.

The helicopter slowed its speed as it approached the barge. Rows of various colored metal containers the size of eighteen-wheel trucks were lined up on the vessel's one and only open deck. Less than a minute later, the chopper hovered over the large vessel.

"Agent Dyer?" the pilot shouted. "Are you ready to drop?"

"Ready."

The copilot slid the side door open and released a ladder rope. It tumbled out with a bounce into the windy air, moist with the promise of a rainstorm. The bottom end dangled over the center of the barge and the only section where no steel containers took up space on the deck, allowing her room to board.

Backward, Lelisa crawled out of the helicopter, stepping down on the rope ladder, one rung at a time, and lowered herself toward the barge's deck far below. Wind force battered her, tossing her around like caught fish at the end of a fishing pole. The ladder swung back and forth, around in circles. A wave of panic lodged in her throat. Picturing Sara's sweet face, Lelisa gained courage to continue down.

After she stepped on the bottom rung, she dropped onto the wooden deck, boarding the vessel with a pounding thud. The panic subsided.

"You okay?" a gruff voice asked her in a volume-raised tone obviously to be heard over the swoosh of helicopter blades in motion.

From on her hands and knees like a dog, she looked up at the voice and found a seaman with a thick and bushy beard. "I'm fine." She scrambled to her feet. "Is the captain around?"

"On his way up here. Uh…ma'am? What exactly do you need from us?"

She flashed him her badge. "Agent Dyer. Royal Cayman Islands Police Service. Thank you for allowing me to board your vessel."

The seaman cocked his head to the side. "As I understood it, we didn't have a choice. Could you tell me how that is, ma'am? Agent Dyer?"

Ignoring his question, Lelisa whipped out a photo of the *Persephone* from her pocket. "Have you seen this sailboat at any time during today?"

The man leaned in, studied the photo. "Not that I know." He turned to a burly man behind him. "Rogers? You see anything like this today?"

The man named Rogers poked his head in, oil-stained baseball hat low over his face. He viewed the photo. "No. Not that I remember."

Overhead, the chopper took off, flying northwest. Staying behind on the barge, Lelisa couldn't help but wonder if her husband was right and this was a huge waste of time.

I better be right about this.

Alec stepped underneath the roof of a Jamaican beachside grass hut and slid onto a bamboo bar stool. Caribbean music played via a live band in the corner of a pool deck about twenty yards from the bar. A young couple, probably honeymooners by the look of their sparkling rings, entwined body contact, and that fresh gaze of love and innocence in their eyes, sat on

Alec's right at the square bar. No one on his left. Across from him, two guys leaned against the counter, hitting on the same twenty-something woman with no wit. Sitting in between them, the young blonde flirted with both men in misguided self-confidence.

The bartender spoke to his patrons in a Jamaican accent, his words a mix of American and Jamaican speak. Proof he'd spent time living in America. Florida, according to the snitches in the drug world. And...Alec recognized the voice. Now he had a face to go along with it.

The black-bearded, long-haired bartender was his man.

Jimar Malcolm approached Alec. "Wha' canna get you, mon?" he asked Alec, sliding a white cocktail napkin in front of him on the bar counter.

"What do ya got on tap?"

"Amstel, Red Stripe—"

"I'll take an Amstel."

"You got it."

Malcolm turned to the left and proceeded to fill a clear glass with foaming beer. His profile showed a gaunt man, the tendons in his neck thin, defined cords. His full but trimmed short beard indicated a man willing to spend the time shaving but desperate to cover the signs of aging, stress, and years of drug and alcohol use.

Waves lapped in on the shoreline to Alec's right, the gentle noise relaxing. Two pelicans squawked in their flight low over the ocean and just above the waterline on the beach. The view was mesmerizing. Peaceful. The reprieve supplied him with fresh energy.

I'm not gonna let you down again, Sara. This time it won't take me two years to find you.

But...do I have any control, any power? How can I make that promise, even to myself?

Malcolm removed the full glass out from underneath the tap. Beer dripped off his hand to the ground. He shook his arm to the side, ridding his skin of the excess liquid, then set the foaming beer onto the cocktail napkin.

"Anyting to eat? Kickin' Jamaican wings? Beef dumplin's? Jamaican hot peppah shrimp?"

"Naw. I'm good with these." Alec scooted the peanut bowl his way. It clinked against his beer glass. He popped three salted roasted nuts into his mouth.

About thirty peanuts later, he pushed the empty bowl aside and eyed the pretzels. The need to stuff his stomach? A distraction. Unfortunately, no food in the world would ease his burning worry and agitation. Nothing would.

Except one thing.

Sara home. Alive.

"Hey, Bartender?" he called out, diving into the start of his plan.

"Anotha beer?" Malcolm asked him.

"I'm thinking a shot."

"Whiskey?"

"Got any Wild Turkey?"

The Jamaican nodded. "Sure do, mon."

"Perfect."

Malcolm poured the dark liquid into a rainbow-striped shot glass.

Head back, Alec downed it. The burn in his throat and trachea was an unfamiliar welcome.

"Anotha one?"

"How 'bout you joining me if I buy you one?"

"Sure, mon." Malcolm nodded, his lips curving into a smile. "Le's do it." He poured himself a shot, then refilled Alec's tiny glass.

As Malcolm downed his, Alec tossed his over his shoulder and onto the sand without the bartender noticing. Alec was more than sure Jimar L. Malcolm could easily out-drink him.

Alec pounded his palm on the sticky bar counter and stretched backward with casual ease. "Buy you another one, Bartender?"

Malcolm eyed over his shoulder, maybe at the clock hung on the wooden pole stuck in the bar counter across from Alec. "Yeah, sure. My shif' ends in twenny minutes."

"The bar closes at ten p.m.?"

"Nope. Someone takes ova for me until tree a.m."

"Well, all right then." Alec raised his empty shot glass. "Fill us both up."

The bartender did just that.

At the same time as Malcolm, Alec drank the dark fluid. Both drained their respective shot glass. Ten minutes later, and Malcolm had swallowed three more shots; Alec had dumped all of his next three over his shoulder.

The Jamaican swayed a little on his feet, closed his eyes for an extended blink.

"Let's do another one," Alec said, wiggling his empty shot glass.

"Can't. Need to be soba latta tonight."

"To drive home?"

"No. To sail out."

Tonight? What for, my new friend?

"Ah." Alec nodded. "You're a sailor, huh?"

Malcolm leaned back against the bar counter opposite of Alec and crossed his arms. "Yup."

"I'm one myself. Catamaran is my boat. You? What's yours?"

"Lugger."

"Solid vessel. I'm buying a new Cat. I'm stumped on a name. What's your boat's name?"

"*Jezebel.*"

"Catchy."

"Named afta a woman who could'na stop sleepin' wid cruise ship visitors to de island. De cheatin' slut's name is Juanita, but I nickname her *Jezebel*, den rename my boat de same."

"Ah." Alec snapped his fingers. "Got it. Sounds like the name fits. Ex-girlfriend?"

"No. Ex-wife."

"Bummer."

"Nope, tons of otha hotties out der waitin' to meet me, mon."

"So...sailor. Where are you headed tonight? Sailing the world?"

Malcolm laughed. "Not'ing like dat. Jus' meeting up wid a buddy."

Jason Keegan? "This late at night?" Yet typical timing of criminal activity.

"Yep."

"You gonna be sober enough to captain?"

"No problem. I have sailed wid way more alcohol in me."

Alec didn't doubt that. "How far are you sailing?"

"A few hours out."

Enough said. Time to go.

"Well, Bartender, enjoy your sail tonight." Alec pulled out four twenties for eleven shots and a beer. "Will that cover my tab?"

"Way cova it. Tank you, mon."

No. Thank you.

Hidden behind a shed on a dock about three miles from the bar, Alec stared out at the dark watery surface beyond. The half-moon brightened the sky and ocean somewhat. Heavy cloud cover blocked most of the stars above.

"Stakeouts stink, y'know?" a Jamaican cop said, lighting up yet another smoke, a pile of burnt stubs around his feet on the wooden dock.

"Uh-huh." Alec checked his cell phone for any missed calls. Any messages. Anything useful.

Nothing.

A French Interpol agent, Dubois, played with a switch on his hand radio, an annoying habit he'd done for the last hour. If he wasn't clicking that knob, he was cracking his knuckles. "When's this guy supposed to show up, Dyer?"

"Not sure exactly." Alec glanced at his wristwatch. "It's almost eleven. It shouldn't be much longer."

"Stand-by," Agent Dubois spoke his French accent into his radio. "Ready to roll on demand."

"Copy that," a male voice responded through the radio.

"Inform the other two out there," Dubois radioed out the order.

"Copy that."

Alec popped in another piece of gum. A second one. Chewed and chomped on the sugar-free wad. For years he'd watched NHL and NBA coaches use the vice, especially during the playoffs, to calm the nerves. Maybe it would work for him, a thought he'd had when he first arrived in Jamaica, the reason he purchased several packs of spearmint gum.

"You think three separate boats out der are enough?" Officer Grant, the Jamaican cop, interjected on a puff of exhaled smoke spiraling out of his mouth.

"The three staging boats are strategically spaced," Alec answered around the gum wad. "One of them will be close enough to the general direction the *Jezebel* heads."

"And you don' think this Jimar L. Malcolm won' realize dat boat was posting, waiting to follow him?"

"You don't know about the plan after that, I see."

"Enlighten me, Inspector."

"Grant, we've got four more boats posting farther out, each in separate locations. When the time comes, one of them will take over keeping tabs on *Jezebel's* whereabouts."

"Okay." Officer Grant inhaled a drag. "Den what? More boats posted beyond that?"

"No." Alec shook his head, irritation brewing for this cop's negativity. "The tracking device I stuck on the front of the hull—"

"—only keeps us updated on de *Jezebel's* coordinates. In orda to seize the *Persephone*, we need to be on top of *Jezebel*, no' shadowing from a conspicuous distance."

"That's not poss—"

"—I know why i's no' possible, Inspector. Since dat's de case, we could still lose dis guy."

"You haven't been in law enforcement long, have you?" Alec snapped at the twenty-something officer, obviously too green to know when to shut his mouth. "There's never a guarantee."

Grant tapped the end of his cigarette over the ocean. Ashes fluttered down into the water. "True dat."

"In addition to the explosives scenario," Agent Dubois interjected into the conversation, "if we move in toward the *Jezebel* too close, too soon, Malcolm will simply abort the plans to meet up with the *Persephone*, and then we lose Keegan, probably forever at that point. Capiche?"

"Sure." Grant breathed another drag. "But in losing sight of *Jezebel*, we also lose de *Persephone*, so either way, we lose. Dat's if Malcolm shows up here at de docks at all."

Alec envisioned his fist punching the officer out into stone-cold silence. "Relax, Grant."

"Keep your negativity to yourself," Agent Dubois added, his irritation clear as he cracked his knuckles on his left hand. "You do remember the hostage is Agent Dyer's *daughter*."

Grant turned to Alec. "I getdat, Inspector. I do." He rubbed his hand over his short yet thick fluffy hair. "De reason I'm trying to make sure we don' lose *Jezebel*."

Alec spit the two pieces of gum out into the ocean. "Again, no guarantees. We just do the best we can as law enforcers." *I should accept the truth in my own spoken words.*

I can't. I won't. My best failed Sara once before. This time my daughter won't have two years; she'll be dead in just days. Possibly hours.

Maybe she's dead already....

No. I won't accept that—there's no reason to accept it.

Alec slipped a new piece of gum into his mouth.

Several silent minutes passed. No sound but the lapping of water crashing into the dock poles underneath his feet, and Dubois cracking his right hand knuckles.

Officer Grant flicked his stubbed cigarette into the ocean. "Dubois? Are all you Interpol guys out of de Buenos Aires site?"

Alec chomped on his gum with heightened annoyance. Obviously this officer was a talker, loved to fill the peaceful air with his annoying voice.

Dubois pointed to the darkened ocean. "All the guys out there are. I'm from headquarters. In France. I just happened to be in Argentina for meetings and such, so I was able to fly here quickly."

"Uh-huh. I hear Interpol is manned 24/7. Dat right?" Grant droned on as he dug out an unopened cigarette pack from his pocket.

"It is. Both in France and in Argentina."

"Just de two sites globally, huh?"

"For now."

Grant lit up a fresh stick filled with cancerous nicotine. "Inspector, if de *Persephone* is rigged up wid de works," he removed the cigarette from his mouth, "heavy explosives in de hands of an explosives expert, as you put it—how are we gettin' around dat?"

Out of the darkened parking lot, a figure appeared, the body unrecognizable with the distance and the lack of light.

"That's gotta be Jimar Malcolm," Alec whispered.

From the parking lot to the first dock, a man strode in the dark of night. Malcolm leaped onto the *Jezebel,* rocking her in the slip. After rigging the boat to sail, the bearded man steered the *Jezebel* out of the marina, trekking out into the open sea.

"Westbound boat?" Agent Dubois said into the handheld radio. "Headed your way. Full alert."

"I'm on it," a male voice spoke over the radio waves.

Alec's cell phone vibrated.

"Craig?" Alec spoke into his cell, impatience tightening his neck and back muscles to a constant state of spasm. "What'd you find out?"

"I got intel on the *Jezebel*'s coordinates, Alec. She's headed due west—"

"Along with the tracking, we have eyes out there on her. I know exactly where she is."

"No, Alec, I know where she's headed. I have the actual coordinates."

"How'd you manage that?"

"She's keeping in close contact with the Jamaican weather center. *Jezebel*'s captain, none other than Jimar Malcolm, asked about weather at certain coordinates an hour ago. Coordinates far enough away and isolated enough to be the ideal meeting spot."

"Craig, if we intercept him before he reaches the *Persephone*, we may just capture Keegan."

"Ah...I see your thinking, Alec. Tricky plan, but possible. Very possible. We're gonna nail him, man. This is it."

I'm coming, Sara. Dad is coming for you. Hang tight.

And stay alive.

———————◇◇◇———————

Lelisa stood in the center of the bridge, staring out at the dark endless emptiness of the ocean.

Now what? The barge held no answers. A dead-end.

It's pointless, Lelisa, to head out to a barge or any other moving vessel in the vicinity of where Persephone *disappeared off our radar.*

She heard Alec's voice once again play in her head. Over and over, her husband's words rolled out like a record perpetually stuck.

Stuck. She was stuck out here, wasting her time.

Alec was right.

"Captain?" She turned to face the white-bearded man. "I need to contact the shore."

"The radio room will give you the privacy you need, Agent Dyer."

Ten minutes later, and in the corner of the radio room, she found a lone man.

"Agent Dyer. You're here." The communications officer stood up from a desk covered with a radio and its components. "I've reached the Cayman Islands." He held out a mic to her. "Our radios are programmed with encryption mode to ensure privacy of your conversation."

Lelisa slid into the metal desk chair. "Thank you." She pressed the side button on the mic. "I need to speak with Inspector Craig Hillman," she spoke into the mic, "Royal Cayman Islands Police Service. Grand Cayman."

Waiting impatiently, she scraped her fingernail over an electrical cord laying on top of the desk.

"Inspector Hillman." Over a minute later, Craig's voice filtered through the radio waves.

"Craig? It's Lelisa."

"Are you on the barge? How's it going out there?"

"It's going nowhere. No one onboard has seen the *Persephone,* at least they don't believe so, and in the last several hours, we haven't located anything that even looks similar to her. The barge is headed due south on a tight schedule with their cargo. I'm keeping a lookout, and if I spot *Persephone,* I'll radio her coordinates and convince the barge's captain to follow her enough to keep her in our sights." She rattled off every word like an efficient agent with no emotion, effectively ignoring the burn coating her heart and lining her stomach, spurring on indigestion. "Anything from your end?"

"Nada. Little Cayman and Cayman Brac are clean. We've got Coast Guard boats searching east toward Jamaica, north in the Gulf, west toward Central America, and three heading in your same direction, to South America."

"All of them under orders to maintain a far distance *if* they locate the sailboat?"

"Yep. Close enough to find and then tail *Persephone* but far enough for Keegan not to notice." Craig scoffed. "Gee, we're not asking the impossible, are we?"

"Have you heard from Alec?" she asked, the burn in her organs refusing to be ignored. Not only was her stepdaughter the hostage of a murderer, but her husband was in the field chasing said murderer, a known explosives expert with the drive to kill himself and anyone near him.

"He's checking a lead. A sailboat named *Jezebel,* supposedly en route to meet up with *Persephone.* We're tracking this *Jezebel.* Plus, based off a weather inquiry, the skipper, a Jimar Malcolm, is sailing her to 18.229 Latitude and -79.458 Longitude. Alec is onboard an Interpol boat with a team of law enforcement, cruising at what is assumed to be parallel to the *Jezebel*, waiting for a window of opportunity."

"Do I dare ask the plan?"

"Crossover and intercept her in an area before the suspected designated meeting spot—those coordinates—before she meets up with the *Persephone...*"

Then what, wing it? Lelisa scoffed in her head, apprehension consuming her.

"...to board *Jezebel*," Craig continued over the radio, "overtake her, and meet up with *Persephone* as if Malcolm is onboard alone."

Yep, wing it. Attack and hope for the best.

Not that it wasn't a solid and typical surprise plan for law enforcement, but her husband was running on dangerous flumes ignited from deep within his parental heart.

His only daughter's disappearance ten years ago had buried his soul until she'd been found alive two years later. Sara's abduction now caused the emotional gravediggers to taunt Alec with their shovels, and this time they brought a coffin for his heart.

And mine too.

She loved her stepdaughter, the grown woman who'd become a good friend. Like Alec, she'd be brokenhearted if Sara didn't come home to them. Their two young sons, Sara's half-brothers, would be devastated.

"Craig? It's killing me that satellite imagery can't track *Jezebel* from point A to point B."

"It could if this was a farfetched action movie."

Lelisa plugged the coordinates Craig mentioned a minute ago into her phone for GPS reference when she'd again have service. "Do you know exactly where that is?"

"The coordinates I gave you? In between Cayman and Jamaica, closer to Jamaica."

"Wow, that's way far northeast of me." She groaned and stared out the room's one window and at the night's darkness swallowing up the ocean.

CHAPTER SEVENTEEN

The dark of night imprisoned the sky and the ocean water.

No court system in the world will ever imprison me.

Hours ago when darkness had fallen, Jason flipped on the master switch. The result bathed the boat deck in dim light and streamed a trail of light on their path ahead. At one in the morning, he couldn't run the boat without headlights, directing the way and alerting other various vessels of *Persephone's* presence. But it was a little risky. Sure, he was taking a chance at being spotted, but locating the *Persephone* sailing the Caribbean Ocean would be like locating a particular car driving somewhere on a Texas road.

So…no time like the present.

With a click he shut the motor off. He tightened the jib with a crank, then reefed the mainsail, easing it to a billow. Via two ropes on the wheel to hold the position, he placed the rudder—just in case of any movement—at an angle so the *Persephone* would turn into the wind. By this heaving-to procedure, the sailboat found a balance and eased to a stop. It really wouldn't drift much from this spot.

He was a skipper in robot motion, operating on the last drop of strength he had in him. All of the chaos had robbed his energy bank, when he should be carefree and easily sailing his escape. Instead…

"I've made change after change to the plan!" he yelled out to the empty sea, his temples pulsating. "No more." If anyone else even attempted to get in his way again, they'd regret it with their life.

He stomped down the companionway.

Along with Alec, two Interpol agents, three Jamaican cops, a boat skipper, and his first mate crowded an Interpol speed boat in motion.

On deck at the front, Alec stared out at the endless stretch of black ocean in front of him. If there were space to do so, he'd pace like an angry lion, terrified for his missing cub.

"Our plan is flawed, Dubois," he said to the agent at his right.

"How so?"

"Our window of opportunity to intercept *Jezebel* without *Persephone* spotting us."

"Your point, Dyer?"

"We have no idea where *Persephone* is, therefore—"

"I got it."

"Early intercept eliminates that flaw."

"Agreed.

The screen on the device in Alec's palm went blank.

Unbelievable!

"The tracker just died," he grumbled, sharing the information with everyone standing within earshot.

Agent Dubois glanced over at the device in Alec's hand. "Jimar Malcolm found the tracker? Turned it off?"

"Maybe," Alec said, ticked off and somehow managing to maintain professionalism. "Or it malfunctioned and shut down. Either way, we lost it. How much longer to those coordinates?" He shot the question over his shoulder at Captain Rieser driving the cruiser behind a Plexiglas windshield.

"At this speed? We're about two hours out."

On his wristwatch, Alec noted the time of twenty-five minutes to midnight. "Captain? Turn and head straight for the *Jezebel*."

"Current coordinates, Inspector?" Rieser yelled over the wind and engine noise.

"Unknown," Alec yelled back, fury blazing the fire inside of him, growing bigger and hotter each nautical mile they sailed. "The tracker stopped transmitting."

"I've seen that happen too often. What's the last known coordinates?"

"The last ones I gave you." To avoid slamming the useless tracker on the boat's metal railing like a lunatic, Alec handed it to Officer Grant, returning it to its owner.

Would this plan be a bust?

Was holding onto hope ridiculous?

He clung onto the belief that Sara would return home safely, like she had after her whacko mother beat her and dumped her for dead in the swamp of the Florida Everglades. But her return then was a miracle, a *once in a lifetime* blessing.

God? Where is Sara? Lead me to her.

It was the exact same prayer he'd repeated endlessly for two years when she'd disappeared as a teenager. The fact boggled his mind.

Twenty annoying minutes later, a tiny light shone in the distance.

"Inspector?" One of Officer Grant's Jamaican cop buddies pointed at two o'clock as he stood on Alec's left. "See dat light there?"

"I see it." Alec pressed binoculars to his face, squinted, but it didn't help to spot details of the boat. "Is it the *Jezebel*?" He dug out the GPS in his pocket and studied the screen.

"We're too far to guess at dat structure's size," Officer Grant interjected from the other side of Agent Dubois. "It could be a cruise ship farther in de distance."

Ten minutes passed on, and the circumference of the light's beam enlarged as they neared it. The view in the binoculars was nothing more than a brighter light than it was before.

Still too far away.

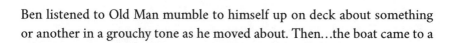

Ben listened to Old Man mumble to himself up on deck about something or another in a grouchy tone as he moved about. Then...the boat came to a stop, and held her position.

He must've heaved-to.

More grumpy words, yet these yelled out....

"I've made change after change to the plan! No more."

From the ray of light filtering down from the upper deck, Ben checked on the EMT across the room from him for a hint on her reaction about Jason's outburst.

Eyes still closed. Her chest still rose and fell in steady rhythm.

She'd fallen asleep several hours ago in a way that seemed out of desperation to escape her fear over… He still had no clue why exactly she'd been so suddenly panicked, as if something had changed, worsening their already dire situation. Regardless, maybe she'd simply worn herself out by freaking out and thrashing around.

Ben heard stomping footsteps up on the deck…then on the companionway. He braced himself for more assaults he couldn't fight off with his limbs restrained.

But Old Man passed through the main salon without any recognition or acknowledgment at all of the EMT or Ben's existence.

"Jason? Can we get some water?"

No response. Nothing. It was as if he'd gone deaf, or chose to forget anyone else was on the boat.

"Hey! Jason? Are you trying to dehydrate us to death? That's your plan?"

Old Man entered the one cabin at the bow of the boat and slammed the door behind him. He'd truly not heard Ben speaking to him, otherwise he would've snapped back with something ugly.

How could he have not heard?

He's lost it.

What's he doing in the cabin?

The Interpol boat drew nearer to the light, closing in on it.

"Inspector?"

Alec whipped around toward the voice, to the skipper speaking to him.

"I hear we're dealing with an explosives expert who doesn't bluff," Captain Rieser went on. "Is there any concern for explosives on the *Jezebel*?"

"Yes, the threat is present."

"And?" the captain said on a shrug.

"Proceed with caution."

"That's it?"

"What do you want me to say, Captain?"

"Inspector, we're in the dark with so much here."

Thanks for the reminder, pal. "So what's the protocol?"

"Don't get blown up."

Alec flashed the skipper one thumb up. "Words to live by."

"C'mon, Inspector. You gotta give me something. You have more intel than you're saying."

"Captain..." Alec stepped closer to Rieser to stop from shouting, and palmed the Plexiglas for support on the racing vessel. "Sure, like *Persephone*, *Jezebel* may be armed to blow. But I doubt it. Jimar Malcolm isn't willing to die, just willing to help Keegan. I don't think friendship is the motivation for Malcolm. It's something strong, though. There's something between those two." Alec rubbed his aching forehead, sweaty from the heat and rattled emotions playing havoc with his head and heart. "Let's just take this one step at a time, Rieser. Stick to the plan."

After the captain finally nodded at him, Alec returned to his spot at the nose of the boat, eyeing ahead at that light.

Fifteen agonizing minutes later, the one light separated into two.

Was that *Persephone* and *Jezebel* out there?

Alec glanced behind them, at the additional Interpol boat following their lead. *We look like one boat from a distance.* "Two lights on one boat, or two boats?"

"Good question," Agent Dubois jumped in with his input, "I'm wondering the same. In another few miles, we'll be able to better judge the distance between the two light sources."

The roar of helicopter blades whirled overhead, the aircraft barely visible in the distance and darkened sky.

"Looks like the Interpol chopper is joining us," Captain Rieser shouted out.

"Pull back on the helicopter, man," Alec shouted at Agent Dubois. He yanked the radio off the man's waist. "Contact them," he said, shaking the radio in Dubois's face. "Do it. Now. The plan is for them to stage farther back. He's too close."

"Relax. I agree." Agent Dubois snatched the radio from Alec's hand and depressed the button on the side of it. "5903? Pull back. You're too close. We've got this. For now."

"Copy, sir."

"Hang back in the air about thirty miles so your presence in the area isn't obvious. Wait for my word to swoop in."

"Thirty it is. I'll be there. Waiting."

CHAPTER EIGHTEEN

Four miles later, the Interpol cruiser closed the gap of watery surface stretched before the two lights in the distance.

Officer Grant lit up another cigarette, his third since the moment they'd hopped on the cruiser in Jamaica. "One boat, Inspector. De two lights are on one—"

"I see that," Alec said, eyeing through binoculars pressed to his face and spotting only one lighted boat in the distance.

Another mile closer.

"*Persephone* is a monohull, correct?" Grant said on a puff of smoke. "*Jezebel* a Lugger?"

Alec nodded. "That's correct."

A Lugger came into focus through the binocs, her sails tied up. No skipper at the helm. The name *Jezebel* written in huge block lettering across the boat's side.

Alec studied his GPS. "Why'd Malcolm stop there?" he spoke his mind. "He didn't reach the coordinates yet."

"Guess away. I am," Agent Dubois said, his words a little muffled around his hands holding binoculars over his eyes. "Could be a trap."

"Maybe they already made the swap." *If so, then Sara's on that boat,* Alec thought, staring at the *Jezebel.*

"Yeah?" Grant interjected in a scoff. "Then Keegan—the explosives expert—could already be onboard, gearing up to—"

"We got it!" Dubois shouted at the officer.

"Relax, Grant." Alec scratched his neck as if he was stripping off a layer of skin cells to reach his itchy nerves driving him batty. "You made a valid point, so let's see how the *Jezebel* responds to our approach."

Not soon enough, they neared the *Jezebel*, isolated and still. No sign of human life onboard.

Alec drew his Sig Sauer P220 from its leather holster.

As discussed and preplanned, the shadow Interpol boat behind them wrapped around to *Jezebel's* starboard, while Alec's cruiser sidled up to her port side. From at the nose of his Interpol boat, he aimed his duty weapon at the *Jezebel's* opened companionway to down below. Next to him, Agent Dubois, Officer Grant, and all the other law enforcers pointed their duty firearms as well.

Ping.

The shadow cruiser pinged one Morse code, a signal for Captain Rieser. Flash.

In a simultaneous second, both Interpol boats flashed their spotlights and flood lights, bathing the *Jezebel* in brightness.

Still no sign of human life aboard.

"Dubois? Stay here. I'll try contact." Alec dashed under the canopy and reached the helm to stand next to Captain Rieser. Alec snatched the mic of the boat's PA system and spoke into it. "Jimar Malcolm? Show yourself."

The boat rocked gently in place. Still no human noise or movement.

"This is the International Police," Alec went on. "Everyone onboard the *Jezebel* come out where we can see you."

Nothing.

"The *Jezebel* is surrounded. If you come on deck and try to start your engine, you will be fired upon."

Still nothing.

"This is suspicious, Inspector," Captain Rieser spoke in a soft and reluctant tone. "Should I pull back?"

Don't you dare.

"No." Alec pointed to the white Lugger. "Get me close enough to board."

Captain Rieser inched the Interpol boat forward, steering parallel to the *Jezebel's* portside. The two boats nearly bumped each other.

"Inspector, have you considered that boat may be set to blow the second you step on it?"

Ignoring the captain's question, Alec hopped over onto the *Jezebel*, his drawn gun in front of him. With a flashlight in his other hand, he scanned down below. The stream line of light shone on nothing human.

Someone jumped behind him. He whipped his head around and found Agent Dubois onboard too, gun drawn and ready to fire. Officer Grant hopped on after.

Alec stepped down the top stair of the companionway, then the second, searching for Jimar Malcolm or anyone else.

A body sprung out from the right and clobbered him with a socking punch, body colliding with body. Together, they sailed in the air to the left and smacked into the boat's hull. The flashlight slipped from Alec's hand.

A jolt of pain seared through him.

Clawing his Sig Sauer with a death grip, he blinked twice. Black and white indiscernible shapes floated in his vision. Weight pressed down on him—Malcolm's squirming body lying on top of him.

"Jimar Malcolm," Agent Dubois's voice shouted. "You got a gun pointed at the back of your head."

The words froze the Jamaican bartender.

Alec snatched the man's gun from his hands. "Get off me."

"I's you, mon," Malcolm said, staring down at him. "From de bar."

Alec punched him square in the face, shoved him away. "No getting anything past you, huh?" He climbed to his feet, slower than typical.

I'm getting too old for field work.

In his midback Alec tucked Malcolm's gun for safe keeping. "Dubois? How about you check around for Sara?"

"You got it, Dyer." Agent Dubois rushed off for the berth beyond the opened area where they stood. Up on deck, Officer Grant stood guard.

On his knees Malcolm watched Dubois rush off. "Sara? Who's Sara? Der is no Sara here. No one here but me, mon. May I stan' up?" He eased to his feet without waiting for a reply.

Alec couldn't care less.

"Hey, Malcolm." With his gun-free hand, Alec snapped his fingers in Malcolm's face. "Focus here. We need to chat. You weren't so talkative over the phone."

"Phone?" Shaking his head, his eyes narrowed. "You mean de bar, mon."

"No, Malcolm. I mean the telephone. I was your strange caller yesterday afternoon."

Malcolm blinked. "Yestaday?"

"Yes. It's..." Alec thought about looking at his wristwatch but changed his mind about taking his eyes off Malcolm, even for a split second. Perps were worse than toddlers. "It's some time after midnight, so yeah, yesterday."

Malcolm's eyes flashed wide, his mouth gaped open. "You were dat guy? Who call me?"

"Yes." Alec badged him. "Inspector Dyer. Royal Cayman Islands Police Service."

"Sara's not here," Dubois said, stepping through the cabin's threshold. "Sorry, Dyer. No one else onboard." He held his hand radio up to his mouth. "Captain Rieser? Take off. Tell the other boat to do the same. Get far from us. Disappear fast out in the distance. We've got it from here."

Malcolm pointed at Alec. "Look, cop," he spoke with an attitude Alec had heard countless times from perps. "I ha' noting to say to you. I didn' on de phone. I still don'."

"I think you do." Alec slammed his fist in the man's gut with a force releasing pent-up anger...and fear. Fear for his daughter's life.

Malcolm collapsed onto his knees.

"Got something to say now?" Alec leaned over him. "Huh?" he shouted in his face.

"No," Malcolm uttered in a strained groan, his left arm wrapped around his abdomen.

"Dyer," Agent Dubois spoke in a warning tone.

"Relax, Dubois," Alec snapped back. He rammed his knee in Malcolm's face. "How about now, Malcolm? Got something to say now?"

Malcolm dropped onto his back, then his side in the fetal position. "Wha' you want from me?" he grunted out.

"Tell me about Sara, Malcolm. Is she safe?"

"I don' even know who she is," he said in a moan, curled up on his side. "How could I pos'ibly know if she's safe?"

"You know nothing about Sara? The abducted paramedic?"

"Wha' abducted paramedic?"

"Jason Keegan's hostage. He abducted a Cayman paramedic."

Malcolm sucked in a pained breath.

"Start talking about Jason Keegan." The son-of-a—

"Keegan?"

"Yeah, Malcolm. You'll spill it all *now*." Alec leaned over the man's curled up body, and swung a punch in his face.

"Oww..." Malcolm pressed his lapped hands over his nose. "You broke my nose, mon!" His words were muffled by his wall of fingers. "I tink you broke my nose. Wha' kinda cop are you?"

"One who doesn't give a rip-roaring how Keegan escaped. I'm not here to drag an accomplice confession out of you. I don't care if you never implicate yourself in assisting his escape."

Malcolm rolled from his side to his back, pounded his bloody palm to the floor. "Den why exactly you here?"

"Don't play stupid, Malcolm. Where's Keegan? Is he on his way here?" Alec's temples pulsated, spurring on a fresh headache. "Start talking!" he shouted.

Silence. No audible words from Jimar Malcolm as he lay on the floor moaning, eyes squeezed shut, body squirming around.

Alec glanced up on deck, noticed Officer Grant's raised eyebrows, clearly not in approval of the beating tactic. But either he'd suddenly lost his ability to flap his jaws, or he finally figured out when to shut up. The small favor didn't do a thing to ease Alec's fiery agitation.

He kicked Malcolm in the ribs. The man coughed, spit blood to the side.

"Dyer," a second warning from Dubois, his French accent hiked up in volume. "Stop it. You've barreled way over the line."

"You think?" Alec snapped back in sarcasm. "Just don't watch, Dubois. Go up on deck. Stay on guard for *Persephone* approaching."

"Grant's got that covered," Dubois fired back. "Dyer, I'm giving you latitude here due to the circumstances. But you're taking advantage."

"I. Don't. Care."

"I do," Malcolm groaned on the floor.

"Shut up," Dubois and Alec yelled back simultaneously at the man.

Alec crouched. "Malcolm?"

No verbal response as he writhed around on the floor on his back.

Alec elbowed him in the lower abdomen. The man's body jerked; he rolled onto his side with a moan.

"Malcolm? We can go at this all night."

He coughed three times, spit more blood. "I'd ratha no.'"

"Then stop delaying the inevitable, and start talking. Where is Jason Keegan? He's headed here, right? To meet up with you?"

Silence.

"Tell me!" Alec yelled, a fresh rush of rage pumping through his blood vessels.

"Inspector Dyer!" Dubois yelled from the top stair, half down, half up the companionway and bending over to see down below. "You—"

"Back off, Dubois," Alec shot back. "I'm not torturing him."

"Physical persuasion, Inspector? Is that what you want to call what you're doing to drag out answers from this man?"

"Call it whatever you want, Agent Dubois. The wording makes little difference to me."

"Why so desp'rate, Inspector?" Malcolm asked in a pained groan.

If Alec revealed the hostage was his daughter—a cop's daughter—it could get back to Keegan.

"I'm passionate about law enforcement. About stopping criminals like you and Keegan." Alec cleared his throat, a little sore from all the yelling. "Malcolm? What time is the meet up?" he prodded on.

Malcolm rolled onto his back, stared up at Alec. "You found me an' overtook my boat. Smart cop like you'self...you figure it ou'."

"I have zero patience left. I ask again, what time is the meet up?"

A few silent seconds of intense glaring passed between them. Alec wasn't going to be the one to flinch first. The staring game was his specialty. So was chicken.

He aimed his weapon at the felon on the floor. "You want a bullet in your leg?"

"You wouldn'."

"Wanna try me?"

Malcolm shook his head. "Wha' time is it now?"

Alec checked his wristwatch. "Almost one a.m."

On his backside Malcolm scooted backward, then sat against the boat hull. His face bloodied, arms wrapped around his middle. "Stop assaultin' me. Dis is police brutality."

Alec studied the man's beaten face, battered body.

I did that.

Guilt surfaced, but he pushed it aside.

This man is a criminal.

"I'll stop if you start talking. I know about the boat swap, so—"

"Obviously, Inspector." Malcolm rolled his eyes, lids puffy and darkening from trauma. "We wait."

"Until? Give me a time, Malcolm."

"Hee'll show wid'in de hour."

"By two a.m.? Keegan will sail here on *Persephone* by two a.m.?"

"Dat's de plan." Malcolm swiped the back of his hand across his face.

Alec snatched up a shirt draped on the galley table and tossed it to him. "Here. Wipe the blood off your face."

"Wha' you care?"

"I don't. But I have nothing else to do, apparently, but babysit you for possibly an hour, and I don't want to stare at your bloody face. Hey?" Alec shouted up to Dubois and Grant. "You two see anything up there?"

"Not'ing but darkness," Officer Grant answered. "Pos'ible Keegan may approach wid de lights off or dim."

"You're catching on that anything's possible, Grant."

"Yes. Sir."

A grueling hour later, Alec envisioned his fists pounding into Malcolm's head until his heart stopped.

I'd never forgive myself.

Would God forgive me?

Alec raised his arm in front of his face in an exaggerated movement and stared at his wristwatch for an extended time. He blew out a long sigh as he stared at Malcolm. "What now? Top of the hourglass is out."

"I'm tinking dis was a setup."

"How?" Alec fired back, his teeth grinding with jaw-aching power. "What do you mean exactly?"

"*I* was set up. Keegan set me up. To take de fall. You know, a decoy."

"To sidetrack all the cops after him." Alec's stubbed fingernails dug into his palms.

"Yeah."

"Nice friend."

"Keegan is no friend o' mine."

Alec grabbed an empty beer bottle off the salon counter and hurled it against the wall. It shattered. "There was never gonna be a boat swap!"

Malcolm winced as he eyed the glass bottle in pieces. "*I* t'ought der was. Aren' you listening, mon?"

Yes. I just don't want to hear it. To face it.

"Maybe Keegan is just running late, Malcolm. Maybe he'll arrive soon."

"I fin' it difficult to coun' on dat, Inspector, but you go for it."

What now?

The only option left? Set up a surprise and hidden blockade at Keegan's destination prior to his arrival on land.

"Malcolm." Alec took two steps to stand over him. "Where's Keegan headed? Where does he plan to dock the *Persephone*?"

"I don' know."

Alec struck his right fist to Malcolm's left cheek; the man's head snapped back. "Why lie for him?" he yelled. "It appears he set you up to take the fall for him. You said so yourself. Decoy, remember?" he yelled even louder. "He must've told you something Monday night over the phone."

Malcolm rubbed his left jaw line. "No' abou' where he's goin'. He specif'cally didna tell me so you cops couldn' find out. Only *he* know where he's headin'.'"

"He and whoever skippered the *Persephone* to Grand Cayman Island. Who is that person, Malcolm? Tell me the name, and tell me now."

"Just a tip, Malcolm," Agent Dubois said, bent over at the waist from up on the upper deck, "the inspector won't buy it if you say you don't know the answer to that one."

"You right, Inspector." Malcolm nodded. "I 'ave no reason to lie. In fact, if I did know where Keegan is headed, I'd tell you jus' so he'd be apprehended."

"Then give me a name, Malcolm. Don't push me. I'm gonna ask one last time. Who captained the *Persephone* to Grand Cayman to pick Keegan up?"

"I tell you wha', Inspector—a name for a break. How 'bout it?"

"You're negotiating? You think you can plea bargain with me?"

"Why no', mon? A free ticket from arrest for a name you desp'rately need—wha' you say?"

"It doesn't work that way, Malcolm."

"Den no name."

"Maybe a lesser charge, Malcolm. But a get-out-of-jail-free card? No. Not in a billion."

"Fine. Lessa charge. C'mon, how 'bout it?"

"How 'bout you give me the name, or I'll slice your leg at the femoral artery with a chunk of glass?" Alec pointed to the broken beer bottle pieces.

Stunned shock flashed across Malcolm's face. "You are violent for a cop."

"Malcolm...I'm just getting warmed up." Alec leaned over, picked up a large glass shard, and pointed it at his prisoner. "You may want to watch your mouth if you prefer to leave this boat *not* inside a body bag."

Every inch of Jimar Malcolm hurt. His gut was on fire; his head pounded in a constant burn of an ache. This cop's beating was ticking him off, but he was powerless to stop it, unless he wanted handcuffs slapped around his wrists, a bullet fired through his skin, or glass cutting him up. He'd learned years ago never to strike a cop, especially an insane cop or one super dedicated to his job, whichever applied to this guy. Then add the fact the two cops up on deck were backing this Inspector Dyer, Jimar was out of options.

Take it like a man.

The criminal charges this inspector would nail him with were a joke compared to the evidence Jason Keegan could turn over on him.

Yeah, but Keegan is obviously long gone.

"Name, Malcolm. What's the skipper's name?" Dyer spoke between clenched teeth as he continued to point a piece of broken glass at him. Rage filled his eyes.

No one was *that* dedicated to their job.

The hostage, the Cayman paramedic—that Sara girl must mean something to this cop.

Or he's jus' crazy.

Jimar didn't want to give up Little Keegan. He'd always liked the kid.

But he's no' worth gettin' sliced open.

"Malcolm?" The other cop, the one who'd searched the *Jezebel* for the Sara girl earlier, stepped down from the upper deck. Stood alongside Inspector Dyer. "Why would you swap for *Persephone*? A sailboat being cop-hunted?"

"I wasn' gonna do dat, mon." This cop, Dubois, had it all wrong. The plan was to abandon *Persephone*, dump her at sea, then he'd sail with Keegan away on *Jezebel* until they split ways for good this time. "I'm no fool."

"Apparently you are," the Dubois cop fired back at him. "Here you are, under police control, and Keegan is nowhere to be found. Not only did he ditch you, he arranged it so you'd take the fall for him."

Jimar rolled his eyes underneath his swelling lids; pain shot up to his forehead and sparked behind his eyes. "Impressive summary, Dubois."

Dyer's fist slammed into Jimar's face.

Crunch.

Can a nose break twice?

CHAPTER NINETEEN

The full moon streamed through the companionway from the upper deck. The boat lights filtered to down below as well. In that light Ben eyed his backpack on the floor, contents spilled. Many hours ago Old Man had dumped it out in search of weapons and whatever else. Apparently he'd found nothing useful, since he'd abandoned all the scattered items.

Ben eyed the EMT scrunched in the corner, still asleep, her rainbow-colored hair tie thing still dangled halfway down her ponytail at her neck.

Leaning forward, he eased upward onto his feet. Bent over with his arms tied behind him, the chair back rested on his, he hobbled his tied-up ankles and padded his way to his backpack. One-by-one, he kicked the spilled items back in, no easy feat with restrained feet, then scooted the filled bag like dribbling a soccer ball toward the exhausted EMT tied up in the corner.

She startled awake at his sudden presence before her. Wide-eyed, she jumped back away from him. Knocked herself into the boat hull behind her.

"Easy," he whispered. "Shh. Be quiet. I'm not gonna hurt you. I promise. I just want to talk."

She stared at him, face blank and unreadable. Without turning her head from him, she looked out the window. A blanket of fear slid over her eyes; her chest panted as if something suddenly upset her.

He glanced out the tiny window but saw nothing beyond black sky and seawater.

What was she so scared of out there?

Maybe it was nothing more than she was eyeing the vast ocean for the show of a vessel to rescue her, yet accepting it wasn't coming. Maybe...he didn't know.

"What is it with you and that window?" he whispered.

Chest panting, her widened eyes trained only on him as if reading him for truth and purpose. Then she glanced up the companionway to the upper deck.

"Jason is asleep. For now." Ben paused to give her time to digest his words and their meaning.

Her head pulled back; her eyes narrowed with skepticism.

"Yes, asleep. Honestly." He jerked his head toward the bow cabin. "In there. Door's locked. I heard him lock it. But he won't want to be stationary for long."

So we don't have an abundance of time.

Even so, Ben couldn't rush her into trusting him. After all, he was Jason's son, and she knew it.

"Are you thirsty? Hungry? I've got water bottles and packaged food in my pack." He toed it.

No reaction. He waited. Several seconds later she nodded with slight reluctance. Her intense fear seemed to subside, although he had no clue why or what caused it in the first place.

"How about I turn this chair around, and you lean your face toward my hands. I'll take the tape off your mouth. We can untie each other somehow. Okay?"

No response.

"Why would you want to keep your mouth taped shut? C'mon. You wanna give this a try?"

Several seconds of absolutely nothing from her but a blank stare.

Finally, she nodded.

He bounced the chair around one hundred eighty degrees. With his back to her, he wiggled his hands. "Lean into my hands. Put your lips at my fingers, and I'll rip off the tape."

Nothing happened behind him, no movement at all. No sound.

"I'm not going to hurt you."

A few silent seconds later, some rustling noises sounded behind him. A warm smooth surface brushed up to his fingers, and lingered. He patted around to get a feel of it.

Human skin. A chin. And...yep, tape.

He fingered his way to the left top of the tape until he reached the edge of it. With the tip of his stub fingernail, he picked at the end. Picked. And picked. He lifted the end free from her skin.

"All right. Ready? Real fast." He yanked to the right, ripping the tape strip off from around her mouth.

He bounced the chair around and faced her red mouth, swollen lips.

"You okay?" he whispered.

She nodded.

"You know, you can speak now."

But she didn't.

"What is your name?" he asked her.

Eyeing him with narrowed brows, she ignored his question.

"Come on. What's your name?"

"Why?" she whispered. She cleared her throat from endless hours of being unable to speak.

"So I can call you something other than 'Paramedic' or 'EMT.'"

"Sara. My name is Sara." She said nothing more. Just stared at him with suspicion glazed in her eyes.

"So...you're just normally quiet. That's your personality. It wasn't only because your mouth was taped shut."

Nothing from her. Not even a physical reaction.

"Sara, I'm Ben. Unfortunately, Ben *Keegan*. Jason's son, as you heard earlier."

She chewed on her lower lip with obvious nervous energy. "You got a flashlight with you?"

"Flashlight? That's what you want right now?" He shrugged, trying to understand her. "Why?"

"And that's strange how?"

It isn't, I guess. "Ah...I don't know."

"Well? Do you have one or not?"

"I do, actually. Inside my backpack."

Beaming a smile, she released a deep breath as if intense relief shot through her. Her left foot edged out to the side, dragging her right leg with it. She toed his backpack and kicked it behind her toward her cuffed hands. She rotated a bit to reach her hands in the pack opening. She dug her cuffed hands around inside. "Where exactly is it?" she said in a whispered panic.

He shrugged again, even more lost in regards to her behavior. "Somewhere inside there. Not in a pocket, if that's what you're asking."

She searched a minute more, struggling with the choking cuffs. "It's not in here."

He glanced over his shoulder but didn't spot it on the ground behind him. "It's not—"

"Found it. Whew!"

Behind her back she finagled with the flashlight. After the sound of a click, a stream of light illuminated the ceiling. Her body heaved in deep relaxation.

This grown woman was terrified of the dark? That was her deal?

"Better now?"

She nodded a bunch of times with rapid succession.

She rolled the flashlight toward her legs and caught it underneath her right thigh. With impressive technique, she used both her legs to trap it between her knees.

O…kay. "Sara?"

She didn't look at him.

"Sara? Hey…"

She faced him, giving him her attention, her face a little red with obvious embarrassment.

Ben decided to ignore it, for her sake. "Do you think you could untie my hands? I'll lower the chair on its side and maneuver my way toward your cuffed hands. If you get my arms untied, I'll untie your legs. Sound like a plan?"

"If I untie you and you leave me tied up—"

"I wouldn't do that, Sara. Why would I do that?"

"How would I know what you would or wouldn't do?"

"Come on. Work with me here. We help each other. Yeah?"

She stared at him for several seconds. "Yeah. Okay."

He bounced the chair around so his hands would face her back. He rotated forward. The chair lowered, and his knees dropped to the floor with a crunch.

Ouch, that didn't feel good.

He leaned to the right. The chair slammed to the thin carpet, smack down on his right shoulder first, then his entire right side. He sucked his groan back down his throat.

"Are you okay?" Sara whispered from behind.

"I'm good," he whispered back. "Tell me which direction to move so you can reach the knots in the rope."

"Ah…go up. Well, I mean what's 'up' for you."

"How far?"

"Just start moving."

He inched his body, along with the chair, upward.

"Stop. Okay, now back."

On his right side, he pushed his body backward.

"A little more, straight back. Then kitty-corner to your upper back."

"Upper back?"

"Think: up and back."

"Gotcha."

He moved upward and backward.

"Stop."

He wiggled his fingers. "I don't feel anything but air."

"A little more. Again, up and back."

He moved in that direction. Bumped into human skin. "Here?"

"That's good."

The rope tugged and yanked. Ten seconds. Twenty. Thirty.

No more movement. No more noise of any kind.

"Sara?" His right arm was tingling since his weight and the chair's was crushing it.

"I can't do it. I can't get the knot undone with my hands behind my back. Can't see what I'm doing. Ben, I'm trying here."

Try harder. "It's okay. Take a break. Try again in a few minutes."

Silence. No movement. No sound. For more than a few minutes.

He didn't want to rush her, push her.

Another minute or so ticked by. He felt nothing. Heard nothing.

"Sara?"

"It's knotted super tight."

"It's knotted excellent. Jason is an expert sailor."

The rope jostled around again. His arm was now numb from lack of blood flow.

Several minutes passed as she continued to work the knot loose.

Then all movement stopped.

"Sara? Talk to me."

"I can't undo it, Ben. My hands are cuffed behind me, you know? Maybe if they were cuffed in front of me so I could see the rope more than just barely over my shoulder." He heard a gulp. A sniffle. "I'm sorry, Ben. I can't get the knot undone."

"It's okay. We'll come up with something else." He squeezed his eyes shut to think. "How about if I placed my feet near your hands, and you try to untie my ankles?"

"How is that going to be any different?"

"It's worth a try." He lifted his left shoulder, his right throbbing and crushed on the floor. "We have nothing else to do, right?"

"True, and I'm not one to give up."

He leaned and rocked to the left, flopped straight down on his back, the chair underneath him. He rotated his right shoulder around, encouraging blood flow. Less than a minute later, he swiveled around on the floor until his feet—dangling in the air—were within her reach. She scooted on the floor, her cuffed hands rattling behind her. She scrambled up onto her knees so her hands—behind her back—came in line with his tied-up ankles.

"How long do you think he'll sleep?" she whispered, eyeing over her shoulder at her working hands.

"I can't imagine much longer. He'll want to get moving soon."

"He anchored us, then went to sleep?"

"We aren't anchored. It's too deep. Most of the Caribbean Sea is too deep to anchor. We're just floating; the sails are pulled in."

"We're drifting around?"

"No. We're pretty much staying stationary with the sails held like they are."

He raised his head and watched her maneuver her fingers around the knot, her back to him.

"I think I'm loosening it. What do you think? Can you feel it? Can you see? I barely can."

No on the loosening.

"Move your left index finger to the right," he directed her since she had limited sight over her shoulder.

Several minutes later she dropped her hands in exhausted defeat.

"I'm sick of this." She planted the soles of her boots on the pipe with a sudden burst of determination. Like she'd done several times earlier, she yanked back from the pipe. Tugged and tugged backward, trying to break the steel pipe loose from the floor.

"Sara. Stop. It's not gonna happen."

In a heavy sigh, she dropped her feet. "I know. I give up. For now."

"Okay, okay. Let's eat something. At least drink. We need fuel. Energy."

Ben rolled onto his left side, flipped up onto his left knee, then right, then pushed his weight backward to sit the chair upright, with him still tied to it. "There are some water bottles and packaged crackers and granola bars in my backpack." He scooted the chair a bit to face her. "Can you grab 'em?"

Again, skepticism swirled in her eyes.

"Sara, I didn't poison any of it, okay?"

She studied him in a silence that unnerved him.

Wow, she was cautious.

"What's the problem? We need to eat something, at least drink some water."

"You're right." She dug out two water bottles.

Simultaneously, they rotated around so their backs faced each other. She handed him the bottle. He finagled the bottle around to be able to twist the cap and open it.

"Can you lay your head under my hands? I'll pour some water into your mouth."

"Okay. This is weird."

"You got a better suggestion?"

"No, not really." She scooted her head underneath his tied hands. "It's like we're playing Twister here."

He chuckled.

"Ready. Go for it."

He glanced over his shoulder, eyed her mouth as best he could, and tipped the bottle, pouring a gush of water into her mouth.

She jerked away, turned her head to the side, and gulped down the water. "Got it." She coughed a little. "Either we're being more quiet than I think, or he's dead in there."

Too bad the second wasn't true.

"Okay, your turn, Ben."

He pivoted his body around so his head matched up with her hands. She tipped the bottle...

...and poured water all over his neck and chest, soaking his shirt.

"Ohhh...I'm sorry."

She tried it a second time. Got most of it on his nose...and in his eyes. The liquid burned like fire. Amazing how the eye rejected H2O. Ben blinked and blinked, wishing for an unrestrained hand to rub his eyes.

"So sorry. Again. I'll do better with the crackers. That will be easier anyway."

"Naw. You go ahead. Eat some crackers or a granola bar or two. I'm not hungry."

"Not taking any chances, huh? I may accidentally stab you in the eye with a cracker?"

He chuckled, still blinking the burn away and not getting far. "Just eat, Sara."

"No, too much work when I'm not that hungry. Let's save the food, Ben. We may really need it later. More than we do now."

"That's true."

Sara manipulated the flashlight in between her knees again.

"Why don't you turn that off?"

"No," she snapped back.

"Sara, we don't want to waste the batteries. A flashlight may really come in handy at some point soon."

"It's really coming in handy now."

"You wanna tell me what that's about?"

"What?"

"Sara."

She shrugged, shook her head. Redness colored her cheeks again. "What?"

Fine. Don't tell me. "We need to conserve the batteries. You know?"

"In a little bit, Ben. Just a little longer." She squirmed in a way that the light from the silver stick shined on her face enough to reveal her left purpling eye.

The visual bothered Ben, coated his stomach with a layer of boiling anger mixed with confusion. He'd never witnessed his father strike anyone in violence, especially a woman.

"I'm sorry he hit you. I'm assuming he hit you several times today."

She lifted one shoulder. "No big deal. I've dealt with much worse from other perps."

"Perps?"

Her eyes widened, a reaction she tried to hide a split second later. "Yeah." She spoke with nonchalance, but he wasn't buying her act. "Perpetrators. Criminals who are my patients."

Huh. Something was off. "You're not a paramedic, are you?"

"What?" she said on a quiet chuckle. "Yes I am."

"Are you an undercover cop?"

"No," she snapped back too quickly, too much on the defense.

Something wasn't right, like she was lying to him somehow.

He gave her one raised eyebrow.

"Ben, I graduated from medic school three years ago, after I earned my bachelors in biology. What higher degree are you working toward?"

"Huh?" he said, a little taken aback by the strange and out-of-place question.

"It sounds like you have an undergraduate degree from somewhere in Florida. What upper degree are you working toward?"

"Ah..." Of all things, why would she ask him this? Now? "Masters in chemistry."

She nodded, and her facial expression indicated she was impressed. "You're developing some kind of new medication for addicts? Is that what Jason was talking about?"

"Yes." He cleared his throat to stall. Was she simply trying to figure him out while subtly diverting their conversation far from his question? Nothing else made sense.

"Meds already exist to treat addiction."

"Not cocaine, and the other one in production has major flaws. Ours doesn't. Sara—"

"What school are you at?" she shot off another question, seeming interested in the topic as well as using it for a diversion.

"University of Miami."

"Really? That's where I earned my bachelors."

"Before going on to medic school?"

She nodded. "Yes."

It sounded like the truth, or a variation of it. Could he drag more truth out of her?

"Sara, you wanna tell me what happened back at the Cayman marina?"

She blinked. Other than that, no response from her.

"You don't trust me?"

"Not enough. Why should I? I don't know you. More than that, you're *his* son."

"Fair enough." Biting his lower lip, Ben blew out a deep sigh of frustration. "Tell me this: was anything he said the truth?"

"Um...one thing."

One? Only one? "The only thing he couldn't lie to me about—he took you hostage?"

"Ding, ding, ding."

Ben felt his head lower, his chin touch his chest. A wave of crushing disappointment socked him in the gut. Hearing her confirm Old Man had lied about everything else stirred up disgust in him, revulsion for the man who'd raised him.

I trusted he was turning his life around. Trusted I was doing the right thing in helping him.

Jason wasn't just a drug abuser anymore; apparently, he'd added convincing storyteller of lies, growing the list of his shady characteristics.

What else was on that list?

"So, Sara, what did happen back in Cayman?"

"You don't really want to hear it."

"That's not for you to decide."

She exhaled. "What do you want from me, Ben?"

"The truth about what happened. I won't get it from him."

"Everyone's truth is different since we all have our own point of view, and—"

"Sara. What happened?"

He waited for her to voice the facts. The facts he so desperately wanted to know...yet didn't.

She was right.

Underneath the stubborn layer of denial, he suspected Old Man's spun story was a string of fabrication. Knew it, even. He just hadn't been ready to accept it.

Until now.

The flashlight flickered, then dimmed.

"I'll turn it off," Sara said in a nervous tone.

Little late now.

She maneuvered the silver light stick behind her, but froze, staring out the window with a haunted gaze.

"Hey. Sara, I'm right here. Look at me..."

She did.

"I'm not going anywhere. You know what I'm saying?"

She turned her head away, eyes closed in obvious embarrassment. Maybe shame. Possibly both.

"Just turn it off. Can you do that?"

"Yeah." She stared into his eyes. Clicked the flashlight off.

He heard her draw a quick breath of air.

"Sara? I'm still right here," he spoke to her in the room lighted only by the moon and the lights on the deck above.

"I know."

"Focus on the moonlight and the—"

"I know, Ben. I don't want to talk about it."

"Gotcha." He paused, dug up strength for the next round. "Sara, just tell me what all went down on the shore at the pier."

"Ben. I don't want to talk at all."

"Hey," he snapped in a hushed whisper. "He is my father."

"Then don't go there. Not now."

"When? I have a right to know. We're in this together, right?'

"I don't know that. I don't know you."

"Sara, fill me in. I'm in the dark here. I don't know what happened between you two or what happened between Jason and the Cayman police. I don't know what he's running from."

"So you say."

"How would I know what happened? I wasn't even there, Sara. I was sailing into Cayman, remember?"

A breathy pause. "Why were you picking him up?" she whispered, yet in an accusatory tone. "I'm guessing it wasn't for a little father-son time on the Caribbean Sea."

"What exactly are you getting at?"

"You know what, Ben. You knew he's a charged drug offender, ditching Cayman. My mouth was taped shut, not my ears."

"You want me to implicate myself as Jason's accomplice? Admit I aided a man charged with drug possession escape his sentencing? Is that what this is about?"

"Ben, you just admitted to committing a felony."

He whistled at his own stupidity but didn't care. After all, it was the truth, and there was nothing he could do to change his involvement. "Yeah, I guess I did. Sara, yes, I agreed to help my drug addict parents, but I didn't know the extent of...I had no clue I was aiding a criminal who abducted a woman and...whatever else Jason did."

Why did I go into this so blindly? So uninformed?

Because I'm desperate to believe Mom and Dad are cleaning up.

In the deck light and moonlight, Sara studied Ben Keegan's saddened face, disbelief in his baby-blue eyes. Or was it guilt? Shame? Something else? Whatever it was, honesty seemed to be his strong suit. It seemed he truly didn't know a thing about his mother's murder on Monday night.

Didn't know his father killed her.

She wasn't going to be the one to inform him. In part because he'd probably toss the truth back in her face, accuse her of lying. Denial of such hard-core facts tended to work that way.

"Why won't you tell me what I want to know? Talk to me, Sara."

Unless she told him *something*, this merry-go-round conversation would continue all night, at least until Keegan showed up, storming out of the berth and demanding answers.

What are you doing, college boy? What did you say to him, Paramedic?

The truth, you psycho.

"Ben, Jason Keegan was my patient."

Ben's brows furrowed together, two lines crinkled above his nose between his narrowed eyes. "What...what do you mean exactly?"

"The bandage on his arm? He was stabbed."

It was obvious to Sara that Keegan had somehow provoked that other psych ward patient. Smart move. Well thought-out executed plan. Impressive.

"By Bubba." Ben nodded. "At the docks."

"No and no."

Ben's lips pursed, eyes squinted. "Okay, by whom, then? When was this? I'm confused."

"Let it go, Ben. For now."

He didn't say anything. She decided it best not to look at him, not encourage him to question her further. So, she focused on her chafed ankles and stretched her neck to the left. To the right. Allowed her mind to wander for a break.

A thought hit her. "You know, I think we have a small understanding of what the Pilgrims went through on their rough, two-month journey in the autumn of 1620."

"What?" Ben sounded super-confused at her change in subject. "What are you talking about?"

"The Pilgrims. The Mayflower. You know, the New America in the 1600s. I think you and I can relate a little bit to the hardship they experienced on that journey over the ocean from England."

He stared at her with one eyebrow cocked.

"Never mind. Just a strange thought." She eyed his chafed and bleeding ankles, knew his wrists were the same.

The skin breakage could become infected by the disgusting sailing rope and whatever germs were embedded in the fabric in direct contact with his open skin.

Her handcuffs and ankle restraints had broken her skin as well. She could feel the warmth of her blood ooze out around her wrists.

Even though the cloth ankle restraints were soft material, all her vicious yanking on them in attempt to free herself had chafed her skin something raw. Sure, a localized skin infection was the least of their problems, but the last thing they needed was high body temperatures and puss-oozing wounds.

She scooted around so her back was to him, wiggled her fingers. "Turn around. I'll try to untie your hands again."

No response from him behind her.

"Ben, if we could get untied somehow, we could ditch this boat on a life raft before Jason wakes up. Row our way to the closest inhabited land."

"I like your sarcasm."

"You don't think it's a viable option?"

She heard a chuckle out of him.

"Hmm, so not a smart idea. Got it." Even if it were, she wouldn't let Keegan sail away and disappear forever without serving justice. Somehow she'd make sure he'd pay for his crimes, for murdering three people, two of which were her friends.

Once a cop, always a cop.

Something Ben had picked up on about her. Luckily, he'd allowed that conversation to drop. She wasn't yet sure if he was worthy of her trust, and her identity as a former cop and a cop's daughter could be information used against her to manipulate all law enforcement agencies to benefit Jason

Keegan and all who supported his choices. If Ben Keegan willingly aided his father to skip out on a prison term, then out of desperation to protect himself against the law, he just may aid his father in murder.

My murder.

Anything was possible, a lesson she first learned as a cop all those years ago.

"Ben?" she prodded after a prolonged silence from him.

Upon hearing movement behind her, she glanced over her shoulder and watched as he bounced his chair around, putting his back to hers.

A few seconds later, warm skin brushed against her fingers. Still eyeing over her shoulder, she worked her fingers around the rope restraining Ben's hands, digging to find a hole to loosen the knot.

She dug, and dug and dug. For several minutes.

No go. The knot wouldn't even loosen.

Cramped up something fierce, her fingers ached. But she kept at it.

God? I'm mad at You. But I know You're there. I know You hear me. Why are You ignoring me? Why has Your answer for the last day to me been nothing but no, no, no?

Why won't You help me?

A wave of defeat washed over her, and she dropped her hands, giving up on the knot.

Giving up on God.

Anger filled her up. She was angry. God had given up on her, so she was going to give up on Him.

But...I can't do this without You; I can't do this alone.

She wasn't alone.

"Ben?" she said his name, their backs still facing each other.

"Yeah? You okay? Are your fingers too sore to move anymore?"

"I just need a break. Ben?" *Do you think God put you in this situation to help me?* "Do you think..."

"Do I think what?"

"Do you think we're here to help each other?"

Silence behind her.

"Is this a religious-thing question?"

"Faith isn't about religion."

"You lost me. Sara, I'm not into religion or church or whatever."

"Oh. You're atheist?"

"I'm…nothing. I don't believe in anything."

Atheist. Got it.

She heard Ben scramble his chair around, obviously to face her. She stayed, giving him her back.

"Nice topic diversions, Sara, with the history reminiscence of the Pilgrims and the religion talk."

"We've got nothing else to do since we can't seem to break free and—"

"Sara, I won't stop pushing you to talk to me. Turn around."

A long and heavy sigh escaped her lips as she stared at the pole holding her captive next to a man she wished would stop talking.

"Sara, if you don't start talking, I won't help you."

"Ben, if you don't stop talking, I'll…" *What? I'll what?* "I'll bleed on you."

He chuckled. "Was that a Monty Python quote? From *The Holy Grail?*"

"Shut up. I couldn't think of anything else."

"Sara, how badly do your wrists and ankles hurt?"

"I'm fine. What about you?"

"I'm good."

"Good, then there's nothing more to discuss." She leaned her head against the pipe and closed her eyes.

"Sara? Turn around. Come on." He paused, obviously waiting for her. "I don't know what's going on here. *You* do. Help me to understand what Jason is up to. What he's done."

"Like I said earlier, Ben, I don't think you want to know."

"Yeah, I do. Shed some light in this darkness I'm trapped in here. If you fill in the blanks, I'll help you. I'll protect you against him."

She scooted around and faced him. Scoffing, she rolled her eyes at him. "Interesting. How are you planning to do that all tied up?"

He scoffed back in clear exasperation. "Wow. You're an unusual woman, Sara. Are you *trying* to negotiate yourself out of my help?"

She didn't know what she was trying to do.

She leaned back against the pole and squeezed her eyes shut.

An atheist was offering to help her—*an atheist*—and he sure seemed sincere. Caring.

It hit her, the truth about her faith hit her—it was a fantasy. Ben was the only one listening to her. God was there, but He didn't care.

For the first time in her life, Sara turned her back on God. Furthermore, *she* didn't care.

"Sara, listen to me," Ben said, his voice softened, pained. "Since as long as I can remember, I begged my parents to stop cocaine. *Supposedly*, this last possession charge convinced Jason to clean up—he was done. Forever. I was willing to help him flee Cayman so he and my mom could turn their life around."

Hmm. Sounded realistic. Sincerity and pain blanketed his eyes.

"What about your mother?" *Where do you think she is, Ben?*

"She tried to quit several times over the years. Always fell back in with the drug crowd of her and Dad's stellar friends."

The sadness in his tone saddened Sara. She could relate to that sadness, to the crushing disappointment and horror of your parent's actions. For Ben, *both* his parents failed him.

Gosh, at least my dad is a good man I can count on.

"Where is she now, Ben?"

"Mom? Jason flew her out of Cayman yesterday. He's planning to meet up with her, wherever we're headed. You heard him say that to me."

Yeah, I did. "Oh. Right." Biting her lip, Sara nodded.

At the time, though, she'd been leery and considered the dialogue between them to be an act on both their parts for her ears. However, with all she'd seen and heard between them since, she had no more doubts.

Ben is completely in the dark.

CHAPTER TWENTY

A familiar buzzing hum stirred Sara out of a deep sleep. She blinked to clear her hazy vision and focus on her surroundings.

Awake and aware, she recalled her bleak reality in the flash of an instant.

I'm trapped on a boat way out at sea. I'm a serial murderer's prisoner.

The familiar sound of an overhead airplane gained volume.

She noticed Ben asleep across the tiny room from her. Out of sheer exhaustion, they'd drifted off to sleep at…she glanced at the lighted digital clock on the wall in the shape of a Jack Daniels bottle, and noted a red 5:03…around 3 a.m., so two hours ago, after Ben had replaced the tape over her mouth and shuffled himself back over there.

Best to keep it secret they'd spoken, they'd decided.

The zoom of the airplane seemed to draw Ben awake. Shaking his head, he strained his eyes as if trying to listen.

She nodded big, smiling underneath the strip of tape.

"Don't get too excited," he said in a whisper. "Slim chance that plane is searching for us."

Fine, Mr. Negative. With the tape over her mouth, she could only think those words.

He scooted his tied-up body in the chair to the window near her. He leaned forward, spied out the circular window, head bobbing in every angle. "I don't even see it."

I still hear it, Ben.

"Even if the pilot were searching for the *Persephone* from the sky," Ben went on, "it's easy to miss a boat this size, Sara. We're tons smaller than a tiny uninhabited island, and search planes easily miss those. It's not as simple as you'd think. Did you ever see the movie *Castaway*?"

She nodded, fully grasping his point. The Caribbean Ocean was larger than the state of Alaska. They needed to depend on no one but themselves to get out of this alive.

"Let's remove the tape from your mouth again. Okay?"

She crouched her head underneath his hands, and he ripped the tape strip off.

She sat upright. "I get what you're saying," she whispered. "I realize the combined law enforcement agencies have thousands of square miles of ocean surface to search for this boat. On top of that, they're limited by distance due to Jason's threat."

"Limited by distance? What do you mean?"

"You overheard his conversation with...that cop..." *Pretend you don't know Craig.* "I think Jason called him Hillman, if I remember correctly."

"I heard Jason's side of a vague conversation over the phone, yeah. It sounded to me he threatened the cops with explosives if they approach us."

"No, Ben. He's not threatening to blow *them* up. He's threatening to blow *us* up. Blow up this boat, the *Persephone.* He's willing to risk his own life to avoid capture." She paused for his reaction, but he didn't say anything, his face blank. "Ben, he'd rather die than be apprehended by law enforcement."

"Huh?" His cheeks crunched up; his eyes narrowed. "I...why? Why would he..." Looking off to the side, his cheeks tensed, jaw locked. He went from confused to awareness. "Start talking, Sara," he said, glaring at her with clear warning. "Shed some light so I understand what's going on." He drew in a deep breath. "Is Jason dealing? Did he turn to dealing? Is that it? Give me something."

Okay. "He was my patient, Ben."

"Your patient—yeah, you said that earlier."

"I was treating his stab wound."

"When...all of a sudden...?" He shrugged. "What happened? Wait." He shook his head. "How'd he get stabbed?"

"Another patient."

"You had two patients?"

"No."

"You're not making sense."

"Ben, stop." She glanced over her shoulder at the berth's closed door.

"We're running out of time, you know? We need to come up with a plan," she said to divert his attention. "You got any ideas? I've got nothing."

Well, nothing good.

He nodded, eyeing the door. "I do, actually. I was thinking about it as I fell asleep, considering if it was ridiculous or not. After a couple hours sleep, I realize we don't have a more appealing option."

Hope filled her, the hope of at least the effort of something new. "I'm listening. What is it?"

"We could overtake him, Sara. Overpower him."

"What do you have in mind?"

CHAPTER TWENTY-ONE

A little groggy, Jason climbed out of bed, thankful the muffled female screams had awakened him. He'd only wanted an hour or two of sleep, not five.

On the other side of the locked cabin door, Paramedic was losing her grip.

"You okay?" Ben's voice asked her in a near shout over her screaming.

The kid had never turned away from someone in need. Something Jimar Malcolm knew well.

With her mouth taped shut, Paramedic couldn't speak. Couldn't tell Ben a thing. Couldn't reveal the truth and refute Jason's Cayman marina story.

Couldn't tell Ben his mother was dead.

Jason slammed a half-opened dresser drawer closed, anger exploding inside of him.

Everyone has turned against me.

Malcolm.

Ben.

Annie.

"Why didn't you just leave it alone, Annie?" Jason pounded his fist on the dresser top. "It was none of your business."

On Monday night his wife's betrayal had boiled a fiery rage in him he hadn't experienced in over twenty years.

Annie had created this fiasco. Everything that had gone down on Monday night and since was her fault, her cause. If she would've just kept her nose out of where it didn't belong, he wouldn't be in this plight.

And she'd be alive.

Oh, Annie, I wish you weren't dead. I loved you. I loved you.

Grief stricken to the point his legs weakened, Jason backed up and plopped on the edge of the bed. Staring at the boat cabin carpet, he pictured their kitchen floor, and more of the memory from Monday night played out in his head…

Annie's body lay limp on their worn linoleum. "Get up, Annie," *he shouted down at her.* "You're fine. I barely touched you."

She didn't move.

"Stop pretending you passed out," *he said, kicking her thigh.* "Get up."

Blood spilled from the back of her head, pooled around her hair. Her eyes fixed on nothing; her chest wasn't rising and falling with breaths.

"Annie?" *In a bit of a panic, he squatted down beside her, slid his fingers to her wrist. Then her neck. He moved his fingers around and around on her neck. Nothing; he couldn't feel a pulse on either side.*

No. Not again.

Just like twenty-one years ago.

But…no one knew then. No one will know now.

Inside the berth on the *Persephone*, Jason blinked. Shook his head. Annie's lifeless body disappeared, no longer a vision at his feet.

He didn't have time for this.

After leaping off the bed, he took three steps to the closed cabin door and wrapped his left hand around the knob. On the other side was his son, tied to a chair, and that woman paramedic handcuffed and restrained to a pipe.

Things spiraled out of my control.

Off to his left, the top drawer mocked him. It was empty, contained no bag of coke, just like the rest of the sailboat. That drawer often held a stash of his white candy, the one thing—the only thing—that coaxed his mood. Nothing else could disintegrate the swarm of grief seizing him.

Instead of wasting time, longing for something not within his reach, he needed to focus.

With a click he unlocked the door and flung it open on a creak. The second he stepped through the threshold, something clobbered him from the left side and rammed his right shoulder into the door frame.

"Ben?" Jason noticed the kid bent over and still tied up in the chair.

A split second later, Ben charged at him a second time, swung himself in the chair around, and barreled into Jason with the back of the chair, crushing him to the door frame.

"Cut it out, Ben," Jason yelled, squirming to break free, both arms smashed by the chair. He planted his left foot on the front leg of the chair and kicked out, shoving Ben away.

The kid jumped around and rammed his head into Jason's abdomen.

Jason raised his knee and slammed it in Ben's face. He slipped to the side, but the kid crashed into him again, full body. Jason shoved him. The kid stumbled backward and slammed down to the floor on his back, tied up arms behind him, his knees dangling around the edge of the chair seat.

Jason yanked out the gun from his pants' waistband at his back and aimed at Ben's face.

"Do it, Jason!" Ben barked at him. "Squeeze the trigger. Go ahead."

Jason froze. The gun heavy in his hand.

I can't shoot him. Not my own son.

"Come on!" Ben shouted in a ticked-off voice. "What are you waiting for?"

Jason eyed the life preserver inches near the kid's head. Aimed the gun barrel at it and riddled the thing with six rounds of bullets.

"Don't antagonize me, kid. Stop pushing me! Next time, I'll fill you with bullets. I won't care anymore. Do you understand that? You got it, Ben?"

Needing space from his son without a second more delay, he bolted up the companionway to the upper deck.

Less than a minute later, he finished readying the sails, and he kicked the motor on, cranked it up to top speed. Steering southbound, he heaved air in and out of his lungs, half of him stunned he didn't shoot the kid, the other half ticked at himself for losing control yet again.

I hate people. I hate everyone—they're so maddening!

Up on deck alone, he chose to ignore the fact two people were down under.

Out of sight, out of mind....

I'm out of my mind.

No. He just needed a fresh start. A new life.

Skies were cloudy, but the air warm and humid. The promise of light filled the dawn sky. The sun peaked up on the eastern horizon. No other vessels anywhere on the ocean.

Minutes later some sort of boat appeared out in the distance. A little after that, Jason spotted another boat. Just like yesterday throughout the day, other boats showed up around and about, but none of them even sailed close to nearing the *Persephone,* let alone approaching her.

The sound of rustling movements down below caught his attention, and he bent over at the waist to check it out, his arm stretched to the max with his hand on the wheel.

Ben maneuvered himself upright in the chair. Bounced it over to Paramedic.

It didn't concern Jason in the least. What could they do? Nothing. What could she say to him with her mouth taped? Nothing.

Even if she could speak, the Cayman paramedic didn't know the details of Monday night.

The details that plagued Jason as a vivid memory…

After a day of replacing hotel light fixtures and repairing the main air conditioner unit on the Beach Suite's third floor, Jason parked at the curb in his neighborhood inhabited by other hotel and resort employees. He stepped through his front door of a simple and tiny home, but he and Annie lived on the paradise island of Grand Cayman, so he couldn't complain.

"I can't live the lie anymore," his wife of twenty years told him before he even shut the door behind him, broaching yet again the same topic they'd discussed every day for the last week.

Every day she backed down, gave up. Agreed not to call Ben. Just like she'd do tonight. Predictable Annie. She'd never fold and reveal the secret truth to the kid.

The truth that would lead Ben to a deeper truth. One that Annie didn't even know about. A truth that would send Jason to prison for life.

She crossed her arms and scratched her forearms. She was experiencing coke bugs, a cocaine withdrawal symptom, and something that sent her right back to her addiction every time she'd attempted to quit.

Predictable Annie.

"Long day, Annie. I'm tired." He grabbed a cold beer from the refrigerator and his stash of bagged cocaine stuffed inside the cornstarch box.

In the family room, he lounged on the couch, gulped down a huge swig of beer.

After he set his beer bottle down on the coffee table, he arranged two lines of coke.

Annie followed him into the family room, stood over him. "Jason." Tears rimmed her lower eyelids. "I'm calling Ben. I'm finally telling him the truth. You hear me?"

"You've been asking me that for a week, Annie. This is the last time I'll answer—"

"Jason, I just want it over. The truth out. Ben deserves that. I'm not asking you, I'm telling you. I'm calling him. This second." She turned away, heading to the kitchen...and the telephone.

A blazing rage engulfed Jason's core.

He bounded off the couch, rushed at his wife. He grabbed her from behind and whipped her around.

"You will do nothing of the sort, woman, hear me?" he yelled in her face, clawing her triceps.

Her widened eyes glazed with confusion and a fright he'd never instilled in her before. "What are you doing? Let go of me, Jason."

"You will not tell Ben tonight or ever. Do you understand that?"

Her chest panted, her lower lip quivered; she said nothing.

"This conversation is finished. Don't ever bring it up again." He shoved her backward; she stumbled away from him, collided with the wall between the fireplace and the entry to the kitchen, knocking a picture off the mantel. It crashed the on brick area fronting the fireplace.

The topic settled for good, he turned for the couch and his white powdered candy.

"You can't stop me from calling him," she said, reluctance in her tone. No sound of movement from her position against the wall.

He whirled back around at her.

Chest still heaving, her red scratch-streaked arms wrapped around her waist in defense.

That's right, baby, you're under my control.

"You wanna bet?" he said, stepping toward her to hammer it home. "Let it go, Annie." Keeping her backed against the wall, he stood over her, the tips of his shoes brushing her stocking toes, his balled hands at his sides. "It's none of your business anyway."

"Not my business?" she whimpered back in agitation and anxiety, two other withdrawal symptoms common for her and clearly heightened due to their heated conversation. "How can you say that? Of course it's my business." She scratched her chest in a pathetic attempt to rid herself of the insect-crawling sensation.

"Jason, you asked me to lie to him all those years ago, and I did for selfish reasons. But I can't keep this lie anymore. He deserves to know the truth."

"Last warning, Annie." He clawed her shoulders, digging the tips of his stub fingernails into her skin with muscle-squeezing force. *"Forget the truth."* Fired up, he glared down at her with consuming anger. *"Got it?"*

"Stop it, Jason. You're hurting me."

That's the idea, Annie, my love. That's the idea.

He wrapped his hands around her throat but without pressure.

She gulped. "You've never treated me like this before. Why are you acting this way?"

"You're cornering me. Leaving me no choice."

"What are you talking about?" Panting her breaths, she squirmed away, slipping to the side.

He allowed it, plotting a new tactic.

Intimidation only worked so far. She was obviously determined, and he couldn't babysit her 24/7 for the rest of his life. "Annie—"

"You can't stop me from calling him." She stomped her foot in the entry to the kitchen. *"I will call him and tell—"*

"Why would you do that? Why risk losing him forever? He already refuses to have much, if anything, to do with us. Remember? You tell him that, we'll never see or hear from him again. Don't you get that?"

"You may be right. But I can't lie to him anymore. I can't live this lie anymore."

"Ben doesn't want to speak with either of us. Have you conveniently forgotten that?"

"No."

"Then you should know you won't be able to keep him on the line long enough for him to hear anything you have to say."

"Yes, I will. My first words will be that I've quit. I haven't had any cocaine in six days, and I will remain clean. For me. For him. Then I'll tell him the truth about...about...that..."

"You can't even say it to me," he said to slam her with self-doubt in hopes of preventing her telling the kid. *"And your drug free days won't last, Annie. Like all the times before, you'll return to the white powder, baby, you always do."* He

leaned into her face. "Your conversation with Ben will only be a few seconds, because he won't believe you'll stay clean, 'cause you can't do it!" he shouted at her.

"I am doing it. I'm getting the help I need to stay clean. I'm done with that stuff. Done poisoning my body with it. It took losing Ben for me to be strong enough to quit. He removed himself from our lives because of our cocaine addiction—"

"You're addicted, Annie. I'm not. My body isn't addicted. It's not physical. My personality needs it in order for me to play nice with others."

"What difference does that make? The why doesn't matter to Ben. Our drug use pushed him away because he couldn't be a part of our destructive behavior anymore. His strength to remove himself from us has given me strength to stop the self-destruction, and part of that self-destruction is keeping the lie going. I will reveal the truth to him because I can't lie to him anymore. It isn't right. It never was."

"So you're gonna get him back in your life by telling him you're clean and staying clean, then tell him the one thing that will push him away forever?" Jason barreled out a laugh. "Excellent plan, Annie..."

You idiot.

He laughed more. "Excellent. Brilliant."

More laughter rolled out of him, confident that through his ridicule, she'd listen to his logic and understand that revealing the long-buried truth to Ben was a grave mistake she'd forever regret.

"You're not getting this, Jason. I've been doing drugs most of my adult life. When I turn fifty next month, I want to be drug free and have Ben be part of my life again...if he can accept the truth I reveal to him. If he can't, I'll accept that, knowing I've finally been honest with him."

She backed into the kitchen, gradual steps, staring at him for a reaction. She leaned back against the counter, the cordless phone inches from her reach.

Hands on his hips, he stepped into the kitchen after her and towered over her short stature, his patience thinning. He dragged his arm across the dish-filled counter, sending all the dirty dishes crashing to the floor. "You—"

"This is not about me, Jason!" she shouted. "It's all about Ben. Just like I'm

getting clean with or without you. I'm telling Ben the truth with or without you."
She picked up the phone.

He snatched it out of her hand and whacked it against her right temple.

Her head snapped to the left, and he slammed it into the cabinet door; she col-
lapsed, smacking the back of her head on the edge of the counter, then crumbled to
the floor.

Ben squirmed in the chair, the seat bent a little from all his thrashing around, but all four of the legs were still stable.

If I could break the legs off...

He let the thought linger in his mind.

"Sara?" He swallowed, his throat dry from the start of dehydration. "I'm sorry," he whispered to her. "I blew it. Again."

Head cocked to the side, she shook her head in disagreement.

"Yeah, I did."

Somehow I'll take him out next time.

He didn't voice the promise she'd no doubt view as empty.

She looked off across the room. Over the next several seconds, at times she squeezed her eyes shut, other times she stared off glossy-eyed.

He had to give her some hope. "Hey, Sara? Somehow I'll disarm him. Stop him. I won't let him hurt you."

She lowered her head. He followed her train of vision.

Chafed, the skin over her ankle bones raw and caked with blood. Even worse with her wrists, due to the metal cuffs digging and rubbing. Same with his own wrists and ankles. The more they both pulled against the restraints in attempt to free themselves, the more damage to their skin, causing swollen, open wounds.

The ideal playground for infection.

Before he'd replaced the tape over Sara's mouth a few hours ago, she'd expressed concern for infection, especially since neither of them were drinking to maintain fluids and help balance out blood loss. As Sara pointed out, the sailing rope was patched with brown stains, indicating a plethora of germ cells.

"Sara, look at me."

She did.

"I won't let him kill you."

She planted the soles of her EMS boots on the pipe yet again and, yet again, pushed up in another desperate attempt to snap it loose from the floor, a futile attempt that wouldn't pan out. But like Ben's attack on Jason, he understood her need to try...yet again.

Ben glanced over his shoulder at Jason up on deck, speeding the boat to destination unknown. Bent over and glancing down there, the selfish snake was laughing at Sara's wasted actions.

Actually laughing.

Ben's nerves rubbed under his skin like stabs from a hot metal rod. He envisioned slamming his fist square in Old Man's face. A second time. A third. Fourth.

His anger didn't dissipate, and neither did his doubt.

When Jason docked this boat, how could Ben protect Sara when he couldn't even protect himself?

Spent in all ways a man could be, Ben looked out the window. Hopeless, he stared at the sun rising farther and farther out of the ocean and higher into the sky.

CHAPTER TWENTY-TWO

Out the window Ben noticed the sun sinking, easing its way toward the ocean surface on the western horizon.

A whole day gone. Wasted.

The endless stretch of ocean rolled underneath the *Persephone* as they continued to sail in a southward direction.

Are we headed to South America?

A few feet from him, Sara was still tied up in the corner, her hair band nearing the end of her ponytail and barely hanging on. An exhausted boredom that had swallowed him up many hours ago seemed to have done the same to her. Like him, all day long she'd either slept or stared off, at times with a blank gaze, others with fear etched on her facial features.

Once they arrived at…wherever, would he fail her? Old Man had ugly plans for her, no doubt. Tied up to this chair, there was nothing Ben could do to stop him.

I can't take the helplessness anymore.

He jolted up, the chair resting on his back. The companionway wasn't big enough for him and the chair. He wouldn't fit.

"Watch out, Sara," he said to her. "Huddle up."

He whacked the right rear chair leg against the galley table. Again. Again. And again.

It didn't break.

He beat the same leg against the side of the companionway stairs. Again. Again. And again.

I can't take it anymore.

I'm breaking free of this stupid chair.

"Ben?" Jason yelled down.

Ignoring the old man, Ben beat both rear legs to the floor, over and over, as he swung himself backward then forward. Backward and forward. Slamming the legs to the floor.

"Knock it off, Ben," Jason shouted.

That's the goal, Old Man. Knock the legs off. Break this chair.

Ben swung the chair at the galley counter and slammed the legs against the edge of it. And slammed it, and slammed it. A sense of ballistic behavior overwhelmed him, and he continued smashing parts of the chair to various parts of the boat. Nonstop, he swung himself in the chair around the room, banging it against any hard surface he could find at the right height.

Jason poked his head down the companionway. "What's all the racket?"

A racket-filled minute later, Old Man barreled down under and stood over Ben.

"You're losing it, kid." His father shoved him.

He stumbled, fought to stay on his feet. Losing the battle, he crashed to the floor.

Bang. A deafening shot rang out. Ben's left ear hummed with a constant ring. A fiery sensation pooled in his left shoulder. His body numbed, his mind blanked.

Did the old man shoot me?

He shot me, didn't he?

Ben blinked a few times to clear the haze from his vision. Glancing at his left shoulder, he saw coiling blood in a hole. A bullet hole.

He really shot me.

No. Couldn't be. This is a dream...a nightmare.

"Next bullet, kid," Jason shouted over him, "will be in your chest." He stormed off, slamming the berth door closed behind him.

Sara winced at the door slamming shut, a reaction leftover from the sound of gunfire.

"Ben?" she shouted, her voice caught in the tape. "Are you okay?" she continued on, even her own ears unable to decipher her muffled words.

Ben lay on his back, arms tied underneath him, unable to press his hand to the bullet wound to control hemorrhaging. The sight of him bleeding out of his left deltoid muscle was torturous to a paramedic unable to reach him. All she was able to do was sit there and watch him bleed.

He could bleed out.

She planted her boot soles on the pipe one last time and pushed with every ounce of energy she could scrounge up.

"Argh…" she groaned out as she pushed with her leg muscles.

Not getting anywhere, she collapsed yet again in defeat.

Ben rolled onto his left side. "Holy…! That hurts!" he yelled out in sheer agony, but he'd found a way to compress the wound.

Smart guy.

He must be stunned his own father shot him.

"This is all you, Jimar Malcolm," Jason's voice ranted from inside the berth, easily passing through the wall. "You created this mess," he shouted louder, clearly to himself, since no one else was in there. "You made me shoot my own son. You will pay for this, Malcolm." A pause of silence. "You will pay." Another pause. "Don't tell me that. Don't you dare go there."

Here he goes again. The man is delusional. Losing his mind beyond the point of return.

In the opening up to the upper deck, Sara noticed the sun setting again. Instead of panicked fear of the dark, a rush of panicked fear of watching Ben bleed to death hit her.

Her heart pounded underneath her ribs like a drum on a crescendo.

"Hang in there, Ben," she yelled out in a muffled cry into the tape. "I'll talk you through this. Keep lying on your shoulder. Keep the pressure on it."

His eyes fluttered open, then closed. Open, then closed.

CHAPTER TWENTY-THREE

A layer of sweat coated Sara's forehead and armpits. With the possibility Ben could bleed out—internally if not externally—on the floor, and Jason losing his grip on reality inside the cabin, she was losing her hope.

"Dang it, kid!!" Jason yelled on the other side of the wall. "You made me shoot you. Why'd you do that, Ben? Why? Malcolm messed things up for me, but you forced me to squeeze that trigger, son. *You* did."

The berth door whipped open, and Jason marched out. A can of cola in one hand. An over-the-counter medication bottle in the other, the word acetaminophen on the label.

"Here." Jason stuck the opened soda can in Ben's face. "Drink this." With his other hand, he held out three oblong white pills. "Take these. It will help with the pain."

"What do you care?" Ben said in a weak retort.

"Just take 'em."

"Or what, you'll shoot me again? What are they?"

"Generic Tylenol. Stick your tongue out, and I'll place 'em on there."

"Don't want any painkillers."

"It's OTC acetaminophen, Ben. Don't be a fool. You have a bullet wound. With the pain, you're not thinking clear, or you're just trying to be macho. Don't. Take these."

No response from Ben as he lay there unmoving, eyes closed. Sara craved to snatch Keegan's gun and shoot the scumbag in the face.

"Do you want them or not?"

He needs morphine, Keegan. You got any of that?

Ben stuck out his tongue. Bent over him, Jason slipped the pills on it, then poured some cola in his mouth.

"Drink some more so you won't get dehydrated."

Caffeinated drinks are diuretics, you idiot. The opposite of hydrating.

Keegan turned to Sara. "Paramedic? I've got a basic first aid kit onboard." He opened a cabinet. From inside it he pulled out a fat red pack with the Star of Life on it. "You're gonna patch him up." He pointed the kit at Ben, semiconscious on the floor. "Kid, you will not bleed to death out here on this boat. You don't deserve that."

An odd sense of understanding passed over Sara as she witnessed a killer's struggle between good and bad, the battle between being a father and being a fugitive murderer.

Somehow it made him seem even scarier.

He's so volatile.

The drug addict needed his drug of choice to get himself under control.

Keegan dropped the medical pack between her and Ben and unlocked her handcuffs.

She socked him in the gut.

He backhanded her. "One punch and you actually thought you could escape me?" He laughed.

"Jason," Ben said with a pained voice struggling to speak. "Don't—"

"Shut up, kid. I'll hit her if that's what needs to be done."

After he grabbed her hands, Keegan squeezed her bleeding wrists together in front of her. She winced at the pain of raw skin rubbing. With a snap he slapped the cuffs back on.

"I was gonna let you work cuffless, but forget it."

Hands cuffed in front of her, Sara reached for the tape over her mouth.

"Don't do that." He aimed the gun at her. "Keep the tape on."

She nodded to calm him. Cuffed hands in her lap, she unzipped the first aid kit.

Keegan lifted Ben off the floor and rested the chair upright on its legs. He groaned out, face contorted in a wince. Blood seeped out of the bullet hole.

"Press your palm over the wound," she instructed in a panic, her words muffled by the tape.

Shrugging, Keegan shook his head.

She pointed her cuffed hands to Ben's shoulder, pressed her palms together.

"Uh…right. Got it." Keegan pushed his right hand to Ben's bleeding deltoid. Blood seeped through his fingers.

With her hands cuffed in front of her, Sara thumbed through various types and sized bandages, a few packs of 4×4 sterile gauze, one self-adhering roll bandage, and one triangle wrap sling. A bottle of disinfectant. Even a box of steri-strips.

Sufficient enough for now.

Keegan skidded Ben's chair near her. He flitted his eyes open, but said nothing. His head wobbled around.

What is he thinking?

Was he really lethargic or just acting to trick Keegan somehow?

Glaring at Keegan, she tried to stand up but couldn't. So she hollered a scream through the tape.

"This isn't gonna work with you sitting. Okay, got it. You need to stand up."

She nodded.

"Fine." Jason unknotted the restraints from the pole but kept her ankles tied together.

She eased up to her feet. A wave of dizziness caught her offguard, and she swayed, then collided with the wall.

"Whoa," Ben said, his eyes half-closed. "You okay?"

She nodded at him. Then screamed into the tape as she glared at Keegan.

"Nope, tape stays on, Paramedic. Work without words."

Clearly the criminal didn't want her telling Ben a thing.

Already have, you psycho. And I'll tell him more if I get the chance, just to spite you.

Out of habit she verified the expiration date on the plastic bottle, then poured copious amounts of antiseptic over and into the bullet hole in Ben's deltoid muscle.

He winced with a groan.

Hang in there, Ben.

If they were in the back of her ambulance enroute to the ED, she'd simply dig into controlling hemorrhaging and not give a fig about infection, but way out on the ocean, days away from land and medical care, infection was a concern.

She opened all of the 4x4s and pressed the stack of them to the blood-oozing wound. Often, bullet wounds created little external bleeding, as the bullet acted as a plug. But for Ben, his deltoid was hemorrhaging moderate to heavy, maybe due to a nicked left brachiocephalic vein. It couldn't be an artery since the human body contained only a right brachiocephalic artery, no left. His lethargic behavior indicated heavy internal bleeding, if it wasn't an act.

She peeked underneath his arm. No mushrooming exit wound. No exit wound at all.

Should I try to take the bullet out or leave it in place?

She couldn't decide. If she removed it, she could use the steri-strips to seal up the hole, but the internal damage may be too extensive and cause him to bleed out internally.

She peeked under the stack of gauze. The hole was centered in the medial deltoid, the thickest of the three muscle sections. It appeared to be just soft tissue damage, muscle and tendon only, not bone or joint.

That was the good news.

The bad? She could see and feel bullet fragments embedded in the wound.

Bullet stays in place. A surgeon can remove the pieces later.

She lined five steri-strips and stretched them over the wound, sealing the skin as best as she could. She topped the strips with the bloody stack of 4x4s, then wrapped the roll bandage around and around, covering all the 4x4s in place over the steri-strips. Then she wrapped the self-adhering bandage over the roll bandage.

"Good job, Paramedic." Keegan patted Ben's bandaged wound. "No surprise, though. As a reward, you want to use the bathroom?"

She nodded.

He waved the gun at the opened door. "Go ahead. Sashay your ankles on over there, sweetheart. Hands cuffed in front of you should be good enough."

Ankle bones banging against each other, she shuffled her way inside the tiny room with a simple sink and toilet. She nudged the door shut.

A minute later, after flushing the toilet, she searched around but found nothing weapon-worthy.

She opened the door to the end barrel of a handgun.

"Break over, Paramedic. Get back to your pole and sit down."

For a few seconds, she stood there, glaring at him, considering all kinds of martial arts moves in an attempt to bring him down to his knees, at which point she'd slam her cuffed hands to his head a few times and knock him out with the thick steel.

"I know what you're thinking, Paramedic. Stop. You'll lose. I don't want to be forced to kill you, but I will if you push me."

He cuffed her hands behind her again, grabbed her upper arm and shoved her on the floor by the pole. He tied the ankle restraints to the pole. She elbowed him in the chin. He punched her in the stomach.

In jolting pain, she heaved over. Nausea assaulted her.

He laughed. "You're just not getting this, are you?"

He bolted up the two stairs to the upper deck. Less than a minute later, the boat sped off with a jerk, heightening her nausea. Behind the helm stood an outline of Keegan's body in the light from the half-moon, his face obscured in the darkness.

The night air breezed down from the upper deck and touched Sara's face with warm humidity, easing some of the nausea. Dusk long gone, lights from countless stars above blinked in the sky with a slight glow.

Nighttime is here.

Not again...in the dark with no light.

"Sara?" Ben whispered. "Is your stomach okay? Did he hurt you?"

She sniffled, lifted each shoulder one at a time and wiped her eyes and cheeks dry.

"Hey...are you okay?"

She nodded.

"Thanks for bandaging my shoulder."

She nodded again. His mental status improved post-wound care, indicating possible hemorrhage control. Also, the 1500mg of acetaminophen—one pill over dosage for an adult—seemed to be kicking in for him. A little too much, too soon?

Maybe those pills weren't acetaminophen.

"Sara, we need to talk," Ben whispered. "Lean over here. I'll take the tape off."

She leaned her head underneath his hands.

Rip.

The tape strip yanked off her mouth.

"He clearly does not want you talking to me," Ben whispered.

"Clearly," she whispered back, hidden low and behind Ben from his father's line of sight.

"Why is that exactly?" He blinked a few times as if to clear his brain or vision. Or both.

"This is what you want to talk about? Ben, what is it you want me to say?"

"Want?" Squirming, he winced in an obvious battling of pain.

"It's good he didn't give you ibuprofen."

"Like Advil?"

"Yeah. That med is a blood thinner, so it increases blood flow, which encourages bleeding. Just to be safe way out here, best not to take any of it. How's your shoulder?"

"It has a bullet in it. Don't change the subject."

She eyed around him and up on the deck.

Keegan's left arm gripped the wheel, his left leg bent a bit in a relaxed stance. She couldn't see anything more. Wind howled around the sails, creating heavy noise.

He probably can't hear down here.

"Ben? Your father isn't just a drug abuser."

"Go on."

"His crimes go deeper than that," she whispered, treading carefully.

"Obviously. Just say it, Sara." He winced out of clear pain. "Say what you're trying to say."

Maybe she could somehow guide him to figure out the truth...but who would guess their own father murdered their mother? Sure, it happened; spousal homicide was the most common murder. But denial was a powerful tool and the brain's keen defense mechanism.

Something she knew all about.

It wasn't easy for her to admit her mother beat her to near death, then dumped her body in a swamp when she was sixteen years old. She'd never get over that horror; she just learned to live with it.

"Sara?" Ben whispered in an intense and impatient tone.

Say little. Be vague. Force him to draw his own conclusions.

Hmm, where to start exactly?

"There wasn't a guy named Bubba at the marina," she whispered.

Ben swallowed, more like gulped. "You're saying Jason was on his own."

"Yes." She bit her lower lip and chewed on it.

"What happened, Sara?"

"Jason overtook my ambulance. Forced us to divert from heading to the hospital and instead drive to the marina."

For a split second, Ben glanced over his shoulder, probably to verify his father's whereabouts and focused attention. "Forced?" he whispered, eyeing her again. "How?"

"A cop was onboard with us. In the back. Jason snagged his firearm."

Ben ran his tongue over his top front teeth and smacked his lips. "Why the police escort?" he asked as if lost and confused.

Oh, boy. I'm sinking farther and farther in this pit of quicksand.

With her right pinky and thumb, she twisted her pearl ring around her finger. "Jason was in police custody."

"Obviously. Why, Sara?"

I could say I don't know. Why lie, though?

So this conversation will end.

"It's that bad?" he prodded with intensity yet wincing in pain. "Fine. Don't cushion the blow. Just say it. Tell me."

"He was charged with a serious crime. I don't know the details." True to a certain degree.

"Why don't you tell me what you do know. Like, what happened inside your ambulance."

Did he really—right now—need to know everything that happened, including his mom's murder?

"I told you."

"Sara," he snapped her name in a whisper, pained impatience dripped in his tone and spread across his agony-filled face. "What else? There's more."

He shot and killed my EMS partner and a cop. "I was driving. Like I said, a police officer was in the back. My partner was also in the back, attending our patient...Jason..."

"And?"

"I heard gunfire."

Ben squeezed his eyes shut. Flashed them back open. "He shot the cop."

Since it wasn't spoken as a question, she didn't say anything. Just stared back.

She gnawed on her lower lip; her heart pounded underneath her ribs with a thudding bang. She had no clue what Ben was thinking or how he'd respond next.

Should've just kept my mouth shut.

"You're saying my father is a murderer?"

She twisted her ring even faster. Yet slowly she nodded.

His head dropped, chin knocking his chest as if crushing disappointment overwhelmed him.

A welcomed silence settled in, and lingered.

Sara glanced around his arm and up at the deck. Jason was in a zone, sailing ahead without any regard at all for the two of them.

Ben's head popped back up. "The man I knew would never kill anyone..." Trailing off, he shook his head in what appeared to be a denial he struggled to understand. "He was never violent. Or explosive. Just the opposite. Things don't add up."

"Yeah, Ben, they do," she spoke in the most compassionate tone she could dig up underneath all her compounded emotion and exhaustion.

He slammed his eyes shut again in what seemed like a battle against both physical and emotional pain. She didn't know what to say, so she said nothing.

"I've never seen him like this. So...intense." He fluttered his eyes open. "When he said Bubba shot a cop to death at the marina, he lied, but only about who pulled the trigger. *He's* the cop killer. *Jason* is a cop killer."

It hadn't happened *at* the marina, but...

"Yes."

Ben's chest heaved, nostrils flared. All denial vanished. "What happened to your partner?"

"Um..." Sara's heart squeezed from the reminder Russell was dead. "He didn't make it either."

"Jason murdered him, too." Ben shook his head, his face scrunched in a facial expression of sheer heartache. "I'm so sorry, Sara."

Too choked to speak, she swallowed the lump of grief. Cleared her throat. "Russell was a good man, and he left behind a pregnant fiancée. Owen, the cop? He was a good man, too."

Ben's chin dropped again to his chest as if a swirl of overwhelming emotion zapped the strength in his neck and it could no longer hold up his head.

If anyone could understand him, relate to him...

Her mother was violent. Explosive. Nearly killed her, and she too often struggled with accepting that atrocious reality. Sometimes the truth was so ugly.

Ben, I know what it's like to have a crazy killer parent.

"He killed a cop and a paramedic," Ben said, looking down at his feet, "then he abducted you. I'm so sorry he's doing this to you, Sara." A beat of silence. "He's claiming his body isn't physically addicted. You heard him."

"Ah...I'm not following," she replied to the top of his head, confused on the sudden topic.

"He's addicted to how cocaine affects his behavior, keeps it under control. Happy, I guess. He's not chemically addicted; he's psychologically addicted. Coke subdues his anger. Without it he goes..." Ben trailed off, still staring at the floor. "I'm not trying to rationalize his behavior."

"I know you're not. I get what you're saying. I've seen psychological addiction numerous times in EMS. Bottom line, though, addiction is addiction, just like you told him."

"Yeah. I know. I know."

"Ben? I understand what it's like."

"What?" he said, his head snapping up.

His eyes glazed over with an array of overwhelming emotions and a physical pain in need of morphine, a mix she'd seen in her patients countless times.

She studied the bandage on his shoulder for any seeping blood. Nothing but white. Hemorrhage under control, but his bullet-holed shoulder no doubt pained him.

"I understand what it's like to have a parent who's..." she shrugged, groping for the right word, "who's—"

"Nuts?"

She managed a half-smile, a show of compassion, hopefully. "Yeah. My mother's in prison for attempted homicide."

After a brief moment of silence and Ben simply staring at her, Sara's nerves rubbed together under her skin.

If I don't elaborate, the connection we're building will break, and this is all I have anymore. Out in the vast ocean with a killer, Ben Keegan is all I have.

"She beat...someone, and stuffed them in a trash bag and dumped 'em in a swamp in the middle of the night." She cringed inside, not sure if that statement of truth would somehow backfire on her.

His eyebrows furrowed deep in obvious disbelief. "Whoa. Who?"

Why did I share the details with him? "Ah...that would be me," she blurted it out in a whisper, fulfilling her need to sympathize with him to soothe him.

He stared at her for a few awkward seconds. "Wow. That's quite a story, Sara."

Something inside her abdomen clenched, and she felt exposed. "Are you saying you don't believe me?" she snapped back in an angry whisper.

Does he think I'm playing him?

"Hey. Actually, I'm wondering if that's the reason you're terrified of the dark."

"Oh." She lowered her head. Embarrassment flooded her insides and dissipated the anger. "You picked up on that?"

Another stretch of awkward silence.

The quietness between them bothered Ben. He didn't know what to say to Sara next. What could he say? *Sorry my dad is causing you additional fears, upping your anxiety to the max?*

No. Ridiculous and pathetic.

A pounding throb seized behind his eyes. His vision blurred. A blanket of grogginess crawled over him, zapped him of strength and a clear head. He rested his temple against the pole.

Something isn't right. Suddenly I feel...whoa...

His body swayed, out of his control.

"Ben?" Sara's voice spoke his name in slow motion, a dragged-out syllable that went up in pitch with progression. "Is...it...the...pain?"

"Pain?" he heard his own voice say. "What pain?"

"Your...gun...shot...wound," Sara spoke in that same dragged-out slow-mo playback.

What did she say?

What am I saying?

I don't know.

"It just hit me. All of a sudden."

"What...did...Ben?"

"I don't know."

"You...look...like...you're...gonna...pass...out."

"Feels like it."

"Ben...he...drugged...you. Those...pills...not..."

Blah, blah, blah, she continued on.

"...probably...crushed...more...in...the...soda..."

Nothing made sense, nothing was clear...except for one thing.

"Sara, he's gonna kill you when he docks this boat." His head flopped around like a weebble-wobble.

"I...know."

CHAPTER TWENTY-FOUR

A sense of awareness startled Ben awake. A ray of blinding sunlight shined through the companionway, lighting down below. It bathed the upper deck in brightness.

A fog captivated his brain. Still tied to the chair, he blinked a few times, but his hazy vision didn't clear. Grogginess swarmed him. It hit him.

Old Man drugged me.

Ben scoffed, a small part of him stunned. The memory of his father shooting him, though, reminded him there was nothing shocking about it, not after the events of the last day.

Sara.

He turned his head to the left, glanced downward.

Sara wasn't there.

The bloody ankle restraints gone, no longer tied to the pole.

"Sara?" he yelled out, his heart pounding with a sudden burst of panicked energy. "Jason?"

Silence.

He looked out the window. Land stretched out in front of him. All forest, no buildings. The view was the same out the window on the other side of the boat. Jason had docked them in an isolated area. The shoreline served as the boat's anchor in the front half.

"The boat's beached," he spoke out loud to himself.

Ben jerked up to his feet. The chair rested on his back. A shot of agony stabbed his wounded shoulder. A heavy painkiller could numb it, but there wasn't a chance to obtain one anytime soon.

He swung the right front chair leg to the pole. Banged it and banged it against the steel. And banged it nonstop for what seemed like a minute or so. In response, his bandaged shoulder throbbed with pain.

Crack.

The chair leg snapped off. The piece of wood flew across the galley, slammed into the refrigerator with a bounce. Three separate pieces dropped to the floor, one a larger chunk than the other two.

He whacked the back right leg to the pole. After six times, the leg cracked off and snapped in two. He did the same with the left rear leg, slamming it to the pole at an angle until it broke off. Then the left front, but it dangled, half on. Two more whacks against the pole, it dropped to the floor.

Ankles still tied together, he hobbled up the companionway, finally able to fit through with just the chair back and bottom. He stumbled up onto the deck, landing smack on his knees.

Crunch.

The bag by the wheel was gone, the bag containing weapons, explosives, and a detonator.

Kneecaps aching, Ben stood with a groan. Hunched over, tied to what was left of the chair, he scanned his windy surroundings. No buildings of any kind, just green foliage beyond the beach. A tree-covered hill led to mountains in the far distance. By the direction of the sun above, the mammoth range looked to be south of where he stood.

"That's gotta be the Andes."

Old Man just left me here shot and no town in sight?

The last bit of his denial disintegrated.

His father was a criminal, a murderer who didn't care a bit about his son...or anyone else.

A loan fisherman stood on the beach about forty yards to the left, pole in hand, line cast out. Ocean water lapped on his lower legs with each wave break on the shore.

"Hey, sir?" Ben shouted out.

The man jerked his head toward Ben, and waved in a casual hello response.

Casual wave? I'm tied to a chair, man. Do you see that?

Obviously not. And obviously, he hadn't heard Ben banging below deck. How could he not have heard? Distance? Wind and waves? Made sense.

Ben placed his knees on the boat bench, allowed all his weight to hold there. He inched forward, one wiggle at a time, until only his tied-up ankles dangled over the edge of the bench.

The boat rocked side to side with each gentle lap of incoming wave. The nose of the boat was lodged in the sand. No ropes held it down.

The shallow seawater stared back him, taunting him to jump overboard.

Even with his hands restrained behind him and his ankles tied together, he couldn't drown in less than a foot of water.

He inched himself forward, toward the boat's topsides. Knees touching the raised ledge, he lifted one knee at a time and rested his shins—and his entire body weight—on the ledge. He propelled himself off the boat, landed in the ocean on his knees with a splash.

The salt water stung his cut ankles with a fiery burn. The bandage over his throbbing shoulder stayed dry, white and intact.

He scrambled to stand...and nearly face-planted in the shallow ocean water. Without limbs in motion, controlling his body was near impossible. Finally, he stood on stable feet, no swaying.

Bent over in the chair, he hopped forward. Twice. Three times. Four. Until he reached dry sand on the beach.

He glanced up to spot the fisherman. The man was striding over to Ben, his face scrunched in obvious confusion mixed with shock.

He spoke in rapid Spanish for several seconds. The only words Ben recognized were *señor* and *delincuente*—sir and criminal.

Terrific, a language barrier. This ought to be interesting.

According to Ben's college transcript, he was fluent in Spanish. Sure, book Spanish, and that was years ago, in his undergraduate days. Yet, he always knew enough to communicate when necessary.

Still bent over and tied up, Ben looked up at the man. "El cuchillo," he said, asking for a knife to slice the rope tying him to the chair with no legs.

"Whoa." The olive-skinned man stepped back, distrust flashing in his deepened brown eyes. "Cuchillo?"

"No. No soy un criminal. Es un...secuestro." Ben explained he'd been abducted.

"Aliens?" the man said, head pulled back.

This guy doesn't have a clue what I'm saying.

"No, not by aliens. A man. Hombre. He tied me up."

"Hombre malo."

"Sí. A bad man. Hombre...took a señorita, too."

"Dos?"

Ben shook his head. "Not dos senoritas. Señorita también." He explained the bad man also abducted a woman.

"Ah," the man nodded, "también. Sí." More nodding. "Donde estan?"

"I don't know where he took her. No donde estan. Matar señorita."

"Matar?"

"Sí. Kill her." *If he hasn't already killed Sara.* "Hombre malo matar policía. Señor, por favor. Ayuda? Help me? Ayuda?"

"Help. Sí. El médico?"

"No, no doctor. Está bien." Ben explained he didn't need a doctor right now.

The fisherman pointed at Ben's bandaged shoulder with white gauze and tape well intact, then his bloody wrists and ankles with swollen open wounds.

"No está bien?" the man questioned, shaking his head in clear confusion.

"I'm fine, señor. No médico. El cuchillo?" Ben asked again. "Cortar la cuerda," he went on, asking him to cut the rope.

The man nodded. "Cortar en la caja," he said, nodding toward his tackle box laying lopsided on the sand about twenty yards away.

Within a minute, the fisherman returned with a knife. After he swiped the blade through the sailing rope tying Ben's ankles together, he sliced the rope trapping Ben's arms to the chair. What was left of the chair plunked down onto the sand in the shallow seawater.

Ben arched up in a stretch, standing straight up with stability and no resistance. His neck, back, and thigh muscles ached. He planted his palms on his hips and leaned backward. He shook his stiffened arms out to the side.

He spied his surroundings and spotted a cell phone tower in the near distance up a tree-covered foothill leading to the mountains in the far distance.

From his front pocket, Ben dug out the cell phone Malcolm had given him on Tuesday, and noticed it still had battery life.

SEARCHING.

Twenty seconds passed. Impatience welled up inside Ben. The fisherman poked his head in and eyed the tiny phone's screen, still searching for service.

"Mal servicio de celular."

Bad cell service? No kidding. "Yeah, I can see that."

The cell phone beeped. Searching complete yet slow. Spotty service at best. The local weather displayed on the screen, and the word *Colombia* popped up. The screen blackened without Ben catching sight of the city name.

Colombia made sense with the time and speed they'd traveled from Grand Cayman. Ben again studied the mountain range in the far distance.

Yep, those are the Andes.

He punched in 911 on the cell.

Beep, beep, beep. Then…nothing. No ringing. No…nothing.

"Señor, número de emergencia? 911?" Ben asked the man if the emergency number around here was 911.

"La policía? Policía Nacional de Colombia?"

Ben nodded. "Is it 911?"

"No."

"Qué es?"

The guy rattled off a bunch of numbers within a sentence.

"Whoa. No. Tres números for policía. Just three numbers. Just tres números."

"Uh…" The man shook his head.

Come on, man. My Spanish isn't that bad.

Fine. I'll look it up myself.

Ben clicked onto Google. Waited. Waited. Waited some more.

The screen froze.

One bar flashed on and off. On and off.

Is it too much to ask to catch one break? Just one?

The only coastal city in Colombia he could think of was…

"Cartagena?" he said to the man. "Is Cartagena near?"

"No," the man said with a shake of his head.

"Qué Cartagena?"

"Cartagena?" He pointed northeast. "Lejos."

"Lejos? Lejos?" Ben shook his head. "I don't understand."

"Fair."

Ben thought about that for a few seconds. "Do you mean far? Cartagena is far away?"

"Far. Sí. Ah…cerca 480 kilómetros."

"About 480?" Ben figured out the math conversion in his head. *Whoa…three hundred miles.*

"480. Sí. Mi casa. Teléfono. Policía."

Hmm, should I trust this guy?

Out on the isolated Colombian shoreline, Ben had nothing around but this fisherman's home phone, a way to call the police.

"Cómo se llamas?" Ben asked the Colombian his name.

"Mateo. Y tú?"

"Ben."

"Ben, mi casa. Policía." Mateo took two steps, waved his fishing-pole-filled-hand as an encouragement to follow; his other hand held his tackle box and a bucket with two fish inside.

The smell of fish confused Ben's stomach. He was hungry, but he hated seafood. The smell too awful, the taste disgusting.

He whipped out his wallet, withdrew two twenties, and handed them out to the man.

"No, no." The man hesitated, staring at the two bills. Nodding, he grabbed one of the twenties. "One. Mi casa?"

"Let me get my bag." Ben rushed off toward the *Persephone*. "Esperar," he said over his throbbing shoulder, asking the man to wait.

Free from ropes, he easily hopped back on *Persephone*, although his aching body protested with a whine, especially his shoulder. Once down below, he retrieved his backpack.

Standing in the center of the galley that had been his and Sara's prison cell for two days, he stared at the pole she'd been restrained to, and considered praying for the first time in his life, praying for her safety.

Praying for her life.

But he didn't know how to pray, didn't even know where to start. More than that, it'd be a total waste of time.

Something Sara didn't have to waste.

Once back on the beach, Ben followed Mateo for about a hundred yards. His sore legs cramped up from two days of being restrained to that chair. Nothing in sight but ocean, sand, and thick green foliage, rising up to meet the Andes in the far distance.

Is Old Man dragging Sara up into that mountain range? Makes sense. It is the ideal place for a criminal to disappear.

"Close," Mateo said on a nod.

"We're getting close?" Ben asked to verify.

"Close. Sí. Ben, que hombre malo?"

Who is the bad man? My father is the bad man.

Ben didn't want to scare the Colombian or tell him details yet uncon-
firmed as the truth. Conjecture, surmise, and Sara's story was all Ben had at
this point, plus the little he knew as fact in this outlandish and mammoth
story with tons of sharp angles. What he did know for certain was kidnapping was a federal crime. Since both Sara and Jason were US citizens, the
United States, Cayman, and Colombia would share in jurisdiction.

"Una larga historia, Mateo." Ben explained it was a long story and left it
at that.

"Ah...sí."

Mateo veered off the beach and onto a foot trail leading into tall foliage.
Following behind him on the narrow trail, Ben punched 011 on his cell
phone, knowing the three-digit number connected to an emergency line in
parts of the world.

The call didn't go through.

He tried 911 again. Nothing.

"Mateo, donde? En el pueblo? Town? Village? El nombre?" *Where exactly
are we?!*

"Cercano Turbo."

"We're near Turbo, Colombia?"

"Sí."

Never heard of it. "Donde?"

"Cercano Panamá."

Then three hundred miles from Cartagena sounds right.

"So...we're *near* Turbo, which is near Panama. What is this town's
name? El nombre?"

"Village. San Juatania."

Definitely never heard of it.

A minute later they reached a grass bungalow, a shack-like house, set
back about two hundred yards from the beach. Mateo headed for the door
at the end of a dirt driveway that curved around the bungalow to the other
side and off toward a road disappearing in the thick foliage.

"Teléfono?" *Here?*

"Sí...and the Internet."

"The Internet?" Ben said, a bit shocked.

"Sí. Computer. Teléfono."

Once inside the tiny and disheveled home with no air conditioning and jam-packed with clutter, Ben scanned around for a bathroom. The short trek to the house had kicked all his systems back on in full force, including his kidneys.

"Baño?" he said to Mateo. "Por favor."

"Sí." Mateo pointed down the hall to the first door.

Anxious to call the police, Ben finished in the cramped and disordered bathroom in a rush. As he stepped into the kitchen, Mateo held out a phone.

"Policía," he said on a nod, bouncing the phone in the air toward Ben.

"Gracias." Ben took the phone. "What's the number?"

"Policía." Mateo pointed to the phone.

"Oh. Okay." Ben pressed the phone to his ear. "Hola?"

"Policía Nacional de Colombia," a male South-American-accented voice spoke over the line.

"Sí. Hablo Inglés?"

"Yes, I do. How may I help you?"

"Excellent, you speak English. The Cayman fugitive, Jason Keegan, is in Colombia. Do you know who I'm talking about?"

"Yes, of course. You say he's here in Columbia? Where?"

"He beached the sailboat, the *Persephone,* in a remote village. San Juatania."

"San Juatania. Yes, it is small. Near Turbo."

"That's what I hear. I believe he's headed up into the Andes."

"What makes you think so?"

"He'd be stupid not to, you know? In fact, I think the Andes are the reason he sailed here. It makes sense."

"It does."

"He took the woman EMT with him. I'm guessing he's dragging her up there. Up into the Andes."

"You're saying she's still alive? You know this as fact?"

No, I don't. But since he didn't leave her on the boat, it makes sense. "Until he's confident he's escaped off radar, he'll need her for a human shield."

"Which won't be for long."

You think? Ben snapped the two words in his head for his ears only.

"I've dispatched officers out to you, sir. Stay on the line with me until they arrive."

"How do you know where I am?" Ben asked, thinking and confused.

"Um…the caller. The caller gave us his address. Stay where you are, sir. Stay on the line with me until—"

"The caller?" Unease spilled into Ben and crept on his skin. "Mateo?" He scanned around for the Colombian fisherman.

An eerie silence floated inside the empty house.

"Yes. Mateo."

Something isn't right.

Ben allowed the silence on the line to linger.

This dispatch officer should be hounding me with questions about Jason. About Sara. About me, especially my name. About everything that—

"Sir? Are you still there? Don't hang up."

This was not the Colombian Police—this person was hired to waste Ben's time, keep him occupied.

"Hey…are you still there? Hello? Hello?"

Ben slammed the phone into its cradle on the wall.

CHAPTER TWENTY-FIVE

Mateo was a friend of Old Man's.

No friend of mine.

Where'd the Colombian disappear to and why?

Ben snagged a steak knife and Swiss army knife out of a kitchen drawer. Ignoring the throbbing pain in his left shoulder, he pocketed the army knife and slipped the handle of the steak knife into his shorts' waistband at his midback, covering it with his t-shirt.

Peeking out of the kitchen window for Mateo's whereabouts, Ben whipped out his cell and found the service two bars strong.

Score.

He dialed Jimar Malcolm for some concrete answers. After four rings, voicemail popped on.

"Jamaica Dude? Man, you manipulated me into a big criminal mess. No wonder you sent me in your place. Did you know Jason killed a Cayman cop and EMT, and he abducted another EMT? If you don't want to be dragged into this, Jimar, tell me where he's headed. Tell me his plans, or I'll make sure the authorities know you're involved. You'll be charged with accessory to homicide. Call me ASAP."

A computer in the family room corner beckoned him, the background on without a screensaver in place.

The PC wasn't locked.

Ben darted across the room, slid onto the flimsy wooden chair in front of the computer, and clicked on Internet Explorer. Less than thirty seconds later, he hopped on the front page of the Cayman news; his eyes flashed wide open at the header of the day's top news article:

WHERE IS JASON KEEGAN?

The search is still on for escaped psych ward patient...

"Psych ward?" Ben spoke the two words out loud to the empty room.

...Jason Keegan, charged murderer. Interpol is assisting Cayman Inspector Craig Hillman in the hunt. Keegan shot and killed thirty-one-year-old police officer Owen Hinders and twenty-four-year-old paramedic Russell Wilson. Keegan then abducted twenty-six-year-old paramedic Sara Dyer as a hostage in order to escape the police barricade on Grand Cayman Island...

Sara's words replayed in Ben's head: *"He was my patient. Another patient stabbed him."*

Why was he in a psych ward? And why'd another psych patient stab him?

Wait a second...Old Man didn't shoot the cop and Sara's partner until the marina, so whose murder is he charged with?

Ben's mind raced for answers, hoping he'd find them in his research. Two things on the Internet search history caught his attention:

Expedia

Map of the Andes Mountains

Footsteps from behind startled him. He whipped around in the chair and found a Colombian-looking little boy, maybe aged eight, trotting into the room from down the hall. He waved at Ben with sad eyes.

"Hola," Ben said on a wave.

"Hello." The boy smiled, lips together, dark brown eyes downcast.

With his torso, Ben blocked the disturbing news page from the young child. "How'd you know I speak English?"

The boy shrugged, whatever that meant exactly, then plopped on the floor near the worn couch and played with a scuffed-up wooden train set.

"I just need to use your computer. Is that okay?"

"I don't care."

"Your English is great."

"My papa teaches me."

"Is your dad's name Mateo?"

"Yep."

"Your dad's English is good?"

The boy nodded. "Real good."

The jerk had pretended ignorance. *No hablo Inglés.* What an actor.

Just like my father, the storyteller. The liar.

"What is your name?" Ben asked the young boy with messy black hair.

"Felipe."

"Felipe? I'm Ben. Do you know where your dad is?"

"Nope."

"He's not in the house?" Ben pointed down the hall. "Back there some-where?"

"Nope."

A gaunt woman strolled down the hall from a back bedroom. "Mateo?" she screamed out the name. She continued on in rapid and angry Spanish to no one in particular.

Strange woman.

She gave Ben a bored half-glance, then kicked the little boy aside. With-out a word or any noise of protest, Felipe tumbled over onto his side. Ben fought against the urge to kick her.

She snatched up a half-empty gin bottle from a chipped side table dam-aged with multiple glass rings, and plopped down on the torn-up couch. Bottle cradled in her arms, she sprawled her body on the cushions. Her eyes fluttered closed.

This living environment reminded Ben of his own childhood.

"Felipe? Is she your mom?" he whispered, jerking his head toward the couch.

"Yep."

The little boy's life was a mirror image of Ben's at the same young age, lost and alone and caught in the world of his parents' addictions. The haunting image stirred buried memories up to the surface, memories he didn't have the time to deal with, so he pushed them back down.

Felipe drove the train set toward Ben's feet and tapped the side of his right foot with the caboose.

Tap. Tap. Tap.

It seemed like more than just playing, more like trying to gain Ben's attention.

Still tapping Ben with the caboose, Felipe glanced over his shoulder and at the snoring woman, then looked up at Ben with a sense of desperate communication.

The boy fingered the top edge of some sort of business card inside the caboose. Underneath the card lay something circular, colorful and made of cotton. Ben caught the word *Cayman* on the card; he snatched it up.

INSPECTOR ALEC DYER, ROYAL CAYMAN ISLANDS POLICE SERVICE

Dyer?

Ben glanced over his shoulder at the computer screen, focused in on Sara's last name written in the news article.

SARA DYER.

Was Sara the Cayman inspector's relative? Daughter, probably. That was it—no wonder she was so cognizant of law enforcement terminology and procedures. She wasn't an undercover police officer; she was a cop's daughter.

"Ben?" Felipe whispered, picking up the colorful cotton item from inside the caboose and handing it to him. Handing him a distinct hair tie with a rainbow of colors.

Sara's hair band.

"The nice lady needs help," the boy whispered. "Papa was mean to her, and that guy was really mean to her."

At least Sara is still alive.

"Where'd the mean guy and the nice lady go?" Ben whispered back, his pulse quickened, anger building.

"A friend of Papa's picked 'em up."

"To go where?"

The boy shrugged. "They took stuff."

"What kind of stuff?"

"Food and drinks and blankets."

Supplies for trekking through the mountains?

"And bad stuff. They took the bad stuff."

"Do you mean weapons?"

Felipe nodded. "And that yucky stuff they sniff."

How'd Sara know she could count on this young boy to help her?

Ben glanced at the alcoholic woman lounged on the couch, passed out. He'd place odds on her being a drug addict. Maybe Sara had been kind and caring to Felipe, something so opposite of his mother. Regardless of how, Sara had clearly made a connection with the little boy.

Ben shoved Inspector Dyer's business card and Sara's hair tie in the front pocket of his shorts, then clicked on Google and typed in *3 digit Colombian emergency number.*

112 popped up in numerous headers. He filed the number in his mind, and clicked back onto the Internet search history.

Expedia: someone had researched one-way flights from Medellín to Bogotá, two Colombian cities.

Map of the Andes: Ben clicked on the map link, studied the three separate maps, and hit Print. After the printer spit out several pages, he folded them up and pocketed them.

"Felipe? I'd like to go hiking. Is there a store near here where I could buy supplies?"

"We got a town. There's stores there."

"Where's the town?"

"Out our driveway and go right."

So follow the first map I just printed.

Ben dug out his cell to dial 112-emergency.

Bang, bang, bang, bang, bang.

Someone fired five shots in the near distance outside.

Backpack strapped on his left shoulder, he slipped out the front door and searched around the dilapidated property.

No gunman. No Mateo.

Instinct told him to hop in the beat-up old truck and take off, but Ben couldn't leave that little boy inside with his unfit mother. And taking the boy was kidnapping.

He had enough felonies piled on him at the moment.

With the surrounding foliage, he couldn't see anything beyond maybe ten yards. He jumped into the bed of the blue, rusted truck and leaped into a tree. The pain of hoisting himself up caused a yell to escape from his lungs, but he caught it in his closed mouth. Eyes squeezed shut, he didn't move for a few moments, just hung in the tree, waiting for the pain to subside.

He couldn't wait anymore.

Up he climbed…until a visual of the ocean came into sight.

Mateo had sailed the *Persephone* out about a hundred yards and was now rowing back to shore on a life raft. The sailboat was nose-down into the sea and sinking, apparently from five rifle-sized bullet holes somewhere crucial in the hull.

The Colombian was hiding the *Persephone.* Smart.

Had the original plan been to sink her with Ben onboard, tied up down below and unconscious in a drugged sleep?

Ben jumped out of the tree, popped open the truck door. No keys anywhere inside it.

He raced back inside the house. The screen door slapped shut behind him. The noise didn't even stir the woman's slumber. The little boy stood in the center of the family room, eyes downcast and appearing to be desperate for love and guidance.

I remember that look from my childhood bathroom mirror.

"Felipe? Do you know where the truck keys are?"

The boy shrugged.

Ben rushed to the kitchen, patted down a stack of haphazard papers on the counter. Opened drawers and cabinets.

No keys.

He dashed down the hall, searched the nightstand and dressers in both bedrooms.

No keys.

"Papa is coming," Felipe said from half-down the hallway, eyes wide with panic.

Screen door slammed shut.

Ben darted out of the bedroom and into the bathroom. Quietly shut the door. Locked it. As he stood in front of the cracked and soiled mirror, he whipped out his cell and dialed 112. The line rang twice.

"Policía Nacional de Colombia," a male Colombian voice said over the connection.

"Hablo Inglés?" Ben whispered.

"Yes. Sir, what is your emergency? Why are you whispering?"

"That's part of the emergency," he continued in a whisper. "The Cayman fugitive, Jason Keegan, is in Colombia. Do you know who I'm talking about?"

"Jason Keegan? Yes. Where he is, sir?"

"He beached the *Persephone* in a village, San Juatania. Near Turbo."

Ben heard fingernails clicking on a keyboard in rapid motion.

"Do you know anything about the paramedic? Is she with him?"

"Yes, he's got her."

"Sir? What is your name?"

"Someone who cares about bringing Jason Keegan to justice. Someone who cares about Sara Dyer's safety. Keegan grabbed a ride headed to Medellín, dragging her with him."

"You know this for sure? Did you see—"

"I know the ride as fact. He researched flights from Medellín to Bogotá."

"I've notified security at the airport in Apartadó, and dispatched units there. It's the closest airport to Turbo."

"How close?"

"Fifty kilometers."

Ben did a quick math calculation in his head. Only thirty-one miles. "How far is Apartadó from San Juatania?"

"About thirty kilometers."

Eighteen miles.

Was Jason heading to the Apartadó Airport? With Sara in tow? No way. Airports weren't safe for Old Man right now, even if he didn't have a hostage with him. He needed to lay low in the Andes for a bit. That scenario made the most logical sense.

"I've also dispatched units along the road from Turbo to Cartagena," the operator went on.

"It doesn't make sense he'd head there. He researched a detailed map of the Andes."

"Maybe he just wants us to think the Andes are his plan."

"Possibly but not likely. I'm guessing he'd assume no one would ever know he was in San Juatania." *In this house.*

"I'm dispatching officers to the Pan American Highway southbound from San Juatania. Sir, did Jason Keegan change his appearance? Is he still wearing the cop uniform?"

"I don't know for certain. Can you track my location via the cell phone I'm using?"

"To San Juatania, yes."

"Is the cell number coming through?"

"Yes."

"Good. Update Cayman Inspector Alec Dyer. Let him know his daughter is in Colombia."

"Another operator is doing that right now, sir. What's the address of your location?"

"I have no idea. The man who helped Jason Keegan is named Mateo. He has a young son named Felipe and a drunk wife. I'm inside their home, a grass bungalow about a quarter mile from the beach. Somewhere in San Juatania."

"Are you being held there against your will?"

"I don't want to leave the little boy in this environment, but—"

"Is he in danger?"

"It's not happy and healthy. His mother is passed out on the couch. The boy trusts me. How 'bout I get him out of here and you arrange for a unit to take over care of him until—"

"That's kidnapping, sir. Do not take the boy anywhere. Just sit tight. We'll find you."

Yeah, after Sara's dead.

Time was wasting.

CHAPTER TWENTY-SIX

Steak knife out in front of him, Ben opened the bathroom door. No one was near the threshold, waiting to pounce on him.

He heard Spanish dialogue drifting out of a television set down the hallway. He slipped the knife handle in his waistband at his back and covered it with his shirt.

In the family room, he found Mateo in a side chair next to the couch, flipping through TV channels, a beer in his hand. The woman still lay sprawled, passed out on the couch. Felipe played on the floor with colorful wooden blocks, the paint chipped off and worn.

"Ah…amigo," Mateo lifted his beer in the air, "la cerveza?"

Stalling me more. Wasting my time—that is this guy's job.

Mateo didn't offer any lame excuse to explain his whereabouts, and Ben didn't ask for one. Not the ideal time to confront him in English or any other language, not with a child around.

Play it cool. Play along.

Ben shook his head. "No, no cerveza," he answered, wondering if Jason had told the Colombian Ben's weakness to beer.

That was a long time ago.

Mateo pointed toward the bathroom. "No se siente bien?" he said, asking Ben if he wasn't feeling well since he'd spent much time in there.

Ben decided to ignore the question and glanced down at Felipe playing, lost in his own world of trains and painted blocks. The boy was a survivor, just like Ben.

"Mateo?" He eyed the fisherman. "Tengo que llegar a casa," he lied, saying he needed to get home.

"Dónde está su casa?" Mateo asked where his home was.

"Far. El aeropuerto." Ben spoke the word airport. "Tomaré un taxi," he went on, explaining he'd call a cab. He pointed to the cordless phone hanging on the kitchen wall as he stepped toward it.

"No," Mateo said, leaping to his feet in what appeared to be a jolt of panic from losing control of Ben. "Voy a darte un paseo." He offered to give Ben a ride. "Grande aeropuerto 350 kilómetros."

Ben calculated the figure into miles. Over two hundred miles to a large airport. "Pequeño aeropuerto?" Playing along, he asked about a smaller airport closer in distance, wondering if Mateo would lie about Apartadó and say there wasn't one.

"Sí. Pequeño aeropuerto thirty kilometros," Mateo explained a small airport was only eighteen miles away.

"Dónte? La ciudad?" Ben asked what city, surprised to hear the truth from the con artist's mouth.

"Apartadó." Mateo dug keys out of his front pocket.

No wonder I couldn't find the truck keys.

Apartadó was on the way to Medellín, so once Mateo dropped him off at the Apartadó Airport curb and drove away, Ben could catch a ride to Medellín.

But…what was the Colombian's exact job here? Something more sinister than sinking a sailboat to hide it from law enforcement? It seemed highly unlikely he'd simply drop Ben off anywhere, unless it was to bury his dead body in a remote grave.

"Apartadó Airport." Mateo opened the screen door. "Sí?"

Waiting for a taxi to arrive in this secluded area wasted precious time Sara didn't have. The thought of leaving Felipe behind here in this environment caused Ben to picture himself punching Mateo out cold and removing the boy from his unsafe home.

Yeah? Then what? Then what?!

I can't take him where I'm going.

"Ella es bien?" he said to Mateo, asking if the passed-out woman was okay, thinking of Felipe's safety alone with someone unable to properly care for him.

Mateo glanced at the woman on the couch, slapped the air. "Ella esta bien. Ella siempre toma una siesta en la mañana," he said, explaining his wife was fine and always took a morning nap.

Got it. She just sleeps and drinks.

"Que tai tu hijo?" Ben pointedly asked *What about your son?*

"Está bien."

He's fine? No, but I get it—this isn't fine, but it's normal for the little guy. I get it all too well.

"Felipe?" Ben spoke the boy's name to gain his attention, and he did. "Adios." He waved at him, conflicted about leaving him behind.

I can't take him where I'm going.

For now, the boy was safer here instead of amongst any crossfire. Ben had no idea how things would play out.

He stuck out his fist to the little guy. Felipe punched it with his own.

"Vamonos." Mateo waved his hand in the opened door, urging Ben to head out first and now.

Play along. Play it cool.

Ben didn't hesitate; he simply walked out the door and headed toward the truck. As he passed the front license plate, he made a mental picture of it before climbing into the passenger front seat.

Mateo slipped behind the wheel. A slight bulge appeared at his waistline, midback. A bulge shaped as a handgun. Ben didn't have a firearm, but he had two knives.

A mile down the dirt road, it remained quiet on their drive. No shared small talk. No further cordial game play. Even if Mateo knew Jason's current location and ultimate destination, Ben could probably only drag the info out of the man if he put a knife to his throat.

What if I ended up killing him? Could I really live with killing Felipe's father?

A village in the distance came into view. Another half mile, they drove nearer to it.

"San Juatania?" Ben pointed at the windshield.

"Sí."

Ben needed supplies and a ride. San Juatania seemed just the place to obtain both. Why wait? The sooner the better to ditch Mateo.

The dirt road ended and turned into a paved two-lane road. A street sign stated San Juatania was only a quarter mile away.

"Parar en el pueblo. Tienda…para comprar algo ami novia." Ben asked Mateo to stop in the village so Ben could buy something for his girlfriend, an excuse hopefully the Colombian wouldn't confront as a lie.

"Pero en el aeropuerto."

"Airport too expensive. Mucho dinero."

No response. More silence. The tension between them thickened. It was like the calm before the storm of battle.

They neared the exit for the village. From that view San Juatania resembled a flea market. Outdoor vendors in the dirt streets, various stores in buildings behind the varied vendors. All deco adobe Spanish. Quaint.

Had Sara been here?

"Mateo? Taxi al aeropuerto from San Juatania."

"No. Mí aeropuerto. Entrar en aeropuerto." Mateo explained he planned to go inside the airport with Ben and watch him board the plane.

Terrific, the fisherman wouldn't leave him alone until he flew out of Colombia.

"No, Mateo." *Playing along with the airport thing is wasting even more time.* "No." Ben pointed to the village. "San Juatania."

The truck spun off onto the shoulder, gravel kicked up at the sides.

"Whoa," Ben said.

The truck skidded to a stop with a shriek. "Let's cut the crap, Ben," Mateo said in perfect English, drawing his firearm from his backside and pointing it at Ben. "I'm done playing stupid."

Hardball now. Fine. "More stalling, Mateo, or do you plan on firing a round at me?"

"Is it necessary, or will you do as you're told?"

"Which is what?"

"I drive you to Apartadó. To the airport there. I'll buy you a ticket home. You leave. No talking to the cops. No going after your dad. Just leave, and go on with your life. Forget everything that's happened. Forget your father."

"I can't just *go on* and forget the crimes his committed." Ben couldn't fathom his mom going along with any of this criminal activity, especially holding a female paramedic hostage. "I can't just *go on* and forget my mother. Where is she?"

"I don't know. Why do you think I would know?" Mateo answered too quickly, just like a lying scumbag, and his face was blank when the sudden change in topic should've confused the Colombian.

"I thought you were done with the stupid act, Mateo? Do you or do you not know where my mother is?"

A breathy pause with a tense jaw line. "Jason is my friend."

"After all you're doing for him, I'd hate to think he was your enemy.

Mateo, he's your friend, but he's *my father*. I want to help him. Help him turn himself in before he's gunned down."

"He doesn't trust you."

"He's not thinking straight right now. How well do you know him?"

"Well enough. He will avoid prison at all costs. Sounds like straight thinking to me."

"Mateo...where's my mom?"

"I don't know. Why do you think I do?"

Ben needed another tactic angle, a straight forward one. "Did he ask you to kill me?"

"He asked me to drive you to the airport, make sure you get on a plane headed to Florida, and that's what I'm gonna do."

"You really want to get deeper involved in his crimes? Did he pay you well enough?"

Silence as the Colombian continued pointing a gun at Ben with a steady hand.

"Mateo, I'll pay you two thousand American dollars to help me help him."

"Two thousand?" Mateo said on a chuckle, either because the amount was miniscule or he didn't believe Ben had it.

"Yes, two thousand." Jimar Malcolm had already transferred the two into Ben's bank account. The other eight would never get transferred, but so be it. He no longer wanted a cent.

"You got it with you? In cash?"

"No, Mateo. But I can—"

"Forget it. I don't hurt my friends, gringo."

"Obviously *I'm* not a friend of yours. Still, stop pointing that gun at me. Lower it, Mateo, nice and easy."

"Don't think so. Ben, you can be bought. Especially since going home gives you the chance to avoid any accomplice charges. Jimar Malcolm is the only person who knows of your involvement, and he won't tell anyone. If you know Jimar, you know he hates talking with the police. So...what do you say?"

I can't leave Sara in Jason's hands.

Ben couldn't assume the Colombian police would trek after Jason and safely extract Sara from his control.

I can't leave Sara.

"Ben, if you avoid the cops and just fly back to Florida, your dad will give you an additional five thousand. Total of fifteen. Just leave. Leave now. You don't have a choice anyway. I'm not giving you one. You are going to the airport and gettin' on a plane for Florida. Understand?"

Ben pictured himself whipping out the steak knife and stabbing the Colombian, but an image of Felipe flashed in his mind—the boy beside the grave of his father, Mateo. Ben couldn't kill the little guy's papa, regardless of the fact the man was a criminal and a bad father.

"Mateo, do you think you're gonna push me around inside an airport at gunpoint and force me to board a plane?" Ben chuckled. "How will that work?"

Mateo cackled as if mocking Ben. "It wouldn't. That's not the plan. Ben, take the money and the plane ticket home."

"Or...?"

Mateo chambered the first round.

The cell phone inside Ben's pocket rang.

The sound distracted Mateo, and the gun drifted a bit.

Ben grabbed the man's gun-arm, shoved it to the side. Mateo slammed his fist in Ben's right eye. The punch caught him by surprise.

The phone rang a second time.

Ben grabbed for the gun, nearly swiped it from his Mateo's hand.

Another punch, this one to Ben's nose. Seeing white stars, he reached behind and underneath his shirt and whipped out the steak knife. He pressed the end tip to the Colombian's skin over his trachea. Mateo froze.

"Keep your arm down, Mateo. You point that gun in my direction, I will slice open your windpipe."

With his free arm, Ben reached behind, fiddled around for the handle and popped the door open. He jerked backward, out of the truck, backpack hanging off his shoulder. He slipped down to the ground, out of the Colombian's sight.

A bullet whizzed by Ben's ear, holed the half-opened door.

He leaped away from the truck and lurched forward, skidding down an embankment several yards. The cell phone continued to ring as he bounded up to his feet, jumped over a bush, and took off in a run toward the San Juatania exit.

A truck's engine roared behind him. Ben glanced over his shoulder.

Wide-eyed and heart in his throat, he watched as the blue truck gunned right for him, his body the target.

Ben darted off road, crossed onto the dirt, dodged left into a patch of brush trees and thick flowery bushes—jumped over a colorful poisonous–looking snake—and ran his fastest pace.

The phone stopped ringing.

Over his shoulder he spotted the blue truck driving on the exit ramp.

Ben dashed behind a thick cropping of trees and headed for the village. Truck out of sight for the moment, in his knife-free hand, he dialed 112.

"It's me again!" Shouting as he ran, he cut the operator off, the same voice as earlier. He sucked in a breath. "Jason Keegan's accomplice—the Mateo guy—is chasing me."

"Chasing?"

"Yes, he's trying to run me down with his truck, blue, license number JXD-584." Ben sucked in another breath. "I'm running to San Juatania. Almost there."

"I see that. A San Juatania cell tower is picking up your signal."

A long buzz sounded on the phone, indicating voicemail. From Jimar Malcolm? Did he finally return Ben's call?

"Sir? I'm dispatching officers to San Juatania now."

"If they question Mateo, it may lead to finding Jason Keegan." Ben sucked in another breath. "And saving Sara Dyer's life."

Ben hung up as he rounded the first building in the village, heaving air. A convenience store three down caught his attention. Backpack slung over his shoulder yet slipping again, he dashed inside.

He grabbed a red basket and tossed in packaged raisins, peanut butter crackers, beef jerky, protein bars, and granola bars.

A quick glance out the window, but he didn't see a blue truck anywhere.

He darted down the next aisle over and dropped more stuff in the basket: a first aid kit, a bottle of acetaminophen, a container of antiseptic wipes, bottled water, batteries for his flashlight, a lighter, a travel sewing kit, a roll of duct tape, and a compass.

Inside his backpack, he had extra clothes and warm gear, even a raincoat. His socks were blood-stained but not soaked. He was thankful he was wearing solid running shoes.

He stepped to the back of the two-person line and listened to the cashier speak English to the customer in front of him. He had finally caught his wind again and steadied his breathing so as to avoid stares.

He glanced out the window again. No blue truck out there.

After twenty long seconds, Ben moved to the front of the line, slid his fully stuffed basket on the counter. "Do you know the best way to get to Medellín?"

The guy whistled. "Turbo to Medellín is the worst section of Colombia highway."

"Okay." *Too bad for me.* "So it sounds like I'd need to get to Turbo first?"

"Yep. No road from San Juatania to Medellín."

"Why's it the worst section—"

"Gringo, it's like only three hundred kilometers but takes like eight hours to drive."

Ben did a quick calculation and came up with a speed of less than thirty miles an hour. "And why is that? You talkin' traveling by bus?"

"Nope. Not just buses take that long. Most of Route 62—"

"What about traveling on the Pan American Highway, not Route 62?"

"That's what I'm trying to tell you, gringo. Route 62 is the section of the Pan American Highway between Turbo and Medellín. Much of it isn't tarmacked, and it's beat up from mudslides and stuff."

If Ben had any doubts before, those all dissipated—no breaks for him on this little journey Jimar Malcolm had coerced him into taking this week. None.

"No matter. I don't have a choice. I gotta drive to Medellín. Now."

"I'll take you," a man with a Colombian accent said from behind Ben.

Ben whipped around. "You're headed there?"

A guy wearing a checkered shirt shook his black hairy head. "No, but you'll pay me, so I'll take you."

"How much?"

"Two hundred American dollars plus gas money."

"Deal."

Sounds of gunfire boomed outside.

Everyone inside the store ducked out of reflex, except for Ben. Maybe only twenty yards from the store were two cop cars, driver doors open, cops behind each door and firing their duty weapons at...Mateo's blue truck.

Thirty seconds later the truck's windshield was riddled with bullet holes. The glass shattered. The driver door popped open. More rounds of fired bullets, these into the truck's driver door, holing up the metal something fierce. Gunfire busted the old door window to pieces. The destroyed hinges collapsed the door to the ground.

"Crazy stuff out there," the cashier said, hiding behind the counter.

"No kidding," the man wearing the checkered shirt answered.

Mateo darted around the side of a building. In pursuit, both uniformed cops bolted off, gun arms out in front.

Ben's hired driver popped outside from the convenience store.

Ben followed suit, then rushed over to the opened door of one of the police cars and snagged a handheld radio from inside.

Inside the checkered-shirt guy's jeep a minute later, Ben listened to the voicemail recording from earlier.

"Hey Little Keegan," Jimar Malcolm's voice spoke on the message. "So t'ings no' goin' as Jason planned. Dat's de breaks, mon. Kid, you deserve better dan 'im for a parent. I 'ave no idea where he's headed. If I did, I'd lead de cops righ' to de rat jerk. Did you know he set me up as bait to get dem off his trail? I won' let him get away wid feeding me to de pigs like that. He will soon deeply regret dat."

A slight pause in the voicemail message. "Charges are stacking up agins' me, Ben." A cough. "Little Keegan?"

Another cough, but it sounded forced, like a stall tactic.

"To ba'gain, I had to give you up. Sorry, kid. 'ated to do it. I 'ave always liked you.

CHAPTER TWENTY-SEVEN

With the side of his tense arm, muscles bulging in anger, Alec swiped five empty cans of Pepsi off his RCIPS office desk. All except one dropped into his trash bin with a clank. The one stray can bounced onto the linoleum flooring.

The sixty ounces of sugary caffeine had worked, but staying up 24/7 proved useless in finding Sara.

Elbows on his desktop, he buried his face behind his palms and wished his heart would simply stop beating.

I'm getting nowhere.

No leads to Sara's whereabouts. The wake of the *Persephone* nonexistent.

I just want to die. Fall asleep and die.

But I have two young sons and a loving wife.

Somehow, that didn't comfort him. Didn't soothe the constant burning ache in his chest wall. Didn't ease the emptiness darkening his soul.

"Alec?" Craig's voice interrupted his pity party. "We've got something."

Jerking upright, Alec dropped his hands and found his best friend inside his office.

"A Colombian arrest…" Craig filled him in on the brief highlights of the shootout in San Juatania between a man named Mateo and the local police.

"And this is a link to Sara how?"

"Call this number." Craig slipped a piece of paper in front of Alec.

Alec whipped out his RCIPS issued cell phone, a blocked number on caller ID. "Who is this?"

"I don't know."

Alec froze his fingers over the number keypad on the cell screen. "Then why am I calling it?"

"Some man," Craig tapped his index finger to the piece of paper, "using this cell, called the National Police of Colombia, claimed Jason Keegan beached the *Persephone* in a small coastal town in Colombia, and is dragging Sara up into the Andes. She's alive, Alec." Full-face smiling, Craig pumped his fist in the air. "Keegan still needs her alive."

Hope weaseled its way over the darkness, lighting Alec's mood. "What's this cell phone guy's name?" he dialed the first four numbers. "Who's the cell registered—"

"It's a burner cell."

Leery, he stopped dialing. "Then why are you so certain this guy's story is legit?"

"I'm not *certain*. But, Alec, he asked the Colombian police to call you, update you on Sara."

"Did he? Hmm." Alec dialed the cell number.

"Yeah?" a male voice answered after only two rings.

"Who is this?" Alec asked.

"*You* called me, buddy."

"Fair enough. This is Cayman Inspector Alec Dyer. How is it that you know where my daughter is?"

"Jason tied me up alongside her on the *Persephone.*"

Hope rising, Alec's heart pounded.

Craig scribbled on the piece of paper in front of Alec: *Friend or foe?*

Needing more time to assess the man on the other end of the phone, Alec shrugged at Craig.

"Why'd he tie you up?" Alec said into his cell. "For what purpose?"

"I'm in his way, Inspector."

Alec fought himself to maintain control and not to push the man to elaborate. Questioning was an art, and timing was essential. "How do I know you're not helping him, that this isn't—"

"I have a bullet in my shoulder."

"Jason Keegan shot you? Today?"

"Yesterday."

Gun shot wound yesterday? "You didn't seek medical care in Colombia, or did you but lied about who shot you?" Otherwise the Colombian police would've contacted Alec and informed him the hunt for Jason Keegan was on in their country after he shot...whoever this man was.

"I don't have time for doctors, Inspector. Besides, for now I'm good.

Sara bandaged up my shoulder and said the bullet is acting like a plug to control bleeding."

Alec felt his lips curve into a smile. "Sounds like Sara."

"Inspector Dyer, do you know about the Colombian man named Mateo?"

"I was just informed, yes. He's now in police custody. Where does he fit into this?"

"Jason hired him to sink the *Persephone* while I was in a drugged sleep onboard."

"Keegan drugged you?"

"Yes, so he could take off on shore with Sara in tow."

For Craig's viewing, Alec crossed out the word foe but drew a question mark next to it. "Drowning two problems at once, but that didn't happen," he said into the phone.

"Actually, Inspector, Mateo sunk the *Persephone*. Riddled her hull with bullets a couple hundred yards off the Colombian coast."

"To hide her."

"From you, from all law enforcement. Why else?"

"What is your name?" Alec asked on a cringe. He needed to work this conversation as an interrogation, but pushing this man could result in a dial tone.

"I don't see how telling you that fares well for me."

"Understood. How about telling me if *you* captained the *Persephone* to Cayman?"

Silence over the line, except for breathing…and the sound of an engine in the background. A car engine maybe, traveling on a noisy terrain, perhaps.

"Will you at least tell me where you are?"

"I'm headed after Jason."

Curious? Stupid? Something else? "Why, exactly?"

"So he doesn't escape and disappear forever."

"Trekking after Jason Keegan to apprehend him is a job for the National Police of Colombia. At the moment they have jurisdiction. Let them handle—"

"Inspector Dyer, do you really trust the Colombian police to catch up to Jason in the Andes and be in time to save Sara's life?"

Alec didn't know what to say to that. The question shocked him a bit, but the concern for Sara could be an act. He circled the word friend on the scratch paper, but wrote a question mark by it.

Craig nodded.

"I sure don't," the man on the other end of the line went on. "Jason is too far ahead and too motivated, and he'll do anything to disappear. He loves to blow things up, Inspector, and I'm not just talking about Fourth of July fireworks, although he loves those, too. He's carting a bag full of explosives. You get my drift?"

Alec ripped off a full blank piece of paper from a large yellow pad near the stapler, and wrote, *Gotta be Ben Keegan, the son.*

Why? Craig scribbled back.

Makes sense.

"Ben?" Alec breathed the name into the phone.

Silence on the other end.

"Ben, how do I know you're not helping your father?"

The silence continued.

"Ben? Are you still there?"

"Is that what Jimar Malcolm told you? That I'm helping my old man?"

"He said *you* sailed the *Persephone* into Cayman on Wednesday morning. Is that not true?"

No response.

"Ben? Talk to me."

"Do I need an attorney for this conversation, Inspector?"

"You tell me." Alec slid his PC mouse to the left and clicked, opening the research pages he'd scanned earlier and pasted into a word document after he'd questioned Jimar Malcolm for hours.

Ben Keegan, Jason Keegan's only child. Twenty-six years old. No priors. No record of any kind, not even a minor traffic violation. University of Miami grad student with excellent grades. Residence address unknown. Address on Florida driver's license no longer valid—an elderly couple owns and lives in the former house of Jason and Annie Keegan since the time the Keegans sold the house and moved to Grand Cayman Island.

"Is Malcolm out on bail, or did he waste his one call on me?" Ben said over the phone.

"He posted bail this morning."

"Then he used his one call wisely, to his lawyer. Sounds like he made a nice deal."

"Sounds like he's been busy telling you all about it."

"No." Ben whistled as if Alec had said the stupidest thing ever. "That's not how it is."

"Then tell me how it is."

"Inspector, Sara trusts me."

Taken aback by the words in the subject change, Alec shook his head. "Really? I find that extremely difficult to believe, Ben. Can you prove that statement?"

A pause.

"She shared with me why she's afraid of the dark."

Afraid of the dark? Sara? No. She didn't have a fear of the dark.

Or...did she?

<Alec had always been close with his daughter, but Sara didn't tell him everything. A more accurate depiction was to say she was a private person, something she hadn't been as a teen...before her mother nearly beat the life out of her. She was a different person post that trauma, no longer light-hearted and chatty. She refused to even hint at why Officer Scott Holland broke up with her all those years ago. Simply, she'd said, *We were happy; then we weren't.*

Alec scrambled for a response for the son of the man who held Sara captive, supposedly in the Colombia boondocks. Nothing came to mind.

"So...you want me to elaborate, huh? Inspector, being beaten and stuffed in a trash bag then left for dead in a swamp in the middle of the night would certainly cause fear of the dark in that person."

A grapefruit-sized lump clogged Alec's throat. The simplistic recap of the violence, of what his wife had done to their daughter years ago, stirred up fresh emotions and picked at his massive scar from that wound. Even if he could speak, he didn't know what to say in response.

"Is your silence an indication she lied to me about that?"

Alec heard a scoff escape his lips, and he found his voice. "You don't believe her? Ben, why would Sara lie about something like that?"

"You tell me," Ben tossed back Alec's earlier words, yet in a very different context.

Alec warned his emotions to leave his scar alone—it was a healed wound, and even Keegan snatching Sara away couldn't slice it open. "No,

Ben, she didn't lie. You claim Sara trusts you, yet you didn't believe her about something like that? That doesn't mesh."

"The last few days it's been difficult to decipher what's reality and what's not. Too many lies mixed with the truth. Can you appreciate that, Inspector?"

"What lies, Ben?"

"Jason's. He spins fabrication to suit his needs. So…Sara's *mother* really is in prison for that heinous crime? Wow, no wonder we relate so well."

Alec scribbled out the question mark by the word foe, but second-guessed it. "Ben, how do I know you're not catching up to help your father?"

"You mean other than the fact *I* called 112 Colombian emergency to alert the authorities and you of his whereabouts?" The kid's voice rose an octave. "How 'bout that instead of hanging up on you, I'm talking with you? Inspector, I don't care what happens to him. Not anymore. Trust me when I say I'm headed after them to help Sara."

The kid sounded passionate about Sara's welfare. But…was son like father? Was Ben Keegan a phenomenal actor, too?

"Why is it so important to have my trust?"

"Will you provide me with backup? With law enforcement support? If not, at least stay off my back. Leave me to this."

Here it was. The catch. "You're asking a lot, Ben."

A pent-up release of air blew out over the phone. "Is there a warrant out for my arrest?"

"What do you think?"

"I think I'm trapped in Jason's heap of serious crimes. Sara told me he killed two people—a Cayman cop and paramedic. But from what I understand, he was charged with homicide *before* both of those murders. Can you explain that?"

"Isn't it self-explanatory?"

Another heavy sigh. "I had no idea he was fleeing Cayman on murder charges. No idea."

"You expect me to believe that?" Alec snapped back. "You're saying you somehow failed to see all the flashing lights from the police barricade at the marina? Gimme a break," he punched the air, "you knew he was running from the Cayman cops."

"I thought the charge was drug possession. That's all. That's what Jimar Malcolm told me."

The twenty-six-year-old has no idea Daddy beat Mommy to death? If so, I'm not gonna be the one to tell him. If he does know, if he's playing me...what does that mean for Sara?

"From your silence, Inspector, I assume you don't believe me."

"It's difficult to believe you, Ben, since Jimar Malcolm claims he didn't know the truth either. From my shoes, neither you nor Malcolm are trustworthy."

"I can appreciate that, Inspector. But of course Jimar knew. That's why he manipulated me into taking his place in captaining the *Persephone* to Cayman."

Sounded logical. However, this young guy was Jason Keegan's son, the second to last person Alec should trust. "Ben, was your mother on *Persephone* as well?"

"No."

"Do you know where she is?"

"I don't. No. But no way is she involved in all this. Leave her out of it, Dyer. Her only fault is she's a drug addict. She would never do anything illegal to protect Jason."

"Unlike you."

"I wasn't protecting him," Ben's voice upped in volume and intensity.

"I'd love to hear that explanation."

"Inspector, Malcolm told me my parents quit drugs. For good."

"You believed that?"

"I did. Several months ago I told them both until they were done with the drugs, I was done with them. I couldn't watch them live like that anymore. Malcolm claimed they were starting clean somewhere new to be a part of my life again. They needed my help getting there."

"You couldn't turn your back on that."

"No, Inspector. I couldn't."

Understandable.

But is it true? Or is he lying only to save himself?

Craig jotted down a few chopped sentences on the yellow piece of paper.

"Ah...Ben," Alec said as he finished reading Craig's message, "I hear you believe your father is headed for Medellín. Explain how you came to that knowledge."

"The history on Mateo's PC indicates the last research was Expedia for flights from Medellín to Bogotá. The dates of travel didn't save in the history log."

Alec scribbled on a blank section of the paper: *I'm flying to Colombia.*

Cell phone still glued to his ear, he leaped to his feet and swiped past Craig, who said nothing in response to the four words but instead followed Alec out the door and down the hallway.

"We're covering the Medellín Airport," Alec informed Ben one of things Craig had jotted down.

"Local cops won't find him there, Inspector."

"No, not yet. We're giving him time to get there."

"Add more time to that. With the terrain it's an eight-hour drive to Medellín. You know he'd be stupid to travel under his own name. And he's not stupid."

Alec pushed through the doors of the RCIPS stucco building and out into the Cayman late morning warmth. "You're saying he's scrounging up an identity change, complete with passport and disguise."

"That would be my guess. When I was in high school, he helped two drug buddies of his in Florida disappear off-radar. To my knowledge both men are still free and untraceable. I never knew their crimes, so don't ask. At the time I assumed drug dealing."

"Now you're not so sure?"

"I just learned Jason is a killer, so my world where he's concerned is a house of cards."

Alec tried to push away the pity he had for the twenty-six-year-old, but it hovered like a gnat. Too revved up to drive, Alec tossed Craig the car keys.

"Dyer? I have a call coming in." A pause on Ben Keegan's end. "Interesting. It's Jimar Malcolm." Another pause. "I'll ignore him. I've got nothing to say to him. Inspector, please. I'm on your side. Sara's in trouble. She needs someone who's in the Andes, someone near her. That would be me. I'm your best viable option. Help me help her. When I bring her safely to you, I'll face whatever criminal charges against me. Just not now."

Alec popped his passenger car door open with an angry force. "Ben, if you don't follow through with your words to me," he punched the car's roof, "if you're feeding me a load of bull, I'll make sure you never again see the world outside of prison walls. That's no threat. It's—"

"—a promise. I hear you, sir."

"Do you really, Ben Keegan, the son of the man I'd like to kill with my bare hands?"

"Yes, Inspector. Every word."

Alec plopped in the passenger seat. Craig slid behind the wheel and cranked on the engine.

"Ben, how you gonna find 'em? Huh? *If* you're right, and *if* you're telling me the truth, your father and my daughter could be in any car or truck anywhere along the Pan American Highway. Do you know much about that winding mountain road? You don't even know how far ahead of you they are. What's your plan?"

"What's yours, Inspector? Sounds like you're on the move. Something I said? Are you heading to the Cayman airport?"

"Answer my question," Alec shouted, punching the dashboard. "What's your plan, Ben?"

No answer came.

A ding sounded on his cell phone. The familiar noise indicated a new incoming email. Jimar Malcolm's name was in the sender's column. After placing Ben on speaker, Alec opened the email from the Jamaican bartender.

Inspector, I believe you'll find this attachment interesting at first...then helpful.

Alec opened the attachment.

"Man, Inspector, you sure wait on an answer," Ben said over speaker phone.

"Ah...yeah." Alec scanned the attachment, a copy of an official document. "Do you have that answer for me, Ben?"

"I'm working out the details as I move."

"Uh-huh. Ben? Where's Ginger Rink?"

"Ginger...who? I don't even know who that is. A woman I assume?"

"You've never heard the name Ginger Rink?"

"No. Didn't I just say that? Who is she?"

Alec didn't know what to say. Yet.

"Inspector Dyer? Hello?"

Still didn't know. He needed time to process, time to research. "I'm still here, Ben."

"Inspector, I may lose you soon. Not the best service way out here."

"Ben? Answer me this: what makes you believe for certain Sara is still alive?" Alec's own question haunted him. He wanted proof, something to cling to. Now.

"I'm not *certain*, but I refuse to believe otherwise."

The kid's concern for Sara seemed so genuine, like he'd be devastated if she didn't survive.

"You claim your father is dragging her along with him as he travels up and through the Andes. Why would he do that?"

"He still needs her alive and with him, otherwise he would've left her on the *Persephone* tied up alongside me, right?"

"That's logical. Sure." But he wanted more to keep his hope alive.

"Inspector, are you playing dumb for a reason?"

"You being disrespectful for a reason?"

"I'm thinking he's keeping his human shield until he feels assured he escaped for good. You haven't thought of that?"

"There's no guarantee. There never is, Ben."

"We're running out of time, Inspector."

I know.

CHAPTER TWENTY-EIGHT

In the backseat of a four-door black truck on a meandering mountainous road in the Andes, Sara's headache worsened. The twisty drive on the Pan-American Highway swung her restrained body side to side like a pendulum and had caused her head to start aching hours ago. The rocky terrain prevented any speed over two miles an hour—a gross exaggeration, but she wanted out of this truck. Off this dirt road. More than anything, she longed to stride away from Jason Keegan as cops read him his Miranda rights.

If she couldn't get that, she'd simply go for several pills of ibuprofen. Chafed and caked in blood, her reddened wrists stung with throbbing pain. Seconds after Keegan had shoved her in the back of this truck, he'd cuffed her hands in front of her.

How thoughtful you are, Keegan.

The change in position from behind her to in front of her eased the soreness in her arm muscles and joints, the only bit of good news. Next to her in the backseat, Keegan held a gun on her, ready to fire at any given second. The intimidation and threat kept her from lashing out at him and from popping the truck door open a second time in order to jump out and escape him.

Soon after she'd met their driver, she covertly tried to convince the Colombian man to help her, but she realized the two men were longtime friends and accepted her efforts were pointless. This man Keegan called Diego would rather laugh in her face than aid her in any way.

The swerved road cut into the Andes at a steep incline and decline. Lush green foliage, thick and dense, welcomed viewers to enjoy the sloped sight lining each side of the road. Out the opened front windows, an array of noises from unknown animals rounded out the Colombian tropical rainforest experience.

Too bad she couldn't enjoy it.

The spectacular sight was mesmerizing, relaxing, peaceful...until she remembered the maniac who'd dragged her there against her will with the assistance of a pointed gun and handcuffs while under the influence of cocaine.

Maybe Keegan had snorted a stash on the *Persephone*. She doubted it, though, since his out of control behavior on the sailboat indicated no. She'd witnessed him and Mateo sniff lines together at Mateo's kitchen table, allowing her time to interact with Felipe, the sweet little boy stuck in a nightmare childhood. One thing Keegan hadn't lied about? Filling his system with cocaine caused his mood to lift and brought him more in control of himself. She had firsthand proof of it.

Speaking of the scumbag murderer sitting way too close to her, Keegan was fixated on one of the maps he'd printed off at Mateo's house. He studied the area outside the window, then the map again. Fifteen minutes later he again studied the surroundings and then the map.

"This is good." He tapped on the driver's seat headrest. "Here's good, Diego."

"Here?" the Colombian driver spoke in a South American accent, eyeing in the rearview mirror. "We're about twenty miles from Medellín."

"Twenty. Yep. That works. You know what to do from here?"

"That's already in progress, my friend." Diego stopped the truck without bothering to pull over to the shoulder. Not that it mattered since no one was around on this dirt road but them. She'd seen several buses, multiple SUVs, and other vehicles as they traveled, but nothing in the last hour.

She'd drifted off to sleep at one point for who knew how long, although she guessed it hadn't been too long. No matter how exhausted she was, since this ordeal had started, she struggled falling and staying asleep. Understandable, she reassured herself.

"You know the timeline?" Diego asked Keegan.

"I know the timeline."

Diego twisted around in the driver seat and handed Keegan a cell phone. "Confirm with this. You'll receive a call when the time is right. The incoming call number is the only one in the address book. Don't answer any calls unless it's that number."

"Got it, Diego." Keegan poked Sara's shoulder with the gun tip. "Out, Paramedic."

Her pinky and thumb twisted her pearl ring. And twisted.

No point in arguing or asking any questions. So, with her hands cuffed in front of her, she popped the door open and climbed out with her ankles still tied together.

She waddled around and found Keegan slapping his palm to the back of the truck. Off it drove, in the same direction…toward Medellín. Apparently the direction Keegan was headed.

Strange.

"Keegan, why'd we get out here? Looks like your friend is driving in the same direction—"

"Do you really think I'm gonna explain anything to you?"

"No. Stupid of me to ask." She scanned around. *So this is where he'll kill me.*

Not one building in sight. No civilization of any kind. No other vehicles. No other people. Just the two of them in the tropical forest of the Andes, only now they were on foot.

Standing there on the road, Keegan dropped two stuffed backpacks, one a huge climbing pack. He whipped out a knife from his pocket and rushed toward her.

This is it.

"Keegan—" A shiver of terror slid over her as she jolted away from his oncoming assault, and stumbled on her restrained ankles.

He gripped her arm and stopped her fall.

"Keegan—" *don't stab me* "—you don't need to do this."

"Yes, I do." He leaned over, swiped the blade to the cotton restraints, and freed her chafed and bloody ankles. He jumped away from her before she had the chance to kick him in the head. "You can't climb with your feet tied together." He slipped the knife back inside his pocket.

The rush of fear calmed inside her.

"Let's go." He pointed the gun barrel to a steep trail leading up mountain.

The dirt road of Route 62 snaked on the side of the peak. The foot trail dug right up it. She glanced over her shoulder. Another trail led down-mountain.

"We're climbing from here? The twenty miles to Medellín?"

"Just move."

This won't end well for me.

"So…me in front. Gun to my back. Sounds like fun."

"That's what you call fun? That's a sad life, Paramedic."

Not anymore. If I live through this, I'm going to live my life better. Not so scared and isolated.

If. That's a big if.

Keegan slipped the large pack over both his shoulders, then the smaller one just over one. "Don't make me regret taking the tape off. Get moving."

For now, she'd play along. For now…until an effective plan formed in her brain.

She stepped onto the narrow trail and studied up ahead. Her EMS boots would serve well as climbing boots, although a bit heavy with the steel toes. In this heat and humidity, her uniform would soon be drenched in sweat. "You got any shorts or a t-shirt in your backpacks?"

"Nothing in your size, sweetheart."

With her back to him, she stuck out her tongue and gagged but didn't bother to snap at him to never again call her any endearment, in a scoff or otherwise. Without concern for anyone other than himself, this man did whatever he wanted.

One foot in front of the other, Sara climbed up the trail. *For now, I have no choice.* Each step ached, her body cramped up from two days tied-up under a boat deck, then stuck all day inside a truck.

Ten minutes later her leg muscles loosened up from the stretch of unrestrained movement.

It felt good. Normal.

Normal?

She glanced over her shoulder. Keegan still trailed her by a few feet, gun out, pointed at her.

Not normal at all.

Downhill behind them the road was now out of sight. Ahead, the rocky trail dug its way uphill. The grand forest lined it on both sides. The tree tops stretched far above her head, reaching for the clear baby blue sky. Compared to inside Diego's truck, the various animal sounds were crisper and louder.

No one's going to find me out here. No one in the world knows I'm in Colombia.

Except Ben, if he's alive.

"Keegan?" she said, still climbing. "What about Ben?"

"What about him?"

"Is he...alive?"

"What makes you think otherwise?"

"First you shot him. Then you drugged him up. He was still sedated when you hauled me off that sailboat."

"I did not sedate him."

"Of course you did," she snapped back over her shoulder as she continued climbing. "Why lie about it to me?"

"Shut up, will you?"

"Fine, Keegan. I hate talking to you anyway."

"That's a relief."

Thirty minutes later her calves cramped up. The word dehydration flashed in her mind in red neon. The small amount of water Keegan handed her to drink at Mateo's and then in the truck wasn't near enough for this arduous climb, not when she'd drunk nothing the last two days.

"Can we take a water break here?" She pointed her cuffed hands to a moss-covered boulder off to the right.

"A break? We've been sitting in a truck for hours and hours. It'll be dark soon. We need to cover more mileage than this before nightfall. Keep moving."

To reach the area you plan to kill me and bury my body?

She turned around and faced him. "No."

"No?"

"No."

"Paramedic, you want to be shot in the arm just like my son?"

"Want? Yeah, Keegan," she rolled her eyes, "that's what I want."

He pointed his gun at her, chambered a round. "Is it?"

She felt her eyes flash wide open. She couldn't find her voice. What could she say to calm such a volatile person anyway? Anything she'd say from here would probably tick him off more and get her face blown open.

"I didn't think so. Don't spit your sarcasm at me, Paramedic, or I'll cover your mouth with tape again. Keep climbing. Go."

Interacting with him was like walking on eggshells. *Stop antagonizing him. Just keep him calm. For now that's my plan.* So, she followed his demand and started up the trail again.

About twenty minutes later, the rush of flowing water sounded off to the left, but the river or stream wasn't visible. She took a moment to enjoy her beautiful surroundings. The smell of wet pine and bark drifted up her nose on a deep inhale. The adoring chirps of rainforest birds and insects relaxed her tensed neck.

An hour later the sun dropped its way down farther, threatening to darken the sky before too long. Her brain still failed to conjure any kind of plan beyond play by Keegan's rules.

I'm done with this.

Mouth dry, calves cramping up, she halted.

"Problem?"

She turned around. "Other than you pointing that gun at me? Keegan, can we stop here? I need some water."

"No." He bolted toward her; she darted backward out of instinct. He pressed the gun to her deltoid, same muscle, same arm he'd shot his son. "This is going to play out *my* way, not yours."

You keep thinking that, Keegan.

But...I have no control over him. None.

Think of something. Now. Something that won't get me shot.

"What's your way, Keegan? Climb in the dark? Even though we're far from the treacherous glaciers of the Andes, climbing in the Andes's tropical forest at night isn't smart. We need to—"

"Thanks for the travel alert, my little trip adviser." He winked at her, cockiness planted across his face. "I know what I'm doing."

"I'm so reassured."

"Glad to hear it." He waved the gun up trail. "Go. Do not stop again. If you do—"

"I got it."

What's my next move?

No intelligent answer struck her. So up she went in silence.

Knee-high foliage lined the narrow trail. Some of the bushes' green tops dangled over, encroaching in the space. The sun's disappearance in the low west, plus the heavy tree coverage, darkened the area. It would soon be impossible to see her feet with each step.

"Keegan, night is creeping up," she said with a wave of panic clutching her abdomen.

Dark, it's gonna be dark soon. Pitch black darkness.

"You noticed that, too, huh?" he tossed back at her like a jerk. "Okay, Paramedic. Let's park it off to the right. See?"

She scanned to the right of her. A break in the foliage-infested area welcomed passersby to rest. "I see it." She stepped off-trail and aimed for the rest place.

At the dirt-covered ground, she plopped on a rock, her feet pointed down-mountain on the steep incline.

Keegan eyed around the area for exactly who knew what purpose. In search of some sort of cave to hide for the night?

"You're just wasting time, aren't you? Keeping hidden until you can...what? Arrange a ride to Chile or something?"

And before he takes that ride, he'll kill me, stash my body in the ground somewhere up here.

"We've been through this. Do you really think I'm gonna tell you my plans?"

Yep, he was biding his time, waiting for things to fall into place to meet his needs. He could be headed anywhere on this continent, anywhere in the world, to ultimately hide and live in plain sight for the rest of his life.

Skin overheated, Sara lifted her shoulder to her sweaty face and wiped off the moisture. Maybe it was more than just the humid heat and the exercise. Maybe her body temperature was rising from a skin infection in her wrists. Maybe she was just freaking out. No puss oozed out of the opened wounds. Red streaks circled her wrists, but that didn't mean she needed antibiotics.

Keegan dropped the smaller bag on the ground and turned his back to her. The sound of his fly unzipping gave her pause to think, and an idea took shape. As he urinated, she eyed the bag, then a boulder taller than she with foliage surrounding it.

In the encroaching darkness, she leaped to her feet, took two huge gaited strides, then kicked the bag high above the boulder. It sailed over the rock. She dashed behind it.

"What the...? Paramedic?" Keegan's voice spoke with a bit of alarm. He sniffled loudly, the sound echoing. A second sniffle, even louder. "Where'd you go?" A pause. "Toss me my bag right now, and I won't beat you senseless *when* I recapture you."

She kneeled behind the boulder and spied around the edge of it and the surrounding foliage, but didn't spot Keegan's beady little face anywhere.

Is he hiding from me?

With her hands cuffed in front of her, she unzipped the bag, spread it open to scan the array of items inside, and found the most precious things she could at this moment—firearms!

Yep, he's hiding. No wonder he's desperate to get his bag back.

An opened plastic side pocket near the top caught her attention. Inside a Ziploc bag, she found coins...and a tiny key. The key to the handcuffs?

Hope-filled, she slipped the key in the lock near her wrists, and *click*, the cuffs unsealed.

Wasting no time on celebration, she yanked out a .357 Sig pistol and found the magazine cartridge full. After finding a 9mm Luger fully loaded, she clicked the safety on and stuck the handgun in her midback. She rifled through the remaining contents inside the bag and catalogued in her mind all the ammo, medical supplies, bottled water, and packaged food.

Touchdown!

.357 Sig in front of her face, she glanced around the boulder again. Still no sight of Keegan.

"Wheeeere...arrrre...yoooou?" he said in a creepy sing-song manner.

It sounded like he was crouched behind a grouping of rocks at two o'clock from her boulder.

I'm behind the fifth boulder in the second row on your right.

She held back the sarcasm—even though it would relax her, it'd fire him up and give away her position. She scanned in that two o'clock direction for any sign of a human body. Nothing.

"Just like a parent of a toddler, I shouldn't have taken my eyes off of you, even for a second."

Heart bounding, her lungs rushing air in and out, she maintained her silence. With her pinky and thumb, she wiggled her pearl ring, toying with it.

"You can't hide from me forever, Paramedic," he snapped, sing-song tone long gone.

The pistol shaking in her hand, she fought the terror squashing her confidence. She hadn't fired a weapon in over eight years. If Keegan clobbered her, somehow gained control over her again, would he finally just kill her without hesitation?

"I should've killed you earlier," he hissed.

A rippling onset of chills spread down her arms.

It's like he read my mind, heard my thoughts.

Instead of freaking out and hiding in silence, she needed to command the conversation, intimidate *him*. Draw him out and blow him away.

The .357 still aimed in front of her face, she warned her hand to get a grip and stop shaking.

I can do this.

She scanned around for Keegan again. "So why didn't you?"

Keegan's head peeked out from a group of rocks at two o'clock, then disappeared the split second he spotted her. "I don't have the luxury of taking any chances. I may still need you, my little human shield. I wasn't sure I was free of cops yet. I'm still not sure."

"You're right. You aren't."

"How's that?" the voice behind the rocks snapped. "You know something I don't?"

"*I'm* a cop, Keegan."

"A cop? That's not possible." A pause of silence. "Are...are you saying you're undercover?"

"I'm a former cop. Florida State Patrol."

"You're telling me you left the force and became a paramedic? That's—"

"The truth. So, Keegan, how's this going to play out?"

CHAPTER TWENTY-NINE

In ongoing silence for endless hours, the checkered-shirt guy continued to drive the old truck on the tedious dirt road curving around in the Andes. Impressive—Ben was doubtful the beat-up hunk of metal could make it this far. In the passenger seat, he studied the printed map zoomed in on a one mile radius, then he scanned the surrounding area to the left of the road leading to Medellín.

We're getting close.

"In about another mile, drop me."

"I thought you wanted to go to Medellín?"

"Not all the way. Drop me just up ahead."

"Here?" the hired driver pointed at the windshield. "At sunset?"

"Yeah. Here. At sunset. We're hours yet from darkness."

"It's your money."

They chugged their way up over the crest of a hill. Just beyond it three Colombian cop cars sat parked on the road's shoulder. No cops anywhere in sight. Ben spotted the trail leading up the mountain on the left side of the road and a trail leading down-mountain on the right.

"Okay, drop me here. Here's good."

"You hang with cops?"

"If the situation dictates for it."

"Whatever." The driver pulled over to the side of the dirt road behind the last Colombian police SUV and shoved the gear into park.

Ben handed him all the cash he had left and climbed out of the truck. "Thanks for the ride."

"Thanks for the cash."

The truck swung around and headed back the way they'd traveled the last several hours. San Juatania to Medellín wasn't even two hundred miles total from each other, yet with the road so rocky and barely maintained, the journey took three times as long as it would've on a paved highway.

And Medellín was still another twenty miles plus from here.

After gulping down two more acetaminophens with a swig from a bottled water, Ben jogged up the trail, his shoulder throbbing. The pills barely lightened the pain, and the relief wore off way too soon, but he'd hate to think what he'd feel like without the generic Tylenol. He was lucky the village store back in San Juatania carried the medication. After this mess was over, he'd need surgery ASAP to remove the embedded bullet.

He was still trying to grasp that Old Man had shot him.

The trail wasn't a steep incline to his standards—he jacked up the incline on the treadmill at University of Miami daily for forty-five minutes. Even so, after about only twenty minutes on this trail, he was growing winded and exhausted, mostly from a lack of food, fluids, and sleep the last two days.

Too bad. He had ground to cover in order to catch up to the old man.

He also had a phone call to make before no signal existed out here. Cell in his hand, he dialed Inspector Dyer as he continued to jog.

"Ben?" the inspector answered after one ring, static fuzz on the line.

"Is the signal spotty on your end?" Ben huffed and puffed as he continued up the mountain, the pain in his shoulder a deep throb, but the bandage still white.

"Some. Not terrible, though."

"Dyer, the Colombian cavalry went in, up the trail in pursuit of Jason."

"How many uniforms?"

"Not sure—" Ben sucked in a breath "—but I found three parked National Police of Colombia SUVs at the trailhead. The one I told you was on the map Jason printed out. I already texted you those coordinates."

"Based on the dispatch time, the uniforms can't be far ahead of you."

"That's what I'm thinking." Ben leaped over a fallen tree branch lying across the trail. "I'll catch up to them, and to Jason and Sara." *She's got to still be with him.*

"Ben? Any ideas on why he'd be so sloppy at Mateo's house?"

"You're considering the possibility of a trap or wild goose chase? Jason trusted Mateo to either drown me inside the *Persephone* or drive me to the airport for a flight back to Miami. My old man assumed I'd never search Mateo's PC, assumed cops would never discover he docked in Colombia."

Ben huffed and puffed to catch his breath. "Still trying to figure out if I'm on your side or not, huh?"

"Of course. But so far you and everything you've told us checks out. It also seems you're right—with little coercing, the weasel Mateo revealed to Colombia investigators that Jason is trekking through the Andes."

"The confirmation is encouraging, Inspector, but I find it difficult to believe Jason told Mateo where he's headed. My father wouldn't tell any-one, to make sure he wouldn't be found."

"The information wasn't exchanged between Mateo and Jason." The static on the line worsened. "Mateo simply based it on the gear and supplies he handed Jason, per his request."

"Oh." *Makes sense.* "Inspector, where are you?"

"Just landed in Colombia. I'm headed your way. Ben? What'd Jimar Mal-colm want earlier when he called? Did he leave you a voicemail?"

"No."

But he sent me the oddest text message after I'd ignored his incoming call.

What did the text mean? Ever since it popped up on his phone, Ben couldn't fathom any possible answers, not that he had much time since to ponder it. Why would Jimar ask something like that? Maybe autocorrect on the guy's cell changed the intended message to the bizarre one?

"Inspector, what all did he say to you?"

"Some topic in particular you're driving at, Ben?"

"Dyer, is there something you know that I don't?"

"About?"

Gunfire echoed in the mountain air.

"Did you hear that?" Ben picked up his pace, pushing his body to the max.

Sara?!

CHAPTER THIRTY

The psycho just missed the side of my head.

Sara's right ear buzzed from the bullet that ricocheted off the top of her cover boulder and struck the tree trunk behind her, splitting bark chips.

Part of her considered telling Keegen he didn't need her anymore, so by all means take off and leave her alone. The cop in her refused to encourage him to escape. She'd no way allow him to ditch incarceration for triple homicide and avoid what he deserved—a life-term prison sentence. If not locked up, he'd kill again. The last few days proved he'd kill anyone in his way.

"Paramedic? I regret cuffing your hands in front of you."

"I bet you do." How long could this standoff continue? The hint of darkness drawing near toyed with her mind.

Don't think about it.

"Crafty how you snagged my pack and darted behind that rock with cuffed hands. Do I have enough ammo in there for you?"

"All I need is one bullet."

"I doubt that, Paramedic. I'm sure your time off the force spent in EMS has made you a rusty shot, and I'm guessing you weren't any good in the first place."

"Guess again."

Ben ran over a hillcrest, and down slightly. Then the trail leveled out a bit. A man stood in place on the trail up ahead, chugging from a canteen. A few more running steps, and Ben noticed the navy blue uniform—a cop's uniform—on the man.

The last conversation Ben shared with Inspector Alec Dyer popped up in his head.

Are you still trying to figure out if I'm on your side, Inspector?

Of course, Ben.

This police officer just might place him under arrest. Probably not, but it was a possibility he'd rather avoid.

"Perdóne, señor." Ben jogged around the uniformed cop. "Buen dia a escalar, no es asi?" he continued, asking him: *Isn't it a nice day to climb?*

For an idiotic split second, Ben thought about swiping the cop's gun from its holster. A pocket knife and a steak knife may not be enough to stop Old Man.

I'll make it enough.

The officer bent over, huffing and puffing. He plopped down on a rock and waved his hands as if to stop Ben, so he upped his speed and ignored the cop.

The officer said something in a breathy panic. The Spanish word el peligro—danger—was the only word Ben comprehended.

Ben kept on running.

After another hundred yards or so, he glanced over his shoulder. The panting cop was no longer in sight.

Where were the other Colombian police officers?

Ben continued through the tropical rainforest in a run. Pain shot up his legs from his ankles. Red swollen rings encircled the skin. Luckily, no thick yellow gunk seeped out of the cuts infected by the dirty sailing rope. Just redness on his wrists, no oozing puss there, either.

Another half mile or so, he found another cop in uniform, sitting on the ground next to the trail. He cradled his right foot as if he'd sprained his ankle.

"Está bien?" Approaching the officer, Ben asked if he was okay.

Without waiting for an answer, Ben passed him in haste. He didn't plan to stick around and offer help, since the injury was apparently minor.

He'll live.

The Colombian officer rattled off a bunch of Spanish words, too fast for Ben to comprehend, but he picked up a few: *cautious, situation, armed criminal.*

As the cop continued steamrolling in Spanish, Ben continued on in a run. Less than a minute later, the cop's shouts faded into silence, and he disappeared into the foliage of the rainforest. Ben scanned the area ahead, searching.

Where are you, Old Man?

The image of his father shooting Sara played over and over in Ben's mind, offering an explanation for the earlier gunfire...and causing anger to boil in his blood vessels.

The roaring flow from a river sounded off to the left somewhere, but he couldn't see it.

With every running step, his shoulder pulsed in throbbing pain. At times it was so severe, nausea warned him the wound could no longer be ignored. When he focused on the memory of Sara's pretty face, her stunning eyes, her kind demeanor, he was able to put it out of his mind—a distraction to subside the pain.

Helicopter blades whirled overhead, faint but clear enough.

Not a smart move, Inspector Dyer.

Ben dialed on his cell, but there was no service. He whipped out the hand radio he'd snagged from the cop car in San Juatania, turned it on, and pressed the button on the side.

"National Police of Colombia? Can you hear me?"

Static and crackles over the short wave radio frequency.

"Who is this?" a male voice asked.

"Are you the Colombian police?"

"Yes. Authenticate your ID."

"I'm not a Colombian police office. I'm the civilian heading after fugitive Jason Keegan."

"How'd you obtain the radio—"

"Does that really matter? Look, who ordered the helicopter? Not a smart move. Jason Keegan could blow it up from the ground. Sir, pull that copter out. Pull it out now."

"The National Police of Colombia doesn't take orders from you."

"You're working with Interpol and Cayman Inspector Alec Dyer, the crazy son-of-a—" With a lift of his finger from the button, Ben cut himself off and regretted losing his temper.

A silent minute passed by over the radio as he continued running, and kicking himself for allowing panic to consume him a moment ago.

"Sir, are you still there?" a voice spoke over the radio.

"I'm here," Ben replied.

"Inspector Dyer is on the line to speak with you."

Dyer? *Oh. Great.*

Radio still in hand, Ben waited to hear Sara's father through the device.

"Ben? You're talking to the crazy son-of-a... What can I do for you?"

Out of embarrassment and avoidance, Ben decided to ignore Dyer's greeting. "A helicopter, Dyer? That's the plan? It's a bad move, Inspector. Not smart. You're gonna get your daughter killed and stuff blown up around here. Call off the chopper. Now." He lifted his finger to hear the inspector's reply.

"Sounds like you're protecting Daddy."

"We're back to that?" Ben snapped. "Really? Fine. You figured me out, Inspector. You're too smart for me."

"Knock it off, Ben."

"Call off the chopper, Dyer."

"I didn't order it. It's just a fly-by, has nothing to do with Keegan. Relax."

"You know that for sure? Maybe the Colombian police ordered it."

"To spot Jason? Not that I know."

Ben stopped running and studied the helicopter overhead. It hovered in place, maybe two hundred yards north behind him. Six parachutes billowed out. Bodies dropped, legs dangling underneath each.

"Guess what, Inspector? Six people just parachuted out. Sure appears to be law enforcement of some kind."

Inspector Dyer exhaled a heavy breath of obvious irritation. "Reinforcements, I assume. I didn't know about this."

"Jason isn't going to respond well."

"I agree, but *how* he'll respond is the question."

"It's possible they're here to help him. What do you think?"

Before Ben could hear the inspector's response, a whiz hissed on the move somewhere in the sky. Like a Fourth of July firework at an annual professional baseball game.

A pop burst.

The chopper exploded into fiery pieces. Gray smoke billowed.

Ben's heart skipped a beat. Wide-eyed, he froze, his chest stopped exhaling and inhaling.

"Dyer?" Ben shouted into the hand radio. "They aren't here to help

Jason. He just toasted the helicopter! It must've been him. Copy?" He lifted his finger off the side button.

"Copy that, Ben," Dyer said in an angry growl. "What all can you report?"

Ben paused before speaking, the reality hitting him. "Wreckage pummeled at least two of the parachutists. No way those guys made it."

"How far do you think you are from the place of detonation?"

"You're asking where is Jason's location? Hard to tell. Several miles south of me, at least."

"What are your coordinates?"

Ben consulted his compass. "6.349421 and -75.684128. Dyer? She's still alive. Sara is still alive."

"Why do you say that?" Hope spilled out with the Inspector's words.

"I refuse to believe otherwise."

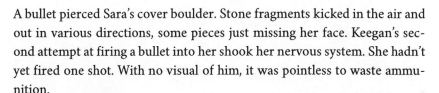

A bullet pierced Sara's cover boulder. Stone fragments kicked in the air and out in various directions, some pieces just missing her face. Keegan's second attempt at firing a bullet into her shook her nervous system. She hadn't yet fired one shot. With no visual of him, it was pointless to waste ammunition.

"What's your plan, Keegan?" she shouted behind her hiding spot. "Blow up everything that flies over us?" She still couldn't fathom it, couldn't wrap her brain around the fact he'd blown that helicopter down, along with the people who'd parachuted out.

Determined. Ruthless. Crazy self-absorbed nut bag.

"What did you do, Paramedic?" he shouted back in a rage. "How'd you do it? How'd you give away our position? Our location? How'd you draw the authorities here? Do you have some kind of tracking device on you? Is that—"

"You just gonna fire an endless barrage of questions at me? I didn't do a thing."

"You're lying. A helicopter—"

"You want to explain how I could've done anything without your knowledge? I've been tied up and at your side since Grand Cayman Island."

I need to draw him out of hiding somehow, if even just a portion of his body. Preferably his head.

"Keegan? Are we gonna do this until we either run out of ammo or fall asleep?"

"What do you suggest, tough girl?"

What do I suggest?

"No answer to that, huh? You know what, Paramedic? You need to fire ammo in order to run out of it."

"Is that how it works? Thanks for the insight, Keegan." She ignored the urge to play into his coercion. If she released her anger and fired at him, she'd only waste ammunition. "Keegan? I'll ask again—how's this going to play out? Clearly you could blow me up, I get that. So where do we go from here?"

"Obviously we've got company. Your cop buddies are advancing on me. So I need you alive."

"Then stop shooting at me."

CHAPTER THIRTY-ONE

Cracks of rapid-approaching footfalls forced Ben to whip around, steak knife out in front of him. In the dusk-lit warm air, two men dragging parachutes attached at their waistlines rushed toward him.

"Hands up," the one in front said, aiming a handgun at him.

"Whoa," Ben lifted his arms above his head, knife still in his right hand, "easy with that gun. Who are you two?"

"Who are you, sir?" the same guy retorted.

The other man said nothing as he, too, pointed a firearm at Ben.

No way out of this. If I run, I'll be shot. "Just trying to help a female paramedic held captive by Jason Keegan. Is that why *you're* here?"

"Ben?"

Not knowing what to say, Ben didn't respond.

"I'm Cayman Inspector Craig Hillman. I work with Alec Dyer. Sara calls me Uncle Craig, that's how close I am with the Dyer family."

The muscles eased in Ben's tensed-up shoulders and neck.

Hillman? The name sounded familiar. Hillman. Hillman. Aha, yes, the voice on the other end of the radio from Old Man back on the *Persephone* as they sailed away from Cayman.

"Don't tell me," Ben pointed to the sky, "an Interpol tactical team flew in via helicopter to drop in after Jason."

"Fine. I won't tell you that."

Not a smart move, Hillman.

Ben decided to keep the comment to himself. Not only was the inspector pointing a firearm at him, he'd just lost fellow law buddies in that explosion. Not a good time to tick him off.

The man standing next to Hillman maintained his silence.

Hillman raised a handheld radio to his face. "Two in position," he spoke into it. "Hillman and Tinsdall."

"Copy that," a voice over the radio spoke. "The other four?"

"They're down. The helicopter explosion took 'em out. No rescue. Recovery only."

Meaning all four are dead.

"Copy."

"You're our inside man?" The other guy, Tinsdall apparently, broke his long silence and finally spoke to Ben.

"Ah..." Ben's mind raced for a response, "if that's what Inspector Dyer is calling me." He shrugged. "Sure. That said, I'm gonna lower my hands now. How 'bout you two lowering those guns?" Without waiting for a reply, he eased his arms down, slipped the knife handle in his waistband at his mid-back.

"What's your intel?" Tinsdall asked Ben, not lowering his pointed gun.

Hillman didn't lower his firearm either.

Ben eyed Tinsdall straight on. "I'm guessing you're well aware Jason Keegan is a cop killer and explosives expert. What else do you need to know?"

"How to ambush him."

"Ah...couldn't say. I'm a lab chemist. I can tell you he'd never go off trail. If we stay on this," Ben pointed south behind him, "we're following him. But listen, when we catch up to him, you can't push him. He'll have no problem killing Sara before shooting himself in the head."

"Then what do you suggest, man in charge?" Tinsdall's ego sounded bruised.

"I'm not in charge. *Jason* is running this show."

Gunfire rang out south of them, echoing in the sky. Ben whipped around.

A second shot.

A third.

He took off in a southbound run, ignoring Hillman and Tinsdall and their guns pointed at him.

Sara fought against the dire inclination to dart over to the shot Colombian cop lying lifeless on the ground.

There's not a thing I can do for him, no pulse to verify. He's dead.

Keegan had fired first but missed the approaching cop. The uniformed officer had fired back, hitting the boulder protecting Keegan, who then fired his rifle again and struck the cop in the face, exploding his head like a pumpkin. It reminded Sara of the Zapruder Film, of the horrific view of that final gunshot in 1963 the day President Kennedy was killed.

If I don't draw Jason Keegan out and shoot him, his killing spree will continue.

In law enforcement and EMS, she'd seen his kind countless times. He'd kill anyone in his way to get his way.

The cocaine he'd snorted with Mateo that morning, and the lines he'd sniffed in Diego's truck, no longer kept his violent bursts under control.

"Keegan? You got any more coke?"

"You want some?"

"Not for me. For you. You're right, it—"

"—makes me nicer?"

"Is that the new term for less violent? I didn't get that memo." She couldn't help spouting off her mouth. She despised sweet-talking and brown-nosing. But she wasn't ignorant to negotiation. "Keegan? No one else needs to get hurt." *Killed.* "Let's figure out a way we can make that happen. What is it that you want?"

"You know what I want."

"Then go. Leave."

Jason Keegan listened to the woman's words, and scoffed to himself.

Yeah, right, Paramedic. So you can seize the opportunity to fire a bullet into my spine.

He had no idea how good a shot she was since she hadn't yet fired. So, she was either patient and methodical or just biding her time until more of her pals arrived.

The cops would never stop hunting him. They'd do everything and anything to capture him and rescue their precious paramedic, a former police officer.

And I'll do anything to escape.

He could no longer park himself here until his new identity and passport were developed. Change of plans, yet again. He had to move, and now. The Andes contained endless nooks and crannies where he could hide out for days without even one human being finding him, but he needed Paramedic alive. Still needed her as his human shield, just in case. Killing her did the opposite of benefit him, and there was no reason to silence her—she knew nothing beyond what the authorities knew about him. Just like inside the ambulance and on the *Persephone*, he needed her in the Andes until he safely scrambled away and forever disappeared.

"If you leave with me, no one else gets hurt," he yelled out to her. "No more gunfire. No more explosives. Toss out both the 9mm and the .357 onto the ground and leave with me. Deal?"

She didn't say anything. No movement. No sound.

"Make a decision, Paramedic."

With her at his side, the authorities would be cautious. They wouldn't attack him in any way that placed her in any potential harm.

But will she surrender herself over to me?

If he stayed much longer, continuing to coerce her, he risked being apprehended.

"Keegan, how do I know you won't shoot me down after I dump my weapons and approach you?"

"You don't, other than understanding it'd be real stupid on my part. I need you, Paramedic. Alive. Tick-tock. What's your decision?"

"Jason Keegan, you're under arrest," a male voice shouted off to the right in the near distance.

In that direction, Jason spotted three human figures on the run toward him. He aimed his Barrett M82 at the one closet to him and fired.

The assault rifle exploded the man's chest open at the base of his throat. The body dropped to the ground like a rag doll.

Gunfire whizzed near him. The other two men darted for cover, one behind a boulder, the other behind a tree with a mass of bushes surrounding the trunk. Neither man was visible, but neither had a solid shot at him either.

Jason readied more explosives. "Paramedic? Toss and go. No one else gets hurt. Agreed?"

Silence from her.

To hammer his point home to her, he assembled C4, inserting a detonator into the block. He fired it at the boulder in front of one guy. Just before it hit, causing a small but effective blast, both men darted off farther back, on the move for new hiding spots. They disappeared out of his sight before he had time to fire off any more rounds of anything.

"Well, Paramedic? What's it gonna be? You want two more deaths on your conscience? You can stop this."

"Stop talking to her, Keegan, and start talking to me."

Ben suppressed the urge to interject and speak his mind; instead, he listened to Inspector Craig Hillman shout out to Old Man. Now wasn't the time for Ben to do anything but keep quiet.

"What do you wanna talk about?" Old Man shouted back. "About how you're way under armed? Who are you?"

Behind a cropping of dense bushes and a thick tree trunk a few feet from Ben, Hillman dabbed at the blood on his forehead and cheeks from shrapnel his face caught by the exploded boulder. "You don't recognize my voice?"

A long pause from Old Man. "Should I?"

Ben rubbed off blood on his left forearm caused by several pieces of tree bark that broke off when struck by flying boulder pieces. "Hillman?" he whispered to gain the inspector's attention. "Toss me a gun."

Hillman shook his head. "Not a chance," he whispered back.

"Why not?"

"You're *his* son." Hillman pointed in Jason's direction, then chambered a round on his rifle. A pile of shell ammo lay on the ground next to him.

"I understand that, Hillman, but this is about Sara. She's over there thinking she has no control and no choice. To protect us, she'll give herself up to him. If you're the Uncle Craig you claim to be, you'd know that. We need to take him out. Take him out now."

Inspector Hillman's narrowed eyes glared suspicion daggers at Ben.

"Did you develop laryngitis suddenly?" Old Man yelled. "You still there, mystery man?"

"I'm here, and my name is Cayman Inspector Craig Hillman."

"Hillman. You're *here?* In the Colombia rainforest? Impressive, Inspector."

"Let's talk about what you want now, Keegan."

"Your precious paramedic knows but refuses to comply."

Ben watched Hillman aim his rifle around the tree trunk and squeeze the trigger.

Pow.

Old Man laughed. "Hillman, we can do this until you run out of ammo."

"Inspector, you got any explosives?" Ben whispered.

"I have firepower to match, yes," Hillman whispered back. "But I won't risk hitting Sara. She's too near him."

Ahhh...got it.

"Paramedic? If you don't come over to me, I'll blow these two guys to pieces," Old Man shouted out. "If you haven't noticed, they aren't taking the hint and retreating to the next mountain over."

"You win." A handgun, maybe a 9mm, flew out a few feet from behind the boulder where Sara's voice drifted. "I'm coming."

"Sara, no," Ben blurted out, "stay put!"

"Kid, is that you?" Old Man sounded stunned yet ticked off. "What are you doing here? You shouldn't be here. You should've taken that flight home."

Scanning around, Ben didn't spot Sara anywhere. Good, she listened to him. "Well, I didn't."

"Why?"

"You need help."

"You're here on *my* side?"

"No, that's not the kind of help I'm referring to, Jason."

"When Jimar called you, Benjamin, you agreed to help me."

"Not like this, I didn't. I didn't agree to any of this, Jason. I don't know who you are anymore. I don't know if I ever did."

"So you're here to help take your old man down. That it, college boy?"

"You're a murderer. You killed a Cayman cop and a paramedic."

Pause. "What do you want me to say, college boy?"

Anger boiled inside Ben's blood vessels. "Why? Why would you do that? *Tell me!*"

Silence, a long angering silence from the old man.

"I know you were charged with homicide *before* you killed those two public servants. So...who did you murder? Was it Ginger Rink?"

Another long pause. "Where'd you hear that name, kid?"

"A cop asked me about her. Asked if I'd ever heard her name."

"What else did the cop ask?"

"If I knew where she is."

"Do you?"

"I don't even know who she is, Jason, so that's impossible. Who is she?"

"Maybe that's Paramedic's name."

"No. You heard me call her Sara just a minute ago."

"Right. So, Paramedic? *Sara?* You're on a first name basis with my son, I see. Seems you two are pretty chummy. You think he's a good guy, unlike me?"

"Unlike you, he has a heart," Sara's voice snapped back.

"Paramedic, we both know Hillman is some sort of cop. Friend of yours?"

"Where are you going with this, Jason?" Ben shouted out, confusion swimming in his head.

"She didn't tell you. Ben, she's a cop."

She lied to me?

Or is Old Man messing with me, another tactic to benefit his cause somehow?

"So what? I know all about Sara Dyer, Jason," Ben ventured, seeking the truth from Sara. "You're right, we are chummy."

"Yeah, Keegan," Sara's voice cut in, "I already told Ben I *was* a Florida cop years ago when I lived there."

She lied to me. Why?

"Paramedic? *Sara Dyer*, is it?" Old Man yelled out. "If you don't do what I want, I'll blow the two of them up."

"You'd blow up your own son?" Hillman countered, joining the conversation.

"Hillman, you're new to our little party of three. I shot my kid in the shoulder yesterday, purposely. Paramedic? You've got one minute to comply. You know the consequences."

"Ben? Craig? Pull back." Panic poured out of Sara's voice. "Retreat now. Get out of here."

"We're not gonna do that, Sara," Ben retorted. "Regardless that you're a former cop able to handle yourself, I'm not leaving you here under his gun." He'd do whatever possible to guarantee Jason would never again get his hands on her.

Until Hillman found a way to control this situation, Ben needed to control the conversation. *Keep Old Man talking. Distracted.*

"Jason? Jimar Malcolm sent me the oddest text earlier today." Still baffled by it, Ben thought back to the exact wording without viewing his cell phone. "Asked me if I've ever seen my birth certificate. You wouldn't know anything about that, would you?"

Pause. "What kind of game are you playing, kid?"

"No game. His question confused me."

"Same here. Strange thing for him to ask."

"No kidding. In thinking about it, I've never seen my birth certificate. You handed it to the DMV when I got my license at sixteen, and you and Mom submitted my passport application when I was seventeen, preparing for that Europe summer scholarship. I've never looked at my birth certificate. Never had the need. So what's the story? What's he talking about?"

"Malcolm is stirring up trouble. Pitting us against each other."

You put us on opposite sides, Old Man. "Why would he do that?"

"Take the heat off himself."

"That makes no sense. His question is so specific. What does it mean?"

"What do *you* think it means, kid? 'Cause I have no idea."

"Bull. Was I adopted? Is that it, Jason?"

"No."

"Then what's the deal?"

"Ben? This ploy to distract me? Kid, it's nothing more than a game you and your cop friends here will lose."

"You're the one playing the games, Jason. The lying stops here and now. Tell me the truth."

Silence from him. Silence from Sara. Silence from Hillman.

Ben eyed the inspector. Did Hillman have a plan, other than hide behind a boulder and point his gun for the opportune time to fire at Old Man and take him out?

Frustration choked Ben's nerve endings and clenched his fists. "How does my birth certificate relate to what you're running from?" he yelled.

"It doesn't," Jason yelled back.

"Keegan?" Hillman interjected. "If you don't tell your son, I will."

Tell me what?

CHAPTER THIRTY-TWO

Sara's mind raced for a way to keep the conversation topic far from Ben. The here and now was not the time for him to learn his dad murdered his mom; he'd be crushed any way he heard it, but finding out like this...brutal. The mystery with his birth certificate seemed freaky, and not the time for Ben to unravel it. Even more than that, if she didn't do something, Keegan would eventually blow Ben and Craig to pieces and any additional law enforcement who showed up.

I have some control here, and I need to take advantage of it.

"Keegan?" she shouted, twisting her pearl ring. "Let's leave. Just you and me. Right now."

"Sara—"

"Lay off, Ben." She eased to her feet and tucked the .357 Sig in the front waistband of her EMS pants in clear view for Keegan. The steel rubbed against her bellybutton. With her arms above her head, she stepped out from behind the grouping of trees and her protective boulder. She kicked the 9mm farther out in front of her. "I'll go. No one else dies. Okay?"

"Just like that? Now you'll leave with me?"

"I can prevent more death. So, yeah, Keegan. Just like that."

"Sara—"

"Shut up, Ben," she snapped at him. "This isn't your decision." Arms still stretched above her head, she lifted her left leg and stepped forward, one step. With her right, another step.

"I don't like this, Sara," Craig yelled out. "You are not doing this."

"Clearly I am," she yelled back, stepping over the 9mm. "Relax."

Step by step, she eased her way closer and closer to Keegan's hiding spot behind a boulder.

Draw him out, then take him out.

She stopped walking. "How do you want to work this, Keegan?" Standing there in the open, she was exposed, vulnerable. But he didn't want her dead, at least not yet.

"Just come around the side, over to me."

Then what?

She didn't move, didn't respond.

Draw him out, then take him out.

She pictured an enormous clock with a loud second hand ticking off the seconds.

Tick. Tick. Tick.

"Where are you, Paramedic?"

"Right here in plain sight."

He didn't poke his head out like she'd hope, giving her the green light to jerk a move, withdraw the Sig, and fire at him.

A hand pressed against the small of her back. She whipped her head around...and faced Ben, smack behind her.

His index finger over his lips encouraged her to remain quiet. In his hand, the 9mm.

"You've got five more seconds, Paramedic. Get your tail back here."

Less than two seconds later, Ben and Craig's hiding area exploded in a gray puff of smoke. Tree limbs and rock fragments swelled in the air.

"That didn't give her even two seconds, Keegan," Craig's voice off to the right somewhere dissipated Sara's terror.

Keegan fired more C4 in Craig's new direction.

Sara bolted for Keegan's boulder, crouched down behind it. The Sig leading her, she peeked around the rocky edge.

Keegan wasn't there.

She whipped around, found Ben again. Squatting, he held the 9mm aimed to fire.

"Did you see where he went?" she whispered.

Ben shook his head, eyeing around.

"Paramedic? I've got Hillman. He's mine."

"Not true, Sara," Craig's voice shouted out. "Don't listen to him."

"He's lying," she whispered to Ben.

"Which one?"

"Craig," she rushed the name out in urgency. "Both their voices came from over there." She pointed to where the explosion cloud settled. "Keegan came at him."

"I will blow Hillman's face off, Sara Dyer, if you don't show yourself."
Keegan's voice.

She popped up, the Sig down along her side. The barrel brushed her
thigh.

"Fine, Sara," Ben whispered down at her feet. "I'll cover you. You draw
him out and I'll end him, but do it from right here."

"How's that gonna work? You told me you have no experience firing a
weapon."

"You gotta better plan?"

"I'll draw him out *and* take the shot," she whispered, then took a slow
step toward Keegan's new hiding spot, heart in her throat.

"Sara…" Ben spoke her name with heightened urgency in his whispered
tone, stopping her advancement. "When's the last time you fired a gun?" He
pointed to her shaking gun-filled hand.

"Cover me, okay? Just don't hit me."

"I don't like this plan, Sara. Hillman?" Ben shouted. "What's the deal,
man?"

Nothing. No response from Uncle Craig.

For a brief moment, Sara squeezed her eyes shut, grief swarming her
chest wall. Then she took a slow step forward.

"That's it, Paramedic. Keep coming. You've got only seconds before I
shoot Hillman's face."

She bolted straight toward Keegan's voice.

"Gotcha."

Sara snapped her head to the right.

Knelt on the ground, Keegan aimed a gun at her. Underneath his knee,
Craig's throat, a brown paper-wrapped explosive jammed in his mouth, his
arms trapped under his body.

Do something. Now.

She threw her body at Keegan's, propelling him in the air. She grabbed
his gun-hand. The firearm flung off. Together they skidded on the dirt, her
gun still clutched in her hand.

Tangled up together, he lodged her chin in the crook of his arm in a
chokehold. She twisted out of his grasp, but he wrestled her on the ground.
Tiny rocks and sticks dug into her back as he clobbered her gun-filled hand.

Bang.

Sara screamed out. Unimaginable pain rocked her body. Tensed up, she clawed the gun, willing the agony to subside.

Keegan squeezed off a round.

He released his grip on her and scrambled away.

Gunfire resonated in the mountain range from two single shots nearly on top of each other.

"Sara?" she heard Ben shout out her name. "Sara?"

From hip to toes, her left leg tingled. Part of it numbed. Nausea assaulted her, but she had no stomach contents to heave up. Black and white shapes floated around in her vision, her eyes flittered closed.

He shot me. Keegan shot me.

A blowout? Seriously?

Alec couldn't believe it.

Balled fists planted on his hips, he glared at the parked Colombian Police SUV lopsided on the side of the dirt road.

"The spare is damaged," Officer Gomez said, confirming what the three of them had believed when they'd taken it out of the SUV. The Colombian uniformed cop tossed the useless round rubber in the back of the SUV with an angry shove.

"I'm hoofing it from here." Alec strapped on a backpack loaded with supplies, including a multitude of weapons and ammo, and darted off on the dirt road.

"I'm with you." Detective Rojas, a Colombian detective, joined Alec at his stride, backpack on, holstered duty weapon at his waist.

"I know this mountain range well," Gomez said as he caught up to the two of them. "Up this way." He stepped off road and up the mountain. "We'll meet up with a trail."

The officer apparently not only knew the way, but the guy looked fit, like he could handle the Himalayas.

Alec held up a bit, allowing Officer Gomez to take the lead.

The dusk sky darkened the distance filled with dense forest.

"I have three head lamps if either of you need one once darkness sets in," Gomez said over his shoulder.

"Maybe the moon will be bright enough to lead us," Detective Rojas spoke up, in a bit of a huff and puff.

"I doubt that," Alec input his thoughts. "Gomez? How far, how many miles, kilometers, whatever, to those coordinates?"

"Not far. The tire blew at the tail end of our drive from Medellín. Lucky."

"Dyer?" The detective's voice drifted over Alec's shoulder. "You really believe the son is innocently caught up in this thing? That he hasn't a clue the extent of his father's crimes?"

"Detective, instead of taking off and disappearing," Alec sucked in a couple of breaths, "Ben Keegan called the Colombian police to help my daughter and capture his father." Another breath in. "Then he discussed the situation in length with me over the phone."

"Maybe just to clear his name once we catch Keegan."

"Maybe. Maybe not."

"You really think he wants his father brought to justice?"

"I think it's possible he doesn't want Keegan to kill anyone else, especially my daughter." Alec drew in more air on a pant. "I think he may be a good guy, a noncriminal. All my research so far backs that up, and every time I've spoken with him, I get that sense."

"You're thinking your daughter is still alive because of this Ben Keegan." The detective took in air. "Jason Keegan's son."

"She may have a chance out of this because of him, yes. But not for much longer."

CHAPTER THIRTY-THREE

Sara rolled onto her back from her side. Shooting pain ricocheted inside her entire body and burned in her left thigh. With all the strength she could scrounge up, she pressed her left palm over her bleeding gunshot wound, compressed her left femoral artery with four fingers of her right hand. Inside her closed mouth, she stifled the groan from excruciating pain. The agony stirred the nausea in her gut.

"Sara?" Ben dropped down at her side. "Sara...Sara!" He sounded panicked. He placed his hand over hers on her thigh wound and stacked his other hand on top with more force.

Blood seeped through their fingers and pooled on her leg's skin, coating her blown-open EMS pants leg.

I could bleed out up here in the Andes.

Her vision hazed. She blinked several times before seeing the compact-sized boulder at her right, dusk shadows splayed on it.

"Sara? You're the paramedic. Tell me what to do." Ben's voice was tight.

"Sara? Honey..." Uncle Craig's voice drifted inside her foggy ears on the other side of her.

"You okay?" she asked him.

"Are *you* okay?" He brushed her cheek with his knuckles. "I'm fine."

"Then go," she voiced her thoughts. "You have to go after Keegan. Stop him."

"Sweetie..." His voice spoke like a caring father. "I'm not leaving you like this."

"We don't have a choice." She swallowed, the burning pain intolerable. "Go. Ben's here. We can trust him. Uncle Craig? Trust him."

"I got this, Hillman," Ben interjected. "Go after Jason. Shoot him down. Right here in the Andes. Stop him from ever hurting anyone else."

Uncle Craig cupped her face, kissed her forehead. "Hang in there with us, honey." He sniffed back emotion. "Ben—"

"No need to warn me, Hillman. I'll take care of her. Bet on it."

"I'll hold you to that." Craig climbed to his feet, strapped on a stuffed pack and toed another one on the ground. "This is a med pack, a little limited." He placed a radio in Ben's lap. "Keep in touch with me. Got it? TAC Channel 18."

As Craig took off in the dusk-filled air, he slipped on night vision goggles. "Hillman here," he spoke into a second handheld radio.

"Authenticate yourself." Sara heard a voice crackle over the radio waves.

"Charlie. Yellow. Brown. Tango. Dog."

"Go head, Inspector Hillman."

"Got a GSW patient down. Send in a med chopper to the coordinates I radioed in earlier."

"Copy that."

"ETA?"

"Unknown."

"Copy that. I'm in pursuit of the fugitive. Hillman out."

"Copy. Base..." The voice faded out as Uncle Craig disappeared in the darkening night air.

Ben moved his top hand off their stacked hands. "This is a ton of blood, Sara. The bullet isn't acting like a plug here. Not like in my shoulder."

"I might have a femur fracture from the bullet piercing the bone."

Even if we control external hemorrhaging, I could bleed out internally.

The words hypovolemic shock repeated in her head like a mantra and spurred on the start of a headache.

With one hand still pressed over hers to her thigh, Ben unzipped the med bag. A flashlight leading his way, he thumbed through the supplies inside. "Sara, tell me what to do."

"Direct pressure is best to control bleeding. Second is a pressure dressing. Are there trauma shears in there? Use 'em to cut my pant leg off. Do you know how to dress a wound?"

"I'm not new to wound care. I meant beyond that, Sara." With black-handled trauma shears, he sliced open the front of her left pant leg, like a medical examiner opening a chest cavity.

"We need to prevent shock. Elevate my legs on something. A rock, maybe."

Arms underneath her, he scooted her.

"Oww…" she screamed out, her eyes squeezed shut. "Wait. The GSW is in my thigh. Don't elevate."

"GSW?"

"Gunshot wound."

"Got it. Shock from blood loss?"

"That's it." Eyes closed, picturing herself soaking in a relaxing bubble bath, she concentrated on slowing down her pulse and respiratory rate. Not panicking eased pain and helped the human body with damage control and healing.

"What about elevating your right leg? Could that help with shock treatment?"

"It can't hurt."

"How high?"

"Eight to twelve inches."

One-handed, he positioned his backpack underneath her uninjured leg.

"Apply a pressure bandage."

"How?"

"I'll walk you through it. First, feel inside the bullet hole."

"You've got to be joking."

"Please. Feel around, not too deep. It's not that disgusting."

"It's not that, Sara. We'd need to lift our hands, releasing direct pressure. That's not a good idea. Is your thinking clear enough here? Pain can—"

"Way out here, I can't follow normal protocol. I need to know…do you feel bone fragments? Loose crepitus bone? The bullet?"

"Way out here, does that really matter? Sara, it sounds like you want to know…as the patient. Step back from yourself."

She processed what he'd said. "You nailed it. I hear you. If there's any saline in the bag, use it to irrigate…" She trailed off, clenching her teeth and envisioning a pain stick in her mouth. Lightheadedness swarmed her. "Normally, I'd just focus on hemorrhage control, but stuck up here in the Andes for who knows how long, infection control is vital."

"Got it. Pour copious amounts over the wound and into the wound. Like the whole bottle?"

"Keep some of it to moisten the gauze."

"Really? Interesting. This is gonna hurt. You want some kind of numbing agent?"

"Forget an analgesic. Just go. Just do it."

Cold fluid flowed over and into her pained thigh.

She screamed inside her closed mouth.

After what seemed like forever, the burning flow finally stopped.

She noticed the near-empty plastic bottle. "Ben, grab all the 5x9s. Packaged—"

"—sterile gauze pads. I know." He poured water from a drinking bottle over his hands, washing her blood off. He dried them on his shirt, snapped on a pair of medical gloves, then ripped one gauze pad open.

"Moisten a few with saline and pack as many as you can inside the bullet hole. Then—"

"I got this, Sara. Just rest." After ripping a bunch more open and packing her wound, he stacked dry ones on top.

"Roll bandages. Get all those."

"Yep, already on it," he said, digging around inside the bag. "Found 'em."

One by one, he wrapped each white roll bandage around her thigh, covering the 5x9s and compressing them over the bullet hole.

"Okay. Now what?"

"Is there a traction splint in that backpack?" She chuckled a little.

"A what?" He peeled off the medical gloves.

"Joking. It's not gonna be in there. How 'bout any cold packs? Any cold packs in there?"

He rummaged around inside the med pack. "I don't feel anything cold."

"No. One-time use packs. Squeeze 'em and it triggers—"

"Ah. I'm searching."

Several seconds passed by with sounds of items being rifled through.

"Found some." He whipped out two white packs, squeezed, and shook them. Laid them on top of her bandaged leg.

"How about pain meds? Any of those?"

"Morphine." Smiling, he whisked out a handful of vials. "We've got morphine." He pulled out more vials. "And fentanyl."

Potent prescription opiates zonked out her mind. "No and no. Any acetaminophen?"

"No? Why the heck not?"

"I want to wait on the heavy stuff."

He yanked out a bottle of generic Tylenol and didn't question her reasons. "And I have some in my backpack. We have enough for both of us."

"Great. Two of those."

He placed two white oblong pills on her tongue, tipped her head up, and held a water bottle to her mouth. "It's possible the bullet didn't fracture your femur," he said with hope.

"Since neither of us has x-ray vision, we can't know for sure."

"It feels fractured, that it?"

"I don't know. I don't want to know, not now. I just…" She squeezed her eyes shut. "Just knowing I'm way out here, far from a medical facility of any kind, worsens the pain somehow."

He gathered her hand in his, her blood sticky on their joined palms. "I'm gonna get you out of here, Sara." One-handed, he peeked under the ice packs. "No blood is coming through. We're looking good. Did I wrap the bandages too tight? How's your circulation?"

"Fine."

He squeezed her hand with tenderness. "What else can I do?"

"Nothing. We just wait."

"Wait for the chopper."

"Yep." A fresh swarm of nausea hit her. The pain so intense, for an irrational second she wished Ben would slice off her leg.

Eighty plus times less potent than fentanyl, a dose of morphine sounded rational and logical. "Is there any morphine in capsule form?"

"I didn't see any pills other than acetaminophen. Don't trust me to give you an injection, eh? Sara, as a chemist I'm—"

"I know. It's not you. It's…I don't know." High above her, stars twinkled, the moon a perfect gray circle in the clear sky, darkening to blackness by the second. "It's getting really dark. I freak out in the dark."

"I know. It makes sense why. Sara, I'm so sorry about what your mom did to you."

"So am I."

Tell him about his mom. It's time.

"Ben?"

Her nerve slipped, courage disappeared. "How'd you find me?"

Chicken. Don't change the subject. Just tell him, you chicken.

I can't.

"The search history on Mateo's computer, and his son."

"Felipe?" The image of the adorable seven-year-old popped into her head. She'd almost escaped Mateo's house with Felipe's hand enfolded in hers while his dad and Keegan snorted away in the kitchen. A gun to the back of her head had stopped her.

"Cute kid, right? Felipe handed me your hair tie and Inspector Dyer's business card. Smart to take a chance on the son. Good call, Sara. After I filled in the Colombian police, I spoke with your dad."

"Whoa. You did? Is he freaking out?"

"You know he is."

Silence between them stretched a bit, but it wasn't uncomfortable. It was shared exhaustion and fear of the unknown with the uncertainty of their situation in the dark Andes rainforest.

"Ben? How's your shoulder?"

"Bullet's still there."

"The bandage looks good."

"You did an excellent job."

"Hand me two syringes, and I'll inject us both with some morphine."

"I don't want any, Sara. You take—"

"Wait," she said, stopping him from removing vials and syringes from the med pack. "You want to be alert out here. So do I, until I can't take the pain anymore."

Which is right now.

"All right…I can't take it anymore."

Without a word Ben followed her instructions and injected her with a dose of morphine.

He slipped the used syringe in a tiny sharps box. A sudden rush seized her, a synthetic control over her central nervous system. A few seconds later, the sensation dissipated, but her body milked the morphine to ease the captivating pain.

"Any relief yet, Sara? Is the painkiller kicking in?"

"Meds don't kill the pain, just take the edge off. It's doing that."

Could she survive out here until a rescue crew reached her? Was she bleeding out internally?

A twinge in her heart encouraged her to pray, to step into God's awaiting arms eager to envelop her with love and comfort.

Not this time. I'm still mad at You.

Day three of what seemed a never-ending nightmare, and she still couldn't believe her life was yet again being threatened at the hands of a violent individual, self-absorbed and unstable.

It wasn't fair.

No, life wasn't fair. Get over it. Accept it.

"Do you know how to pray?" Ben asked her.

She was stunned. Maybe it was just coincidental. It wasn't possible he'd heard her snap at God in the privacy of her mind a moment ago. Maybe he hadn't asked her that. Maybe her ears made up words that…what? She didn't know.

What do You want from me, God?

Maybe He wanted her to hear Him through Ben. Maybe He hadn't ignored her the last three days and…

Maybe…who knew. She was too tired to figure it out. In too much pain to care about anything anymore. She fluttered her eyes closed, giving up on herself.

"Sara? Are you okay?"

Do I look okay? Do you, Ben? Look at where we are, and we both have a GSW and a bullet embedded in our flesh.

She opened her eyes and looked up into his big brown ones. Eyes so curious and full of hope.

What an optimist.

"Come on, Sara. Tell me how to pray. It can't hurt, right?"

An atheist asking her to teach him to pray? An atheist? Hmm, that sure seemed like God's method of intervening. Seemed exactly His technique to bring her back to Him.

"No, it can't hurt."

It may not help, though.

"Just talk to God, Ben. Like a good friend, your best friend. That's it. Nothing fancy. No rules. I try to always start with praise and thanksgiving before I dive into whining, but I often forget." *Or choose not to.* "You've never prayed?"

"No."

"Ever been to church?"

"No."

"Ever read the Bible?"

"No."

A true atheist, raised and life-long. And he was asking her to educate him on prayer at the only time in her life she turned away from God, blamed Him, transferred all her anger onto Him.

Huh.

Coincidental? Knowing God the way she did, she found that impossible to believe. God's timing was perfect. Always.

How 'bout her timing?

"Ben? There's something you should know."

"About praying?"

"No. Ben—"

"Sounds serious. Later, okay? You need to rest. Just rest now."

"No. Talking with you distracts me. Takes my mind off the pain."

"All right," he spoke with reluctance. "What is it you want to tell me?"

"Ben...*before* Jason killed my partner and a cop, he was running from homicide charges."

"So I've heard."

She closed her eyes for a brief moment to gain some strength, both physical and emotional.

Spit it out. Quit stalling.

She looked up into his face. "On Monday night, Cayman police found Jason in a catatonic state at a murder scene."

"Catatonic?"

"Means he—"

"I know what it means, Sara. Are you saying he committed murder and fell into catatonia?"

"He committed murder, yes."

A few silent moments ticked by as she gave him the time to process.

Ben cleared his throat. "You're saying he brilliantly acted catatonic to avoid arrest, then successfully escaped the psych hospital to avoid facing homicide charges."

"That's it. Ben..."

Keep going; don't stop now.

"He's charged with murdering...his wife."

Ben's upper body jerked upright and visibly stiffened. "His wife?" he snapped back, his voice cracking. "Mom?"

"Yeah." Stinging tears filled her eyes. Her heart broke for him. "I'm so sorry."

Shaking his head, his brows furrowed deep. His lips curved downward in a frown as if he balanced on the fence between denial and puzzlement. "No. I don't...understand this."

She decided to say nothing more in order to allow what she'd revealed to him time to stick in his brain and form the beginning of grief and acceptance.

Staring off at something in the distance, he seemed stunned into silence. Shaken into shock.

In her head, she scanned through a list of comforting words. All fell pathetically short.

Silence stretched on, and on. Grief emanated from him, in his lingering silence, in his stiffened body, in his saddened eyes and trembling lip.

He was understandably crushed. Devastated.

He leaped to his feet, meandered a few steps away. "You knew." He looked down at her. Redness rimmed his lower eyelids. He blinked, his breathing heavy. "All this time, you knew whose murder he was charged with." His voice rose in volume, the anger stage of grief spilling out. "Why didn't you tell me sooner, Sara?" he snapped. "Why keep this from me? Why?"

"I...I didn't know how to tell you. I'm sorry."

He rubbed a shaking hand over his face. "This...it just doesn't make sense to me. He'd never hurt Mom. Never. Not Mom..." Mouth opened, he paused. No words escaped out. "But..." he trailed off.

She sensed his confusion, his reluctance to accept the facts as facts, his deep inner struggle to grasp the harsh truth. And she hurt for him. Ached for him.

Hands on his hips, he stared off in the distance again, eyes glossed over with emotion. "But after everything I heard from him on *Persephone*, everything I saw him do..." He shook his head as if disappointed and disgusted. "He isn't the same...he isn't the man I knew." Betrayal swam in his angry eyes. "The man who raised me."

"Drugs really mess with the brain."

"Sara, he's taken cocaine my entire life, for years before I was even born. No, something's changed. Something happened. Something caused him to snap. He didn't just...kill Mom during a heated argument or because being a cocaine addict altered his brain chemistry."

Sara envisioned shrugging as a way to express herself in response. She tried to actually shrug as she lay on the ground with a bullet in her thigh. "I...I don't know, Ben." She didn't know what else to say to him.

The idea that this week was nothing more than a nightmare she'd awake from toyed with her mind like a cruel delusion. And one she fought against playing into.

Leaning over her legs, he peeked under the cold packs. "Still no blood coming through. How are you doing, Sara?"

"How are *you*, Ben?"

"Do you know what happened that night?" he asked instead of answering her question. "What led to my mom's...death...?" He planted his hands on his hips again and stood like a stone statue. "To her murder?"

"I don't know anything about that."

"Sara, why'd you tell me this now? Why now?"

"I didn't want you to hear it in a malicious way, exactly how Jason nearly told you earlier."

Ben blinked once. Twice. "You stopped him. That's when you came out of your cover and surrendered to him." He stared down at her, grieving heartache spread across his face. "You didn't need to do that. You were thinking I'd jump out to attack him and get shot."

"It crossed my mind. He shot you once already, Ben. We both know he would've succeeded in nailing you and Craig with explosives."

Ben sat down beside her again. "Sara, what's the deal with my birth certificate? How's that come into play here? Twenty-six years after my birth, what does it mean now?"

"I don't know anything about that, either."

"Fine. We don't need to discuss this anymore. Rest."

"I am resting. I'm lying down, aren't I? Ben, I've told you all I know. Honestly. I wish I had answers for you, but I don't."

"I believe you, even though you lied to me about being a cop."

"Ben—"

"No need to explain. I'm kidding." He winked. "Why'd you leave the force?" he said, giving Sara the impression he needed a break from discussing the trauma whirlwind in his family.

"All the death and ugliness in EMS and law enforcement wears on you, of course, but in EMS I have the chance to reverse the outcome. To save a life. Also, I wasn't who I thought I was. Literally." She wanted him to know he wasn't alone, remind him she could relate. "After my mom dumped me in a swamp, believing she left me for dead, I crawled to the road. A mentally unstable woman picked me up."

"Mentally unstable. How'd that play out?"

"I didn't make it home to my dad until two years later."

"Two years?" He sounded incredulous, something she well understood even all these years later.

"Two years. I suffered head trauma and retrograde amnesia. I believed I was that woman's daughter, who actually died in a house fire years prior. The woman believed I was her daughter."

"Wow."

"I know." Why was she sharing this with him? "I can't believe I'm telling you all this. I barely share anything with anyone."

"Well, we've shared quite a day together. Actually three days." He smiled, a sad, lips-pressed-together smile. "You obviously healed well from the head trauma."

"I did. I recovered from brain damage. It wasn't permanent."

"Unlike the memory loss. But your memory returned two years later? Just like that? That's what happened for the sister of one of my buddies. A year after her car accident, bang, for some unknown reason, it all came back to her, except for the accident itself."

"Sometimes that's how it happens. For me...I was a cop, searching the Everglades for the remains of a teenaged girl murdered by her mother two years prior."

"Wow. Seems I don't know what else to say than that."

"No one ever does." *Including me every time I looked in the mirror as my face healed.*

Facial disfigurement was too strong a word; however, the trauma had changed her appearance to the point she no longer resembled herself. Dad had paid for plastic surgery to repair her asymmetrical cheek bones, fractured nasal bridge, and deformed forehead.

Even after all they'd been through together the last several days, Sara suddenly felt awkward around Ben, though she wasn't sure why. She turned her face away from him.

"Sara? We can stop talking about this. You need—"

"I *need* to talk it about," she said, facing him again. She swallowed, feeling herself drift down an uncharted stream, but for some reason she trusted the flow of it. "Will you listen?"

"Of course." He cleared his throat. "Of course. Sorry. I just didn't want you getting upset." He slipped his hand in hers. "Talk. I'm here."

"You're a sweet guy, Ben Keegan. You probably *were* adopted—no way you're blood-related—" She cut herself off. "That didn't come out right. Even if he is your—"

"Don't apologize. Heck, Sara, you of all people can relate to having a murderous parent. You have more to say about that. Tell me."

Where was I? Oh yeah. "While I was searching for the teenager's body in a Florida swamp, the area seemed so familiar. So eerily familiar. When the case detective told me the victim's name, it hit me...*I'm Sara Dyer.* Everything flooded back to me." She swallowed again as if unclogging her head from trapped memories haunting her mind. "I wasn't ready for it—didn't want to be ready for it—but it was time."

"What do you mean?" he asked with obvious genuine interest.

Talking it out with someone who could truly empathize—instead of only sympathize—broke through her concrete barrier separating her from the vista of healing.

"For two years, my brain didn't want to remember. Didn't want to deal with what my mother did to me. It was easier...safe...to pretend to be another person, someone loved and cared for by their mom. At least that's the Florida State Police psychologist's theory."

"It's logical."

"It is."

"I don't get it, Sara. How do you recover from something like that?"

"You don't. You learn to live with it."

"Sara, I'm not gonna hang on to this stuff with my father and learn to live with it. I've got to somehow let it go."

"It's not even over yet, Ben," she ventured as kind as possible.

His jaw line tensed in a locked and bulging position. "I noticed that," he snapped, then tilted his head up. "Where's that med chopper?"

Sara looked up at the night sky, at the darkness.

Instead of panic or fear, she felt...relief.

Relief?

Relief.

A sense of peace filled her, like a healing drug. An ointment that turned an old wound into a scar with only one application. She'd never felt anything so simple yet so powerful, so...maybe it was just in her mind.

Is my newfound inner peace just a fantasy, like my life-long faith?

Why do I doubt so today?

"Sara?" Ben stared down into her face. "You know why I don't believe in anything?"

Whoa. The timing...again. Like earlier it couldn't be coincidental.

God? Okay, I hear You. I'm listening.

Wait...she never stopped listening; He stopped responding.

"Jason actually believes," Ben went on, "and I quote: *Since Jesus died on the cross for our sins, we can do whatever we want, and it's fine. None of us are able to be good, so Jesus's death makes up for all the bad we people do.* Now, Sara, how ridiculous is that?"

"That...that is ridiculous. Sounds like justification."

"Before I was thirteen, I knew his philosophy was definitely wrong."

"But you didn't know what's right? Still don't?"

"With all the ugliness in the world, there must not be a God, no higher power that cares about people. We're on our own."

"That's your philosophy?"

"Sara, what loving God would allow an anti-addiction medication to cause cancer? My mom's best friend was trying to get clean. The only anti-addiction med for cocaine gave hundreds of patients liver cancer before being taken off the market."

"Oh. That's tragic. Very sad. Ben, you'll develop a safe and effective medication."

"Not in time. I'm too late to help my parents. Sara, what loving God would—"

"Ben, God doesn't *allow* bad things to happen. It doesn't work that way. Bad things happen. That's just life. He isn't to blame when something goes wrong."

Gulp. Wow, maybe she needed to remember that as much as Ben needed to hear it.

No "maybe" about it.

God? I'm so sorry I doubted Your goodness. Humans are like that, as You know. I apologize for myself, for all of us idiots down here. We're trying. We're all trying in our own unique way.

"Sara, you seem so certain God is the real deal. How?"

Ben's question was so blunt and powerful, it stirred fresh energy in her that had nothing to do with the combination of acetaminophen and morphine working in her system to numb some of her pain.

I'm gonna be okay. Whether I live or die on this mountain, I'm gonna be okay.

Will Ben?

Since she wasn't just referring to his medical crisis, time for the spiel she'd thought of on her own and first shared as a fourteen-year-old girl to a middle-aged woman at the county library. She'd retold it countless times since that summer day.

"It's logical, Ben."

"That's a response I've never heard before. Care to explain?"

"The components of a computer didn't form together in the air and somehow develop the first computer or any computer since, right? Humans designed computers, something complex and extraordinary." She waited a beat, for any negative reaction or recant from him. She had a spiel for any negative recant, too.

"Hmm. I'm still listening."

A typical reaction up to this point, and the less exhausting one.

Good, my pain is less, not deadened.

"But a computer, Ben, isn't alive. It doesn't feel or think. It doesn't grow, procreate, create, heal itself, or die. All living organisms were created by something far greater than humans. Think of it this way—in order for something created to be alive, something alive had to create it."

"That is a logical viewpoint. I can understand believing it."

"But you won't? You see it as *buying into it?*"

Ben's mind continued to process all Sara had said, and not just about religion.

Mom is dead? Mom is dead.

Since the moment she'd told him, he fought against accepting it, desperate to ignore it. It hurt too much. But denial had never been a crutch he used.

My dad murdered my mom.

An array of emotions entangled his heart. Grief was awful.

"Sara…" he looked down at her, swallowed.

"It takes time, Ben. Give yourself time."

To grieve? No...to believe.

Sara Dyer was the first person not to extend him the holier-than-thou attitude when discussing this topic.

It was refreshing.

Sure, he knew Old Man's philosophy was way off-base and Planet Self-Absorbed thinking, but talk to God like a best friend? That sounded hokey, bizarre, like an occult or something. And...God doesn't *allow* bad things to happen, which suggests he could stop them but didn't? That sounded like a heartless controlling puppet master.

"Sara, I'm a scientist. A chemist. Science explains how—"

"Humans created computer science, Ben. The science you're talking about? Something way more intelligent and powerful than us created it. God is something humans will never be able to truly grasp or understand. That's why it's called faith."

Huh. Solid argument, yet again. In fact, she sounded logical. And far-fetched at the same time. So...the scientist in Ben resorted to his knowledge and educational background.

And hit a dead-end.

Just like the big bang theory, the primordial soup theory was flawed. No matter how science attempted to disprove God's existence and prove the universe developed via chemical stability, in the end all theories failed at proving chemical stability possible.

"Ben, earlier you wanted to know how to pray. Now you're debating against God's existence?"

"It's an ongoing debate, isn't it? Sara, science recognizes that amino acids do not react to form proteins, and that nucleotides do not react to form DNA. That said, they must be chemically activated to react with something, but whatever the something is, this process must occur without water since the activated compounds react when in water and breakdown, so it's impossible."

She followed him easily. "My study group in medic school detoured discussing this one night. You're talking about the big unanswered question: how can proteins and DNA form if the activated compounded required to form them cannot exist in water?"

"That's it."

"Ben, you're admitting that science—"

"—can't explain how the universe—including any living organism—formed."

The radio on the ground near the bag crackled. "Inspector Craig Hillman?"

"Ben, that's my dad's voice."

"Yeah, I recognize it." Ben snatched up the radio, held it in his palm.

"Hillman?" Inspector Alec Dyer's voice again. Followed by...

An eerie silence stretched on over the radio waves. Still no answer from Hillman.

"Sara, I'm sure Craig is okay." He was? No. He wasn't sure of anything. He depressed the side button. "Inspector Dyer?" He lifted his finger.

"Who is this?"

"Ben."

"Where's Craig? Why's he not answering?"

"He's a little busy right now, Dyer. What's the ETA on that med chopper? Do you know?"

"I don't. He's busy doing what, exactly? What do you mean? Wait...this isn't a secure radio line. Watch your words. Keep it simple. Who has a GSW, Ben?"

Wide-eyed, Sara shook her head. *Don't tell him,* she mouthed, begging Ben to evade the truth.

"Sara..."

"Please. He'll freak out."

Her beautiful face looked so desperate.

"A cop," Ben said into the radio.

"Thank you," she said once he lifted his finger off the button.

"I don't like lying to him, Sara."

"Sounds like you two trust each other."

"We kinda do, yeah."

"Oh." A stunned expression blanketed her face.

"A Colombian cop? Interpol?" Dyer's voice questioned over radio waves.

"I'm not answering that, Sara. I won't extend this charade."

"Ben, where's Sara? Do you know?" Dyer's voice again.

"Here with me," Ben said into the radio, raising a spread palm at Sara as a warning to let him speak his own words.

"Seriously?" Dyer again.

"Seriously."

"Ben." Sara waved her head toward her chest. "Lemme talk to him."

He placed the radio in front of her face and depressed the side button.

"Hi, Dad." She gripped the radio, taking it from him.

"Sara, honey!" Relief spilled out of his voice. "Where are you? How are you?"

She pressed her index finger to the button. "Out from under the control of a killer. Thanks to Ben." She smiled up at him as she released the button.

He didn't know how to react to what she'd said, so he didn't at all.

"You're really okay?" Dyer asked.

"It's been a nightmare," she said, obviously striving for vague.

"What's happening, Sara? Where's Craig?"

"Chasing Jason Keegan."

"Honey, you don't sound good."

"Just tell him, Sara." Ben gathered her hand in his and squeezed. "He'll deal with it."

Whirring blades of a helicopter sounded overhead in the distance. The noise grew in volume every second.

"Sara?" Dyer again.

"Dad, the chopper arrived."

"You sound relieved." A pause. "You're the GSW patient, aren't you, Sara?"

She sighed. "It's in my thigh, Dad, so no big deal."

"Come on, Sara. Don't forget who you're talking to. We both know a thigh GSW can be serious. Any GSW can be, especially way out here."

"Out here?" she said to Ben.

"He's in Colombia. Hiking up, not far south of us."

"He's *here*? No. No, Ben, my half-brothers are young kids. My step-mom...if anything happens to him—"

"That's not gonna happen." Confusion had Ben shaking his head.

Sara stared up at the sky.

"Sara, look at me." She did. "Your dad is an excellent cop, right? Why are you so worried about him?"

"Working a case involving loved ones...emotions don't play into things well. Ben, I'm his only daughter, and with what happened with my mom..." she trailed off, her emotions and magnitude of the situation—past and present—too overwhelming.

"I get it."

In the night sky about two hundred yards away, spotlights and floodlights shined down from a helicopter's belly, streaming through the darkness.

The eerie sound of a firecracker on the move whizzed through the air high above.

Pow. Boom.

The med chopper exploded into pieces. Burst into flames. In the spine-chilling fiery light, various sized and shaped pieces spit in all directions and showered down.

"He's completely lost his mind," Ben uttered, sadness enveloping him.

My father just murdered more people.

And Sara's in deep trouble.

CHAPTER THIRTY-FOUR

In the stream from his flashlight, Ben studied Sara's pale face, her closed eyes, her still body. The last twenty minutes she'd drifted in and out of consciousness. Earlier, she'd been so alert.

I'm losing her, and there's not a thing I can do about it.

"Sara, how's the pain? Talk to me. How you doing?"

"I'm here..." She trailed off, sounding groggy.

"Maybe I shouldn't have given you the second dose of morphine. Did I overmedicate you? Is that it?"

"You've only given me two doses...right?"

"Yeah."

"You could inject more, if I'd let you."

"Oh." Then was she hemorrhaging inside and soon even surgery wouldn't be able to save her? "Sara, if there is a God, why would He allow you to suffer like this? You're one of His faithful believers. Why isn't He helping you? Why—?"

"Not getting exactly what we want, how we want it, when we want it..." Tears rolled out from the corners of her eyes, trickled down over her temples and into her hairline. "Sometimes what we believe is best, isn't for the best. Good things come out of bad things, and *when* is important. Timing truly matters." Her eyes fluttered open. "Thank you..." She gulped, the flow of tears streaming out of her eyes. "Thank you for forcing me to remember that."

He didn't know how to respond to all the new rationale. He'd never thought of religion as logical. Earlier, she'd given him enough to consider on the subject, and he was still processing it.

Her eyes drifted up and stared at the night sky above them. "You know, the dark isn't so scary anymore. Nothing is scary if you just let go and trust."

"Trust God?" He ventured a guess.

"You're gettin' it, Ben. You are gettin' it."

The pound of footsteps on the ground and rustling of foliage sounded behind him.

Ben whipped around, the 9mm pointed and ready to fire at anything sinister. The flashlight stream didn't find anything amidst the foliage, nothing human, no wild animal.

The sound of approaching footfalls increased in volume. Still no visual.

The 9mm Luger still aimed in front of him, Ben tossed the flashlight and slipped on the night vision goggles he'd found inside Tinsdall's pack, the cop who'd parachuted down with Hillman and Jason had executed in the throat without a care.

The clear view through the NVGs eased Ben's unsettled nerves, but not for long. No one was there now, but it sounded if he or she or it was fast nearing.

"Sara?" he whispered, keeping his eyesight in the direction of the incoming footsteps. "You still with me?"

"Fear of what that is kicked me awake. What is it? You see anything?"

"Not yet."

From out of the darkness, a human body appeared, a parachute trailing behind him on the ground. Night vision goggles on his face.

"Inspector Hillman?" the man said.

"No. Ben Keegan."

The man nodded with a sympatric express written on his face. "I'm Paramedic Kolton."

Ben slid his NVGs to his forehead and stuck the gun in his waistband near his bellybutton. "I'm stunned. You survived that explosion?"

"I parachuted out about a minute before the chopper exploded." Removing his NVGs, he kneeled at Sara's other side, performing a quick visual exam. "Ma'am? What's your name?"

"Sara."

"The Cayman paramedic?" Kolton dug out medical supplies from his hefty backpack. "The hostage?"

"That's...the...one," she uttered on a squirm.

"Move a rock to elevate her right leg on it instead of using that bag."

Ben rushed to do what the paramedic asked of him.

Kolton prepped a vein in Sara's arm for IV access. Within thirty seconds the line was inserted, the enclosed fluid dripped into her system.

"Hand me some tape." Kolton pointed to his pack while holding the IV bag up in the air.

Ben dug out a roll of tape, then watched the paramedic use multiple tape strips to secure the IV bag to the top of the rock elevating Sara's uninjured leg.

Kolton pushed the ice bags off Sara's thigh and on to the dirt.

"They're not cold anymore, but I left them on as weights, added compression."

"I get it. Sure." The medic unwrapped the top layers of the white bandages...until he reached bloody ones underneath.

"Wow." Concern coated Ben's stomach at seeing the red soaked layers. "I didn't—"

"This is to be expected." Kolton dug inside his med pack and withdrew...

"Is that...a tampon? You're gonna control bleeding with—"

"It only looks like a tampon. It's called X-STAT, a homeostatic device. Investigational until recently when the FDA approved it. It's the first of its kind." The medic cut away the bloody bandages, inserted the tip of the device into Sara's bullet wound, and pushed the syringe-like plunger. "I'm injecting a bunch of tiny sponges. They expand fast and swell to fill the wound hole."

Wow. "Very cool."

"Yeah, no joke. It's ideal for wounds occurring many hours from a civilized surgical facility."

"I hear the military loves the X-STAT," Sara interjected.

"I'd bet on it. An x-ray detectable marker is inside every sponge."

"Once a surgeon gets in the wound cavity, they're all easily found and removed."

"You got it, Sara. Hand me fresh trauma supplies," Kolton said to Ben.

Like a surgical assistant, Ben unwrapped and handed the medic gauze pads and bandages as he applied a fresh bandage.

"Let's verify circulation." Kolton scrambled to Sara's feet, removed her left boot and sock. "You feel this?" he asked, touching her toes.

"Yes."

He felt something on the top of her foot. "Strong pedal pulse. Can you move your toes?"

She wiggled them, moaning a little in pain.

After returning to Sara's side, Kolton strapped on a blood pressure cuff on her right arm. Inserted stethoscope buds into his ears, and pumped up the cuff.

"BP is a little low," he said after about twenty seconds.

"Due to blood loss," Sara said. "It's expected. What is it exactly?"

"Ninety-eight over sixty. Not dangerous, if it stays there." The paramedic listened to her chest with the stethoscope. He did other stuff Ben assumed was all an assessment of her condition.

"Fentanyl, morphine, or toradol?" the paramedic asked her.

"I think I'll pass."

"Way out here in the Andes, I will force a pain med on you. Let's go with morphine since a secondary effect is swelling reduction."

"The reason I allowed Ben to give me two doses IM."

"Oh."

"IM?" Ben asked.

"Intramuscular," the medic supplied the answer.

"I also took two acetaminophens a bit before that."

"You know that's not a contraindication. Let's add some fentanyl for a rapid onset and short duration. You've gotta be hurting."

"You talked me into it."

"You bet." After Kolton injected a filled syringe into Sara's IV catheter, he raised his radio in front of his face. "Paramedic Kolton to dispatch."

"Go ahead."

"No one but me survived the chopper explosion. I'm with the GSW patient, treating her now. Copy that?"

"Copy."

"I'll stage here until I receive updated info and orders. Copy?"

"Copy. We'll be in touch ASAP. Dispatch out."

"Paramedic Kolton out." He clipped the radio to his waist.

"Kolton?" Sara spoke, the groggiest Ben had seen her. "He has a bullet in his shoulder," she said, pointing her elbow at him. "Jason Keegan shot him."

"I'm good." Ben raised his palm at the paramedic, wanting the guy to focus on Sara. "She patched me up well."

"You want something for the pain?"

"After you're done treating Sara. I've taken multiple acetaminophen dosages today. So something stronger, but still mild. This day is far from over."

"I hear you. Help me with this, will you?" Kolton pulled out a metal contraption thing with straps of some sort.

"What's that?"

"A femur traction splint." After he unfolded it via the hinges, he arranged the splint beside Sara's bandaged leg. "Carefully lift her entire leg."

Ben positioned himself beside her bandaged thigh. "Ready for this, Sara?" he asked, looking at her eyes squeezed shut.

"Sure," she mumbled in a groggy slur, thanks to the morphine.

With one hand underneath her thigh, one hand underneath her calf, Ben eased her leg upward in a gentle lift. Kolton slid the traction splint in place under her entire leg, hip to ankle.

"Hold her foot, Ben. Pull it in a gentle stretch."

Ben crawled to Sara's feet, cupped her left ankle in his palm and gently pulled her foot, stretching her leg out.

"Oww," she screamed out.

"Pain from this is excruciating," Kolton explained to Ben.

"Then why do it?" He couldn't help but snap the question back.

"Just wait." Kolton immobilized Sara's leg with several Velcro straps as she winced. He strapped on the thing like a metal cast, then cranked a lever near her ankle with a final click.

"Ahhh," Sara blew out in relief, her body sagging in relaxation. "Definite fracture."

"I'm lost," Ben admitted. "What does she mean?"

"She's saying the relief of pain she felt when I turned the splint tight proves her femur is fractured," Kolton explained.

"Is that the pain med talking?"

"No. What she said is accurate. EMS 101."

"What else can I do to help her?"

"Nothing. There's nothing I can do, either. We just wait for our sky ride to show up."

"Sara?" Ben said and gained her attention, eyes half-open. "Craig may need my help out there. Maybe I should go." But he didn't want to leave her.

"That's not a good idea," the paramedic interjected. "You're a civilian."

"He's right, Ben," Sara slurred out. "Let the cops handle it."

"*Cops*? With an S? Sara, Craig is alone out there. No back up. He could use some help. We can't take a chance Jason will escape."

"It isn't your job."

"You're a *paramedic*, so it's not yours either, but you went after him and got yourself shot."

"Hey…it happens. Even to the best of cops."

"I know. Sorry." He gathered her hand in his. "Sara, I've gotta help stop him."

"You're not a cop, Ben."

"Neither are you anymore. He's my father, Sara. I need to do this. Need to try."

Yet instead of darting off, reluctance froze him in his spot on the ground at her side, holding her hand. Why am I hesitating to leave?

"Ben? My dad is out there somewhere," she spoke in a medicated-relaxed voice. "Not just Craig, right? I'm remembering that right?"

"Yes," he jumped at the reminder, planning to work it in his favor. "I need to help your dad."

"No. I mean Craig isn't alone. He's got Dad. Craig will keep Dad in check. Hopefully."

"Sara…" *Would he leave if she continued to be adamantly against it?* "Cop or not, I could help." *How?* "Somehow I can be of help. Three against one—"

"You've never even fired a gun, Ben. Even though I'm doped up on morphine and fentanyl, I remember that."

"Actually, I fired at him as he took off. Both Craig and I did. I hit him, Sara."

"Sounds like she's worried about you, bro." Kolton wiggled his brows up and down several times.

"We just met a few days ago." Ben couldn't think of any other response.

"Whatever you say."

"Could you give us a minute?" Sara said to Kolton. "A little privacy."

"I know when I'm not wanted." Smiling, the paramedic stood up and took a walk a few steps away.

"Keegan's shot?" she asked Ben. "You got him?"

"Yep. It took two bullets, but I got him. In the shoulder blade, I think."

"Impressive. A moving target is…" She blinked a few times as if fighting off dizziness from the IV pain med. "Ben? After the last few days of what we've been through…" Liquid pooled in the corners of her eyes. "…I do care." She gulped. "You could get hit by crossfire." She sniffled. "Or Jason could finally finish you off."

He kissed her hand, then set it down on her abdomen. "What if your dad needs help?" Ben twisted the full chamber on the 9mm Luger and stuck it in his waistband. "I can't leave Inspector Dyer hanging."

She inhaled a deep breath. "I'm torn. I want Dad to have all backup possible…but Ben, you're no cop."

"I'm fast learning."

He jumped to his feet.

"Looks like you're ready for that morphine." Kolton came up and withdrew a syringe from the med pack.

"Half dose. This will be mild?"

"I wouldn't call morphine mild, but you'll still be able to think straight and run." Kolton lifted Ben's sleeve and injected the liquid into his shoulder muscle.

"Ben?" Sara uttered his name in a choked voice.

He squatted down next to her, snatched up his flashlight, and wrapped it in her hands folded over her abdomen. "You keep this."

"I'm good now, remember?" Her words refuted her wavering voice.

"Keep it anyway. Just in case."

"*You'll* need it out there on the move. It's dark."

"I've got night vision goggles." He leaned over her face, kissed her cheek. "Stay strong, Sara. Do everything this paramedic tells you." Ben lingered over her, ignoring the desire to say more, to stay by her side and somehow help keep her alive. "Pray that we capture him? Okay?"

"Pray? Really?"

"Yeah." He brushed the back of his fingers to her soft cheek. "Praying can only help, right?"

"Yes."

"I'll be right back, Sara."

"Promise?"

He couldn't. Instead of promising something he didn't know without any doubt he could pull off, he smiled down at her and winked.

Before he changed his mind about leaving her there, he dashed off.

She was in the capable hands of a paramedic, so why did he feel as if he were abandoning her?

He stopped, dead in his tracks.

"No, Ben," Sara's faint voice spoke behind him. "Keep going. There's nothing you can do for me here. You're right, you need to go."

He whipped around and faced her. "I know. I..." *I don't know what to say.*

"Tell me later, okay?"

"Later. You got it." He started to turn but couldn't leave. "About Jason...thanks for your honesty."

Thanks for your honesty? Before he sounded any more like an idiot, he dashed off.

As he ran, Ben slid the night vision goggles back in place over his face, then dug his arms into Tinsdall's pack, stunned that only slight pain radiated in his shoulder wound.

Morphine is a god!

Gun pointing his way, he followed the trail.

It had been utterly quiet in this direction since Craig Hillman took off. Nothing from him. No sound from Old Man, either.

How far ahead are they?

Did Craig catch up to Jason?

What's going on up ahead?

As his breathing turned to quick pants to accommodate his speed, Ben's mind raced with plausible scenarios. One after the other, possibilities flashed in his brain like an endless reel of movie trailers. With each one, an array of emotions swirled in chaos, suffocating him. If Jason died from a bullet out there, the truth died with the old man.

The truth surrounding the death of Ben's mom.

The reason behind the sudden fascination with his birth certificate.

The truth about my life.

CHAPTER THIRTY-FIVE

A pair of NVGs strapped to his face, Alec raced up the dark trail, Officer Gomez in front of him. The detective had tripped a mile back, landed on his knee cap, and could no longer bare weight on his leg. He'd stayed on a rock, urging the two of them on. It took maybe a half a second of encouragement for Alec to bolt off.

"Gomez? My daughter is the GSW victim."

"Sorry to hear that. Where's she hit?"

"Thigh."

"Oh."

"Yeah, not good."

It didn't matter who was suffering with a GSW up there—even a paramedic and former cop as well as a daughter of a cop—no law enforcement agency would authorize a third chopper to descend on the area and risk losing it and its occupants. Risk losing more.

Understandable.

How many is it now that Keegan murdered in his quest to forever disappear?

"Interpol base to Inspector Alec Dyer," a voice drifted out from his waist radio.

He snatched it, depressed the side button. "Dyer here, go ahead," he said on a huff and puff as he continued to run.

"Inspector, this is a secure line. Boise PD needs to speak with you."

It was the news he'd been waiting on since the moment he'd found pertinent research info during his flights from Grand Cayman to Medellín, which led him to contact the Boise, Idaho Police Department.

"Go ahead, Boise PD."

"Inspector Dyer?" A male voice spoke over the radio waves. "Detective Price here. We found what you're looking for."

"Tell me."

"We discovered skeletal remains buried in a field near the banks of the Boise River less than a hundred yards from the house Jason Keegan rented over twenty years ago. Caucasian female, height 5'6", age twenty-five to thirty-five at the time of her death, which looks to be about twenty years ago, based on the preliminaries."

So far, the description fit to a tee.

"Homicide?"

"No doubt."

"ME know the method yet?"

Paper shuffling sounded over the radio line. "I'm looking at the prelim report now. Um...right radial fracture. Cervical fracture. Mandible fracture. Contused occipital bone. Several cracked ribs. Both cheeks fractured. At this point it's looking like she was beaten to death and bled out, either externally or internally or both. We've already processed the paperwork for the father's body to be exhumed for DNA confirmation and received clearance to have the process expedited."

Hurry it up. I need evidence and all the facts ASAP.

"You think you'll hear anything today?" Alec asked, still on the run.

"Anything's possible. I'll be honest, Inspector, count on today. The father's grave site is inside our county limits. I told the lab guy if he wants to date my baby sister, he better rush the results. Suddenly, he stuck our case at the top of his to-do list for today. You owe me for this."

"I'll pay up. Two weeks all expenses paid vacation in Cayman. That's our deal. Listen, I'm trekking through the Andes after a fugitive. Reception is spotty at times. If I don't pick up, leave me a voicemail and text me. Hopefully I'll get at least one of your messages."

"You got it, Inspector."

Two seconds after Alec finished that radio communication, he heard two men yelling in the dark distance, words undistinguishable. He reclipped the radio to his waist.

A gunshot rang out.

"It's not far ahead of us." Gomez increased his speed.

"That's what I'm thinking." Alec followed.

The next quarter mile, the volume of yelling between two men heightened.

"Gomez, one of the men is Cayman Inspector Craig Hillman. I know that voice. The other sounds like Jason Keegan."

Alec followed Gomez for another hundred yards.

"What's the plan, Dyer?" the officer said over his shoulder in a near whisper. "We're almost on top of them."

"First get there."

"After that?"

"Take cover somewhere without Keegan knowing our arrival. Listen to the exchange of words. Be patient. Play things right."

"No details spelled out? I like this plan. Be patient and go with the flow."

"Glad you like it."

"No, no, Hillman," Jason Keegan's voice scoffed somewhere off the right of the trail. "You have it all backward."

"You have it all backward." Inside a dark cave, Jason yelled back in annoyance, then snorted another line he'd arranged on the lens of his sunglasses.

This conversation with Inspector Hillman prompted his mind to replay the memory from eleven days ago, a week before his wife's death.

"I never knew her name," Annie said, sitting Indian style on their bedroom floor, their fireproof safe open beside her, a legal document in her hands.

"Well, now you do." Jason shrugged. "So what?" On the outside he tried to emanate a cool nonchalance, but an internal rage boiled inside of him. The same level of rage that had captured him one night twenty-one years ago. "Let it go, Annie."

He needed a line or two.

Three lines later in front of the TV, a wave of exhilaration soothed him like nothing else could. Plopped in the center of the couch and flipping through the channels, he marveled at how in control of himself and his surroundings cocaine gave him.

Life on coke. Nothing better.

Down the hall, their bedroom light flickered out. No more words or noise from Annie. Clearly she'd gone to sleep for the night.

Inside the cave Jason snorted another line, remembering how Annie had badgered him on the topic again, every day after that night for a week, and every day they fought about it...until Monday night, the night she pressed him to the max, refusing to let it go, even picked up the telephone to finally spill the truth to Ben. That night, nothing in the world could control Annie's mouth, so Jason had shut her up for good.

CHAPTER THIRTY-SIX

My dad killed my mom.

Mom is dead.

Ben was still weeding that information into his brain to settle for acceptance and understanding as he ran on the trail in the dark of night.

Grief, however, overruled. The crushing pain of sorrow and mourning captivated his thoughts and sidetracked his energy. It felt like a sucker punch, a dozen or so in the torso, knocking the wind out of his chest and abdomen. He couldn't shake the intense sadness burning him. No morphine dose could erase or speed up the grieving process.

He heard voices off to the left of the trail, near the edge of a cliff. He dashed in the direction. The volume of their tones increased, the words not yet discernible. Through the NVGs, he spotted a uniformed cop and a plain-clothed man kneeling together behind a minivan-sized boulder and two tree trunks.

About twenty yards back from them, Ben hunkered down behind four trees grouped close together, each trunk thick, providing adequate cover for him. He peeked around the side of the tree on the far left side.

"Keegan? Come on," the plain-clothed man yelled out; the voice sounded like Alec Dyer's.

So, the inspector found Old Man.

Dyer checked something on his cell phone. "Let's talk about how you passed your wife off as Ben's mother all that time."

Ben stilled; his head spun.

Little Keegan? 'ave you eva seen yo' birt' certificate?

"Inspector," Old Man's voice drifted out from...maybe inside a cave straight up head. "Annie not only welcomed the idea, she suggested it."

What? What am I hearing?

"Ben went along with it?" Dyer prodded on, unaware Ben was there and listening in a state of mass confusion.

"The boy was in kindergarten."

Sheer numbness seized Ben.

"You're saying he doesn't know," Dyer continued. "Too young to remember his mother and young enough for you to just slip the new mom in the old one's place."

The way his body and mind swayed, Ben felt as if he were belted in a seat and riding on a rickety and unsafe rollercoaster, steamrolling backward.

Get me off of this thing.

"Inspector, Annie raised him, so she's my son's mother. How is this relevant?" Old Man spoke in a chilly indifference.

This isn't happening. This isn't real.

Yes. It is. Deal with it.

"What about your son's birth mother, Keegan?" Craig Hillman's voice spoke up ahead and a little off to the right, but Ben couldn't see the inspector with the dense foliage and hilly terrain. "Where is she?"

My birthmother? Mom didn't give birth to me?

"Not that it's any of your business, Hillman, but she walked out on us. Left me and Ben. We never heard from her again. Ben didn't deserve that."

"She just vanished?" Dyer countered.

"The boy needed a mother," Old Man went on, not missing a beat to ignore Dyer's comment.

Vanished? My birth mom disappeared when I was in kindergarten?

"That's where Annie came in." Dyer checked his cell phone again as if waiting for an important text or something.

"Where are you two pigs going with this pointless conversation?" Old Man spoke with such cool confidence.

Cool confidence? Ben shook his head. *How is that possible?* The old man was trapped inside a cave with several armed cops right outside the only opening, the only exit. How could he possibly be so calm and confident? Clearly the nut case had some cocaine—compliments of Mateo—and was sniffing it in there, been inhaling the booger sugar off and on all day.

"Furthermore, why do you two even care?" his loser father continued.

"I care," Ben blurted out, finally joining in the conversation. He couldn't help it.

Dyer whipped around and eyed him through NVGs, so did the uniformed cop.

"Ben?" Old Man said, shock in his tone. "How long you been here, kid? Listening in?"

Long enough, you lying, murdering loser. "Why don't you tell me what this conversation is about?"

"I asked you a question, son."

"And I asked you to elaborate." *Do you ever tell the truth, or are you a master at evading it? Let's find out.* "Where's Mom?" He dove in and changed the subject since he couldn't tackle everything at once. Even though he knew the answer to this question, he needed to hear Old Man say it, admit he'd killed her. Murdered her.

"Ben, this isn't the time."

"When is? At your funeral?"

"Who says I'm dying any time soon?"

"From what I heard, death is what you want if you can't escape and disappear. Since you're stuck in a cave over there, with no available escape route, death is on his way to you, Old Man."

"What's your point, Ben?"

A ding sounded on Ben's cell, indicating an incoming text. It was from Inspector Dyer.

Sara?

Ben texted back: *She's good. No lie.* He lifted his arm high, thumb pointed up.

Dyer responded with a thumb up.

"Tell me what's going on, Jason," Ben answered Old Man. "It may be your only chance."

"Make the dying man talk? No thanks. I've got nothing to say."

"Cut the crap, Old Man. Just tell me where Mom is. I *deserve* to know."

"Dead. She's dead, Ben." A cunning coldness radiated out of his creepy tone, matching the words he spoke. "Get over it."

Chest heaving, Ben closed his eyes for a few seconds and dug deep for the courage to remain calm and behind his place of cover, instead of rushing toward his father and punching him out cold.

Play stupid. Get answers. "What exactly do you mean…dead?"

"Dead. What don't you understand? It's self-explanatory. She isn't worth any grief, though. She lied to you, kid. All those years, she told you she's your mom, pretended you're her son. Truth is, Ben, she didn't give birth to you. She's not your mom. You didn't even meet her until you were five years old, okay? So knowing that, why do you care she's dead?"

"*What?*" Ben snapped, anger soaring through him. "Do you hear yourself? Of course I care. She was a loving mother to me for as long as I remember and—" he swallowed the grief swelling his throat, somehow breathed through the tightness in his chest "—*you killed* her. *You murdered* her. That's what this is all about. For days you've been running from homicide charges, and committed additional murders to escape." Ben spoke the words, but his brain was still trying to catch up and process. "I know the truth."

"Well, good for you, kid. The truth will set you free."

"Snort some more coke in there, you heartless psycho," Ben shouted, his fists balled on the boulder in front of him. "Maybe it will help you sound less crazy."

"Keegan, it's over," Dyer said, stepping into the conversation. "There's no way out of this. You're stuck in there."

"Then come on in and arrest me, Inspector."

The situation boggled Ben's mind a bit. All of them—Old Man, Inspector Hillman, Inspector Dyer, and the uniformed cop—all four refused to move from their positions. Sure, Old Man was trapped in a cave, but he'd blow up anyone who attempted to approach him.

Ideal time to get answers.

"Jason, who's Ginger Rink? My biological mother?"

"Yes." Spoken without hesitation and without any emotion.

Ben had no memory of her, of Ginger Rink. Nothing. All of his childhood memories included only the loving woman he called Mom, Annie Keegan. "Where is this woman? Ginger Rink? Where has she been for over twenty years?"

"She left us, Ben. Didn't want to be bothered by us anymore."

"If that's true, Keegan," Dyer shouted, cutting in, "why'd you tell friends, neighbors, Ginger's father, and Ben's elementary school that Ginger earned a promotion and was already living in California waiting for you and Ben to join her? Yet the next day you moved to Florida?"

"Change of plans. Last minute."

Ben's head spun even faster, trying to grasp Dyer's words, the meaning behind them.

"Ben?" the old man yelled out to him, some emotion back in his tone. "Kid, the truth was too horrible. I was ashamed and broken up that she left us. So I moved us to Florida. To start over. Give you a happy life, hoping I'd meet someone new who could be a mother to you. Someone I'd fall in love with, and I did. With Annie Webb. Mom. I married her, Ben, within a year. She's been more than my wife all these years. She's been my best friend."

"Then why'd you kill her?" Ben snapped back, hearing sincerity in his father's voice and remembering his words as the truth.

Silence from the old man. No scramble for a lie. No denying or refuting. No response whatsoever.

"You have nothing to say to that, huh?" Ben gulped to keep rising heartache at bay in his gut. "Dad...help me to understand."

Was Old Man's display of sorrow and grief nothing more than a transparent act Ben should read right through?

"I know you two loved each other. I know it." A sudden anger burst coursed through him. "What happened?" he yelled. "Why'd you...why? I don't understand this. Tell me why you murdered Mom...Annie...whatever. Why?!"

Inside the cave Jason clawed a handful of dirt on the ground next to him and squeezed the mound. The dry soil filtered through his fingers.

Why, kid? Because she was going to tell you. Gonna tell you that you aren't her son, and you'd start asking questions about your biological mother and her whereabouts....just like you're doing now.

Another memory floated in his mind...

Ginger Rink drifted into their family room from their kitchen. "Jason? We need to talk."

He didn't respond. Didn't even give her any indication he'd heard her. She'd probably just harp on him about something stupid. He loved his girlfriend, the mother of his five-year-old son, but hated her incessant nagging. Did it really matter if his dirty socks and shorts lay on the floor or if the yard work was long overdue? They lived in a thousand square foot, two-bedroom, one-floor dump of a rental house in a meager neighborhood. Who gave a rat's tail if their landscape was mostly weeds and dirt patches? A hard-working man deserved to hang on the couch and watch ESPN on his day off.

"Hey...Jason?" Ginger grabbed the remote from his lap, clicked the TV off. "Are you listening to me?"

"Not cool," he snapped, and claimed the remote back in his possession. He punched the On button. The television screen flashed with colorful images in motion.

"I don't want to live like this anymore."

Her nagging was a nuisance, but he no way wanted her to walk out of his life.

He pressed the Off button on the remote, jerked upright from his slouched position on the old but comfy couch, and gave her his full attention. She just needed some coaxing, some tender words and kisses.

She'd never demanded marriage, so no need for him to ever offer it. When she'd discovered she was pregnant with Ben, she'd learned she was lucky—Jason didn't abandon her and the unborn baby. Most guys would've. Smart girl not to push her luck.

Maybe she was finally demanding marriage now.

Will I oblige?

"Come here." He patted the ratty cushion, willing to allow the conversation to flow.

She plopped down next to him, one leg tucked underneath the other.

"Okay, talk." He curled stray hair strands around her ear lobe and kissed her cheek.

"We need to stop. I need to stop."

"O...kay. Stop what?"

"The drugs, Jason. I don't want to do any more cocaine. I'm done."

His mouth dried. It felt like a hidden trap door whipped open underneath his feet and he dropped out into a bottomless pit of darkness. Down, down, down he fell.

He'd rather her demand marriage.

"I'm stopping, Jason," she said, patting her chest. "No more for me. Ever."

Stunned. He was stunned. "Just like that?"

"That's right. Just like that. Yeah, the withdrawal will be a killer, but I'll fight through it, and this time I'll beat it. I'll win."

He felt his eyebrows pinch together. "This time? What do you mean?"

"I've tried to quit before." She stabbed her index and middle fingers in the air. "Twice."

No way. "What? When?"

"First time? Less than a year after we were hooked. Second? About two years ago."

Stunned. She stunned him again. He had no idea she'd tried to quit twice and failed. Huh. "What makes you think you can do it this time?"

"I hate the way I look. Hate the way I feel. My immune system is shot. I'm sick all the time."

A flood of panic choked Jason. His palms slicked with sweat. He couldn't live without cocaine; he didn't even want to try.

Nose candy made life sweet, more tolerable. Kept him happy and in control.

"I'm not stopping, baby. Sorry. Not happenin'."

"Jason...I flushed it all down the toilet. All of it."

He jumped to his feet. "You what?" he yelled down at her on the couch. Just days ago he'd bought their new stash, a huge one that would last them months. "Thousands of dollars' worth of stuff is floating in the sewers? You better be joking." Fear slid over him, the fear of not having his next fix to control his mood.

She knew all the hiding places in their house since she was the one who chose each ideal location no narcotics cop would ever find...or anyone else. Dealers and other users could break in and steal their stash. He'd seen and heard it happen to others too many times to count.

She leaped to her feet, her petite stature well under his average male height. "Why would I joke about that? It's gone, Jason. All of it, and unless we don't want to eat or pay our rent, we have no money to buy more. It's over."

The anger building inside of him pinnacled to a rolling boil. "You can't force me to quit."

"I just did."

Rage exploded to the surface. His hand balled into a tight fist and struck her face square on with a punch. Another punch. Another one.

It was as if he were out of his body, watching another man beat the mother of his young child.

What seemed like only a minute later, Ginger was sprawled on the floor in their family room, bleeding and motionless. Silent.

The entire room was destroyed. The coffee table overturned and broken, the television on the ground in pieces, and wall hangings shattered on the carpet.

How had it all happened?

Jason jumped backward, away from her lifeless body. "What have I done?" *he uttered.*

She can't be dead. She's unconscious. Yes, that's it. Unconscious.

He leaned over her body and checked for a pulse in her neck. Nothing. He checked her wrist. Nothing. "Come on, baby!" *he yelled. He checked her neck again, everywhere, both on the left side and the right. Nothing.*

Ginger was dead, and he'd killed her. Beaten her to death....

Now inside the cave, Jason shook his head, ridding his mind of the twenty-one-year-old memory that had flashed in his head on fast-forward mode.

"I lost my mind, Ben," he shouted out to his son somewhere outside the cave, answering the kid's question.

I lost it when I beat two different women to death, twenty-one years apart.

"You're insane?" Ben's voice shouted back. "That's what you're saying, Jason? That's the reason you murdered Mom?"

His son's words caused yet another memory reel to play out in Jason's head...

"Jason, I can't live this lie anymore. I'm telling our son the truth—"

"Reality check, Annie. He's not our son. Ben is not your son. You could never have children."

"Not my son? How can you say that? His birth mother left him when he was a one-year-old baby, you told me. Since age five I've loved him and raised him as if I'd given birth to him, as if he were my biological son. How much more of a son could he be? Exactly what I'll tell him, Jason. My honesty will win his heart, I just know it. I know Ben. Just like I'm getting clean with or without you, I'm telling Ben the truth with or without you. Now...are you with me or not?" She picked up the phone.

He snatched it out of her hand and whacked it against her right temple. "Not."

The memory ended, leaving Jason staring at the cave wall.

I killed two women I loved, the two deaths melding together as one in my mind.

And I can't escape it.

"Yeah, Ben…" Jason answered his son. "Insanity explains it."

What else could he say?

"I'm stopping you right there, Keegan," Dyer's voice cut in after being silent for a bit. "Don't try to feed your son any more lies."

It was impossible to know what these cops had proof of as pure fact versus what all they only suspected. They could refute any lie Jason spewed off…but so what. It didn't matter anymore.

No need to scramble my words to fit the truth or a variation of what could be passed off as the truth. Dead or alive, my life as Jason Keegan is over.

Yes, but…he didn't want to hurt Ben more. The kid didn't deserve it. The truth was better left hidden from him.

"Keegan?" Inspector Dyer's annoying voice drummed on some more. "Tell your son about the charade, your acting stunt Monday night, or I will."

"Don't bother, Jason," Ben shouted. "I already know you played catatonic next to Mom's murdered body when cops arrived."

"Clearly, kid, you educated yourself on the facts after ditching the *Persephone* and coming after me."

"Then, Keegan? Tell him about Boise."

"Boise?" Jason shot back at Dyer. The inspector was fishing. Fine, Jason would play along for now. Until he thought of an effective plan to get out of this death trap of a cave. He was a sitting duck in there. If he popped out without a plan, it'd be a turkey shoot, he the turkey.

I've got to get out of here. Escape my life and start over in Australia.

Or die trying.

"The city in the state of Idaho?" Jason went on, trying to sound confused and unaware. "What about it, Inspector?"

"Cut the innocent act, Keegan. We know Ben was born in Idaho and you moved him to Florida when he was five years old."

"So you can read his birth certificate and the history on my Florida residence. No brilliance on your part there, Inspector Dyer." This cop had no proof of anything, only suspicion. He was fishing without any bait. Desperate to draw out answers. Shooting for some kind of confession.

Ridiculous. The Cayman police already had enough to hang him on multiple counts of murder on Cayman. So why the third degree?

"Incidentally, Keegan, during the same exact timeframe you moved to

Florida, Ginger Rink vanished, yet no missing person's report was ever filed. It's like she simply no longer existed."

That's right. And with the supposed move to California, no one even noticed, including her own father since they hadn't spoken in years anyway.

You've got nothing, Dyer. Nothing even resembling proof.

Even if the cops did, so what? It no longer mattered.

No one would take him alive, not the three cops out there, not his own son. He refused to spend the remainder of his life in prison.

If he fired everything in his arsenal at them, he'd soon run out of ammo, and way before the four of them together ran out of theirs.

Jason peeked out of the cave at the dark cliff, listened to the roaring river below. If he lurched off and jumped into the river, he could swim his escape in the darkness of night.

"Hey, Keegan?" Dyer's droning voice continued on, annoying him even more. "Why don't you tell your son what happened in Boise?"

He didn't know what to say other than, "Why don't you shoot yourself, Inspector."

CHAPTER THIRTY-SEVEN

Boise?

Ben was lost.

I moved from Idaho at age five? All this time I thought I was born in Florida.

"Cut it, Keegan," Inspector Dyer snapped as he checked his cell phone yet again, apparently impatient for something to appear on it. "I know what happened in Boise."

"I don't know what you're referring to," Old Man replied in faked befuddlement Ben read right through.

The old man isn't lost.

"No more acting, Keegan," Dyer hammered on, full of contempt. "The catatonia was your last stint anyone will believe. Let's talk about what happened to Ginger Rink."

"I told you, Inspector. My girlfriend left me and our five-year-old son. What can I say? She's a bad mom. Took off to who knows where a long time ago. We never heard from her again."

"No one did, Keegan. No one. Can you explain that?"

Ben's head spun to try to grasp the words and the meaning behind them.

"Ben? Kid, this cop is revengeful against me for kidnapping his daughter. He is Paramedic's father."

"I know that!" Ben yelled, fresh anger mixing with confusion. "What I don't know is anything about Boise. Anything about Ginger Rink. What is Inspector Dyer talking about?"

"Yeah, Inspector," Old Man shouted. "Where are you going with this?"

"Twenty-one years ago, Keegan, Ginger Rink's social security number stopped earning income. No known residence after the Idaho rental home when you and Ben moved to South Florida. No more credit or financial records. No taxes filed. No driver's license after her Idaho license expired seventeen years ago. No marriage license anywhere. No record of a death certificate."

"And that proves what, Dyer?" Old Man said, keeping his cool. "That maybe she changed her name and slipped into a new life in California or somewhere else. Maybe she's living on the streets. Maybe she's living in a remote location overseas. How would I know?"

"We found her remains, Keegan. Buried in a field near the banks of the Boise River. Less than a hundred yards from the house you rented. She has no living blood relatives. Her father died a few years ago, and DNA on his exhumed body proves those remains are Ginger Rink's."

Ben was done. Done listening. Done processing. Done just sitting there, accepting ugly truth after ugly truth.

I can't stomach it anymore.

A flaming anger burned inside of him, sparked his nerves at their ends.

9mm Luger aimed and leading the way, he dashed off to the right and forward, toward Old Man's hiding spot inside the cave, ahead of Craig Hillman about fifteen yards.

"Ben," Dyer whispered with intensity, behind and to the left.

Ben ignored the inspector's attempt to stop his movements. Instead of stopping, he jogged hunched over, darting from tree to tree, boulder to boulder for cover.

Old Man murdered two women, my birth mother and the woman I knew as Mom. He'd take me out without a second thought.

This is what my life has come to.

He found Inspector Hillman hunkered down behind a boulder and joined him there.

"Ben?" Hillman propped up his NVGs on his forehead. "You left Sara," he said, voice choked a bit. "Is she—"

"No." Ben left his NVGs in place. "She's alive. A paramedic is with her."

The inspector rubbed his forehead and sighed. "Whew!"

"The medic parachuted out before Jason blew the second chopper."

"What are you doing here, Ben?"

"I'm here to help take Jason down. I'm done with this. With him. Aren't you?"

"So...your plan is...?"

Ben pointed to the cave. "Draw him out of there."

"Then what? Ben, you will *not* fire that weapon at him. Give—"

"I won't? Isn't the goal here to take him out?"

"You're not a cop, Ben." Hillman pushed out his hand, palm up. "Give me that gun."

"Relax. I'll only fire if you guys need me. Think of me as back-up."

"Ben—"

"I need to do this, Hillman. Need to help capture him." No medication Ben—or anyone else—could ever develop would help Jason. He was too far gone.

It was too late.

CHAPTER THIRTY-EIGHT

Inside the dark cave, walls splashed with light from his lantern, Jason sniffed up two lines. The throbbing pain in his right shoulder blade eased a bit. A third line, and the pain subsided to numbness. Before he'd encountered Inspector Hillman smack on his tail, he'd bandaged his gunshot wound—packed the hole with balled-up gauze and applied stacked gauze pads with tape. Difficult to do only one-handed, regardless of his left-hand dominance. Hours ago when he'd wrestled with Paramedic—right before his son fired two bullets at him—his right forearm started to bleed through the bandage, so he'd taped more roll bandages over that wound as well.

In arranging his escape from Grand Cayman, he'd left nothing to fail. His only thought since Monday night? He'd get away with another murder—Annie's murder—or die trying.

Staring at the bag now empty of the numerous explosives it had contained this morning, and only two grenades on his body, he'd never felt so cornered in his life. So trapped.

It's now or never.

He switched the lantern off and stuck it inside his bag. Stuffed pack strapped on his back, a grenade in his hand, he darted for the cave opening. Lingered there just inside, listening to the roaring river below the darkened cliff. His heart rate sped up; his gut knotted into a ball.

Now.

After yanking the grenade pin, he popped out of the cave. Dashing for the edge of the cliff, he tossed the grenade over his shoulder to buy himself some time to—

Bam.

Pow.

Two separate sounds, a split second apart. One the grenade, the other...

A bullet had pounded into the back of his left knee. Out of his control, he collapsed to the ground without warning. Fiery pain shot up his leg to his hip, down his leg to his toes.

The bullet placement was a clear message: the cops wanted to take him alive.

And off to prison I go.

A steady spill of anxiety flowed through him.

On his stomach, he crept toward the edge of the cliff, dragging his bleeding body. A blood pool trailed underneath him. He'd rather risk death with the dive than be apprehended.

"You're not going anywhere," a voice behind him said with command.

Ignoring the agony in his body, Jason scooted like a dying cockroach.

If I can just...

Digging his toes and elbows into the dirt for support, he inched his way to the drop-off only a few feet away.

"No, you don't, Old Man." Ben's voice boomed behind him.

The sound of a round chambering caused Jason to hustle his movements even quicker. The tip of a gun barrel pressed against the back of his head; he froze, stiff in place.

Do it, kid. Squeeze one bullet into my brain. Give me death.

"Ben, lower the gun," the commanding voice floated into Jason's ringing ears. "You don't want to fire that weapon."

"I don't?" The kid snapped back. "What would you know about it, Dyer?"

"Did you really just ask me that? Ben, you should know I'd love to blow him away, too."

Blow me away? Go ahead, Inspector Dyer. Give me what I want.

Tormenting pain radiated throughout Jason's body. He couldn't decide where he hurt the worst.

Fire the gun, kid. End my life.

"Give me that gun, Ben."

"Dyer, he's killed...how many people in total has he killed now? Huh?" the kid yelled. Obvious heartbreak rolled out with his words. "He murdered my real mother, a woman I don't remember even existed. And he murdered the woman I thought was my mom. He also murdered—"

"I know, but Ben...son. He isn't worth going to prison for. And if you fire, if you blow him away, it will be first degree murder. Lower the weapon."

The steel barrel pressed deeper, harder into Jason's skull. He had no words. Nothing came to mind. He just wanted it over, wanted to...stop hurting his son. Wanted...

Death or escape.

He found the strength to drudge forward, inching his way to the cliff edge only a couple feet from his fingertips. The gun tip remained shoved to his head, moving along with him, his son's feet shuffling beside him.

"Ben, listen to me." Dyer spoke in that annoyingly calm voice cops faked.

Jason inched farther, dragging himself closer to the edge. Pushing through the agony to near his escape route.

Shoot me or let me dive over the cliff.

"Don't give him what he wants," Dyer continued as if the jerk could read Jason's mind. "This shouldn't end with his death."

You assume, pig, I won't survive the jump.

Maybe. Maybe not. Chances existed he could survive the impact with the water and he'd swim away in the dark and escape to Australia. So, he picked up his crawling speed, ignoring the protest from his knee, his shoulder, and his forearm in the form of a jolting sear of pain in each.

"Ben," Dyer's droning voice again, "this doesn't end with him getting off easy by dying here today. No. He will live the rest of his life in prison, the one exact thing he desperately doesn't want. He's gonna die in a maximum security prison years from now."

A foot slammed down hard on Jason's lower back, shoving him into the dirt and halting his movements. He reached his left hand into his shirt breast pocket, the dead cop's uniform pocket, and withdrew his last grenade.

He slipped the ring in between his teeth, and pulled.

A hand reached over his shoulder, snatched the grenade, and tossed it over the cliff. Five seconds later a blast resonated up the cliff wall. The ground shook for a split second.

The shoed-foot still rammed his core into the ground, encumbering him there in place. Two arms grabbed his hands and whipped them behind his back.

"Inspector Dyer? Is that you back there?" Jason spoke to the night-darkened dirt mere inches below his nose.

"It is." Warm circular steel encompassed his wrists, locking them together with a bone-chilling click so similar to the sound of jail bars sliding closed. "I'll make sure you rot in prison."

The worst possible scenario was in his face.

Hands of unknown origin wrapped bandages around his shot knee, the goal clearly to keep him from bleeding out. Keep him from dying.

There's no way out. I'm caught.

Giving up? Me?

No.

He squirmed, tried to thrash about, but his cuffed hands and trapped legs were forced in locked-down mode. The edge of the cliff mere feet out of his reach, taunting him.

I can't get there.

Come on. Bleed to death. Die from trauma wounds.

"Impressive job, Inspector Dyer, tossing the grenade," he spoke with contempt, aiming to sound indifferent to his predicament, refusing to give the inspector the satisfaction of hearing his ripe fear.

"That wasn't me."

"Hillman?"

"No. It was *me*," the kid's voice snapped out, full of hatred, anger, and heartache.

I'm a failure. I failed my son. I failed...at life.

"Ben?" He uttered his only child's name, despising Malcolm for involving the kid—he should be in Florida, continuing to finish that big degree of his.

"That's right, Old Man. You know what I wanted to do with that grenade? Stuff it in your mouth. But the notion you'll spend the remainder of your life in prison stopped me."

The anger pulsing through Ben boiled hot in his arteries. Bent over, he gripped Old Man's left arm and yanked his body one hundred eighty degrees around, tossing him on his back with his cuffed hands sandwiched between his spine and the ground.

"I hope you're hurting," Ben shouted down at his father in the light from the moon. "Really hurting, you lousy piece of..." He sucked in a deep breath.

It didn't help relieve him of the burn from overwhelming emotions.

As if he had no control over his arms, he found his own fist punching Old Man's face. Again and again. Again and again.

Someone behind grabbed his shoulders, lifted him upright. "Stop it, Ben. He isn't worth it."

Ben whipped around, planted his palms on Dyer's chest. "Get off me." He pushed the inspector away.

He turned to face Old Man again with the intent to use his face as a punching bag some more as he lay on the ground handcuffed. But...the desire was gone. Poof.

I'm not like him—violent and out of control.

Hillman dragged Old Man to his feet, backed him against a tree trunk. The uniformed cop snapped cuffs around his ankles and read him his Miranda rights.

"Jason Keegan, you are under arrest for the murder of Annie Keegan, Owen Hinders, Russell Wilson..." The officer listed other names, then lifted a handheld radio to his face. "Officer Gomez to base," he spoke into it and continued with his status report.

Old Man's nose was sniffling and whistling. Ben stepped back. Hands on his knees, he leaned over at the waist. His heart burned as if on fire; his chest wall squeezed, suffocating him.

All those people dead, at the hands of my own father. Mom...Annie. Ginger...Mom. A Cayman cop. Sara's partner. Tinsdall, other law enforcement, two helicopter pilots, etc., etc.

And if Sara...

Fresh raw anger surged through Ben. "Jason?" He stabbed his index fingers in the air at his old man, who struggled holding all his weight on his uninjured leg as he writhed against Hillman restraining him to the tree. "If Sara doesn't survive the bullet you fired into her..."

"You'll what?" the old man asked, his nose bloodied, his upper lip cut. He sniffled.

"I'll never forgive you."

Then he realized he'd never forgive him for murdering Mom and his birth mom either, but...what did it matter?

It does matter. The anger will eat me up alive.

After a deep breath in, he exhaled, and somehow it released every last bit of his pent-up hatred and rage—Old Man wasn't worth holding on to it.

A sense of finality washed over him.

"Your choices are yours alone, Dad. There's nothing I can do for you. There never was. No one can help someone who refuses to help themselves."

Ben turned away, giving his cuffed and apprehended father his retreating back. Moonlight leading his path, he took off in a run, anxious to return to Sara's side.

"Hey!" Inspector Dyer's voice shouted behind him. He bolted in front of Ben. "We need to talk." His nostrils flared, jaw tightened. "Where's my daughter?"

Ben's brain raced for the right response.

"Why'd you leave her, Ben?"

"A paramedic is with her. Don't waste time talking or placing me under arrest. I haven't heard a chopper, so she's still there." Ben rushed off.

Sara...oh, Sara. He swallowed. *Be okay. Be alive.*

Within a few seconds, Dyer was running alongside him. "How far away is she?"

"A couple miles."

Silence between them as they ran, each huffing and puffing in a near sprinting pace.

"You lied to me, son. You said the GSW victim was some cop."

"Yes, sir," Ben answered on a nod as he ran. "I apologize for that."

"You're not gonna make some excuse? Blame it on Sara?"

"No, sir."

"We both know she begged you not to tell me she was the one shot. What's her condition? The truth this time, Ben, and don't sugarcoat it."

"The medic has her well medicated and in a femur traction splint. External hemorrhage is under control. Your friend Hillman radioed in for a med chopper, but that was the second one blown to bits. The paramedic requested another one. It should reach her soon."

"It may be too late."

"Yeah, I know."

I

CHAPTER THIRTY-NINE

"Silent night... Holy night..." Sara sang out loud, staring at the inside of her eyelids. Tingling pain mixed with hot numbness blanketed her shot leg. She shivered even though her face sweated in the tropical temperature.

"You're singing Christmas songs in May?" the paramedic asked her.

In her medicated brain fog, she couldn't remember the guy's name. "It's a peaceful song."

"Yeah. That it is."

"What if no one ever comes for us?"

"Never? Sara, that's not gonna happen."

"We both know no more choppers will be dispatched until Keegan is under arrest or dead."

"Or runs out of explosives. He can't have an unlimited supply up here. How are you feeling?"

"Groggy. Somewhat numb."

"Half-dead?"

"Yeah. Something like that."

"You want another dose of fentanyl?"

"It'll just make me even more groggy." She stared up at the starry night sky filled with bright light from the full moon. It was all so beautiful. "I'm not afraid of the dark anymore."

"Umm...that's good. Yeah."

In the privacy of her mind, familiar a cappella music played.

What is that tune?

It hit her, and she sang it for her ears only. Jesus loves me, this I know. For the Bible tells me so. Little ones to Him belong. They are weak, but He is strong...

She pictured herself at the foot of the cross, her fisted hands opening up, releasing it all. Letting it go. All her anger. Resentment. Fears. All of it.

She wailed out in uncontrollable sobs. They wrenched from deep inside her and flooded out of her in a steady flow. With that release an incredible amount of belief and trust filled her up. Deep inside in a place indescribable in human terms, she felt belief in God. Trust in Him.

And true inner peace spilled into her.

Think and feel with your soul, she told herself. *Don't get caught up in human details.*

"Sara?" she heard a male voice speak her name. "Are you okay?"

"Let it go."

"What?"

"Everything. I get it. It's not always easy, though."

"What isn't?"

"Being a human."

"Uh-huh. Sara, I'm gonna push another dose of fentanyl. Okay?"

"That sounds nice," she listened to herself say, the words echoing in the contours of her brain. "One, two…" She counted the pretty twinkles in the sky around the big white saucer thingy. "Thirty-seven, thirty-eight… Sixty-five, sixty-six…"

A warm palm brushed her cheek. "Sara…baby…"

She turned her head toward the familiar male voice. She blinked twice. "Dad? You're *here.* You're okay."

"Oh, sweetheart, we're gonna get you outta here."

"Where's Ben? No…don't…Keegan shot him. Nooooo," she screamed, her chest squeezing.

"Sara." A warm hand folded into hers. "I'm fine."

She turned her head to the right, and a handsome face came into view. "Ben?" Tears sprang to her eyes. "You're back. You came back."

"I did. I'm right here with you." Soft lips brushed the back of her hand in a gentle kiss. "You are a fighter," he spoke in a cracked voice as if emotion caught in his throat. "You hear the helicopter, Sara?" Those foggy words rang like sweet music in her ears. "It's nearing us."

The sound of rotating blades whirred in the night sky.

A radio crackled. "What's the update on that orthopedist?" the medic's voice asked.

"A surgical team in Bogotá is on standby," a voice over the radio replied.

"Ben?" Sara eyed his bandaged shoulder. "You need surgery too."

"Is that your expert medical opinion?" Smiling, he winked down at her.

"You don't trust a woman on painkillers?"

A wide stream of light overhead shined down. A rope ladder spilled out of the chopper, dropping a swinging basket gurney with it.

CHAPTER FORTY

Cell phone to his ear, Alec stood outside Sara's hospital room. Down the humid hall from him in the Bogotá hospital, he heard a bell chime. The elevator door swooshed opened. Out stepped Ben Keegan, right hand holding a small sack, his left arm in a sling from surgery five days ago to remove the bullet in his shoulder.

"Alec?" Craig's voice spoke over the cell. "You hear me? Jason Keegan is on suicide watch. They've got him in isolation."

"Apparently he's been crying himself to sleep nightly, begging God to stop his heart. He deserves what's coming—the rest of his life in a prison cell," Alec answered, not regretting his indifference. "How's Baleigh?"

"Rachel loves that dog, Alec."

"Tell her she can't keep him." Alec watched Ben converse with Sara's doctor standing at the nurse's station. "Seriously, tell your girlfriend thanks for taking care of him."

"She's not my girlfriend."

"So you've said numerous times. What are you two, then?"

"I don't know. We don't talk about what we are. We're just...I don't know."

"Well, tell your *I don't know* thanks again for looking after my sons last week until Lelisa got home off the barge. And now our dog until we get back from Colombia. Lelisa and I really appreciate it." He paused. "Hey...Craig?"

"Yeah?"

"Thanks...for..." Alec swallowed, gratitude overwhelming him.

"Buddy, you'd do the same for me."

Ben thanked Sara's surgeon, ending their conversation, then stepped down the hall toward her dad as the inspector clipped his cell phone to his waist, his facial expression serious.

The warm plastic in Ben's right hand suddenly felt like a fifty-pound weight instead of a sack filled with a hot sandwich.

Shoulders back, Inspector Dyer stood erect in front of Sara's closed door. "Smells good," he said, pointing to the bag.

"She loves pulled pork arepas." Ben shrugged.

"They are a Colombian treat. Walk with me, Ben." Dyer headed down the hall toward the wall of windows at the end of the long row of hospital rooms. "I hear you're flying home to Florida tomorrow."

Ben caught up to Dyer's stride. "Ah, yes, sir. I need to get back to work." He was more anxious than ever to finish production on the anti-addiction med. He and Professor Evert were so close to beginning human trials. It was too late to help his parents but not countless other addicts.

"Ben?" Dyer cleared his throat. "You wanna tell me about the two thousand dollars?"

"Is there an arrest for me at the end of this conversation, Inspector?"

"Should there be?"

"An accomplice charge is reasonable. I'm surprised I haven't been charged yet."

"You believed your father was only running from drug possession."

"Why are you defending me?"

Dyer stopped walking, turned toward Ben. "Life is rarely black and white. Most of it is gray."

In agreement, Ben nodded. "Thanks. You didn't have to—"

"If I didn't see it that way, neither my wife nor my daughter would ever speak to me again. Can't have that. They're my diving buddies." Alec Dyer smiled at him, man-to-man.

Ben chuckled. "No, can't have that." Sara had told him her dad had final say in any possible criminal case against him, so Ben didn't inquire for an elaboration.

Dyer pocketed his hands and stood there, staring at Ben. No question, the inspector was waiting for Ben's explanation regarding the two thousand dollar deposit into this bank account eight days ago, the morning he'd flown to Jamaica to sail the *Persephone* to Cayman.

That day was only a little over a week ago? It seemed like months ago.

"Inspector, I setup a trust fund for Felipe, the young son of Mateo. Two thousand isn't much, but I know his grandmother will put it to good use for the boy."

"Yes, she promised me she would."

A spark of irritation narrowed Ben's eyes. "If you already knew I gave the money to Felipe, why are you questioning me about it?"

"That's my job. I'm tying up loose ends here."

"Inspector, I didn't donate that money just to get out of criminal—"

"I know, Ben. I know."

"I never should've taken the two thousand, never should've agreed to help—"

"If you didn't, my daughter wouldn't be alive."

"I doubt that. Sara is extremely resourceful. She knows how to take care of herself."

"Accept my deserved gratitude, son."

"Of course." Ben nodded. "I do. Sir."

"Good. Now get in there." Dyer pointed down the hall to Sara's closed door. "I know you two want to spend your last few hours in Colombia together."

"Thank you." Ben extended his right hand.

Dyer shook it, then he patted Ben's right shoulder. "No, son, thank you."

Less than thirty seconds later, Ben slid Sara's door open and found her beautiful smile lighting up the room the moment she spotted him.

"Hi, there." He slipped into the chair beside her bed.

"Hi, back." She reached out for his hand.

After setting the warm sack on the tray table, he weeded his fingers with hers.

"Ben. Ben!" Little Kyle leaped into Ben's lap.

"Hey, buddy." Ben snuggled the kindergartener.

Jeremy, the older brother, gave Ben a high-five and a cool nod.

"All right, boys, let's give your sister and Ben some time alone." Lelisa Dyer climbed to her feet from a chair on the other side of Sara's bed.

"Thank you, Lelisa," Ben said to her on a smile.

The door popped open. Sara's dad held it wide open with his back. "Boys? Out."

With a mixture of peace and happiness, Sara watched her stepmom and dad share a brief kiss and her little brothers dance around their legs.

"Thanks, Dad."

"For?"

"Being you. Love you guys."

Lelisa blew her a kiss. Dad winked at her, then ushered his wife and sons out the door.

Sara lay her right cheek on the pillow, facing Ben. "I like being alone with you."

"Do you? Then you're ready to take our hospital dating to phone calls and texts?"

"No emails?" she teased.

"Only if you come visit me soon."

"Well, sure." Her smile widened even more. "It's a date."